REVERIE

SHAIN ROSE

DEDICATION

To Gladys Tesmer:
Your never-ending love, your unsurpassable beauty,
your quick wit, and the exceptional brilliance of
your soul still shines as bright as the sun. You will
always live on through each and every one of us.
Cancer was never, ever a formidable opponent
in extinguishing your dazzling light.

CHAPTER ONE

VICK

"**Y**OU'RE FIDGETING," **THE** man with eyes as dead as stone but as piercing as a sharp knife pointed out.

"I am not." I squirmed one last time in the black dress. The tulle hung loosely over my waist and down to my mid-thigh. Unfortunately, the corseted lace across my bodice left little to the imagination.

I should have ordered a size up.

My best friend, Brey, was marrying a musician-turned-music-app-nerd and every person was recognizable past the lush, expansive row of bushes. If I was going to walk down the aisle as a bridesmaid, I needed to look freaking amazing doing it. I just didn't know how if I couldn't take a breath. I pulled at the strapless sweetheart neckline digging into my cleavage one last time.

"Are you about done? You'll look fine if you just stop squirming like a bee flew up your dress."

Jett Stonewood. The groom's brother. And the devil of a man who Brey paired me with for this ceremony. The other bridesmaid had been paired with Jaydon, the younger, fun-loving brother of the groom. Jett, on the other hand, was who you talked with if you wanted humor to die, your smile to disappear, or your belief in all things joyful to disintegrate.

Still, my knees buckled a little when I saw him in his suit. Stonewoods wore suits better than any other men on the planet. Jett wore his best. His broad shoulders set a perfect line for the jacket to sit on, accentuating his thick neck and strong jaw. Every part of him screamed masculinity and my body responded.

I licked my lips, turned toward the ceremony, and pointedly ignored him as best I could. The music started, a soft instrumental version of one of Jax's songs. His one album had gone triple platinum, an album he admitted he wrote just for Brey. Then he effectively retired, saying he wanted her to hear it and didn't care about the rest of the world.

My eyes watered thinking of their story.

Lush green rolling hills swelled up from the horizon of the private golf course. Clouds as white as cotton fluffs spotted the blue sky. The centerstage's gondola overflowed with stargazer lilies and roses. The backdrop of it all was the sea, lapping at the sand. The sun hit the clear water in such a way that it looked as if diamonds sparkled everywhere.

I peeked around the corner to get a glimpse of everyone before Jett and I had to walk.

Jett growled, "What are you doing?"

"Just trying to see how it all looks," I whispered.

"Probably about the same as it did when we rehearsed."

I wasn't sure if he was trying to be rude. So I shrugged. "The wedding planner said the sun would start to set over the ocean. The shimmer on the lilies with the Swarovski crystals would be out of this world."

He looked toward the sky and took a deep breath, like my presence was an annoyance he could barely handle.

Yup, definitely trying to be rude.

Before I could say anything more, the wedding planner cued us. I gripped Jett like my life and reputation depended on it as my heels sunk into the sand with each wobbly step.

I did not want to fall face first in these heels when my best friend was about to get her happily ever after.

When we passed the wall of lush shrubs, I closed my eyes.

Beep. Beep. Beep.

It was a sound I heard only in my head. The same rhythm every time. The same high note, sounding off that I was still alive.

Barely.

I opened my eyes and drowned out the beeping with what was right in front of me. The sun shined on precious stones that had been positioned in white-and-red bouquets along the aisle. The flower arrangements stood tall in glass vases. They'd decorated pillars with more crystals and draped tresses of flowers around and above us. The sun basked every guest in their best light. With the waves crashing in the background, the music couldn't have sounded better.

"This is stunning," I whispered to Jett, choking back a sob.

"It's ridiculous," he said under his breath.

His words were so final, and filled with such anger, I forgot where I was. I halted to glare at him.

He nudged my arm, widening his eyes. "What are you doing?" he whisper-yelled at me.

"How can you say that?" I said behind a forced smile as I took measured step after measured step. "This is the perfect day with the most amazing couple."

"You're just as delusional as everyone else."

My jaw dropped. "Excuse me?"

"This marriage is bound to be chock-full of problems. Probably won't last. Most of them don't. And we'll have to pick up the pieces when it falls apart."

"Marriages last when they're meant to be together and those two are soulmates."

A chuckle—dark and bleak—rolled out of him.

As we neared the altar, I tried one last time to change his mind. "This is going to be a moment in your life you'll never forget. This is your brother and your future sister's happily ever after."

He made eye contact with me for the first time. I gasped at how strikingly blue his eyes were. The blue was direct, cutting. It sliced away at my happiness, so vivid and so stark that it seemed to mock anyone who dared to dream of anything. "Vick, everyone should know by now, there's no such thing as happily ever afters."

With that, his arm dropped mine like I was a very hot, very diseased potato. He turned to make his way over to the groom's side.

I twirled toward the bride's side and made sure I strutted with extra pep in my step.

I'd get him to change his mind by the end of the night.

I could make anyone believe in happily ever afters.

CHAPTER TWO

JETT

EVERYONE CRIED AS Aubrey and Jax said their vows.
Everyone except me.

Maybe I wasn't meant to be a groomsman. My eyes were as dry as the Sahara in a drought. Shit, even my father shed a tear.

Senior Stonewood, the man who'd molded me into who I was, stood next to my mom looking prouder than ever before.

It was quite possible that everyone had amnesia. My father leaned down to say something my mom smiled at. People would have said they looked in love. Yet, I remembered the year my mom kicked my dad out. They'd screamed at each other about his long hours, about the business coming first.

My mom broke down, crying so many nights, her depression nearly overtook her. She begged him to let her be his first love. My dad swore she was. Still, he couldn't commit to anything but his enterprise. The investments pulled him away time and time again.

On those nights, I remember soothing her as she cried on my shoulder while shielding my brothers from her pain and despair at the same time.

Then I grew up. My mother had been so determined to keep us away from my dad's business that I gravitated towards it. Wave after wave of arguments ensued over my staying with my father. My mother had overcome the sadness and morphed into a ferocious woman who could match my father's ruthlessness one-for-one when it came to the job of raising her children. She didn't want me to turn out like him but also didn't want to suppress my dreams because she feared history repeating itself.

Today they held hands like they missed one another, like they had forgotten the past.

Love hadn't conquered all with them, and somehow everyone thought it would conquer all for Jax and Aubrey.

The bar presented the only solution to my problem. I needed to catch amnesia with a drink or two. The outdoor hut with long stalks of hay and twigs for a roof held every type of alcohol, and I could smell the fruit mixed with rum as I approached. The bartender welcomed me with a wide smile across his tanned face.

The groom and my baby brother, Jaydon, walked up next to me.

Jaydon questioned Jax as they both leaned onto the bar. "When do you think the reception music will start?"

Jax chuckled and nodded out at the guests mingling on the sandy coast we'd reserved for a happy hour. "Are you planning something?"

"I might have one or two people crash the party." He smiled like we had nothing to worry about, like just anyone could show up.

"You can't have some girl off the street come to the reception, Jaydon. It's asking for trouble. They could be the media or ... " I started in on him.

"Lighten up, man. We're in Kauai. The media's not trying to fly to the island to get a shot." Jaydon waved me off.

"You're the most famous person here," I ground out, trying to keep my frustration at bay. He'd been acting for years now and tabloids loved to put him center stage. "You should understand how detrimental crazy paparazzi can be," I responded.

"Oh, I understand. I'm just not going to let them dictate my fun," Jaydon said.

Jax sighed. "You're not having strange women at the reception, Jaydon. Aubrey will kill you and then me for allowing it."

"I'll ask her." Jaydon scanned the crowd.

"If you do that right now, I promise I'll help her kill you," Jax grumbled.

Jaydon didn't seem to care because he started texting someone. I snatched his phone away.

"What the fuck, Jett?" He made a grab for it, but I held the phone out of his reach.

"You're not bringing a girl that hasn't had a background check into this event. Everyone signed an NDA. No one outside our circle comes in. End of story."

Jaydon stared at me a second longer and then slumped into the bar. "You two are fucking buzzkills. Brey would let me bring someone in."

Jax snorted.

Jaydon continued, "She might have married you, but she's still my best friend. She's nice enough to give me the opportunity to get laid here."

"Yeah, she's too fucking nice to you. And everyone. Which is why we have to speak up for her." Jax tapped the bar and the bartender appeared, aligning three hand-cut crystal lowball glasses on the shined wood. He poured whiskey in each.

"She's not always that nice." I broached the subject everyone had been avoiding.

Jaydon laughed and sat down on one of the barstools. "She can be a sass pot. Girl knows when to lay down the law."

"If you say so. You're already married but it's still something you should consider, Jax," I said and slid Jaydon's phone back to him.

Jax turned to me and handed over the glass of liquor. His blue eyes held a warning when he asked, "Consider what?"

Maybe I should have backed off. "Her dad's in prison. You and I both know the media can twist a story."

Jax turned to set his glass on the bar and faced me again. This time, I saw the anger. His muscles bunched with it, and his jaw ticked. Behind him, Jaydon stood up—his phone forgotten—with the same look in his eyes that Jax had.

They both wanted me to retract what I'd just said. They wanted me to apologize and say I didn't mean to talk badly about Aubrey Whitfield.

Aubrey Whitfield, the love of his life, was intelligent, inspiring, and driven. In fact, I'd offered her a job investing with me at Stonewood Enterprises after she'd graduated. My team consisted of extraordinary people and she'd overcome her father burning down her childhood home. She took risk after risk. The girl was strong. Perfect for him and for our family, considering the media that followed it.

But they were naive to think the media wouldn't have a field day with how quickly they were getting married. And stupid to think it wouldn't take a toll. I needed them to last, not crumble under the pressure.

And most people folded under the institution of marriage because the titles, the expectations, the compromises—they pushed people to the brink. My parents were a perfect example of that.

If I had to be the one to consider every angle, I would. Fact was, her father was in prison for arson and the homicide of her mother. My brother was a Stonewood and a retired musician. With his fame and her father's notoriety, the press loved to watch their every move.

"She has done well with being in the news, Jax. I'll give her that. But what happens when she gets stressed? What then?"

"Then she gets stressed, and we handle it," Jax replied, his tone flat and void of emotion.

"You have to consider that fifty percent of marriages end in divorce—" I started.

He cut me off. "I went to visit her father for years, Jett. I made it my business to be there, bring him to his knees, and make sure he never bothers us again."

Jax had climbed a metaphorical Mount Everest to make sure Aubrey's father never had the money or authority to come in any contact with his daughter again. I didn't agree with the amount of money he'd lost by disassembling her father's company, but I understood that he'd done it for her. "If you say so."

His eyes narrowed, a glare meant to wither me. "I've considered every aspect of this relationship more than you can ever imagine. Repeat what you just said and you'll regret it."

"Someone has to protect the family…"

Jaydon snorted and crossed his arms. "Brey's never tainted our name and she never will. If anything, she's lowering her standards by marrying Jax. He doesn't deserve her."

Jax shoved him. "Fuck you."

"What? You know damn well you don't deserve her."

"Look," I reasoned with them both. "You're married, it's all fine. In the future, if everyone folds under the pressure, the divorce will be—"

"Jesus," Jax sighed as if he was tired. "You deserve to get your ass beat."

"Are you kidding me, Jax? I'm trying to make every angle clear." I rubbed the five-o'clock shadow that had spurted one or two gray hairs over the course of last year.

Jaydon's gaze ping-ponged between us, and then he pointedly placed himself between Jax and me. "Come on, you two. We don't need black eyes tonight."

"You're lucky I love my wife and don't want to cause a scene," Jax said.

"No, you're lucky. You forget who taught you to fight?" I glared at him over Jaydon's black-suited shoulder.

The muscle in Jax's jaw worked as his ice-blue eyes shot anger my way.

I deserved a beatdown. He was right.

Running my family's investment company was taking its toll on me. I was taking my stress out on them, on this wedding. I didn't have time to vacation in Kauai, even for something as important as my brother tying the knot.

I straightened my tie and adjusted my suit jacket. "Look, Dad's not been present at work lately. He's spending more time with Mom. Trying to make things work." I resisted the urge to state another point in the case of why the institution of marriage wasn't a smart move. My parents were a perfect example of consistent compromise, of my father not getting to do what he loved. "He can't work and make Mom happy, which means more work is falling on my team. We have a lot of clients that need my attention."

Jax stopped me. "I don't give a fuck about a job. I work there too, remember?"

Jax worked on algorithms. Not deals, not major companies under our name folding, not managing the work of thousands. The weight of people's families having dinner on their table each night sat on my back. That work didn't stop because of a wedding.

He continued on, "You're a groomsman. Start acting like you care."

I ground my teeth together as I once again held on to the words I wanted to say.

Jaydon tried to play peacemaker again. "This is supposed to be bonding time between brothers."

I sighed and nodded my head. "Jaydon's right." I patted his shoulder as we both stared at Jax. "Sorry for bringing it up. I just want what's best."

Jaydon turned toward me and let my hand slide from his shoulder. "You didn't let me finish, Jett," he growled, his glare even meaner than Jax's. "It's bonding time, so let's not talk about my best friend like she's not worth a damn or I'll help Jax hide your fucking body, you prick."

I rolled my eyes and turned toward the bar. "Guess I'd better drink the whiskey down and shut the fuck up. Seems you two aren't into seeing reason anytime soon."

They turned away from me and the bar to walk off, leaving me with the toothy bartender.

"What can I get you?" he asked.

The bridesmaid I'd walked down the aisle with literally skipped up beside me. "Can you get him a strawberry daiquiri? One for me too, please."

Spunky, full of life, and exasperatingly happy, Vick didn't appeal to me. Nor did her taste in drinks, but the bartender spun around to make them anyway.

I pushed the heel of my hand to my temple to ward off the migraine I knew would come from irritation. "You can take both of them. I don't want strawberry anything today."

"They're great, I promise. It's the best drink to have in hot weather like this. You'll see." Her smile didn't reach her eyes as she tried her best to keep a cheerful face.

The girl was pretty. She had long blonde hair that swung with its own weight when she walked and a tall enough frame that she could pass as a model. The black dress she wore accentuated her curves, small waist and substantial chest. With high cheekbones and full, pink lips, her face had perfect symmetry.

Her personality was the problem. The fucking prancing around needed to end here. "Where's Brey? Shouldn't you be getting her a strawberry drink?"

Her honey-colored eyes widened. "OMG." She actually said the letters. "She's only drinking white wine today. She can't spill on that dress. And these drinks"—she grabbed hers as the bartender set it down and shoved mine over to me—"have way too much alcohol in them. This bartender doubles down on the daiquiris, I swear. Being that impaired on your wedding day never ends well."

I grabbed the drink. "Well if it's got as much alcohol as you say," I shrugged. "Bottom's up."

I clinked my enormous glass to hers and took a big gulp. The rum overpowered the saccharine taste to the point that I coughed and almost spit up on her dress.

She smiled wide this time, like she'd won a private fight between us. "Told you it packs a punch."

She stood tall, chest puffed out and eyes sparkling when she got the best of someone. She clearly relished in getting the best of me. For the first time that day, I was a little less perturbed and a lot more intrigued.

"What did you say you do for a living?"

She waited a second before she answered me. She stared out at the horizon and the ocean below it, then dropped her gaze to where most of our family and friends were dancing and mingling. "Brey didn't tell you?"

I chuckled. "Brey and I discuss business. She doesn't share what's not important. I know we're looking at buying up the company you work for. Your job isn't really a factor in that."

She stiffened at my bluntness. "I would think everyone's job is a factor if you want to keep people happy."

"It's not my job to make everyone happy."

"Right. Well, the owner of the company I work for strives to do that. He won't sell unless he knows his employees are taken care of."

"Everyone sells for the right price, honey."

"You'd be surprised what Steven has turned down. I promise he's not in it for the money."

I leaned back on the bar and studied her. Those eyes turned a molasses color when she got fired up. She stood her ground with me, and I liked it more than I thought I would. "You're sure about that?"

She folded her arms over her chest and glared at me. "I'm sure."

I shrugged and downed the rest of my daiquiri before I turned to place it on the bar. "So, what do you do within the company that makes you so sure?"

"I … well,"—she cleared her throat—"I'm one of the associate contract lawyers for Samson and Sons."

"Samson and …" I recall chuckling a bit at the name when I'd first read over it. We would have to drop it if we acquired them. I couldn't help but smirk as I cleared my throat. "Doesn't matter. An associate who knows what the owner wants?"

She flipped her ponytail over her shoulder like she was fluffing her feathers. "Look, Steven and I have known each other a long time. Our families go way back. I interned with the firm, and I'm climbing the ranks fast. He's confided in our team—and in me—time and time again. We trust him to do what's right for the company."

"If you say so." The bartender appeared again. This time, I ordered our drinks. "We'll have two tequilas straight up."

"I don't want—"

I cut her off. "I tried yours. You'll try mine."

"It's disgusting."

"It's much healthier than what you're drinking."

"And you think I'm trying to be healthy tonight?" she snapped.

"I think we're both doomed to feel the effects of our drinks tomorrow. Let's just enjoy what the bartender serves us."

"Fine." She narrowed her eyes. "But, if I finish this drink, you have to dance to one song with me and look like you are having an enjoyable time. It's your brother's and Brey's day. We have to make it the best. For them."

I sighed and shoved her drink toward her when the bartender brought it over. "If we keep getting drinks, I'll be able to look like I'm having a magnificent time."

She rolled her eyes and brought the glass to her lush lips. She tipped it back fast, letting the liquid flow into her mouth.

The sun-kissed skin of her neck bobbed as she swallowed. She'd probably been out prancing along the beach every day before the wedding, singing the praises of the sand and seashells.

She didn't cough at all. I was surprised when she kept gulping and finished the drink right then. She set the glass down without a wince.

Her triumphant smile met her eyes this time. "You ready to dance?"

Before I could answer, she spun around so fast her blonde hair whipped me in the face. Then, she was bobbing up and down as her heels carried her to the open dance area on the beach. Aubrey and Jax swayed near a speaker, along with their friends.

I grunted and downed my drink before I made my way over.

The beat of the music moved the crowd, pulsed through the bodies. I sidled up close to Vick and shrugged when Jaydon raised his eyebrows at me.

Vick lifted her hands above her head and rolled her hips while she smiled at me. "I love this song."

I rocked just enough so I looked like I might be dancing. "Do you love everything?"

She laughed at my question. "What's there not to love?"

She didn't give me time to answer, just spun and dropped down low to the beat. Her friends hooted and egged her on. She bounced a little, watching me. Her antics were immature, but I had to admit she looked hot as hell doing it.

Pole dancers looked good while they worked too. It didn't mean they should do it everywhere.

As if Vick read my mind, she leaned into me and slid her body up mine to bring herself back to her full height.

She was being ridiculous, I thought.

She was fucking hot, my dick thought.

I stepped back from her, but she followed me. "Jett, the song's not over yet and you don't look happy at all. This wasn't part of the deal. Are you a man of your word?"

She moved toward me, like a little fox trying to outwit me, and I pulled my frown into a slight smirk.

I slid my arm around her tiny waist and yanked her into me. I moved against her as I leaned down to whisper in her ear, "Sure am, Pixie."

She narrowed her eyes. Then she twirled around and that damn ponytail flew into my shoulder, sliding off it like golden liquid as she walked a few feet away. When she turned back around, her eyes were back to big, honey-colored saucers filled with joy. "Can you do anything other than step side to side?"

I undid the top button of my white collared shirt and when the next song's beat hit, I stepped up to her challenge. I did the damn dance with everyone else.

After one more song, I nodded to Vick. "Man of my word. Off to get another drink."

The woman cracked another grin, like she had an unlimited supply to give out. "I'll come with you."

I headed toward the bar. "I don't want another daiquiri."

"Suit yourself. I do though."

I ordered her another one while I ordered myself more tequila. When the bartender set the drinks down, her hand shot out to grab mine, and she gulped it like a damn shot. When I protested, she held up a finger. "I just need a second before you get all crabby about it."

"The bar is open, woman. Just order one of your own if that's what you want." I tapped the bar and signaled for another.

She stared out at Brey laughing with Jax as she asked, "You don't want to celebrate them. Why?"

"It's complicated."

"Simplify it for me."

"I don't believe it'll last this way. So, it isn't worth the effort."

"So, you think love isn't worth the hassle?"

"Honestly, it isn't."

"What about life?" She turned to me and waited for the answer. The happiness bled out of her eyes, the warmth of the honey sapped away, leaving a worn, dismal mahogany behind. Her stare was cavernous, holding secrets behind layers I wanted to see, to learn, to experience.

When I didn't reply, she lowered her gaze and grabbed her daiquiri. "See ya on the flip side, Mr. Stonewood."

I didn't respond to her trying to end our encounter. I followed her instead. She wove through the crowd and we passed a few tables and chairs in the reception area.

She jumped when she glanced around and saw me standing behind her. "What are you doing?"

"Following you."

"I'm aware. You held up your end of the bargain. We're done playing now. You can go be all dreary somewhere else."

"Why did you ask me if life is worth the hassle?"

She focused on a table covered in a milk white cloth in front of her. Her bubblegum pink lacquered nails ran over the linen, working out the wrinkles. "Well, there are a lot of obstacles."

I nodded, but she continued watching her own efforts to iron out every flaw in the tablecloth.

"Like love, life has hurdles. Peaks and valleys. It's give-and-take. It's a freaking feat just to live. And to love ... that deserves serious recognition. So, I wondered what you thought of it all being as pessimistic as you are."

"I'm not pessimistic. I'm realistic."

She peered at me, through me, into something so much greater than me. "And isn't reality the saddest thing there is?"

She waited for my answer with a different type of smile. It didn't spread across her face, and it didn't light the room. She concealed sadness behind it, and she crossed her arms over her chest like she wanted to keep that sadness locked up and hidden from everyone.

"You've been buzzing around this beach like a little pixie, excited to be a part of reality. Now it's sad?"

"I push the bounds of reality to be happy. You have to fight for joy."

I sneered at the ridiculous answer. "You don't change it, Pixie. Reality is what it is. It's all we're given."

A piece of her hair had fallen loose, and she moved her manicured hand to push it behind her ear without answering me. Her somber movement and the way she heaved a sigh fascinated me. Her plump lips parted, and her tongue wet her lips. She ran her gaze up and down my body and those eyes warmed up again.

Her silence hovered in the air, making me wonder exactly what she was thinking. Something had shaken her enough that we'd moved past her default happy personality. I wanted to unravel her and find out what was behind her facade.

"Reality is reality," I continued. "Get lost in it with me?"

She tilted her head. I didn't wait for an answer from her. I walked toward the hotel rooms.

I heard the clicking of her heels behind me and knew that even with the copious amounts of alcohol I drank that night, I would not forget my time with her.

CHAPTER THREE

VICK

ALCOHOL WASN'T TO blame for me following Jett on Brey's wedding night.

He spoke of reality, and it jarred me into wanting to experience something other than happiness.

Jett was the epitome of the reality I didn't focus on. I focused on flowers, sunshine, rainbows, and holidays. He focused on mud, darkness, rain before the rainbow, and probably memorials instead of holidays.

He lived in the dark while I lived in the light.

Opposites attract, though, and I was curious as to how the other side lived.

I was also a little tired. Tired of trying not to be jealous of the love Brey and Jax had, tired of not having a date myself. I was so tired of searching for Mr. Right at a wedding when Mr. Wrong was right in front of me.

Jett could barely smile when he danced with me. Still, he could dance, and he could turn me on just as much or more than any nice guy I was going to run into.

I followed him along a grassy pathway and peeked back at the wedding. No one noticed me leaving. My friends were all lost in their own bliss.

We created that. My friends and I had come together to coordinate this celebration of love and life. We planned the reception, tasted the cakes, ordered the flowers, decorated the space, and sent out the invites.

We made a day so perfect no one should have been negative about it.

Yet, there he was. Jett Stonewood. Mr. Negative.

The man had everything going for him. He practically owned a multibillion dollar company, had a family that loved him, and was in Kauai celebrating his brother's happiness. He looked like a freaking god. He stood half a head taller than me even though I wasn't short and I was in heels. His crystal-blue eyes popped against his obsidian black hair. The way he filled out a collared shirt had just about every woman at the wedding salivating. And his face. His freaking jawline and cheekbones and full lips. The combination, honestly, was unfair to every other man.

So how Mr. Everything could also be Mr. Negative was very confusing to me.

Frustrating.

Exhilarating.

Interesting.

I blamed my lack of foresight on it.

I hurried along behind him. He never slowed down for me or looked back. I wondered if he even knew I was following him. When I stumbled over a rock in the path, though, he spun around and caught me before I fell.

"Careful," he grunted.

I mumbled a thank you as I righted myself and tried to step back from him.

He slid his hand down my arm and threaded his fingers through my hand. He slowed his pace as we walked toward the hotel.

I looked out at the horizon and pointed. "This is the most beautiful sunset I've ever seen."

"It's the same one you see everywhere, Pixie," he replied with a smirk, like he knew I had a point.

I laughed. "You know my name's Vick, right? And, come on, it's setting over the same mountains they used to film *Jurassic Park*. It has every color bleeding out into the ocean. It's not the same everywhere and you know it."

"Real is real, doll. It's the same."

I halted on the path, and he turned to look at me. "Sometimes seeing something in a unique light brings a whole new view. You have to admit that."

He squinted at me. He dropped my hand and stepped back. Then he tilted his head as he dragged his gaze up and down my body. "You're in a different light in this sunset."

I didn't shrink at his assessment. I was confident about how I looked even if I was standing in front of one of the most attractive and powerful men I'd ever met. "And? Am I different?"

I didn't realize I was searching for a compliment until he replied with an insult. "No different, Vick. You are who you are. You look how you look. A sunset isn't going to change that."

I rolled my eyes and shoved past him. When we got to a fork in the path, I stopped and asked, "Which way to your hotel room?"

He halted at the fork too. He put his hand on the small of my back before he asked, "You sure you want to come to my hotel room? Will you remember any of this in the morning?"

He wanted to make sure I hadn't drank too much. Or that I wouldn't regret the decision I was about to make. He was giving me a way out, and for some reason that made the way out much harder to take.

"Which way?"

"We should probably call it a night."

I glared at him. "Which way, Jett?"

He sighed and turned to his right without answering. I followed.

Our hotel rooms sat on the edge of cliffs that overlooked the ocean. They were more like condos or suites, so big and inviting that they each had their own entryway. We walked up to his door, and he swiped the keycard while looking at me. The beep sounded, and he twisted the handle but didn't look away. "We walk in here, we lose the facade, Vick. I'm too on edge to play any games or recite some fairy-tale poetry you might want for your happy ending to your day."

I shrugged and walked right past him into his place. "I intend to make you recite poetry because you want to, Jett. It's never forced. It's—"

I didn't finish my sentence because he grabbed my face and devoured my mouth.

I gasped in surprise, but he didn't let up. He dove in deeper, pressing his body against me. The way his tongue tasted mine, the way he didn't hesitate but gripped my face like it was the only thing he ever wanted made me feel like we had something more than just tonight.

He kissed me like he wanted there to be more.

Maybe I imagined it, because then he pulled back and held my face in his hands. His blue eyes looked almost black, and he stared at me like he wanted me to see into his thoughts. "This is reality, Vick."

I leaned in to kiss him, and I didn't hold back. I wrapped my legs around him and let my dress bunch up. I felt him against me. He was long, hard. Ready.

He slid his hands down to my butt and groaned when he felt just a thong beneath my dress. He lifted me up and carried me to his bed.

I didn't look around or take in how he had set up his suite. I didn't care. When he fell back onto the bed with me on top of him, I lifted myself so he could slide my dress over my head. Then I was back on him, sucking his bottom lip, biting it, and working his belt and zipper underneath me.

His hands slid up my back, and one wrapped around my ponytail. He pulled it hard enough that I leaned back and moved to the side. Then he was on top of me, taking over. He ravaged my neck, biting it roughly and then licking it better. He didn't waste time taking off any more of his clothes. He grabbed protection, slid my panties over to the side and plunged into me.

I was ready for him, so ready that I orgasmed on his first thrust. I pulled him close and screamed into his shoulder as stars brighter than the freaking sunset burst through me.

I rode my high and he let me, watching me the entire time in the darkness of that room.

When I came down from it, legs still wrapped around his waist and him still deep inside me, he said, "You're in the darkness now. You want to know if you look any different than when you were under the light of the sunset?"

I barely comprehended what he was talking about but I nodded. "Sure," I mumbled in a state of shock at how blissful it was to get off by none other than Mr. Negative.

He looked down at where our bodies connected and then back up at me. "Still the same. You look exactly the same. Truth, doll."

I shrugged, not caring that he hadn't given me a poetic line. I'd just had a fairy-tale orgasm.

His next words seared into me though. They left a tattoo on my heart.

"Beautiful as fucking ever. Most beautiful thing I've seen in a long time. Light or dark. Under any light." He waited a beat. "Truth."

Then he rocked back to thrust into me hard, not giving me a moment to respond.

I blame alcohol for the idea of love that swirled in my head. He balanced me and showered me with compliments throughout the night. His whispers of how perfect this was, how good I felt, sparked my own dreams of a wedding day, of a happily ever after.

The way his hands smoothed over my skin like it was made of pure gold and the way he ran his nose along my nape.

He wanted me the way I wanted him. I knew it. He wanted the love, the future, and the commitment.

Like stars glittering against the night sky, I felt like I shined damn brighter than ever before with him beside me.

After we made love again, he fell asleep, and I raked my eyes over his entire body. He breathed in air like he dominated it, his muscles rippling with the effort. The frown he normally wore disappeared, as if his dreams freed him from the drain of reality. He looked at peace and he needed that. Worrying about every war the world waged at every moment of the day wasn't healthy.

I could attest to that. Once upon a time, there was no happily ever after for me.

I fell asleep after snuggling into his arms. I was excited for what the morning would bring. We would talk over the future and enjoy the sandy beaches of Kauai.

His arms weren't around me when I woke. I stirred and found not even a sheet covering my body. I woke up cold and sat up to look around.

The sun shined into the bedroom, and I smiled as I breathed in that humid air, listened to the rustle of the trees, and thought about our extraordinary night.

I stretched and winced a little, knowing I would need water and ibuprofen to fend off the headache that was sure to come after the amount of alcohol I'd consumed. Even more so because Jett had ravaged me last night. I was sore in places I wasn't sure I'd ever ached before.

He strolled in from the bathroom, a white towel hanging from his hips and a few stray droplets of water glistening on his chest.

Part of me couldn't believe I'd slept with that amazing specimen all night long. Every muscle cut into the next with precision and they moved in beautiful sync with one another as he entered the room.

He hadn't looked toward me yet as he dried his hair with another towel. I let the sheets hang loosely on me as I tried for a sexy rasp, "You look good this morning."

Jett jumped in surprise and then his whole body went rigid. "You're still here?"

I frowned. "Well, yeah. I just woke up. I figured we could lounge in bed…"

"I don't have time for that." He stepped back as if offended by my suggestion.

I scooted off the bed and found my dress in a ball on the floor. "You're totally right. We should start the day off by getting outside to explore this amazing island. Do you have some sweats I could borrow? My dress…" I held it up and shrugged, knowing that guys loved when a woman wore their clothes. I hoped he'd think I looked cute standing there completely naked.

I was excited to see his face when I slipped on the shirt he would give me, excited to spend the day with him too.

He didn't move to get me a change of clothes though. He stared at me like gum on the bottom of his shoe. My smile dropped a little.

Did I imagine that look of annoyance?

He raked his eyes up and down my body and then rolled them. Dramatically. "You can't just wear that dress for a minute to get back to your place? It can't be far from here…."

"But I thought we—"

"We?" He spit the word out like it was gasoline in his mouth. "There's no we, Pix."

"Last night was…"

He held up a hand to stop me. "Last night was last night. Now last night is over."

"But you said—"

"Nothing to make you think this would last till morning. Honestly, why did you even stay the night?"

Shock ping-ponged through me. And the reality that he'd spoken so damn highly of dropped down on me like a lead weight, crushing all my hopes with that one question.

"I stayed because I thought we were enjoying each other."

"I enjoyed fucking you. I think it's safe to say you enjoyed that part too."

I wanted to throw my dress at him, but I didn't want to retrieve it completely nude. So, I took my time stretching out the wrinkles all while I looked at him.

He didn't shrink away from my glare. He met it head-on by crossing his arms and pointedly looking at my deliberately slow movements. "I don't have all day, Vick."

"Wow, you know my name now. Not your little pixie anymore, huh?" I fumed. "And you had all night. You can spare me a precious few minutes of your day so I can at least look presentable when I do the walk of shame."

"Oh, please,"—he turned toward the living area—"half of the island is probably doing the walk of shame. You could call it a normal stroll at this point."

"Where are you going?" I quit trying to smooth creases from my dress and threw it on as I stomped after him. "You don't get to whisper sweet everythings in my ear all night and then act like a complete jerk the morning after."

His face held a question. "'Sweet everythings'?" He burst out laughing, like the answer he found was the most comical thing ever. He laughed so hard he bent at the waist and held himself up on the island counter near the living area. The towel barely clung to him as his whole body shook.

Maybe he's joking with me. Maybe he's laughing because he's about to tell me he really does see us going somewhere.

"You." He wiped his eyes quickly and then shook his head as he righted himself. "'Sweet everythings.' That's ridiculous. You know what a one-night stand is. I know you do."

My laugh died as my jaw dropped.

"Come on." He rolled a finger in front of him, motioning for me to start moving. "Let's get moving. I need to get dressed."

I snapped my mouth shut. I straightened up. And I stepped up to face the terrible morning this was turning out to be.

"You know what?" I stalked toward him, not waiting for him to respond. "You're exactly what is wrong with this world. Don't tear me down because I had a fucking hope that this was more, you dick."

His eyebrows slammed down. Good, I wanted a reaction.

"I know where I'm not wanted. And I'll walk out of here happy, Jett. You want to know why?"

He lifted one shoulder, but he watched me like I finally wasn't a joke to him or just a one-night stand. All of a sudden, I had his attention. His sapphire eyes held mine, and they didn't look away. It was almost like he wanted my disdain. When most people would have shied away from being reprimanded, he reveled in it.

"I'm thankful I enjoyed a couple orgasms from you and now I get to leave you and all your negativity behind. I thought you might be deeper than it, that you just saw this world differently from me, but you're only searching for grim places, and I've been down that boring road before. I want the light, and I'm good enough at finding it that I can honestly say"—I slipped my shoes on, glancing at him while I did—"this will be one of my better mornings because I got to leave misery—you—in the dust."

With that, I swung open his front door and flipped my hair over my shoulder as I walked out.

Smiling.

CHAPTER FOUR

JETT

THAT GIRL WAS something.

I smiled as she turned to leave. I waited for her to turn back and catch one last glimpse of me. I wouldn't have minded one last look at her too.

Sleek and well-packaged woman that she was, her body would drive any man insane with her long legs, tiny waist, and curves in all the right places. I wanted her to turn so I could see her face and the smooth, soft skin right where her jaw and neck met, the place I now knew drove her fucking crazy when I bit at it.

I wanted to see those honey-colored eyes burning with resentment and fight in them. She bled confidence when someone cut her. Surprisingly, I found that blood attracted me.

I prided myself on not caring about the women I brushed off. I never gave them a promise, just like I hadn't given Vick one. Yet, she targeted the jugular by calling me on my flaws and leaving me to think about them.

Normally, women knew what a one-night stand looked like.

A shiny outlook on the future blinded her to all we had last night. I wasn't the one at fault, but there I was questioning myself.

She was the best I'd had in a long time. I practically got hard just watching her walk away. My body wanted her in a way I didn't want a lot of other women, but I wasn't stupid. I knew I could find someone to fill her shoes any day of the week. There were billions of women in the world and she was only one of them.

She was only one, and yet, when she didn't look back at me, I almost went after her.

Almost.

She flipped her long blonde hair like it was waving goodbye and good riddance. I had wrapped that hair around my hand and owned her last night. Saying goodbye shouldn't have been that easy for her. To most of the women I slept with, it wasn't.

I shook off our encounter and got to work. Businesses had to grow. Money had to be invested. I had to focus. The world my family built had to run and run well. People depended on that. I wasn't in Kauai to play around.

I took breaks here and there.

Jax and Jaydon would have killed me if I didn't.

But I wanted to take my own life when I found out that day one of our excursions was a paddleboard lesson on a private beach across the island. We sat in a large van, piled on top of one another. And our driver looked completely incompetent.

I surveyed the van. "Put your seatbelt on, Jaydon."

He smirked, "Sure, Dad."

Everyone else complied without me pushing further. If I had to be the one with the stick up my ass so that everyone would live, so be it.

Somehow, Vick ended up next to me. We didn't talk because, thankfully, I'd brought my laptop so I could catch up on emails.

I lost my patience after watching cars take turns to cross a one lane bridge though.

"Who booked this?"

Vick jolted a little at my tone, and Brey answered meekly from behind me, "I did. I didn't know there would be so much traffic or that there was only one lane."

Jax's hand was on her thigh and he smiled like we had all the time in the world. "It's fine, Peaches."

Vick wiggled next to me like excitement was about to burst out of her. "We get to take in so much of the island. Look out that window!" She pointed as she practically shouted, "The fog hugs those mountains like a cocoon around a caterpillar. I love this! I could spend days doing this."

I grunted. "No one has days to spend bouncing around a damn island."

The tension in the van thickened. No one responded to my lashing out at Vick, and the woman just looked down at her phone as if she hadn't heard me.

Suddenly, from her phone, I heard an excited weedy voice, "Vicky! You FaceTimed me finally."

Her face lit up like a firefly in the middle of a warm summer night. "Steven," she breathed and held her phone just far enough away from her face that he got a damn good angle of her neckline. The neckline I had ravaged the night before. "Kauai is gorgeous."

"I told you it would be. How was the wedding? Brey and Jax with you?"

"Everyone's here!" She swung her phone around to showcase all of us. Then she practically dangled her phone out the window. "And we are enjoying the freaking fantastic views. Isn't it absolutely breathtaking?"

His low hum came out as a squeak over the phone's speakers. "Vicky, I really wish I could have come with you. My apologies to you all. I'm sure the wedding was amazing." Then he cleared his throat and said in a voice I am sure he hoped was casual, "And I see even Jett's taking a break from work to sightsee."

She angled the phone so we were both in the frame for Steven to see. "Jett's still working. Laptop came along for the ride."

Steven chuckled, but it was strained. "I see. Well, good to meet you through the phone, Jett." He didn't really think that. Anxiety bled out of his smile. "I know we may do business together soon."

"Right. My lawyers and the financial team are reviewing some details before we reach out. I know you've been working closely with them and my investment reps. I'll be sure to personally take a look before we make our final decision." Because I hadn't looked at all. I didn't scope out every company we absorbed. I trusted my team to do that.

He looked relieved as he sighed into the phone. Then, his eyes shifted over, and I knew from the smile that stretched across his face, he was looking at Vick. "Well, that makes me so happy, Jett. Vicky, you are always influential and indispensable, I swear."

Her friend Katie grumbled behind us about him calling her Vicky, but she ignored it and said, "I'm excited to get back to work. I'll look over the contracts you sent me tomorrow morning."

"Perfect. Call me once you do."

"Sounds good. Talk soon."

He smiled and then the video chat ended.

"Seriously," Katie piped up from behind her. "Can he stop calling you Vicky? You hate that nickname, and I do too. It's fucking gross."

"It is not gross," Vick retorted. "He doesn't mean any harm."

"Harm? Ha! He's practically pissing on you by calling you something no one else does. He wants to bone you."

Vick didn't deny it. She smiled like she hoped that was the consensus. "I hope you're right. We've been friends for a few years, but I think he's starting to really make an effort. Brey was there last time we all went out for drinks and he totally looked like he was into me, right?"

Brey smiled and rested her head on Jax's shoulder. "He seemed thrilled to see you."

"And he sounded sincere when he said he wished he could have made it right?"

Brey nodded.

I went back to typing and cut their conversation short. "Is this ride ever going to end?"

My tone must have come off rude because Jaydon kicked my chair from behind. "Loosen up, you prick. We're not working."

"You're not working," I grumbled.

The conversation in the van went on without me. Rome, another one of the newlywed's friends who'd flown in for the wedding, bothered Katie by continually calling her Kate-Bait. Jaydon complained that he should have been able to invite a few girls. Jax kept telling him to fuck off while Brey kept my two brothers from coming to blows.

I worked.

At one point, Vick leaned right over my lap to take a picture of the view. "You want to trade seats since you're so intent on capturing every damn thing on your phone?" I asked quietly so we were the only ones privy to our conversation.

"We'll never get a better view than this," she whisper-shouted back at me.

"Then put your phone down and look at it."

She glared at me, but clicked off her phone's camera. "Fine. Trade seats with me."

I slid my laptop into the case at my feet and unbuckled my belt. She started to stand but there was enough space for me to just grab her by the hips and lift her. I held her as I slid into her seat and set her in mine. Her eyes widened and stayed on me the whole time.

"What?"

"Don't grab me like that in front of everyone," she whispered so discreetly I could barely hear her.

"Why?"

"Because it looks like you ... we've ... well, you know."

I smirked. "Maybe I don't. Care to enlighten me?"

She rolled her eyes and looked out the window. "Don't be a jerk and don't grab me like you know my body intimately."

I looked her up and down. Then I reached past her to pull her seatbelt down across her chest. I took my time, and I felt her chest heave in a breath, hold it. A little bubble, one I didn't want to exist formed around us. I snapped the seatbelt into place and popped our moment. "But I do know your body just that way, Victoria."

She scoffed, "No one knows about our night, and I want it to stay that way."

"Why?"

"Because!" she said loudly and some of her friends looked over. I was finding she had a hard time keeping her voice down.

"Are you ashamed, Pix?"

She smiled at everyone and they lost interest quickly. "I'm not ashamed. I just don't think it was memorable enough to share."

I hummed low. "Okay. I'll let you have that one."

She pursed her lips like she wanted to say more but knew it wasn't in her best interest. Her honey-colored eyes followed my movements as I reached back into my bag to grab my laptop.

"What are you working on that is so much better than all this, anyway?" She leaned in a little as I opened my laptop, and her blonde hair slid from her shoulder onto mine.

She was so damn close I could have turned and bit the bottom lip I'd spent so much time nibbling the other night. It tasted like a sweet strawberry, and I could smell that she was probably wearing that same lip gloss.

My body reacted, and I was surprised to find I could barely focus on the email I pulled up. "Just business as always. I may need to research that little company of Mr. Stevie's too. Huh?"

She recoiled. "His name's Steven. Or Mr. Samson. And I highly doubt Steven will think your company buying out ours is a good idea, not after our conversation about you not giving a damn about employees."

Her defensive tone tempted me to push her more. "Honey, for the right price, every man thinks my ideas are fan-fucking-tastic."

She narrowed her eyes. "Not Steven."

The bus driver announced that we'd arrived and everyone cheered.

I let Vick's comment go. She could live in her bubble forever. She probably would too, because I wouldn't pay an arm and a leg for a company that wasn't willing to bend to my will. If Mr. Stevie wanted to keep Samson and Sons, he could.

We paddle boarded on the private beach for much longer than I would have liked to. Fortunately, Rome was also one of the clients I personally invested for. We discussed how his clubs and bars were doing and where we could put extra money. It was close enough to a business meeting that I didn't feel I'd completely wasted my day.

When Katie, Brey, and Vick approached us, I figured I could succumb to a little play. They all goaded Rome into going out to paddleboard. Katie and Brey didn't bother with me, as if they knew my answer would be a withering look.

They practically dragged Rome out, but Vick lingered behind, eyeing me in my black swim trunks. "You dressed to get into the ocean. Are you planning to?"

I looked at the bikini she filled out. "I don't think you're dressed for paddleboarding at all."

She crossed her arms. "Jett, I'm wearing a swimsuit. Of course, I dressed for it."

"You barely kept it on with that last fall."

"So, your attention wasn't just on your work this whole time," she remarked, hands falling to her hips.

"If you're insinuating that I was paying attention to you, I can admit to that. Every guy is paying attention to you. The paddleboard instructor can't look away. He's too damn nervous he'll miss when the strings you call a bikini top inevitably come loose." I wasn't kidding either. He was still staring at her even while she talked to me.

I understood though. Vick drew eyes wherever she went, I was starting to realize. She dressed for attention and she got it. She had chosen to wear a bubblegum-pink bikini top and thong today and the color popped against her tan. Her blonde hair was down and slicked back by the ocean water. With her long legs and loud personality, she drew every eye on that private beach.

She put her hands on her hips and leaned in closer. "Jett Stonewood, stop trying to insult me and get your workaholic ass into that beautiful water. No one should be sitting here working, not even you."

I stared at her for maybe a moment too long. She surprised me by not fighting back when I insulted her. Most everyone would have been defensive, would have retaliated in some way. She, instead, wanted me to have an enjoyable time.

Before I realized what I was doing, my laptop was back in its case and I was standing up. She backed up a step, and her eyes widened as I loomed up to her. She didn't shrink away. Instead, she blatantly looked when I took my shirt off.

"Careful, Pix, someone might think you had an unmemorable night with me."

CHAPTER FIVE

VICK

THAT MAN COULD sit on a laptop all day, and somehow, I would still salivate over him. When he took his top off, I wasn't going to look away for anyone. I didn't care if everyone in the world knew I'd slept with him right then.

Kauai somehow made everything more vivid, colors more saturated, life more vibrant. And under that sun, Jett became a man I wanted more and more. His arms looked bigger, his chest wider, his abs more defined. His skin already looked bronze even though I was sure he didn't spend extra time tanning.

I didn't respond to him, knowing that's what he probably wanted. I just met his gaze and held it.

He cocked his head as if assessing me. "Paddleboarding won't make me enjoy this trip."

"Have you ever paddle boarded before?"

He grunted and then walked past me to grab a board. "Of course."

I rolled my eyes. "Not everyone has done it. It isn't just common practice, Jett."

I grabbed mine and followed him out.

"Have you not?" he asked the question like he knew the answer.

"I just learned on this trip."

As he waded into the water, I followed. When he veered around a large rock that blocked the others from view, I did too.

"So, you just suntanned when you went to the beach before?"

I let the cool blue water lap at me while the sun warmed my skin. I breathed in the humid air and felt the breeze in my hair before I answered. "My family only went to the beach when I was young. I haven't been to one since high school. This is my first time."

Before he jumped onto the paddleboard, he asked, "Why?"

I shrugged. "Life sometimes gives you lemons and you make lemonade. Other times, you can't make anything."

It wasn't an answer. We both knew it. I waited to see if he'd pry, but he jumped up on the paddleboard instead.

I got to my feet, the board shaking beneath me, and steadied myself. Jett paddled ahead with confident strokes. When I stuck my paddle in the water, I overbalanced and belly flopped in with a splash.

Jett looked back and laughed. I managed to right myself and paddle a few strokes after him, but it wasn't long before I fell again. Each time I fell, he laughed harder.

Under the sun and in the sparkling water, I could swear Jett was finally enjoying himself.

After about my tenth fall, I stayed in the water and rested my elbows on the board as I stared up at him. "You have to admit this is kind of fun, Jett."

He paddled up so close, looming over me. Droplets of water glistened on his legs and he smiled down at me like Zeus would at an ungodly soul. "I'm getting my exercise in for the day instead of having to work out when I get back to my place, so that's a plus."

"Oh, come on," I whined. "You are the epitome of a bad mood. Nothing will make you enjoy this trip, will it?"

As soon as the words left my mouth, Jett crouched on his paddleboard. His smile disappeared and his brows drew a little closer together. Determination glittered in his eyes.

I took a small step back in the waist-deep water. He jumped off his board, unhooked himself from it, and came toward me. I backed away and tried to put my board between us. "What are you doing, Jett?"

"Showing you exactly what will make me enjoy this trip."

He ducked underwater and suddenly I felt his hands skating around my ankle, removing my board's band. Then, he was back above water, pushing away my board so he could grab me around the waist and bring my body up against his.

I glanced around quickly. "Are you joking? We can't…"

He didn't shift his eyes away from mine for a single second, not even checking his surroundings to see who might be watching us. He just pulled me closer with his hand on the back of my neck and kissed me.

Devoured me.

Branded me with that kiss. He didn't leave room for me to object or resist or even breathe. No part of me wanted to do any of those things anyway.

My stomach flipped, and my heart rate picked up. My mind got lost in the illusion of a world where we were lovers, the only people who existed. The waves lapped at my back, cooling it while Jett heated me everywhere else.

"This bikini top…" he groaned as he kissed down my neck.

"You love it?"

"Me and every fucking man on the island."

He untied the strings around my neck. "Is that a problem?"

"You enjoy men looking at you?"

I smirked and shrugged. "I don't really care whether they do or not. It's all about fun, Jett. Enjoying yourself on a vacation. I enjoy feeling sexy, and if men enjoy looking, I guess everyone wins. They're just looking."

He hummed but didn't say anything else. He let my top slide off of me and drop into the water. The breeze felt liberating against my bare skin. His hands skimmed down my neck to my breasts. "They don't deserve to see this body, Vick. Not like it's a piece of meat. It should be a crime."

I didn't answer him, didn't tell him that his idea of hiding it all away was silly. Because at one time, I'd thought I would never get to display it again or even have a body to display, for that matter.

I looked down at his hands squeezing me. I rubbed my hands up and down his chest. Then, I did what any woman would with Jett Stonewood in front of them. I hooked my arms behind his neck and jumped up to wrap my legs around his hips. He grabbed my ass with both his hands and hummed low in my ear, "Woman, next time we go to a place you have to wear a swimsuit, wear a damn one piece."

I bit his neck. "No fun."

"And we all know you're all about fucking fun."

He slid my bikini to the side. When his fingers brushed over me, I should have glanced around to make sure my friends weren't looking for me, that people weren't catching me in the act.

I didn't though.

Beep. Beep. Beep.

This was my moment and the little sound in my head reminded me of that. In the middle of Kauai's bluest bay, under the brightest sun, with one astonishingly hot guy who wanted me here, and I wanted him.

I catalogued it, saving it for a future daydream when I'd pull it out of my imaginary Rolodex. I noted the way his blue eyes darkened, the way his jaw tightened when I slid my hand down the front of his swim trunks, how he thrust into me and every one of his muscles rippled under me. I would have taken a freaking picture of his face if I could have, so perfectly symmetrical and angled just right that every woman in the world would probably drop their bikini top for him.

I didn't need to record the way his hand moved in me though. He had learned how to work each inch of my body into a frenzy the first night we were together and there in that crystal-blue water, he used every skill he knew to drive me to the edge.

I writhed against him, wanting to race to my release, but he kept a steady pace. "Jett, stop playing with me."

"I thought you liked to play," he quipped as he walked us into deeper water.

I squeezed him hard and quickened my strokes. "I like to have fun."

His hand moved in me, and I moaned. "This fun enough?"

I didn't answer, just rode his hand and stroked him at the same pace.

He grunted, "Looks like you're having a great time, Vick."

He slid another finger in, and I bucked against him. "Jett, can you please ... "

"Please what?"

I moaned, "Please shut up and fuck me here. Please. Please. Please."

He laughed at my chanting but didn't move to take his shorts off. He curled those two fingers in me and rubbed in just the right place.

He kept strolling deeper into the water. And just as I was about to scream, he submerged us.

We looked at each other as I pumped him faster and faster, and he fingered me at the same speed. The water clouded my senses, disoriented me with lack of oxygen, and shook me to my core. When I orgasmed, I didn't see stars or explosions or lights. I saw his blurry figure under the water like a foggy dream taking over my damn mind.

He owned me, held me where I couldn't breathe, couldn't feel air against my skin, or witness any life other than him.

I felt him spasm right after me, his muscles tightening. I saw his neck go taut and knew he was getting off just as intensely as me.

We were under the water, in an unfamiliar world made for us alone. I told myself to forget about the fairy tale, to stop living in reverie, but I lost myself to it with him under that water.

After Jett got me off, he swam away, then reappeared with my swim top. "Here."

I grabbed it and retied the strings as he front crawled over to where the tide had washed our boards out. When he pushed mine toward me, I said, "Should I go around the rock first or you?"

"Or we could both go at the same time?"

I narrowed my eyes at him.

He laughed. "Vick, no one cares what we're doing."

"Speak for yourself. My friends are nosy."

"Are they? Or are you the nosy one and think they'll ask the questions you normally ask them?"

"Brey knows..."

"She might know something is up, but that girl would never ask."

I huffed and straightened my bikini top before I paddled my board toward the rock. "Whatever. It doesn't matter."

"I know it doesn't. We're adults. We can do whatever we want in the damn water."

I ignored him and swam toward Jaydon and Brey who looked like they had resorted to sitting in shallow water looking at seashells.

"Where did you guys go?" Jaydon asked.

I looked pointedly at Jett behind me. "There's some beautiful coral reef on the other side of that rock."

Jett rolled his eyes and walked past all of us without engaging in the conversation.

"Guess Jett didn't enjoy it?" Jaydon practically yelled after his brother to irritate him.

Jett turned to respond, catching all of us off guard. "Oh, the reef was exceptional. Under the water, in this light—absolutely exceptional."

My face heated, my stomach flipped, and my knees went weak enough that I slid down lower into the water to hide my reaction to his words.

CHAPTER
SIX

VICK

HIDING MY REACTION to him for the rest of the trip proved more difficult. His presence weighed me down at every turn.

We would go out to eat and he'd sit next to me as if he thought we'd suddenly become friends. When I ordered a helping of the pig roast, he scrunched up his nose as if I offended him. Then he went on to tell the table about the detriment of meat to our health.

Of course Jett was vegan. His overly practical mind couldn't fathom eating food for pleasure. Food was fuel and, according to him, meat was like feeding your body unleaded when you could have diesel.

Nope, he corrected to electric.

We'd have sundowners on the hotel beach and he'd hover at my elbow like a pesky fly, a very large, very sexy pesky fly.

We would go for a hike and he'd decide to come with, even though he complained the whole time.

On a particularly rigorous hike, he critiqued my hiking style the whole way, telling me I needed better shoes and I was going to fall, and then he smiled smugly when I did.

I didn't give in to the weight of his negativity. Even on that hike, covered in mud from my fall, I made it all the way to the Queen's Bath. The rocks jutted up against one another as we climbed them along the water's edge. A steep slope fed into a pool of crystal-blue water. The surf lapped at the rock surrounding it as one wave crashed in and the bath swelled with more water.

I turned to him and said it would be the best way to get rid of the mud but he scolded me about my clothes getting wet.

So I started to pull my shirt over my head, undeterred, but he growled as he grabbed my arm and told me I'd better fucking not. I wasn't sure if he was possessive or concerned others would judge us, but I let it go. Instead, I waded in with my outfit on and made sure to tell him how amazing the water felt. I sighed and moaned as I washed the mud off, like it was the most pleasurable experience of my life. I told him it was even better because I'd fallen and could wash the mud off.

Then my last morning in Kauai came. I sat on top of a cliff, watching the water down below.

The day was chilly and cloudy, but the sea was calm, waves barely lapping at the rocks. The soft breeze blew through my hair, reminding me to relax and let the wind whisk away any anxieties.

I ducked under the chain fence that kept people away from the cliff's edge and stepped right up to it. All I saw was green mountains and water meeting the clouds on the horizon. Standing on the bluff, witnessing nature in all its glory, made me feel bigger and smaller than ever before at precisely the same time. I sat down and let the feeling wash over me.

"Fuck me, woman. You shouldn't sit so close to the edge." His voice made me jump.

"Jesus! Warn someone when you're behind them. Especially when they're on the edge of a cliff."

"Like I said, move back. There's a reason for the fence," he commanded as he wiggled the chain.

I turned back toward the sea. "I'm not moving."

I heard a low grumble and then he sighed. "God damn it."

I turned to find him maneuvering under the chain before sitting right behind me. I furrowed my brows. "What are you doing?"

He tucked his legs on either side of me and wrapped his arms around my shoulders. "Making sure you don't die on this trip because apparently you have a death wish."

I glared. "No, I don't."

"You went on about a hundred dangerous hikes and whenever you came across a sign saying danger or caution, you did exactly what it said not to do."

I shrugged. "You only live once, right?"

"Can't enjoy it if you're dead because you fell off a cliff."

"I'm aware that I can't enjoy things if I'm dead, Jett."

"Could have fooled me," he murmured as he nuzzled into my neck and looked out at the sea.

I let the conversation die. I didn't want to argue while I took in the sun on the water or the waves breaking against the rock wall. We stayed cuddled against one another for too long. So long that I memorized the way I felt secured in his arms. I memorized how he smelled—like a citrus soap mixed with sea water—and how his chest felt like solid, steady ground against my back. I tried to catch my heart as it fell for Jett but it may as well have been plunging over that cliff. The slope was steep, jagged, and too severe to correct.

Just as I was about to drag myself away from Jett, I saw a movement against the waves. At first, the tiny splash drew my attention because it deviated from the natural current. When nothing more happened, I scanned the water one last time and started to stand.

Jett's hand grabbed my thigh, holding me there. He pointed just a little way from where I had seen the first splash. "Baby whale," he whispered.

I tried not to blink.

Beep. Beep. Beep.

The sound in my head reminded me to absorb this moment as once in a lifetime, as a moment I may have never gotten.

My eyes scoured the water again. I didn't want to miss anything. I stared so hard I began to think I'd imagined the splash. From the water, breaking the slight ripples, jumped a baby humpback whale. Right after, the mother followed. She soared through the sky like she could fly and the sun rays caught the water glistening over her body. She sparkled, she glimmered, she erupted with life.

I didn't realize I was squealing until Jett nudged his chest into my back. "They can't hear you, Vick."

"I saw a humpback whale." I looked over my shoulder at him and he attempted to hide his grin, but his lips curled at the corners.

"Yes, you saw a humpback whale and a baby one too."

"It jumped out of the freaking ocean, Jett." I couldn't be quiet if I wanted to.

"They do that sometimes, Pix."

"This is officially the best trip I've ever been on. I can't believe that happened. I mean, we were just sitting here, and they jumped out like they wanted us to see them, like they wanted to be a part of my day."

"They jumped out because that's what they do. They have to breathe," he deadpanned.

"Fine." I would give him that. "They probably didn't care if I saw them, but still...."

His smile finally came out to play, and it reached all the way across his face, enough to crinkle the corners of his eyes.

He was so appealing when he smiled, like he had all this happiness bottled up in him he didn't want to share with anyone. When he unleashed it, it blinded me to everything but him. The wind had tousled his jet black hair, and his blue eyes mirrored the sea below us.

On the edge of the world, I didn't question myself when I leaned in and kissed him.

He wrapped a hand around my neck and kissed me back.

He tasted of Hawaiian sea and sun and love.

We made out on the edge of that cliff for maybe a minute. Maybe an hour. I lost track of time. I was more focused on how his hands slid over every part of my body he could reach, how his mouth owned every part of mine.

When he finally leaned back to stop us from going too far, he raked his gaze over me and grumbled, "I would screw you on the edge of this cliff if it wasn't so dangerous."

I smirked. "I'm game if you are."

"You have a death wish, Pix." He stood up and pulled me with him, lifting me over the chain with no struggle.

"I don't. I just like to—"

"Have fun. I know. But vacation ends today when we fly back. You ready to face the real world?"

"My real world is still fun. I'm happy to get back to my day-to-day."

We started walking back to our places. "You enjoy the city that much?"

"I'm loving it." I practically burst with emotion. The city had always seemed out of my reach. I was so damn happy to be experiencing the hustle and bustle of it all over the past month that I would tell anyone about it. "The jostling to get to work every morning, the way people are so driven they would literally fight you to get one step ahead. Sounds weird, but the pulse of the city is amazing."

He grunted.

"I'm lucky. I get to work near my best friend and do what I love. Steven gave me a great opportunity."

He nodded. "Yes. Sounds like Stevie really does you a lot of favors."

"He's an exceptional friend."

Jett looked my way, and his smile was slow. "If that's what you call it."

I quirked a brow. "That's what I call it. And I know what you're insinuating. I'm honest. I'd let you know if I'd slept my way into a position. But I'm an associate and Steven hasn't even asked me out yet. I hope he does though."

We came to the fork in the road where our paths separated. Jett didn't stop walking like I expected.

I thought maybe he would confess that he wanted my number, that we should try to give it a go back home. He turned to the right and said over his shoulder, "I hope he does too. I'm sure, even having only seen him on your annoying FaceTime, you would make a picture-perfect couple and your wedding would be just as beautiful as Brey and Jax's."

I glared at him. "You say that sarcastically, but it could happen."

He kept walking away without looking back at me. So I yelled after him, "One day you'll come across the love of your life and your cynical ass will miss it. You'll regret it too. Just wait and see."

His laugh carried over the wind. "Goodbye, Victoria."

I let him go. That man wasn't mine to change.

He was a glorious distraction that I had gotten too wrapped up in.

I had indulged myself and allowed everything I did with him to touch me deeply. But I refused to have regrets.

On the flight back, I wrote him off.

And back in Chicago, I forgot all about him.

Or so I told myself.

CHAPTER
SEVEN

JETT

LIVING IN A city either makes or breaks a person. The constant movement—the way the streets are always alive, the lights always on, the noise persistently vibrating through your walls at night—can drive a person to work harder or fold under the pressure. It can irritate someone into leaving for the suburbs or lull them into the rhythm they were made to follow.

I was made for it.

The city pumped to a steady beat, and I loved knowing that I could alter that beat if I worked hard enough.

Stonewood Enterprises was one of the largest investment companies out there. We bought up businesses and turned them into lucrative ventures. We also invested companies' money and pulled in so much that the market felt our every shift. Stocks moved when we moved.

I called those shots.

I focused on some of the largest accounts as well as a few small clients. One of them sat across from me, back straight as she went over her portfolio.

"I want to make sure this goes back into funds for your family."

I sighed. "Brey, you are family. You were before and now you are legally."

She cleared her throat. "Still, if you could keep this confidential…"

I slammed my laptop shut. The woman, I swear, did this shit just to irritate every one of us Stonewoods. She couldn't handle that my mother and father gave her a trust fund when her dad went off the deep end and her mom died. Now she kept trying to pay it back, much to the irritation of me, my brothers, my father, and my mother.

Her ideas were actually respectable in my opinion, but I wasn't going to honor them. The money had been a gift from my parents, one we all got as their children. They saw Aubrey as one of theirs. It was their choice, not mine. "I commend you for trying. I understand why, and I would probably try to do the same thing. But the whole family's been pretty clear about this."

"You go around them all the time," she quickly retorted.

She had a point. She worked under me exclusively, and as my intern, she knew I had a habit of writing off my brother's and father's business suggestions.

"That might be true, but Jax—"

She cut me off. "He would probably try to kill you, I know. I'll talk to him."

I chuckled. "My brother fooled you into thinking he can one-up me? I'd still beat his ass if he came at me. That said, he has some leverage when it comes to that app of his. I know him. He'd threaten to tank that app if I helped you funnel money back into the family funds."

She sighed. "Can you just think about it?"

"You want honesty?"

She nodded.

"No. You're family."

Her cheeks reddened, not in embarrassment but anger. There it was, the spitfire she tried to hide from everyone.

"It will never happen and every time you ask me, you waste more of my time and more of your time. And your time is my time when we have work to do."

She glared at me, and I waited. I nudged my closed laptop so it sat perfectly straight on my desk.

"Right," she sighed. She knew the conversation was over for me. She opened her laptop and pulled up a list of businesses. "We handled your two biggest clients. They accepted your offers. We'll have a merger happening by the end of next week with the other, and you told the investment team to handle the rest of the businesses. It looks like all but two have accepted our team's offers."

"And the two are?"

She named a company I knew wouldn't accept. I didn't want them to, which was why they hadn't.

It surprised me to hear that Samson and Sons had walked away from our offer though.

"Reason given?"

Aubrey squirmed. "Ah, this feels like something I shouldn't be involved in, but you know Vick too. So, I guess she and Steven spoke. He wants what's best for his employees and didn't want to give up the firing and hiring ability along with retirement plans."

"Hmm," I said as I pulled up information about the company on my computer. As I did, I mumbled, "Tell me more about their request."

"There wasn't a request."

"I'm sorry?"

She smoothed her hair. "I can send you the email, but there wasn't a counter request. They just refused."

"Send me the refusal letter."

Aubrey's eyes widened. "Jett, Vick and I are close friends and—"

"And what?"

"Well," she cleared her throat. "Our communication is a bit informal because we all know each other. I can have her send an official letter today. I only got word from her earlier this morning."

"Actually, I'd like to see the informal e-mail."

She licked her lips and looked down at her laptop. Her poker face was slipping, which meant that e-mail wasn't one they wanted me to see.

Aubrey was a decent intern, good actually. Her investment style jibed with mine. She took risks, did her research, and remained professional. She also never stepped outside of bounds and was exceptionally well-mannered. I liked her from a work perspective.

I also knew she wasn't someone I could fire considering my brother had just married her. So sometimes, in these moments where I wanted to tell her to do as she was told and send the e-mail over immediately, I'd become frustrated with her.

"Brey?"

Her eyes snapped up.

"Send me the email now, please."

She started typing on her laptop. "Okay. Before I do … "

I didn't have time for the explanation and warning she would give me regarding the email. "Never mind. I'll pull it up myself."

"What?" she stuttered out.

I already had her email opening on my own laptop.

"This is Stonewood Enterprises. I need access to all my employee's emails. For security and efficiency purposes. You're being inefficient right now."

She huffed.

I shot her a look. "You'll have the research we need for our two o'clock meeting?"

She got the hint and stood up as she slammed her laptop closed. "Access to everyone's emails is—"

"Company policy, Brey. You read the handbook?"

Her eyes narrowed. Sometimes I wondered if she knew how big a temper she had for someone so small. "Of course I read the handbook. Did you?"

"I helped write the handbook."

"Then you know that the way you are talking to me isn't right. Don't be that boss. Or that brother-in-law."

I felt the need to crack my neck. She had a point. I wondered if sisters-in-law were supposed to be this annoying. "Just be ready at two."

"I plan on it." With that, she walked out, and I took a few deep breaths. I needed to talk to my brother and my dad about her working under me. I couldn't keep reining in my temper around her. I needed an intern or assistant I could yell at if I needed to yell at them, and one who listened to me right when I asked for something.

On that note, I pulled up the email that Vick had sent Aubrey that morning.

> **FROM:** Victory Blakely <V.Blakely@samsonandsons.com>
> **TO:** Aubrey Whitfield <Aubrey.Whitfield@stonewood-enterprises.com>
>
> *Yep. Steven said there was no way he was selling just for the money. He's not going to hand over firing authority to your dick of a boss. He's honestly such a moral guy. I'll draft the legal document later.*
>   *Sorry not sorry we won't be working together :-P*
>   *Drinks at the club on Saturday? Just tell Jax we need a girls' night. He can live without you for a little while. Or he can come and watch us like a hawk. I know he'll pick the latter.*
>
> *Vick*

Such a moral guy? As opposed to what I was? Funny that the woman who'd slept with me multiple times just a week ago didn't have anything remotely nice to say about me when it came to my business.

I rolled my eyes and closed the e-mail. I'd brought little Stevie's company up for no other reason than the principle of the matter.

His numbers were good, his company prospered. There were holes though. Just by glancing over the data, I could see where he could make more money, where he could succeed, and where he was faltering.

His type of business was a dime a dozen. Even so, I found myself wanting to prove a point.

> **FROM:** Jett Stonewood <Jett.Stonewood@stonewooden-terprises.com>
> **TO:** Victory Blakely <V.Blakely@samsonandsons.com>
>
> *Dear Ms. Blakely,*
>
> *I was informed Stevie doesn't want to sell at the price point my team offered. Why don't you have a talk with him and let me know what price point he thinks is fair?*
>
> *Sincerely,*
> *The Dick of a Boss*
>
> *PS Your full name's Victory. You didn't correct me in Kauai. Why?*

I wasn't surprised that she responded almost immediately, and I found myself smiling at her words.

> **FROM:** Victory Blakely <V.Blakely@samsonandsons.com>
> **TO:** Jett Stonewood <Jett.Stonewood@stonewoodent-erprises.com
>
> *Dear Mr. Stonewood,*
>
> *Steven wanted me to be clear it wasn't a monetary issue. I have attached the formal rejection letter. We appreciate*

the offer and hope to maintain a cordial business rela-
tionship in the future.

Sincerely,
Vick Blakely

I stewed over her email for the rest of my work day, which went well into the night. I reread the legal documentation and saw that Mr. Stevie had in fact stated that he wanted to retain his roster of employees through their retirement. It was an odd stipulation and one we wouldn't normally accept.

Yet, I called one of my team members to rework our numbers and offer an even higher payout for the company. It wasn't my practice to adjust stipulations, so I didn't in this case either. I wanted firing power if I needed it—always.

Over my late dinner, I pulled up her email again. Outlook let me know she was available on her personal email, the one I'd grabbed from Brey's contact information, and instead of e-mailing her this time, I messaged her.

> **ME:** You didn't answer my PS.
>
> **VICTORY:** I replied to you on my business account. I didn't feel the PS was appropriate work conversation.
>
> **ME:** Hm. And a cordial business relationship?
>
> **VICTORY:** Yes?
>
> **ME:** In your email, that's what you wrote.
>
> **VICTORY:** Right. Yes, we want to maintain that. What's your question?
>
> **ME:** Were you maintaining that in Kauai with me?
>
> **VICTORY:** This also isn't an appropriate work conversation.
>
> **ME:** That's why I messaged you on your personal account.
>
> **VICTORY:** Want to tell me how you got this account, by the way? And your account still isn't your personal one.

ME: I run this company and it's a family business. I'm not concerned.

VICTORY: Well, I am.

ME: Fine, give me your number.

VICTORY: Yeah, no.

I opened a new window and signed into my private Gmail account.

ME: This is now my personal account. You happy? Answer my question.

VICTORY: Your question is off base and totally rude.

ME: How?

VICTORY: You're insinuating I slept with you to maintain some relationship!

ME: No. I was insinuating you can't have a cordial business relationship after I fucked you and saw you come.

VICTORY: OMG, I'm going.

ME: Give me your number.

VICTORY: No and don't you dare ask Brey. She already feels like shit after you hacked her email.

ME: You know I couldn't care less. I will ask her if you don't give it to me.

VICTORY: The number's in your email… You're really starting to make it hard to see the good in someone when you're such a terrible human being.

I closed the chat and called her.

"Are you serious?" she practically shouted in the phone. "I don't want to talk to you."

"Well, you picked up your phone."

I heard rustling and a sigh. "Yes, because I happen to think you'll interrogate Brey if I don't answer."

"And you're right."

"What do you want, Jett?"

"Why didn't you tell me your name is Victory?"

"Because it's a common mistake everyone makes when they meet me. There's no need to make someone uncomfortable by correcting them."

"I'm not 'everyone' or just 'someone.' I slept with you and spent nearly a week with you on an island."

"And that was a great time. Now the week is over. So, we should probably stop bringing it up."

"Why?" I asked, not really sure I even wanted the answer.

"Why?" she repeated, her voice shrill. "Because, as you made abundantly clear, it was just a vacation fling and we're back to reality now. Like you said."

"You didn't seem to think it was just a fling at first."

"But you reminded me it was, and I'm very happy about that."

I chuckled at her emphasis. She riled so easily and it made me want to rile her more. This girl, so wrapped up in the whimsical little land she'd created for herself, had no idea how bad life could get. Some part of me wanted to show her, to see her light dim a little and then have her explode under me in my bed.

I realized right then that I wasn't done with her and I wanted our fling to last longer.

"Why are you happy about that?"

"Because you and I are oil and vinegar. We don't mix well at all."

"Maybe we do. Have dinner with me here."

"Absolutely not."

"Why not?"

"I'm not a booty call…" she hesitated. "At least I'm not anymore now that we aren't on vacation."

I laughed. "Come on, Vick. Just dinner."

"Honestly, Jett, maybe I would have." I heard her sigh over the phone. "I thought we could be more, but you reminded me we couldn't. And I'm set on finding something serious. I want a boyfriend and a husband and 2.5 kids with a white picket fence."

Her declaration shut down my desire to banter with her. The metaphorical bucket of ice water splashed over my head and dick. "Right. I don't want any of that at all."

"Exactly," she sighed. "We had a good time."

"Good enough to maintain a cordial business relationship?"

She cleared her throat. "That would be ideal. Steven is"—she sighed into the phone in a dreamy way—"such a great guy. I don't want him concerned that my relations with you were anything more than they were."

I hummed. "You told him about us?"

"I'm not telling anyone about us," Vick replied quickly. "There's nothing to tell."

"Right. Cordial business relationship. Got it, babe."

"Okay. So, hope you have a good night."

"Sure. Sweet dreams, Victory."

She hung up without replying.

That night, I couldn't stop mulling over our conversation. I pictured her pacing as she spoke to me on the phone, her blonde hair swaying. The girl was animated as hell, and I was sure she lived her life the same way, with a level of vibrancy that was too loud to turn off.

The next morning, I had my team email Samson and Sons. I wanted a sit-down with them all. Vick thought I was coldhearted when it came to business but there was a reason Steven's company was small and mine was big.

I had nothing to prove. However, that didn't stop the idea from bouncing around in my head, impossible to ignore. I had stopped setting aside my own desires long ago. I found it rarely paid off.

One of my team members stopped in my office. "Jett, Mr. Samson agreed to meet with you next week. He wanted me to warn you that he doesn't see himself negotiating any new terms though."

I leaned back in my chair. "Okay. He say anything else?"

"He went on to explain that he's thrilled with his company at this time." He waved off the rest of the conversation. "He thinks he's playing hardball. Just doing his peacock dance."

I smiled. Jack always had an ear for the ones who were lying or exaggerating. He was one of the best on my team when it came to measuring how well a business would actually do under our name. "So, you think we need to fluff his feathers next week?"

"I think the guy's excited to meet you."

"Most people are."

He rolled his eyes. "Man, get off your high horse. He says he doesn't want to sell, but he's bringing his legal team, which means he's willing to negotiate. I don't know if it's even worth the investment."

"It probably isn't."

He narrowed his eyes a little. Then nodded. "I figured you knew that. Guess you have your own agenda. I'll follow your lead."

"That's what I hired you to do."

He left my office, waving at me over his shoulder.

I got to work and researched Samson and Sons a little more.

What was so priceless about his company and their assets that he wouldn't hand over rights to me?

I knew of only one asset worth hanging onto, and I was starting to think I'd be willing to pay a hefty price to obtain it.

CHAPTER EIGHT

VICK

"I'M NOT DATING** either of them," Katie yelled across the table over the music. The crowd was loud, but not that loud.

"You don't have to scream at us about it." Brey eyed Katie as if signaling her to take it down a notch. The two were probably having some private, telepathic conversation. They had been best friends since high school and inseparable ever since.

I understood their bond in the sense that Katie was a sort of fierce protector of Brey's when they were growing up. They both came from rough backgrounds, but Katie wore her warrior loud and proud. Her hair was chopped at her shoulders with electric-blue streaks through the black. She wore a cut up shirt and even though she was small, her tattoos made her look badass.

Even without all that, her gray eyes could stare down the biggest man in the room and make him wither.

Brey was the complete opposite. She had dark, natural hair, dressed conservatively most of the time and always tried to make everyone comfortable by being polite. People would call her well-bred but her new husband made sure to shake her out of that breeding every chance he got. He loved to see her let loose, and I envied their connection every time I saw them together.

"I'm not screaming about anything." Katie looked at me for support. "Vick, you know what screaming is. Tell her I'm not screaming."

"She's not screaming, Brey." I sighed and put my chin in my hand.

Brey stared at me longer than I wanted her to. "What's wrong, Vick? I wouldn't ask except that … well, something is bothering you, isn't it?"

"I shouldn't have e-mailed your business account," I admitted. I still felt bad about our conversation. She had run to the bathroom immediately after leaving Jett's office to warn me that he'd hacked her email.

"Water under the bridge." Brey waved me off. "Jax said Jett won't hold that e-mail against me."

Katie blew a raspberry. "Jax is lying."

Brey sighed. "I know he is. But I decided I don't really care. Jett shouldn't have done that."

I smiled. Brey held everyone to her own standards, and I was happy to see her stand up for herself when they didn't meet those standards. "Your boss is something else."

"Is he now?" Katie asked and raised an eyebrow.

"Why are you asking me like that?"

"You still haven't disclosed what you two were doing half the time in Kauai."

"And you still haven't disclosed what you are doing with the two Armanelli brothers," I quipped.

Katie narrowed her eyes. "I said I'm not dating either of them."

"That doesn't give us any information. You never admit to dating anyone. Ever."

"Brey knows I'm not dating either of them." Katie nudged Brey.

She sipped her drink before she agreed. "She isn't, but I think Bastian wouldn't mind … "

"Bastian wouldn't mind with anyone."

I whispered what was bothering me. "Aren't they in the mob?"

Brey rolled her lips between her teeth, and I knew the answer immediately.

"You can't date someone in the mob, Katie." I grabbed her drink as she reached for it to buy time. "No. You date questionable guys all the time, but I think we need to put our foot down with the freaking mob, you guys."

Katie leaned in and widened her gray eyes at me. "Keep your voice down. Jesus. It isn't the mob, per se."

"'Per se'?" I threw my hands up. "What does that even mean? Brey, you tell her."

Brey winced. "I can't tell her anything. I love those boys."

"You love them? You can't love people in the mafia. They … wait. Do they do business with the Stonewoods?"

Brey looked toward the ceiling of the club. "This isn't something we should talk about."

"Well, Katie is dating one of them!" I yelled and stood up from my stool. "And you just married Jax. If his business is associated with—"

"Stonewood Enterprises is associated with every business in the city, Vick," Brey stated matter-of-factly.

I pictured guns, violence, murder. *The Godfather* reel started playing in my head, and I blurted, "You guys need to figure your shit out. We could be killed."

Katie—who never seemed to worry about anything—eyed me like I was a lunatic. "You do realize that we aren't in a movie, right? Organized crime isn't what it once was."

"I don't know if you're downplaying the situation or being honest." No one ever really did with her. "And, anyway, you don't think anything is a big deal."

She rolled her eyes. Brey jumped in. "No one needs to worry."

I pursed my lips. "Does Rome know you're dating someone in the mob?"

This time, Katie's eyes bugged out and she stood up. "He doesn't get a say in who I date."

Her words were measured. She narrowed her eyes at me like she was telepathically communicating to keep my mouth shut.

She didn't want me blurting out that I had found Rome and her tangled in the sheets a while back. Rome and Brey used to sleep together too but never had feelings for each other. I had a pretty good suspicion that Katie and Rome's story went deeper and Katie didn't want anyone finding out.

I shrugged my shoulders and crossed my arms. "Then he won't mind if I tell him you're dating one of the Armanelli brothers."

"Don't be a bitch, Vick," Katie spit out.

Brey rubbed her forehead. "You guys, come on. This is a girls' night out. Let's not fight."

"Fight about what?" A deep voice rumbled behind me, and I felt the Stonewood presence before I turned and saw them.

Jax and Jett approached with a few enormous men in suits. Security.

The club was packed tonight, and they didn't need problems with Jax being here. Jax slid his arm around Baby's waist.

"This is a girls' night," she glared at him.

He smiled. "Peaches, we're newlyweds. I get you every night."

Envy shot through my veins. I wanted a man to want me like Jax wanted Brey. Love me like he loved her. Always. Even at her worst.

I glanced at Jett. The man who would never ever want or love like his brother. He stood there staring back at me with nothing in his blue eyes. He didn't feel a sliver of emotion for any woman, not even me, who he had slept with multiple times. Still, even with that coldness, or maybe because of it, he looked lethally gorgeous. Muscles stretched his collared shirt, his rolled cuffs revealed impressive forearms, and his dark jeans screamed casual but expensive.

He didn't smile or nod as we eyed one another. His eyes held that look of control, but I knew what was beyond that wall. He covered up how he eyed the crowd, how he was constantly scoping out the weaknesses of a situation.

Jett wanted to keep everyone safe, everyone in his circle protected.

A club was not the place to protect and still his nature to do so made him seem even more appealing to me. Yet, I knew from just the way he broke our stare, he was completely unavailable.

"So, guess the party's over," Katie mumbled and downed her drink. "I have to meet someone anyway."

I glared at her. She glared back because we all knew who she was going to meet.

"We'll talk more about this later," I enunciated every word, making it clear I meant what I said.

She singsonged in a ridiculous Disney princess voice that didn't suit her, "Sure we will." Then, her tone dropped. "Bye, bitches."

With that, she sashayed away.

I wanted to scream at her for leaving me and Jett as third wheels to Brey and Jax, but she knew exactly what she was doing.

I glanced at Jax and Brey who were already in a deep conversation, whispering to one another. I gave in and looked at Jett again. "I guess we're the odd men out."

He tilted his head a little. "Are we now, Victory?"

"Can you not call me that?"

"Why not? It's your name."

"Yeah, but no one calls me that. Everyone calls me Vick."

"I'm not everyone."

"Oh, please. Don't act like you're someone to me or I'm someone to you." I downed the rest of my drink and realized I needed to take a note from Katie and leave. "I should get going, Brey."

She looked away from Jax like it physically pained her to tear her eyes away. "I'm sorry, Vick. My husband is rude."

"That's right. *Husband*." He emphasized the word and Brey smiled. She couldn't help herself, and seeing her that happy made me smile too.

"It isn't a big deal. I should catch up with work anyway. Steven has a big meeting next week."

Brey eyed Jett. "Yes. One I hope goes well for every single person in the room."

Jax glared at Jett. "Don't be a dick next week, man."

Jett didn't respond to either of them. He kept looking at me. "You drive here?"

I grabbed my purse. "No. I didn't move to Chicago and bring a car. The street is one of the most amazing places in the world."

His face scrunched up like he was smelling garbage. I rolled my eyes and hugged Brey goodbye, then Jax, who offered his driver to me. I shook my head no, telling them I would get an Uber.

I glanced at Jett and mumbled, "Have a good night."

With that, I wove through the crowd. No one readily moved for a girl trying to leave, but I swayed in and out of the dancing masses and patted a few backs while I smiled on. I didn't jostle anyone out of their partying. This was someone's night to remember and another's night to forget. I didn't want to take them away from that.

I made it outside about twenty minutes later after stopping a few times to dance with a stranger or cheer on a few shots being emptied.

I pulled up the Uber app on my phone, but someone grabbed my elbow.

"I'll take you home," Jett grumbled behind me, and when I looked up to see his jaw ticking up and down, I tried my best not to be turned on.

"Are you following me?"

"Unfortunately, yes," he ground out as he steered me toward a black SUV.

I attempted to jerk my elbow away from him, but he just tightened his hold and kept pulling me toward the vehicle. "I don't want a ride."

"Well, I would have considered that before."

"Before what?"

"Before I made my guy wait twenty minutes for you to lollygag and mingle with every person in the club."

"Excuse me?" I shook him off when we reached the SUV. "For your information, I didn't need nor did I ask for need a ride. I am perfectly capable of getting myself home safely."

"No woman looking like you and dressed like you at midnight on a Saturday is capable of doing that." He opened the back door. "Get in."

I didn't move one muscle toward that SUV.

"What the hell is that supposed to mean?" I was capable of a lot more than he would ever know. "Don't be an asshole. If you think women can't—"

"Victory, I don't have time for this shit."

"Good." I looked down at my phone and pulled up the Uber app again. "Then leave and let me call an Uber. You would be surprised at how amazing some of these drivers are. They always have the most unique life stories."

I heard him stalk toward me but didn't look up. I knew he was irritated, I just didn't care.

Until he swept me up off the sidewalk and practically shoved me into the back of the SUV.

I should have screamed bloody murder or kidnapping or something.

"Are you kidding me?" I yelled instead.

He got in behind me. "Give it a rest. I told you no one has time for this bullshit."

"You are seriously the most infuriating human being on the planet."

"Don't count yourself out. Where do you live?"

I eyed his driver, who'd pulled away from the curb. I wanted to withhold my address just to spite Jett, but that would force us to be together in the SUV longer.

I rattled off the street name. "Just a few blocks from the park."

Jett narrowed his eyes. "That's the area you live in?"

I shrugged. "Yup."

He didn't explain why he asked and it made me uncomfortable. I hated that feeling. I sat there as we drove in silence, wondering if he thought it was a good neighborhood or a bad one. Did he think I was below the poverty line or spoiled wealthy?

Or did he think nothing at all as he sat there without any emotion on his face whatsoever.

When we turned onto my street, I finally caved. "Why did you ask if this is the area I live in?"

"I wanted to know."

I waited, watching the city lights dance over his face.

I rolled my eyes as we pulled to a stop in front of my apartment building. "You wanted to know? You aren't going to elaborate?"

When his gaze cut to me, I stifled a gasp. The emotion was there. His steely blue eyes drilled into me when he replied, "Do not take an Uber from that club all the way here ever again."

I didn't know whether to be turned on by his command or offended. With our history, I chose the latter, knowing I wanted more than a romp in the sheets. "Jett, my neighborhood isn't unsafe."

"Do you know how many side streets there are on the way here? Do you know how many bad neighborhoods we passed?"

"I'm capable of taking care of myself."

"You're a tiny, naive girl who looks like a bad man's wet dream every time you dress up. You are a *Dateline* case waiting to happen."

I swung my door open as I scoffed at him. "I'm not naive." I paused and widened my eyes as he followed me out of the SUV. "What are you doing?"

"Walking you to your apartment," he ground out like it was the last thing he wanted to be doing at that moment.

"I don't need you to walk me to my apartment. This is a decent part of town." I crossed my arms and glared at him. He somehow looked masculine even getting out of a vehicle, and then he straightened to his full height. Every time he stood in front of me, I wondered if I'd only ever be a booty call to him or if we could have something more.

"I didn't say this wasn't a decent part of town. Stop being so damn defensive."

I turned on my heel and walked to my apartment's lobby. I didn't need to humor him or anyone else.

Except the driver. Shit! I spun around and raced to the driver's side. I knocked on his window and an older man lowered it. "Yes, ma'am?"

"Thank you so much for the ride tonight. Next time, if there is a next time, we should have a bit more fun, right? What's your favorite type of music?"

He beamed. "Johnny Cash is close to my heart."

"Johnny Cash is getting played the whole way."

We smiled at each other and then I waved goodbye.

I skipped all the way to my lobby, leaving Jett in the street.

I didn't slow down because I didn't want to lose the feeling of joy that flowed through me from making someone a little happier that evening.

CHAPTER NINE

JETT

SHE WAS PURPOSELY trying to drive me insane. She ran in front of my SUV to get to the driver's side where traffic raced by—without even looking.

As she approached me, I figured I would get an apology or a thank you, but she just kept skipping right on by.

I grunted. "You're a real piece of work, you know that?"

Her blonde hair swished with each step. The scrap of clothing she, I am sure, would claim was a dress swayed along with her. The fabric floated around her legs but somehow clung to all the right places.

She looked like my heaven's devil tonight—so pretty I was willing to sin for her. It had probably been a mistake to meet them out, but I couldn't get our phone conversation out of my head. I wanted to know exactly what a cordial business relationship entailed. So, when my brother told me he was going to bother Brey on her girls' night out, I found myself tagging along.

I got the warning on the way there. "Don't keep fucking with her, Jett. That's Brey's girl."

I grunted because it wasn't his business that I was fucking with her in the first place. Or just plain fucking her. Which I found I wanted to do again.

I couldn't understand the effect she had on me. It wasn't like me to go to a damn club to find her looking like a dessert I couldn't resist. It wasn't like me to want to drag her out so no man could look at her. And it definitely wasn't like me to follow her out and watch her flirt with every damn man in the club either.

"Did you see the oncoming traffic when you went to talk to my driver, Vick?"

She scoffed as she opened the lobby door. She walked through and didn't hold the door open for me. I slammed my hand into it and followed her in anyway.

"All right. Not worried about that, I guess. Did you know my driver could have run you over when you practically dove in front of the vehicle?" I said to her back.

She mumbled, "Oh my God."

We made our way to a side staircase. I watched her behind as she climbed them in her stilettos and I'm not proud to say my dick stood straight to attention. Those legs were sculpted to be licked and wrapped around a man. This man.

"I'm surprised my driver didn't follow you home too with this fucking outfit."

She spun around on the top step. "What's your point, Jett?"

I shrugged and looked her up and down. "You have to have some sort of survival instinct, woman."

"I survive by not worrying about dumb shit."

She needed to understand there was a risk to being in Chicago, an enormous city where women were most definitely preyed upon. She whipped around before she entered her hallway. "Do you know that two guys followed you out of that club?"

Her laugh carried through the space. "So what? I was probably talking with them before I left. And, let's not forget, you followed me out of the club, too, didn't you, Jett?"

"I'm not just some guy."

"Aren't you though?" Her tone changed; she enunciated every word.

We made it to her front door, but she didn't move to open it.

"You going to invite me in?"

"Depends on how you want to act."

"Open your door, Victory."

She rolled her eyes and put her hand on her hip. "Jett, I don't answer to you."

"You answer to anyone?"

Her eyes glazed over, like she got lost in her own head. Then she looked down to grab her keys and, I assume, to break eye contact with me. "Everyone answers to someone or something."

I leaned toward her, hoping she would continue her train of thought. I wanted to know why she had that melancholy tone all of a sudden, why her hands shook when she put the key in the lock, why her eyes didn't meet mine for a couple more seconds.

She turned to me, her smile was back in place, but it didn't reach her eyes the way it normally did.

"Say you'll be fun if you come in."

"Don't play games, woman." I stepped toward the entrance.

She pulled the door close to her, blocking the way. "Say you'll be fun."

She enjoyed grating on my nerves. Her eyes sparkled with mischief as I sighed and felt my jaw tick. "I'll be as fun as you want me to be."

"Oh, I want all the fun." She swung the door open wide and stepped back.

I walked in and wrapped my arm around her waist. "You better be worth the trouble."

She started to respond, but I didn't want to bicker. I dove into her mouth and kissed her hard, bit her bottom lip, slid a hand up her neck to hold her jaw as I ravaged that sweet taste out of her.

She moaned and encircled her arms around my neck before jumping up to wrap her legs around me too. I kicked the door closed and shoved her up against it.

She gasped when her back hit the wood. "A little rough?" she said in my ear.

"Next time you go out to a club in a dress like that, expect rough, Vick."

She moaned and rolled her hips. My dick responded a little too fast for my liking. I swept my hand up her skirt and found she was wearing next to nothing under it. "How wet are you for me already?"

"Jett, don't play games."

"Games are what make things fun, aren't they?" I dipped my hand in her underwear, and she hissed. "Tell me, how wet?"

Her honey-colored eyes simmered with heat. I wanted them on fire when I took her this time. I slipped a finger in her and felt her tighten around me.

"Damn, woman," I sighed.

"Don't stop."

"A fucking nuclear bomb couldn't get me to stop." That glazed look in her eye, her body tightening everywhere, the sheen of sweat that made her body glisten—it all made me want to get her off as many times as she liked. When that woman orgasmed and writhed under me, I liked it too much.

It was why I had gone to the club tonight, left work at home, decided to play rather than focus on my responsibilities.

She panted as I sucked on her neck, and I slid another finger into her. She bucked a little and moaned.

I moved my mouth up to her ear, "How wet, Victory?"

She hummed and whispered, "So wet."

"That's right, baby." I worked her faster, giving her exactly what she wanted. She clawed at my back, looked toward the ceiling, and then she screamed. She rode my hand as she milked out every last bit of the pleasure I gave her.

She practically melted against me. Her legs slid down my back as she tried to right herself and stand up.

I didn't let her go all the way to the floor though. I held her little body in my arms and mumbled, "Where's your room?"

She was about to answer and then her phone went off. A twangy country voice belted out something about acting like a lady.

Vick shoved away from me. "Oh my God," she mumbled as she searched for the phone.

She scrambled to silence it.

"Do you need to answer that?" I asked.

"No!" she yelped.

"Kinda late for a phone call."

She wrapped her arms back around my neck. "It wasn't important."

Her lips pursed and her jaw tightened. Her body coiled with so much tension, I could feel it ready to snap. I stepped back to assess, to figure out if we should continue what we were doing.

"What happened to a nuclear bomb not stopping you?" she taunted, determination in her eyes.

I told myself I went to her because she was a willing body and damn good lay. I told myself I didn't care about being the one to unwind that tension. I told myself I didn't care about wanting to make that look in her eyes disappear.

I told myself I didn't care.

Still, I stayed by her side until I saw her happiness return.

CHAPTER TEN

VICK

I CRACKED OPEN ONE mascara-crusted eye. The side of the bed he would have been on was empty.

I sighed. Figured he'd have left before the sun came up.

I couldn't complain though. Jett Stonewood was handing out orgasms like free candy. And, well, I was acting like a little kid with a sweet tooth.

Lying in bed thinking about his bedroom skills would have made for a relaxing and probably pleasurable Sunday. But I had wasted too much time thinking about him already. Jett, I decided, checked only one box for me. I needed someone to check off a lot more than that before I spent any more time on them than I already had on that man.

I jumped out of bed and called Brey. She was the one person I could count on here in Chicago.

"Hello?" she answered on the third ring with her usual polite tone. I don't think I'd ever heard that tone change except when she answered a call from Jax.

"Hey, lover!" I would amp her up for the day along with everyone else if I had to. "What are your plans for the day?"

"Well, Jax seems to think I should stop decorating. I wanted to go shop for a vase but he says"—I heard him yelling in the background—"we don't need any more vases."

"You always need more vases," I disagreed.

"Exactly. I told him he could help me look, but he's laughing and working on his laptop right now."

"What is with the Stonewoods and working?"

"Right?" she sighed. "Actually, I should probably be working because Jett will be on his Monday Rampage tomorrow."

I threw on some athleisure clothing as I responded, "Girl, just call in sick. He can't fire you. Better yet, tell him you can't be there on Mondays. Then you can avoid it forever."

I heard her try to suppress a laugh. "Vick, you know I can't."

"Um, you can. You are his sister-in-law." A thought popped in my head. "Hey! Part of that company is technically yours now. Oh my God, girl. Get your own department out from under him."

"He's not so bad. He just takes work very, very seriously."

"Too seriously."

She stayed quiet, which I knew meant she fully agreed.

"All right. Want to go find that vase in the chaos that is Chicago?"

It took us an hour to meet at HomeGoods but when we walked in together, we sighed like we'd been deprived for years. Our eyes probably sparkled with delight as we tried to scope out all the deals at once.

"Okay," I stepped in front of Aubrey before we started. "We have to find a vase. That is the goal."

She nodded as her eyes bounced around the store. "Yup. Beautiful vase will be found."

I turned to the purses, and my mouth practically salivated. "If we find a few other things, no one can blame us."

Aubrey laughed. "Right." It was her turn to step in front of me. She didn't blink her big green eyes at all when she said, "And no one can blame you if you share your secret about Jett with me either."

If I looked away, she'd know there was more to the story. "I don't know what you're talking about."

She stomped her foot. "Come on! I keep a good secret."

"There's no secret to keep."

"I'm the worst liar, Vick. You aren't much better."

My mouth dropped. "That's so rude!"

She looked up to the ceiling. "I know! I'm sorry."

I was about to tell her it was all right.

"But I'm not really sorry." She wrapped her arm around my waist and we both turned to look at a very nice purse. "We only have each other here in this big city. Katie only visits once in a while, and she's not much good as a confidante. I'm your very best friend here. Like this beautiful purse, I'm one in a million."

I looked down at her, narrowing my eyes a little. "I agree that you're one in a million, Brey."

"And you also agree that you don't want to lose your one-in-a-million best shopping partner?"

"When did you get so ruthless?"

"When I married the love of my life and figured out I hated staying inside my little box."

I sighed. She saw me conceding and her face lit up like a Christmas tree. "You can't tell anyone."

She didn't squeal or jump for joy. Aubrey didn't do things like that. She nodded solemnly. "I definitely won't tell anyone," She winced a little. "Pretty sure Jax already knows though."

I rolled my eyes and grabbed the purse to throw in our cart. "I deserve this handbag for sharing all my crap with you today."

We strolled around the store and put way too many things in that cart as I told her every dumb detail about my encounters with Jett.

She might have squealed once or twice.

"He's so frickin' good in bed, Brey. Like fireworks and explosions good. I want to fuck him all day. And yet, he's sort of the worst human being ever."

Her gaze wandered to the candy in the aisle as we stood in the checkout line. "Everyone has their demons. You know that."

"Right. I make my demons angels though. I like hanging out with people who do the same."

"Jett's too much of a…"

"A pessimist? Or a complete jackass? Or—"

She cut me off before I could get on a roll. "He's the oldest. He cares, just in his own controlling way."

"I don't need that in my life."

She nodded and rolled her lips between her teeth.

"What do you want to say?" I sighed.

"Nothing." She pushed the cart toward the checkout lady and started setting items down on the counter. "It's just I don't normally hear you talk about guys like this."

"I talk about every guy like this," I retorted.

"No"—she shook her head and handed her card over to the cashier—"you claim every guy is a prince and/or your knight in shining armor."

"A lot of them could be."

"Okay. Well, you didn't claim that Jett was."

Huh.

She had me there. "Well, that's because he literally could never be that. He's seriously a devil. Like, take Steven for instance. He would definitely wine and dine me."

She shrugged. "Steven hasn't wined and dined you yet."

I looked down and slumped a little. "I know. I think he's weirded out by the fact that he's technically my boss. But he invited me to the meeting with Stonewood Enterprises this week. He knows he shouldn't invite an associate lawyer to that meeting. I am a nobody in the company right now."

Aubrey straightened. "Hey. You are such a smart lawyer. He wants your professional opinion."

"Maybe." I shrugged. "I'm green though. It doesn't look good to the others who have been left out of the meeting although they've been there for years."

"He knows what he's doing."

I winked. "And he looks good doing it."

She shrugged. "Okay, so we're still rooting for Steven to ask you out, and we want nothing to do with Jett?"

I nodded. "Exactly."

I moved to grab my card so I could split the cost with her like we had in the past, but she stopped me. "Jax is paying for this one. He said you saved him from the near-death experience of shopping with me."

"Oh my God! Why didn't you tell me? I would have bought so much more stuff," I whined.

Her eyes bugged out. "Vick, you don't have to scream about it."

I winced, knowing my excitement always made me too loud. "Sorry!"

My phone went off as we made our way out of the store. We listened to Miranda sing about her broken heart not being her momma's.

"You have to talk to her at some point, Vick." Aubrey eyed my purse which held my phone.

"I know but, for now, my poor mother needs to take a hint. I texted her that your wedding went well."

We walked toward the SUV that was waiting for Aubrey. "I still can't believe you didn't let me invite them."

"My parents are way too much." And they'd reveal way too much about me.

She shrugged. "Want a ride home?"

I looked at her driver holding the door open for us. "No," I chuckled a little. "But that's pretty baller."

She blushed. "It's weird."

We hugged, and she left me in the throng of people on the sidewalk. They weaved around me, and I stayed there just to watch them all keep passing by.

I looked up to remind myself the sky was up there above the buildings somewhere.

Every person who sped around me on the sidewalk of this fast-paced city seemed to be dealing with something so big, they couldn't take a moment to remember how small and how fragile we all really were.

CHAPTER ELEVEN

VICK

I WENT INTO MY work week at full throttle. I wanted Steven to know I deserved that spot at his meeting with Jett.

He passed me in the hall of our office. "Hey, Vicky. You ready for tomorrow?"

I nodded and hoped I wasn't imagining the way his face brightened when he saw me. He smiled at everyone, but I liked to think it lingered with me. The way he tucked his blue button-down shirt in more than most made him look a tad uptight, but his pale-blue eyes always sparkled with friendliness. Unlike the dark-blue ones that appeared in my dreams. His blond hair didn't stand out against those blue eyes either, not the way Jett's hair did.

He was attractive, he just wasn't devastating. I didn't need devastating though. I shouldn't have even wanted it.

"I'm as ready as I'll ever be. Any documents you need me to look over?"

He waved away my offer. "Oh, no. I had my other lawyers take a look, but I doubt Jett will offer me anything that will make me change my mind. This is just a formality."

"Right. We want to maintain a cordial working relationship with him." I repeated the line I'd written to Jett because it was true.

"Yes, exactly." He tilted his head and put his hand on my shoulder. "I like how that sounds. Jett will understand too."

I nodded and leaned a little closer to him. "He has to understand you wanting to keep control of what's yours. He does that with his company, right?"

"Right. And I'm doing the same." He puffed his chest out a little, and I thought about patting myself on the back later for making him feel so great about himself.

"Well, I should get back to it. Let me know if you want to grab a bite for lunch."

His hand dropped from my shoulder like he'd just noticed I was on fire. "Right." He cleared his throat. "I probably need to catch up on some stuff."

I wanted to roll my eyes. He was thinking he couldn't date me, that it wouldn't look good to his employees. But he'd hired me, he invited me to meetings when I wasn't required. He even touched me in the hallways, although it may have been subconsciously. Hadn't he read his own HR handbook? It didn't say anywhere that we couldn't date.

"Okay, Steven." I shrugged, trying to shake his discomfort. "I'll be ready for the meeting, if I don't see you before then."

"Sure, sure." He backed away from me, but I caught him looking me up and down. "He wanted lunch, he wanted so much more than lunch with me. "We'll have transportation tomorrow. I'll see you then."

I turned before he could and sauntered down that hallway like a freaking lingerie model.

Eat your heart out, Steven.

Back at my desk, I woke up my laptop to find a message from an even more frustrating man. This one didn't seem to care at all about work boundaries.

> **JETT:** You ready for the meeting tomorrow?
> **ME:** Yes.
> **JETT:** So, can I be myself in front of Stevie?
> **ME:** I don't know what you mean by that. Just act like a normal human being. Steven knows we are friends through Aubrey and Jax.
> **JETT:** What else does Stevie know?
> **ME:** Can you stop calling him that?
> **JETT:** I don't know. Can you stop calling him Steven?
> **ME:** That's his name.
> **JETT:** No one goes by that name. It's pretentious.
> **ME:** I am going back to work.
> **JETT:** Your work will include me tomorrow.
> **ME:** Goodbye, Jett.
> **JETT:** See you tomorrow. Wear something for me to stare at.

I turned on my out of office auto-reply and googled scrubbing my message history.

God, the man was infuriating. He couldn't separate a damn personal encounter from a business one to save his life. And wasn't that the problem with him? He was so far up his business's ass, he couldn't enjoy life.

The rest of the day, I stomped through every one of my tasks, including choosing an outfit for the meeting the next day. I didn't do it for Jett. I did it for Steven and our company. I had to represent. I also wanted to look nice enough that Steven noticed.

The next morning, I slipped into the Fendi bodycon dress with long sleeves and a high neckline. The dark-beige logos against the black jacquard of the dress complimented my skin tone, and it fit like a glove, hugging my curves.

My mother, ever the crazy driven businesswoman and a micro-manager, had climbed her way to the top of the fashion business. I learned a sharp sense of style growing up and had a closet full of wonderful clothes. I also knew how to pull off a risqué dress and still appear professional. I tied my hair back in a tight bun and stepped into my stilettos. This outfit would not only make people gawk, it would make them see how lethal a lawyer I was.

At work, our legal team buzzed about before the meeting. Mark, one of the senior attorneys, told us all, "We need to be fully prepared to negotiate if necessary and know our number."

My face scrunched in confusion. "Steven said he doesn't want to sell. Why should we prepare to negotiate?"

Mark smiled but looked down his nose at us. "Steve wouldn't be going to this meeting if he didn't want to sell."

"That's not true," I blurted. A couple of senior attorneys looked over at me. Their faces wrinkled in either question or distaste. Most of us junior associates stayed quiet except to ask questions. I cleared my throat. "I just find it hard to believe that Steven would hand all his loyal employees over to that unscrupulous shark for any number."

Mark chuckled. Then the chuckle grew to a full belly laugh. And while I stared at him holding his gut in, I had to school my face into a neutral expression so he wouldn't see my disgust. Mark reminded me of the terrible cliché of a dirty old uncle who was always side-eyeing you. He'd lost most of his gray hair but was holding onto the last few strands with a death grip. And the looks he shot my way always made me feel grimy, like I needed a shower.

He nudged John, another senior attorney, in the side. Those two always looked at me like a piece of meat they wanted to devour in private but a weed in their manicured lawn in public. Most days, I understood. I was the upstart blonde they dreaded would take their place next to Steven. I didn't outrank them, but they knew I climbed a different ladder. I could have the lowest LSAT in the state and they believed Steven would promote me over them.

Maybe they were right.

Maybe Steven was only dragging me along to these important meetings because of the attraction we had toward one another.

But I wasn't dumb. My LSAT results had been one question shy of a perfect score.

They could laugh all they wanted. I might not have earned my place at the table yet, but I was damn capable of getting there. I pushed a few stray hairs behind my ear. "We'll see."

I was sure of Steven's resolve, sure of his righteousness, and knew when he'd said he wanted the best for the company, he'd meant it.

Mark, John, Steven, and a few others piled into an SUV that took us over to Stonewood Enterprises.

The building stood taller than those around it and looked like it curved into the sky. The architectural design allowed for it to be constructed in a way where the windows looked like a wave bent up above the city. It was a physical representation of the Stonewoods' dominion of the business world. Jett and his father had a strong handle on every big company in the city and were large contenders nationally. They dabbled in software, applications, stocks, just about everything that could make money.

The Wall Street Journal claimed that Jett stepping into his father's shoes some years back had driven the company to greater success. He was solely responsible for some of the biggest—and riskiest—investments the company made.

"Steve, what's our number?" Mark asked boldly, interrupting everyone's small talk.

Steven wiggled a bit in his seat. He ran his hand through his blond hair and glanced out the window at the tower. The SUV idled in traffic, but we were only about ten feet away from being able to exit. "It isn't about the number. There's a lot more that goes into wanting to give up control of Samson and Sons."

Mark nodded. When he looked my way, I raised my eyebrows. I couldn't help it. I'd told him it wasn't about numbers.

Mark pushed again. "Still. What's the number?"

I rolled my eyes at Mark. Steven wasn't like him; he didn't crawl around on the floor to pick up dollar bills when they were thrown his way. He wouldn't sacrifice another's happiness for money he didn't need.

Steven replied, "I'll know the number if I see it."

Mark raised his eyebrows at me this time, but I just shrugged. Steven wouldn't see that number, he'd told me. If he had to fib a time or two to get Mark off his back, I understood.

We exited the vehicle and two men met us in the lobby. We made our way to the elevators, and I took in the lobby's layout. Leather couches and oak desks had been strategically placed throughout. The dark browns and ceiling-to-floor windows screamed luxury which was, I am sure, the designer's intent.

No one else really took in the furniture or the design as they walked in. They were mesmerized by the elevator shafts, which curved with the building all the way to the top, while water cascaded down around them.

Steven commented to the two men waiting with us for the elevator, "The architecture of this building has always floored me."

One answered, "Yes, the Stonewoods were very much involved in determining the final look. Jax had a hand in developing the elevator design."

"It's a phenomenal design. Really quite brilliant," Steven said.

The man nodded. "He and his family are quite brilliant." The awe and pride in the man's voice was apparent as we stepped onto the elevator. The doors closed as water cascaded down the glass walls.

Steven eyed him curiously. "You really enjoy working here, yes?"

"I couldn't have asked for a better position. They push everyone hard but get the best out of them too."

Steven nodded.

"This way." We followed the man down the hall to an expansive built-in desk where a brunette sat, her hair pulled back in a severe chignon. "Gloria, let Jett know I'll be bringing Samson and Sons to the conference room now."

She jerked her head down once, as if any more motion would be inefficient. We followed the man through glass doors and down a hall that opened up to more ceiling-to-floor windows. People buzzed between the desks and pellucid cubicles. No one seemed to be tied to one area though. Like a hive, they all worked on something different, but we knew they had built this magnificent thing together.

To the very back of the space, up three dark gray marble steps was the man who made it all run. He stood at the edge of those stairs, like a king. He wore a tailored navy suit with brown leather shoes and a belt to match. His white collared shirt and blue tie finished off the perfect package.

I had seen Jett in the nude, swimming trunks, sweats, and jeans. He looked good in everything, but that suit looked like the most natural thing on him. The man was made to reign over the world, and his outfit showed it.

When he saw me, his mouth tipped up, and he raised one eyebrow.

I looked away, not at all as ready for this encounter as I'd thought I was.

Jett took his time walking down the steps to come shake each of our hands.

He eyed Steven first and put his hand out. "Happy we could meet today. Your company has my attention."

Steven smiled and stood a little taller, not at all hiding his admiration for Jett. He shook Jett's hand vigorously. "I am really happy to hear that. We are looking forward to talking over things."

Jett nodded and turned to shake everyone else's hand.

He saved our exchange for last or maybe I lingered in the back, hoping he would overlook me.

He didn't. He looked me up and down, waiting a beat before putting out a hand. "Ms. Blakely. Always a pleasure."

I nodded. "Yes, Mr. Stonewood. It is."

He motioned to a hall that led to more rooms. "We'll be meeting in the second door on the right."

Everyone turned to follow the two men who had led us up to this floor. Jett waited behind and as I started walking, I felt his hand on the small of my back.

My eyes grew to about twice their size, I was sure, as I turned to glare at him. "Are you kidding me?" I whisper-yelled.

He winked and leaned in to whisper back, "I never kid, Ms. Blakely."

I wanted to say more, but Steven turned to eye us curiously as he made his way into the conference room.

Jett's hand never dropped from my back, even when Steven glanced at us. He kept it there down that long hallway, sending sparks through my body as though he had every right. I almost shoved it off as we entered the conference room but he dropped it to close the door behind him.

I sat in one of the last available chairs which happened to be next to the one at the head of the long table.

Of course, Jett filled that seat. He folded his hands on the table and an expensive watch peeked out from his cuff. Rolex, for sure. "I appreciate you all coming here to further discuss how we can help one another in the future."

Everyone either nodded or murmured agreement.

"I'm sure those of you who have met me know I don't like to waste time. So, we've drafted a new contract," he started.

Steven shook his head, and I was proud of him, sitting there opposite Jett, ready to go head-to-head with one of the most lucrative businessmen in the world. "We don't want to waste anyone's time either. We've already been over everything, and we appreciate the offer. I really like to keep control of things though. My employees mean a lot to me. And I just can't see giving up control of their positions like you ask. I realize that's what you do with most contracts. I can't ask you to change that. So, like I said, we appreciate it but today this meeting won't be about acquisition. It will be about maintaining a cordial business relationship."

Jett's nostrils flared at Steven's last words. He glanced my way, and I shrugged before looking down. I couldn't have known Steven would use my exact words here, but I was proud that he'd taken the moment to stand his ground, to show everyone he could go toe-to-toe with Jett Stonewood and not back down.

He was the light to Jett's dark. He had a blond halo over his head while Jett's inky hair curled up like devil's horns. He smiled sweetly and Jett's smile spread like Lucifer had found his next victim.

Jett cleared his throat. "A cordial business relationship?" His hand went to my thigh under the table. The shock of it shot between my legs as he squeezed and glared at me. "I swear I've heard that phrase before."

I bit my tongue, wanting to kill him, wanting this meeting to be over, wanting to gouge a hole right through the Italian leather of his outrageously extravagant Cucinelli with the heel of my stiletto. Instead, I dug my nails into my hands as I fisted them in my lap, holding my reaction in.

"Either way," Jett looked over his shoulder, and I followed his line of sight to Gloria, the severe-looking assistant. "I think we should consider more than that. Gloria, would you hand out the new contract?"

She stood from her little corner desk, and every man in the room shifted slightly. The woman looked like an hourglass, curvy in all the right places. When she walked, she strutted, and when she passed out folders, she leaned in. I saw the way she'd handled her position at the desk up front. I knew she was handling this in just the right way too. Each move she made was calculated.

Maybe she thought she needed to woo them for Stonewood Enterprises' sake, or maybe she just wanted a date later that day. I couldn't be sure.

Until I saw the way Jett tracked each of her movements, the way she looked back at him and parted her lips when she saw him staring at them.

He had been—or still was—sleeping with that woman.

They didn't do a good job of hiding it either. As I looked around the room, the men's smirks at Gloria and Jett's display showed how camaraderie could so easily be built.

I wanted to roll my eyes. When Gloria dropped my file in front of me instead of placing it in my hand, I glared at Jett and shoved his hand off my leg.

He winked. If I didn't pride myself on being a professional, I would have kicked him in the shin.

Steven's voice drew my attention away from my immature thoughts. "Mr. Stonewood—"

"Jett. We're on a first name basis at this point, I would think."

Steven cleared his throat and then a small laugh bubbled out of him, high and awkward. "We just might be with the number you're offering."

"Good. The rest of the contract stays the same."

Steven nodded fast and blurted, "Sure. Sure."

My eyes bulged, my stomach dropped, the oxygen *whooshed* out of my lungs and didn't seem to come back in. But no one was paying attention to me.

Mark slapped Steven on the back and laughed.

John was mumbling how he couldn't believe it. Everyone talked excitedly. One of Stonewood Enterprises' guys began talking tactics with one of our guys.

I scrambled for the file and skimmed the pages looking for the godforsaken number. When I saw it, I gasped.

Like I said, no one was paying attention to me. Or so I thought. Then I felt his hand back on my thigh, squeezing. I snapped my gaze to his. Jett's eyes twinkled in an arrogant way. "Welcome to Stonewood Enterprises, Victory Blakely."

CHAPTER TWELVE

JETT

THE NUMBER ON that contract was well worth the look on Vick's face. Her mouth dropped open and her cheeks hollowed out as she sucked in a breath. Her lips jutted forward as if they were trying to aid her in sucking in air.

The way she'd walked in today, confidence pouring off that skintight sweater dress, had riled me. I knew immediately I would acquire her company.

Stevie's company would prosper under our name, but most companies would. We didn't even look at companies that wouldn't.

I'd gone beyond our normal MO when I'd set up this meeting, deciding to personally sit down with Samson and Sons.

Stevie spoke up from across the table. "We're honored to be starting this journey with you, Jett."

Kiss ass.

"Great. Seems the people in this room are indispensable to your company. We'll want you all working here starting next week to get everything situated. Gloria will iron out the scheduling details with you."

Stevie looked a little shell-shocked.

I chuckled. "I pride myself on productivity and adaptability. Should everyone here have a desk next week?"

Stevie stuttered as he looked around. "Um, well, uh, sure. Yes. Everyone here has something to offer."

Vick cleared her throat, like she'd finally come out of her shock. "I'm sorry. You expect us to move into this building by next week? Steven, we have obligations, and our colleagues at Samson and Sons are already concerned about the acquisition. Us moving next week will only add to that concern."

"Thankfully, Stevie—I can call you Stevie, right?" I asked as I stared across the table at the man she thought was her perfect match. When he nodded, Vick practically growled under her breath, making me smile. "Great. Stevie doesn't have to worry about that anymore. We'll be taking care of every employee as we always do at Stonewood Enterprises. Lucky for all of you, you'll be in our tower next week."

One guy from Samson and Sons hissed a celebratory yes under his breath, and I saw that most of them were genuinely excited about the move.

Vick's posture was bone straight, her hands rested on the contract as she twirled her pen back and forth furiously. As my people addressed the details, I watched her. Her lashes didn't lift because she wouldn't look up from the documents. Her hands didn't shake but there was extreme tension in each twirl of that pen. I'd ruined her perfect picture of Stevie, and I could tell she was having a hard time accepting that.

Good.

The girl needed a wake-up call. "Antonio,"—my colleague's head snapped up—"would you show everyone around."

"Absolutely."

"I'll have Ms. Blakely catch up with you later. I'd like a word with her."

Vick said, "Oh, that's not necess—"

Stevie stood. "Great. We'll see you both soon."

Vick bit down on her bottom lip, and I was a little concerned she'd make it bleed.

Everyone filed out.

I let the door click shut and then listened to the clock tick to see if she'd say anything first. The woman hated silence.

"I guess we'll be working together," she blurted, clicking her pen like she was trying her best to release her emotion somehow.

"Are you mad?" I asked, wanting her to finally admit that reality sometimes sucked.

She sighed and looked to the ceiling. "No. I'm just—" She dropped the pen and shoved away from the table. "It'll be good. This will be good."

"It's good that Stevie gave up his company after you swore he wouldn't?"

She shut her eyes, scrunched up her face, and then snapped them open to look at me. Honey-colored eyes never looked so mean. "Anyone would have taken that offer. Steven isn't an idiot."

"Could have fooled me."

"What?" She stood up fast. "How can you say that? You barely spoke to him."

"Right. And the grand old speech he came up with wasn't even original. He finished it off with the line you fed both me and him. 'A cordial business relationship.'"

"You don't know that he got that from me," she said.

I stood up and stalked toward her. "I know damn well he got that from you."

She glared up at me and put her hands on her hips. "Think what you want. You have no evidence."

"As a lawyer, you should know there aren't coincidences that big."

I could tell she was biting her cheek, probably trying to hold back from agreeing with me. "Either way, Steven's smart enough to know an amazing opportunity when he sees one."

"Or he's just like every other person in this world, Vick. Money talks. Little Stevie's nothing more than a boy who inherited his daddy's business a while ago and has bent to whichever way the wind blew, the water flowed, and the sun shined. I'm sure those guys have been telling him what to do with that company since the day he walked through Samson and Sons' doors."

She shook her head. "You're wrong."

I smirked. "He doesn't have a backbone, doll. You and I both know it. He'll probably make a perfect husband for you. He'll roll over when you tell him to."

She spun away from me, paced back, then threw up her hands before she stomped around me to grab her file. "It is official. I hate someone. I literally hate you. I thought it was impossible. I really do try to see the good in everyone, but there is not one thing good about you."

The satisfaction I thought I would feel slipped a little. "Surely you don't mean that."

"Oh, I mean it." She folded her belongings under her arm. "Walk me back to where my colleagues are. I really don't want to be alone with you anymore."

"Not what you said this past weekend." I knew I should have quit. Should have left well enough alone. Yet, she'd walked in here today like we were playing chess and she'd already won. She stood tall with so much confidence in that dress. She ran her hand along its logos, as if the dress could have formed a crease.

Acting like that dress was prim and proper was a joke though. It fit her like a second skin. Every guy in the room had been looking at her if they weren't already distracted by Gloria. She couldn't hide the fact that she had legs for miles and curves that every guy wanted to explore. And that high neck just reminded me of all the sensitive spots she had under it.

It ignited a feeling inside me I couldn't name. It snowballed quickly when I saw the way Stevie looked at her, like she was already his.

Did he think that? Did she want him to think that?

"You made it perfectly clear last weekend what we were," she replied.

I tilted my head a bit at her accusation, not knowing exactly what she meant.

Her eyes narrowed and her finger poked my shoulder as she whispered, "You left my bed and my house without a goodbye. Obviously, I was a one-night stand—or whatever number we're on—but I won't be one again."

I stepped back and shook my head a little in surprise. "That's not what that was."

"Oh, please." She turned back toward the door, leaving me behind.

I grabbed her elbow and spun her back to me, pulling her close. "I had work, Vick."

"You always have work." She looked down at my lips. They were so close to her I could practically taste the strawberries.

"Yes, that's true. I really did have time-sensitive obligations though."

"Well, you didn't wake me or leave your number."

"You already have my number."

She shook her head. "So, you wanted it to be something more than—you know what? That's not the point." She stepped back and jerked her elbow out from under my hand. "My point is it shouldn't have happened. I don't ever want it to happen again. I just don't want to be around you. You're …"

I folded my arms over my chest, waiting to hear her description. I wanted to hear her give in to calling me a name, wanted to break down the fluffy wall of clouds surrounding her.

"Come on, Victory, you can do it. I'm what?"

She licked her lips. "You're not what I want. But I'm sure you are for someone else."

"Good save. You almost gave into expressing how you really feel. We'll have to work on that."

"I'm not working on anything with you."

"Oh you are, doll." I pulled open the conference room door. "You work for me now. Starting next week, you'll be working on everything with me."

She scoffed.

When she tried to slide by me, I gripped her elbow again, leaning down to whisper, "I intend to start with working on your honesty. I don't want rainbows and roses; I want the truth."

She didn't turn toward me. She kept her eyes on the hallway and mumbled, "My truth is rainbows and roses."

I chuckled a little. "Would it be rainbows and roses if I took you back inside the conference room to fuck you in this dress? If you were going for conservative, you missed the target by a damn mile."

"Get fucked, Jett."

"I intend to."

She yanked her arm away and stalked down the hall. "Not by me."

"We'll see, Pix. We'll see."

CHAPTER
THIRTEEN

VICK

THE DAY HADN'T gone as planned. I met up with our team and listened to starry-eyed Steven *ooh* and *ahh* over being a part of the Stonewood team. I wanted to be frustrated with him, but he had done the smart thing, the thing I would have done, what anyone would have done.

I couldn't be sure if he'd done it for himself or the company. Either way, it benefited everyone. Stonewood Enterprises always made companies better. I just worried that some of the team wouldn't be able to move on with the rest of us.

When we got back to the office, it was nearing the end of the workday. None of us were allowed to share the news with the others but I knew some associate lawyers caught on. They eyed me with either sadness or disdain. One colleague, Liz, met me as I was exiting the building. "You don't have to say what I already know, but I'm probably getting laid off. So, I think you should know that Mark and John have it out for you."

I rolled my eyes. "Not news to me. They would probably poison me if given the chance."

Her brown hair blew in the wind as we stepped onto the city sidewalk to head toward the L, Chicago's elevated subway. "They would probably poison every one of the associate lawyers if we weren't doing all their legwork for them."

I nodded and wove through the usual stream of people leaving work. "They don't want anyone encroaching on their monopoly of Steven's ear. They practically control his brain."

She laughed. "But you have Steve's ear too, right?"

I sighed. "We aren't dating."

"Really? Everyone says you are."

I nodded when we reached the stairs up to the train tracks. "We're not. Just friends for now. Maybe more in the future." I shrugged. "I'm this way." I pointed to the stairs and she eyed them like they might be infested with bedbugs.

"You want to do an Uber with me?"

I shook my head. "I like the L."

"Huh. Wouldn't have ever guessed that about you." She put her hand on her hip, and I decided she meant no harm with that comment. Once, a very long time ago, I might have thought I would end up just like her, a little privileged by my parents' money. Everything worked in my favor in high school. I saw myself exactly where she stood, with the same mentality, the same outfit, maybe even the same job.

I turned to the stairs that held so much more life above them than people gave them credit for. I surged forward, hearing the man with the guitar who I always listened to for an extra minute. He plucked at the strings and hummed a song that consumed him. I dropped money in his case, and he nodded a thank you without breaking from his song, without opening his eyes. The world had weathered him and his voice. Yet, when he rasped the words to his song, it flowed like a soft breeze through a field, like it was comfortable, like it was home, like it belonged and was right where it was supposed to be.

This L, so full of life, so full of unfamiliar people, and hustle and bustle. This was where I breathed and felt home.

Even on my worst day, I was thankful for the moment, for the opportunity to be right where I was.

My phone buzzed as I got on the train, and when I took my seat, I read my message.

MOM: If you don't answer, I will come to visit.

Miranda Lambert started singing immediately.

"Hi, Mom," I answered, my voice high and bouncy.

"Oh, don't jump right into the sarcasm, Victory."

"I'm not. I'm happy to answer when a warning is attached." I rolled my eyes and looked out the window to the streets we passed below. Night and darkness lurked, ready to overtake the city. By the time I reached home, only the streetlights and buildings would light my way.

"Are you on your way home?"

"Yes."

"What's that noise I hear?"

"I have no idea." She was talking about the train.

"Is that the L?"

I sighed. "Why are you calling, Mom?"

"So, you're on the train? You have a compromised immune system and you're using public transportation?" Her voice started rising. "Do you know how worried we are about you living in that city?"

"Mom, I can't keep having this conversation with you."

"She says she can't keep having this conversation." Her voice was muffled and I knew my father was standing over her, rubbing her back. "Well, I don't want to have this conversation over and over either, Vick."

I sat up a little straighter. "Then, let's not have it. I'm fine and I had a long day at work."

"Work." I heard my mother physically relax, she sighed into the phone like she was deflating and sitting down. "How is work, honey? I am so happy you are working with Steven."

She would be. Steven was safe. He followed the rules, he gave the right impression to parents, without fail he acted like a gentleman.

I knew because my family and his had always been close. Before Steven's father passed away and left him the company, our parents used to double date. Now, my mother stayed in very close contact with his.

"Yes, Steven is a great boss and friend."

"Isn't he? And Darcy called me today to tell me they sold to Stonewood Enterprises," my mother squealed. The Stonewoods were like America's royal family. "I can't believe you know them, that Brey married Jax. Who did Samson and Sons have the meeting with? Was it Jax or Jett, the oldest?"

My mother loved celebrity gossip. She loved talking about almost anything, really. The woman could talk for hours about nothing and everything. I liked to think I inherited her uncanny ability to make anyone feel comfortable.

She could almost fool me into having a normal conversation with her. "Yes, but I didn't say much. I think he's always amicable because he knows I'm Brey's friend."

"Of course, of course. So, are you going straight home?"

As if on cue, the train screeched to a stop, and I shut my eyes as my mother gasped.

"You *are* on the L, Victory Blakely." She hissed my name with venom. "I used to ride it, and I know exactly the way it sounds."

My mother, once upon a time, conquered Chicago by climbing the ranks of the fashion industry here. She took the train every night, walked the streets without supervision, probably did some crazy shit like crossing the street with her eyes closed.

I stood to get off, whispering, "Excuse me, excuse me," as I made my way down to the street. "So, then you know it's perfectly safe for most people."

"You aren't most people."

I tried to focus on putting one foot in front of the other, the sound my shoes made against the cement, the way the fall breeze kept the city air moving. "Mom, can we just not?"

"I told you I would get you a driver or a car."

"I don't want a driver!" I screamed and then scrunched my face to hold back my emotions. "I can't talk. I have to go."

I reached my apartment block and hung up the phone even though I heard her talking. The high rise boasted white-tiled floors in the lobby, as well as a doorman, and an expansive entryway. I never took the elevators, but I knew they were high-end. Just like the building and my apartment.

My mother had made sure of that. She made sure every single thing about my move was a well-laid plan. I should have thanked her. Yet, every day my resentment snowballed and my frustration built. I walked up the stairs to my apartment, each step a nail she hammered into my metaphorical coffin.

She wanted a daughter who would follow her rules, approach life with caution, look both ways and then some when crossing a street.

I wasn't that daughter. I had been, but I couldn't go back. Not after all we'd been through.

I set my work bag down and beelined to my cupboard. The wine I set on the counter stood next to a case of pills. The supplements were also my mother's doing. She and my father had hired a nutritionist out of Portland, the best of the best. I remember her coming to the house, lining up all the vitamins and saying, "Now, these will help. But you have to will it, Vick. It takes the right mentality, besides diet and lifestyle."

My mom nodded along with her. "We're taking every precaution."

My dad, a burly man who never said much, stared at me with pity in his eyes. He didn't want to speak over my mother but knew the nutritionist was too much. He laid his hand on my shoulder, the best way he knew how to support me.

I stared at the supplements next to the wine bottle, then at my hands gripping the counter. My acrylic nails met the cuticle line perfectly. I'd told the manicurist to make them look natural with a light-pink hue. No one ever caught me with my real nails exposed; they reminded me of the time I'd barely had nail growth. They still grew out damaged, worn out far too early for my age.

The manicurist hadn't asked questions and that terrible feeling of discomfort snuck up on me. When she'd started filing my nails, words bubbled out of me. "These nails have just never been pretty without a work of art from you professionals."

She had tsk-tsked and responded, "We'll clean them up, huh?"

I'd averted her discomfort and gained a new nail artist in a new town. Now, she talked a mile a minute at every session and never blinked twice at the wreckage she covered up.

I laid each of the pills on the counter, then swiped them all to the edge and into my other manicured hand. I poured my wine into a long stem glass and threw all five pills in my mouth. They knocked around in there before the wine washed them down in one large gulp.

My nail manicurist, along with my friends from college, didn't know the whole story. They didn't know that those pink nails I used to pop shut the pill case hid just one of the imperfections I'd been hiding for years.

When the leukemia snuck up on my family as I turned seventeen, I'd been a naive social butterfly, fluttering through high school like nothing could go wrong. Sure, there'd been the occasional terrible hair day and awful date, but I'd had friends every which way I looked. I'd had good grades, our volleyball team was going to state, I'd known what I was doing for college.

I gulped more red wine and pulled my laptop from my work bag.

Junior year, during a volleyball game before the state competition, I blacked out. I woke up in a hospital listening to that terrible noise.

The beeping.

Beep. Beep. Beep.

My mother delivered the news with my father standing by, holding her up. Holding my mother, the woman who could plow her way into a CEO position of a Fortune 500 company after coming from nothing, like she was barely capable of standing.

"We'll beat it, sweetie," she'd murmured as the shock of her words barreled through me. The beeping galloped faster and faster. Then and there, in that hospital room, I saw the first look of discomfort on my parents' faces.

"It'll be okay." I nodded. "We'll get through it."

My mom's hand shot out to hold mine and she squeezed it so tight I could feel her love for her only child flowing through it. I remember thinking of all the things I would have to get through. I wondered if I would lose my hair, if my friends would make me a card, if my boyfriend would break up with me.

All those things happened more quickly than I could have ever imagined.

I sat down at my kitchen table and opened my laptop, telling myself I needed to work.

I chugged more wine instead and stared at my phone. I'd hung up on her as if she could control the worry and love that consumed her heart. As if she hadn't torn apart my history trying to find a culprit for the cancer that destroyed her perfect fairy tale. Her family. Her life.

Because cancer did that, infecting not just the patient, but the whole family.

Now, eight years later, I had beaten it and survived.

But my relationship with my mother hadn't.

Our family hadn't.

We couldn't forget. She couldn't stop bulldozing. Or stop searching for answers. Or stop worrying. My father couldn't stop holding her up and staring at me with pity.

And I couldn't stop the damn guilt of never wanting to talk to them, wanting to avoid all the awkward conversations and live harder than I had ever lived before, even if my mother wanted me wrapped in a plastic bubble of supplements, doctors, hospitals, fruits and vegetables. She wanted to place that plastic bubble in her home, in a nice little town away from the big city, and make sure I lived a long, prosperous, very boring life.

I gulped the wine she would scream at me for drinking and got to work, trying to forget about my wallowing. When I couldn't forget, I drank more wine, and found myself mostly incapable of work.

I almost closed my laptop to go to bed, but the green dot next to Jett's name on my e-mail list beckoned to me.

I opened our messages.

> **ME:** This bad day started with you.
> **JETT:** You're up late.
> **ME:** Have to start working like my new boss does.
> **JETT:** I do like my employees motivated.
> **ME:** Do you ever stop working?
> **JETT:** I wasn't working when I was with you last.
> **ME:** You left me to work.
> **JETT:** We're still on that, huh?
> **ME:** I don't know what I'm on. I need to get off it though.

I slammed my laptop shut and unfurled myself from my cramped position, stretching out the stiffness to go to bed. I tossed and turned all night, wondering how I would get through working at Stonewood Enterprises the very next week.

CHAPTER FOURTEEN

JETT

VICTORY BLAKELY DRAGGED the sun out of hiding the very next week when she showed up at work with her crew. She even wore a yellow blouse tucked into a pencil skirt, as if to solidify her joy through colors. A large bag hung from one of her shoulders, and she smiled like she wanted to be here with everyone else who had arrived bright and early with stars in their eyes.

She showed all her teeth to Gloria who was introducing people, a grin so brilliant everyone should have known it was fake. Then she tried to laugh at something Stevie said, but her hand stayed on the handle of her bag, gripping it tightly.

Holding in her real feelings.

I stood in my office, leaning against a floor-to-ceiling glass wall that overlooked the office space below. I seated the best of the best in that space, right there in front of me. The open desk concept allowed ideas to fly freely and honestly. It gave me immediate access to everyone I needed on a daily basis too. This was my empire, and I ruled from a few steps above.

Gloria, like a king's hand, moved down my list of onboarding duties, brutal in her six-inch heels and plum form fitting dress. I noted which men's eyes lingered too long on that violet fabric and filed the information away.

Most men who let their dick overpower them on their first day wouldn't last long at Stonewood Enterprises. It seemed I would do some firing sooner than I had anticipated.

Gloria, efficient and effective in all she did for me, snapped her binder shut. Her dark eyes flicked my way, and she nodded to indicate she'd finished. Last week she'd played up her sex kitten role because I'd correctly guessed it was the right way to butter up the men in that room.

Now, we were back to business, and that woman was the best at it. She knew as well as I did most of the men eyeing her would be gone within a few months. I'd never failed her in that regard.

I pushed off the glass and walked out of my office. I unbuttoned my suit jacket as I stepped down the stairs.

Eyeing Stevie first, I addressed him for the last time as the man I'd relieved of a business. "Happy to have absorbed your company, Stevie. It'll be great having you work for us."

He nodded, eager to please. "Absolutely. I think the acquisition will go through—"

"It's already done, but the rest of your company will move here next month. That said, I have the people I want here now. We'll be moving each of you to departments of need as Gloria said. Today, we have more onboarding that is personalized to your job descriptions."

Gloria handed out files and more of my team appeared.

"My people will get everyone up to speed and show them to their departments. Most of you won't be in this office. I have a very small team operating in here, personnel I need direct access to at all times. Every office throughout this building is a part of our family though.

Remember that you're one of us now. Welcome aboard Stonewood Enterprises, where the sky's the limit for some, but not us."

My canned welcome earned genuine smiles, but Vick's was just as fake as my welcome. That woman wanted to roll her eyes at me, I knew it.

I turned on my heel and went back to my office. This was a normal day for me. We acquired companies all the time.

The only abnormal part was that I'd seated Vick and Stevie at two desks directly in front of my glass office. Gloria didn't question why I wanted an associate lawyer and small business owner there. She eyed me with curiosity when I'd informed her of my decision though.

I wondered too. I told myself that after examining Vick's file—which I did every now and again for new employees—I'd seen brilliance in her: she'd received a near-perfect score on her LSAT, turned down Harvard for a small school, and her mother used to run a Fortune 500 company. Having her on my team might be beneficial, but then again, I had Harvard graduates milling about in other offices.

So, maybe I was thinking with my dick that day too.

I saw most everyone peeling away from Vick and Stevie as they followed their mentors to the elevators. When the two of them were left with Gloria, I watched her give them the news. A high laugh burst from Stevie, a boy not able to control his emotions at all.

Vick's amber gaze cut across the room to my office like a razor, catching me staring at her. She shook her head no and informed Gloria of the mistake.

"I'm just a junior associate. Surely Mark or John should be in this space."

"I'm not mistaken," Gloria replied. "Your desk is this way."

Vick glared at me as she followed Gloria to a desk that was in my perfect line of vision. Stevie was directed to sit across from her. As Gloria gave them more instructions about their day, those amber eyes stayed glued to mine. She assessed the situation while I assessed her.

Game on, Pixie.

I headed back to my desk, determined to focus on work. My father's number popped up on my cell as I sat down. I pressed the privacy button and the windows of my office tinted black so that no one could see in.

"Yeah, Pops?" I answered.

He sighed, "I could have been patching you on an important conference call."

"And they all would have appreciated the father-son camaraderie."

My dad's laugh rumbled through the phone. "More like they wouldn't have said shit to a Stonewood."

I grunted in agreement. "What do you need?"

"We have signatures from the Armanelli family still?"

I glanced at my privacy button to make sure the light glowed red, indicating the room's soundproofing had kicked in before I answered. "Why?"

"They'll be trying to squeeze more from everyone in Chicago soon."

"Bastian and I are good. They won't ask us."

"Bastian's dad heads up Chicago, Jett. He doesn't answer to his boy." His tone wasn't lost on me.

"Dad, making a fucking point through them to me won't help you. You need to hand over the reins if you're not going to steer Stonewood Enterprises with a clear head."

"My head's always been this clear."

I turned to look out of my window at the lake Chicago abutted. The water shimmered in the distance, ever-changing yet always the same. "You keep up, I'll give you that, old man. You don't want to though. Your heart's not in it. Mine still is."

"Your heart was always in it. It's a damn watch ticking to the beat of work. I'm not sure anything will ever jam up those cogs either."

"Nothing will. Except potentially the Armanellis trying to take a bigger cut."

"Bah." My dad's signature sound, the one he saved for my brothers and me, was his way of waving something off. He wasn't going to give such an insignificant thing another thought. I wished I shared his ability to get past his concerns. "Don't worry about it."

"You called specifically for me to worry about it."

Silence hovered on our line. My father's voice was somber when he replied. "Maybe. Maybe I am getting a little tired of it all."

The cogs stopped moving, jerked a little. Dad never admitted to wanting a break. The defeat in his voice shifted something in me. "It's fall, Dad. Mom's been emotional because of the wedding. It's a lot. Take a few days, huh?"

"What if a few days is all I got?"

"Dad, come on."

"I'm thinking I might agree with you after all this time and now you want to fight me?"

I cleared my throat. "Well, you not having your head in the game and half-assing it is still better than most people's full-assing. The company needs you."

"Not true. You and Jax handle things very well."

"Jax is buried in algorithms half the time, and I'm stuck in meeting after meeting. We need you driving the stocks, your connections, your presence."

More silence. "I'm thinking your mother needs me more."

"Dad, come on. Not this bullshit again."

"Love's bullshit to you, son, but without it you wouldn't be here."

"You seem to forget the aftermath. Mom and you used to—"

"I'm aware our relationship damaged your outlook on love, Jett. Your mother reminds me of that more than anyone. But, make no mistake. What you witnessed between us was no aftermath. An interlude, sure. I'll even admit to a break. But we were never done. There's no such thing as an aftermath with us. She's the only person aside from you boys who I will always fight for."

"You didn't fight very hard when the company was at stake and I came to run things with you."

When he didn't reply at once, I figured my attempt to go for the jugular had worked. He needed to pull his head out of his ass though. Our empire couldn't have a lovesick leader and if I had to kick him a little to shake the illness, I would.

"Jett,"—his voice was woven with anger as he sighed my name—"the company is yours. I'm not making the same error twice. Your mother and I are flying back to Kauai for a few weeks. I intend to renew our vows. I intend to make things right."

"I ... you ... are you fucking with me?" My ball of hate for love and happily ever afters grew twofold as I sat there waiting for a reply.

My father didn't respond. He breathed into the phone, and I could picture him with his full head of silver hair, sitting in a desk much like mine, his index finger and thumb pinching the bridge of his nose. After so many years of working with him, I knew he was leaning back in his work chair when I heard the leather creak over the line.

"Dad, I'm not running this company without you."

"You already are. Jax will be there. I'm done."

"You're giving up a multibillion-dollar company that you built from the ground up to run off into the sunset with the woman you think was your first love? You two could barely stand one another ten years ago! And that woman flies off the handle as much as you do. You're putting the company at risk for nothing." I tried to check my rising voice. I straightened a file on my desk. "Let's just back up a step."

"I'm not backing up at all, boy. This is me and your mom. We built this empire for you boys. Don't forget that she was just as much a part of it as I was."

"She wasn't keeping the company afloat—"

"She kept this goddamn family afloat," he yelled. "She worked her ass off to raise you boys and did a damn good job. And she righted my ship so many times, I should give the company to her, not you. Don't make me question my decision."

His shouting knocked me right off my high horse. The man was still my father, still the guy I looked up to, still the one I wanted to make proud even if I wouldn't admit it. "I'm not saying she's not a good mother—"

"You better not be saying anything of the sort."

I sighed. "Can we just back up?"

"I'm not going back. I'm sick of the past where I don't have her, Jett. I'm done. Start drawing up your crew. Get your goals together. You're captain. You better not sink my damn ship."

The phone lit up, signaling he'd ended the call. He might have been done with the conversation, but I sure as hell wasn't.

I stalked out of my office and yelled to Gloria to hold my calls. I took a side door to the stairwell that led directly to my father's floor. The rich mahogany doors screamed old school and clashed with my floor's open concept. Every floor of Stonewood Tower varied in look and feel. The floors we managed represented our individual styles a lot closer than we wanted to admit. Dad's style was always old money and power.

I didn't knock or wait for his assistant to usher me in. She scrambled to buzz a message to him as I opened his door.

He sat behind his large wooden desk, smiling. The expansive piece of wood shined proudly in the middle of the room and a woman with dark hair curled in sleek waves sat on top of it, arms crossed, facing the door. She had a smile on her face to match his.

I groaned and started to swing the door closed as I backed out.

"Oh no, Jett Stonewood," my mother shook her head and the dark curls swooshed lightly over her shoulder. "You get your workaholic ass in here."

"Mom," I sighed and skulked into the room where I slumped into the chair directly in front of her. "I have to get back to work."

"You want to get back to work, you can start with an apology." Her voice didn't hide her amusement.

"If you two wanted a conversation, we could have continued it over the phone."

"I wanted to see my son, not just hear his voice. I shouldn't have to come to the tower to do it."

"Mom, we're busy."

She clucked her tongue. "You're about to get busier. That mean you don't have time for your mother?" She leaned forward, arms still crossed like she was daring me to say no.

I shook my head and looked at my father. "You could have told me you had me on speakerphone."

He chuckled, and I took in his relaxed shoulders, his light laugh, how the lines on his face disappeared when he grinned. Loving my mother always agreed with him; being in her company practically made him a teddy bear.

Without her, he was the most ruthless businessman in the country, one not even the mob would mess with. He'd woven himself into every big business in the city and staked a claim on it. But my mother honed his brilliance, and it showed whenever she came into town.

Dad motioned to her before he spoke. "She wanted to witness for herself how far off the deep end you were."

She nodded and then slid off the table, pacing the office like her opinion of my work habits mattered. "You need to pull back, Jett. Jax will be with Aubrey. Your dad and I are leaving. You can't take on the burden of managing this company alone. You have the most intelligent people working here. They know their products. Trust them. Trust our teams."

"Dad, you can tell her that's the worst business advice ever."

He straightened in his chair. "I don't think you need any advice. Just do as you normally would."

Mom said from behind me, "No. He needs a vacation, Joe."

"Honey, he can't take a vacation when I'm about to resign."

As he said the words, his eyes glazed over and a large grin formed on his face while he looked over my shoulder.

I turned to see my mother with the same damn watery smile on her own. "'Resign,' Joe. I love that word."

"Oh, for fuck's sake," I grumbled.

My mom's hand connected hard with the back of my head just as the words left my mouth. "Watch it. You're treading on thin ice as it is. I'm so sick of your attitude."

"My attitude? You two realize I'm a good son, right?"

"'Good'?" she scoffed. "You're not married, you work fifteen hour days like your father—"

"I don't drink. I don't do drugs. I'm successful. *Forbes* claimed I'm one of the most successful—"

"Success would be a grandson," she mumbled while she glanced around the room and moved to straighten my father's shelf. The awards that sat atop it, the photos of him with a president, the gifts from various businessmen. They were a testament to his accolades. Yet here he was throwing it away for love.

"Love and kids aren't in the cards for me. You have Jax for that."

"I have every single one of my boys for that." Her voice cut through the office as she strode towards me with purpose. Mom was the most forbidding woman I knew when she wanted to be. Her striking blue eyes and tall willowy frame could come across as severe if she maneuvered herself just right. With a tailored pantsuit and deadly heels, she was a starkly beautiful older woman.

Maybe raising three boys and dealing with my father all these years had taught her something about authority, but I'm pretty sure it came naturally to her. "Each of my boys will give me grandchildren, you understand?"

She whispered, but her cold-blooded-killer stare screamed how serious she was.

"Mom, come on."

"Don't disappoint me. I'm so, so sick of being disappointed in you not finding the right girl and settling down."

I stood. "You two have fallen off the sane train. I mean it." I pointed at my father who was grinning like a fool. "You know I'm right."

He shrugged.

If it had just been him, I would have stormed out. But I couldn't leave my mom like that, so I wrapped up that crazy woman in my arms and kissed the top of her head. "Love you, Mom. If you're here after I'm done with work, we can get dinner."

Her blue eyes connected with mine and all I saw was love, no disappointment. "Sure, sweetie. Tell Brey I said hi."

I nodded and walked out.

When I rounded the corner, the damn weight of a whole industry came down on my shoulders. Stonewood Enterprises was mine, and I knew better than anyone that one misstep could fuck it all up.

CHAPTER
FIFTEEN

VICK

AFTER THREE WEEKS of being on Jett's team, we'd fallen into a routine. I'd learned the names of everyone in our space, knew that Josie in marketing got coffees in the morning, that Bob could whip up a legal contract faster than I could boot up my laptop, and that Gloria handled every one of Jett's needs.

Perfectly. With ease.

Much to my annoyance.

I also knew Brey showed up at about 9 a.m. on Tuesdays, Wednesdays, and Thursdays. We decided if we got a lunch break, we would take it together.

We hadn't gotten one yet.

Steven and I barely had time to peek at each other across our desks or discuss the weather. I'd wanted to discuss a lot more than the weather with him too. The man had finally gotten up the courage to ask me on a date now that he wasn't my boss.

Or so he'd said. Yet, with the hours we were working, we hadn't gotten around to figuring out when that date would happen.

In our first week, Jett Stonewood announced his team was about to step in for Senior Stonewood. He was stepping down, and we were stepping up.

I nearly lost my lunch. He handed me and the rest of the legal team about a million files and said he would be e-mailing more over. Contract after contract had to be rewritten or reworked. His father had solidified loyalties with a lot of companies through handshakes and backroom conversations over the years. Now that he was stepping down, nothing could be off the books anymore. Jett wanted everything in writing. He'd said as much to our team before he disappeared.

Over the past couple of weeks, he'd pop up in his office sporadically and then be gone again. Gloria would report that he had flown to New York or LA or some other place. His schedule was booked out for weeks at a time. And then he'd waltz in and nod to us all, stopping at certain desks to discuss anything of importance.

Bob would receive visit after visit about certain wording in an e-mail. Josie would perk up when he had a question about financials.

Steven and I would grind away in our corner, knowing that Jett would never stop by.

Misfits. Outsiders. The ones no one believed truly belonged.

I tried to look on the bright side day after day. Thousands of people were gunning for our seats. We were at one of the top-grossing businesses in the country where innovation met sophistication and thrived.

Yet, the feeling of being left out, of feeling inadequate, of someone passing you by time and time again was like sanding an open wound. If I tried to help Bob with a contract, he would scrunch his nose at me. I attempted to help Gloria rework an approach to a company about an investment, and she let me know she worked better alone. The woman cut right to the chase.

I even asked Josie if I could help her get coffees one day. Her doe eyes went wide, and she backed away like I was poaching her only job. Which maybe I was, but I wanted to do something that would make me feel part of the team.

I sipped my coffee and got back to the contract I was working on. There was a loophole, and I didn't know how to change it without making the other company extremely uncomfortable.

I rubbed my eyes and then took one tiny second to look at my manicured nails. I needed a reset, a moment's break so I could revise this.

The blue on them sort of matched the color of Tiffany & Co. And my manicurist had painted a little bow on the ring fingers. My dress was the same Tiffany blue with a ribbon around the waist, and I wore white stilettos to match it. The ensemble felt airy and fun.

"Victory."

I jumped, slamming down the hand I was examining. The voice vibrated through me and sent shivers skittering down my spine.

"Where's Bob?"

I cleared my throat, embarrassed. "He's at lunch."

Jett surveyed the room and ran his tongue over his teeth. Then he clicked his tongue as if he was shit out of luck. "Let him know I need to see him when he's back."

This was why I looked at my nails. The team handed grunt work to me, but no one trusted me with the real work. It made my eyes bleed and my hands itch for something more.

"Something I can answer for you, Mr. Stonewood?"

His lip curled when I referred to him. "Mister ...? You know what, never mind. Yes, pull up the Benson file if you can."

I already had it up on my computer. I repositioned in my chair and motioned to the contract I had open.

"Ah. So, you see the loophole too." He eyed me with a little more attention this time.

Those deep blues crinkled at the corners, and I felt his assessment of me shifting.

"The wording allows for it. Legally, you could argue they intentionally worded it that way, but it probably wouldn't hold up in court."

He leaned over my shoulder, his chest brushing my hair, and I caught his scent, masculine and fresh. Intoxicating. A distinct reminder of some of the best orgasms I'd ever had.

I wiggled in my seat for reasons I didn't want to acknowledge and shook my head a little to clear it.

"I see your point. How do we fix it?" His voice rumbled in my ear, so close that I could feel his breath on my cheek.

I started to respond, but he lifted his hand to point to a sentence on my screen. "Could we remove that sentence?"

"That leaves you liable if something goes wrong."

A growl rolled from him all the way to my core. "Let me know when Bob gets back. I need him to figure this out by the end of the day."

"I'm working on it." I shouldn't have pushed, but I knew I had this, the answer was right there on the tip of my tongue.

Jett tilted his head just enough that his five-o'clock shadow grazed my ear. "Are you now?"

I turned to look at him, and he was a breath away, so damn close I could have kissed him. I licked my lips, and his eyes tracked my movement. "I'll get it to you by the end of the day."

"See that you do, Victory." He pushed away from my desk and straightened.

Everyone had continued to work. No one stopped to witness him visiting my corner. Only Steven and I were shaken by it.

He leaned over his desk to whisper, "I think he just got back from New York."

"Didn't come back in the best mood either."

Steven chuckled. "Let's do dinner after you finish that today, huh?" I waited for my heart to gallop the way it did when Jett whispered in my ear, but it stayed steady.

I nodded toward him anyway. "That would be great. I'll have it by then. It's right there."

It wasn't right there. It was so far from there I wanted to scream.

Bob waltzed back in after lunch and asked if I needed help. I told him I had it.

I didn't have anything, and I damn well knew it.

Just past seven, Steven clapped me on the shoulder to announce we could do dinner another day because he had to get home. I had to get home too, but I couldn't leave without ironing out this contract.

Gloria was the last to shut down her computer other than me. She glanced at Jett's office, but he didn't seem to pay her any mind because she spun on a heel and left. I expected that from her now. She didn't waste niceties on anyone. Everything she did was calculated. Effective. Almost robotic.

Another hour passed. The glow from Jett's office beckoned to me while I sat at my desk, letting my screen be the only sign of life in the office space. I reworked the whole clause in the contract. I sighed. If Bob could do this, I could do this too. Except I didn't have his expertise or all those years of experience.

Why had I said I could do this?

A notification sounded on my laptop, and I looked to the corner of my screen.

> **JETT:** Go home.
> **ME:** I'm still working.
> **JETT:** On something Bob can finish for me in .2 seconds tomorrow. You're wasting company time and company time is money.
> **ME:** I'm salaried.
> **JETT:** Go home.
> **ME:** Look, I'm working on a few things. If I can't iron it out in the next hour, I'll talk with Bob tomorrow.

The light from his desk clicked off. His entire office in the glass fortress went dark and the city lights flooded in. My body hummed, my heart fluttered like a hummingbird's wings, and the part of my mind where I told myself Jett was never an option turned off.

One of the glass doors opened and Jett walked out, navy suit jacket over his shoulder and the sleeves of his white shirt rolled up. He glided down the stairs like a man so comfortable in his environment it had become part of him.

He'd married himself to the job and it showed. Every person respected his drive, his accomplishments, his unrelenting determination to work harder than every other businessman out there. His employees sat up taller when they encountered him, his clients' jaws dropped when he reported quarterly numbers, his competitors bowed down when he went up against them. His presence alone mirrored that of a stallion in the wild, rare and magnificent.

"Victory." My name rolled off his lips like a command. "I'm tired. Turn off your computer."

"As you should be after flying around the country. I'm finishing up here, but Gloria showed us how to leave with our FOBs. So, no worries. I won't be here too much later." I scanned him. His forearms flexed, and my thighs clenched in response. I wanted to feel them around me again, near me again, even a brush of skin would probably hold me over until Steven and I went on a date.

And I had to go on a date with Steven because Steven was serious. He wanted more than just sex.

I did too. I squeezed my eyes shut to ward off the temptation in front of me and then glared back at my computer screen. I intended to conquer this godforsaken sentence. He must have finally given in because I heard his footsteps retreat, and I smiled to myself.

Without him in his office looking down on me and no one waiting on me to finish, I had all night to figure it out. The lack of pressure instantly motivated me. I'd approach the contract from fresh angles, rework the structure of it, form something new and better. All parties would benefit and walk away happy.

I started typing away with more targeted strokes, hit every key with pizzazz. All I had needed was some space.

A loud pop sounded. I yelped as my screen and all the lighting went dark. I glanced around, but my eyes didn't adjust that quickly to the shadows.

I tried to restart my computer, but nothing happened when I pressed the button.

I reached for my desk lamp and knocked something over. I gasped at the clatter, and then I heard a rustling from behind me.

I whipped around and grabbed the first thing within my reach. My stapler would make a decent weapon, right?

"Hello?" I said, my voice strong. Whoever stood in the darkness couldn't possibly see my hand shaking, I told myself. I inched away from my desk, navigating slowly to the door in order to put distance between myself and that noise.

"Pix," Jett sounded amused as he stepped into the light that cascaded in from the window.

"Are you afraid of the dark?"

"What the heck is wrong with you?" I slammed my stapler down and stalked toward him. I shoved his chest enough that he took a step back. "You almost gave me a heart attack."

"Oh, please." He crossed his arms over his chest. "What are you? Twenty-four? Everyone needs a kick of adrenaline now and then."

"Twenty-five and I get my adrenaline rush doing things I want to do, not having someone frighten me in the dark."

His lips curved up like a joker and he rocked back on his feet as he shoved his hands in his pockets. "What things normally get your adrenaline going?"

My mouth, I'm sure, opened to say something, but he stood there tall and sinister in the bluish glow that highlighted all his best features. The way his muscles bunched under that shirt, the way his hair was mussed just right, the way his eyes sparkled midnight blue … I couldn't form words.

I cleared my throat and pointedly turned toward my desk to search for my phone. When I found it, I switched on the flashlight to gather my things. "I don't have time to make small talk with you tonight. You don't have time, either, as it seems the electrical in Stonewood Tower is down."

"Shame." He didn't sound regretful at all.

Approaching the brink of cracking that contract only to have my momentum stunted by a blackout frustrated me. I lashed out because of it.

"'Shame'? Not really, Jett. I don't think I would enjoy making small talk with my new boss, although it isn't like we've tried it. Instead, I'm completely ignored throughout the day and given elementary tasks as if I don't have a college degree. Even though I got put in the damn all-star room where the sky's never the limit for anyone except me. I'm limited to getting freaking coffee for Gloria."

His teeth shined like a wolf's in the night. "If this job isn't what you pictured it being..."

I sighed and tapped my stiletto toe on the tile. "I just don't see why I was put in this room. You could have put me anywhere. You have a whole legal team on the twenty-third floor."

"Gloria normally assigns desk areas to new employees."

"So, she wanted me in this room?"

"Nope." He popped the P and stalked toward me. "I put you where I wanted you, Victory."

"I'm useless here." I motioned around the space. "Bob's going to figure out the contract that I can't change tomorrow, and I'm going to go back to getting only Gloria coffee because Josie will freak if I get anyone else a beverage."

"Bob already looked at it."

"What?" I recoiled at his words.

"He doesn't know what to do with it either." He shrugged, his large shoulders bunching.

"That's not what you said."

"I know what I said. I did it to motivate you." He sighed and pinched the bridge of his nose. "The Armanellis are going to be a bitch to get under the right contract."

"That's the Armanelli contract? It says Benson." My voice went high.

He nodded slowly and sucked on his teeth. "That's confidential."

"Why wasn't I made aware when I was working on it?"

"That's the meaning of confidential, Pix."

I pulled a little at my sleeve, not sure I wanted to say what I blurted out next. "Legally, Stonewood Enterprises needs to make me aware of that. I have a right to know. I could hold you liable for putting my life in danger."

"I'm not putting your life in danger." His eyebrows slammed down.

"They're a freaking mob family," I leaned in and whispered like someone could be listening. For all I knew, someone was.

He rubbed his forehead. "That's debatable."

"If you're trying to get a written contract with them, that means—"

"It means we get a written contract with them and protect Stonewood Enterprises from whatever they do outside of it."

"Protect? From what? Are they killing people?" Instead of dying from cancer, I was going to die from this. I just knew it.

"You're being dramatic. I didn't take you for so much drama when I met you."

"When you met me, we were on a sunny beach with no stress," I pointed out for the idiot of a man standing in front of me.

"The Armanellis haven't killed anyone in decades." He rounded back to the subject at hand.

"And that's supposed to make me feel better?" I shouted. Then, I took a breath and said with as much disdain as I could muster. "You're a lunatic. I'm not working on this contract."

"You already started, and I need Stonewood Enterprises protected."

"Well, with what is already written, it won't be." My words were jackhammers of truth we both needed to hear. "What are you thinking, Jett? Even if I were to come up with perfect sentences, it doesn't mean anything. They can't be trusted."

"Cade and Bastian have always been trustworthy."

"Then why the contract?"

"Because their father and mine had an understanding. Without my father at the helm, we need to have something concrete, something in writing."

"As if the law will stop someone in the mob." I rolled my eyes and grabbed my bag, so ready to be done with the day. "You're wading into waters no business should be swimming through."

"Coming from you, that's pretty epic." One dark eyebrow raised in surprise. "Where's the silver lining, Pix?"

I blew a puff of air toward the ceiling. "I get that my positivity is somewhat frustrating at times, Jett. I know I'm a lot, okay?"

His eyes widened in shock at my admission. I knew the truth though. My peppy attitude could be a turnoff. Sometimes, I couldn't even handle my own cheerfulness. Some days I wanted to curl up in a ball and wallow in self-pity.

Tomorrow, I could be out of remission though. When you're contemplating death knocking at your door, it's hard to enjoy anything. So, I couldn't live any other way now. This was living life to the fullest every damn day, even when it got tiring, because I'd come very close to not having a life to live.

"I never claimed to be anything different, Jett. But I'm not stupid either. I like to avoid completely avoidable dangerous situations."

"Could have fooled me on vacation."

"Why? Because I wanted to go on a hike or two?"

"You went gallivanting around that island looking for ways to die. You always do. You talk about wanting to feel alive and now you're cowering in the damn corner without even trying to negotiate a contract."

"This isn't cowering," I seethed, poking his hard chest.

"Then you'll be at the meeting tomorrow when we discuss this further?"

"Meeting?"

"Yes. I invited the Armanellis here to see if we can come to a compromise."

"Jett, shouldn't we think about what this means for the company?"

"Bob can come if you don't want to. Jax and Brey will be at the meeting as well."

What an immature way of getting someone to do something.

I narrowed my eyes at him. "Send the invite to my Outlook. I'll make sure my schedule is clear."

"Fantastic. Now, since that's out of the way, are we fucking in my office or here at your desk?"

"Are you insane?"

"Not yet, though I might be on the verge after watching you all day in that outfit. What the hell are you wearing?"

Screw him. This light-blue dress flowed around every part of my body and made me look as expensive as the rings inside the Tiffany & Co. boxes. I twirled in front of him and let the skirt flare at my knees. "You like it?"

"It's distracting, that's for sure."

"In a good way?"

"If you're searching for a compliment, Pix, call Stevie later and ask him. I want to fuck you, not fluff your ego."

I ignored his callousness because his eyes dragged across my dress like he wished he could burn it off me with a look. "We should probably go home, Jett."

I didn't want to, but one of us had to be smart. Who better than the one who didn't own the company? "We can't have sex in the office. There are probably cameras throughout this floor."

I didn't care about the cameras. My heart beat faster just being in his proximity, my legs got weak, my pussy throbbed.

"You're right," he said pointedly. "That's why I turned off the power to this floor."

Beep. Beep. Beep.

Three brief sounds reminding me what it felt like to barely be alive in a hospital bed. They reminded me now to live. Three little pulses telling me to let him take me anywhere and everywhere. I would only live this once. Indulge once. Dive deep down into the place I felt most real and most alive. The time was now. I didn't want to encounter the it's-too-late realizations or the if-only-I-would-have regrets ever again. I had too much experience with that train of thought, and I wasn't going back.

"That's cocky." I shot a pointed look at the bulge in his pants as I backed up to rest my hip on my desk.

He followed and pushed his body right onto mine. "Not cocky. Confident. Now, your desk or mine?"

I breathed him in as he leaned forward to nip at my neck. My nipples tightened under the dress, and I mentally racked my brain for what I might be wearing underneath it. I'd dressed for Steven, not Jett.

He slid his hands under the skirt and ran them up my thighs, then grabbed my ass. "No preference?"

I gasped as he jerked me forward to feel him against me, reminding me just how freaking big he was. How lucky I was to be here with him for this moment. "Oh, God. Just here. Let's do this here. Now."

I didn't want to wait another minute. I grabbed my skirt and slid it up as I hopped onto my desk and spread my legs. White lace to match my white stilettos. I knew the color popped on my sun-kissed skin too. I stared at him taking me in. He wanted to own me, devour me, feed off me. He was there for the feast and would leave me right after.

"So, your desk it is."

I nodded slowly. "I want it right here, Jett. You better devour me and leave me completely ravaged."

When he showed his teeth, no one would mistake it for a smile. Under the city lights, he'd warped into a wolf. "Good. I want you to remember us here when you look up at Mr. Stevie across from you tomorrow."

"You're such a dick."

"The dick who's about to fuck you."

I should have shoved him away right then. This wasn't going anywhere, but my body didn't care. It woke like a damn bear that had been in hibernation all winter.

"In that case," I lifted my hips and slid my lace thong off. Then I spread my legs and planted my hands behind me. "Fuck me good because Steven went home, which means I'm not getting any without you."

He growled and unzipped his pants. "You think he's going to get you off, woman?"

"Oh, he will. Just not tonight."

He laughed as he gripped himself and pumped once, hard. Pre cum already glistened at the tip.

My mouth watered. "Are you waiting for something?"

"Waiting for you to tell me this is your dream. Me and not him. I can see you practically concocting our future together. You and me in a nice house together or some shit."

"Your realities rubbed off on me, Jett," I scoffed. "I'm just here for a good lay tonight."

"Now that, Pix,"—he whispered softly in my ear as he placed his hands right on top of mine behind me—"is the best thing I've heard all day."

He plunged into me. I gasped and arched into him, trying to adjust to how fast the man worked, how quickly he took what he thought was his to take. I had to adjust to how quickly my body gave in to the idea too because I already was trying to grab hold of the orgasm that was about to burst out of me. "We have to slow down."

He fisted my hair and pulled it back so that my neck was exposed. As he dragged his teeth along it, he pumped faster and harder. My legs wrapped around him, wanting him closer. "I intend to keep pace. You can't control how fast you get off, that's your problem."

His rough voice sent shivers down my spine and I almost bucked off the desk when he dragged his hand down my stomach to squeeze the soft spot near my hip. If he didn't want me to sync with him, fine. I took his words for what they were. We were in this, doing this, feeling this. For ourselves.

Sex with Jett wasn't about making him feel good, wasn't about trying to get him to want me.

It was about me. Me getting off. Me feeling good. Me screwing a guy because I wanted to, not because I was making anyone else happy.

The worrying about how I looked on that desk, how my face scrunched in ecstasy, how I might sweat too much, or my hair might not be perfect faded away. Worrying about sex with a man who didn't care about anything except his own pleasure would have been stupid. With Jett's lack of interest, my normal concerns died, and I felt more alive.

I screamed into the office. I clawed at his back and took what I wanted. I dug into his muscles, squeezed my legs hard around his ass and met him thrust for thrust. I didn't wait for him to kiss his way back up to my lips from where he was ravaging my neck, I grabbed his face and brought it to mine. "Kiss me like you mean it for one second, Jett."

"Just remember I don't mean a damn thing. I'll still be only your boss in the morning."

"Boss of the whole fucking city, but sure," I shrugged.

"Damn right." His tongue kept up with our rhythm. His pillowed lips devoured mine and his hands were on my cheeks holding me to him. The kiss barreled me into an orgasm completely unhinged from anything I'd experienced before.

I rode his dick selfishly, milking every ounce of it, feeling my heart beat, my breath panting in and out. He let me set the pace even though he said he wouldn't. When we stopped, I opened my eyes to take in the lights that shimmered outside and his face as he watched me come down from bliss.

His shirt wrinkled where I clenched it at his chest and his hair stuck up wherever I'd pulled at it. He leaned back and his twilight eyes assessed me. "You good?"

"Does it matter?" I yanked him close by his shirt. "We keep pace, Mr. Stonewood." I tightened the hold of my legs around him so he pushed back in me.

"You're still a goddamn knockout, Ms. Blakely. Even under my city's lights."

CHAPTER
SIXTEEN

JETT

ONE OF MY drivers idled outside Stonewood Enterprises, ready to take Vick home. I watched her evaluate the creases in her dress. Then she grabbed her purse to pull out a compact and smooth back her hair.

She sighed. "Whatever. This will have to do." She snapped the compact shut and gathered the rest of her belongings.

"The SUV out front is for you."

She didn't look at me, just kept putting papers in her bag. "I don't need a ride."

"But you'll take one."

She slammed her bag shut. "Do we have to keep doing this?"

"Not if you just take the damn ride offered to you."

"Would you offer anyone else a ride home?"

"Yes. I'd offer everyone a ride home if they were here this late."

Her whiskey eyes rolled all the way back. Then landed on me. "I'm too tired to argue with you."

"Then do as I say. We'll get to that point eventually anyway. This way is faster."

She swiped her stuff off her desk. "Fine." She turned on her heel as she hiked her bag onto her shoulder along with her purse. "See you at the meeting tomorrow, boss."

"Yeah, do me a favor and don't dress like a damn present that's begging to be unwrapped."

Her hair flared out, she spun around so fast. "This outfit is completely professional."

I shrugged. I knew she was right. However, it didn't appear professional when the skirt swayed as she buzzed around the office and my dick stood to salute it. She'd bent over to talk with Bob, and I'd almost called her to my office so I could press the privacy button and have my way with that ass.

Here I was, running the damn show, and I couldn't think past my dick. I'd fired countless men for that very reason. I'd thought about firing a few more because they'd been doing the same damn thing I'd been: staring at her ass all day.

"That bow under your tits makes men think you want them to rip that dress open. I promise."

"You're deranged. You aren't thinking straight. Probably because you work too much. Go home."

"You go home and take the ride."

Her nails dug into the shoulder strap of her bag. "Good night, Jett."

"Good night, Victory."

She walked out of the office toward the elevators, and I watched her the whole way. She didn't turn back to look at me.

Not once.

The next morning, Bob and I combed through the Armanelli files one last time to check every possible angle.

We were fully prepared for the meeting. Bob assured me that he and the legal team had it handled. I knew the Armanellis better than him though. We had nothing handled. As he sat there reworking one last scenario with me, I looked out of my office to see Vick laughing at something Stevie said.

The two grew closer every day. I saw the way she relaxed in his presence, her shoulders loosening and her posture slouching. Her chin in her hand, she rested her elbow on the table, honey eyes gazing longingly at his lips as he spewed something dumb.

I couldn't hear it, but I knew. Stevie wasn't bright. He'd brought no equity to the business so far. The best thing that ever happened to him was his father leaving him the company and my team immediately seeing an opportunity. Stevie would have run his business into the ground. Now, his employees would have a chance to flourish. They wouldn't suffer the boredom of a mediocre, dead-end job.

What Vick thought was so damn funny as she laughed at him, I couldn't understand.

I pulled up my messages as Bob explained he would video conference with Antonio to talk about the club the Armanellis and I owned together. I could recite our agreements about that club in my sleep, but I nodded and let him carry on.

> **ME:** You wore bright pink for our meeting today. With a bow, Pix. We just discussed this last night.
> **VICTORY:** Pink calms people. Also, discussing my work attire is probably not approved in the HR handbook. Actually, I seem to recall it stating that I should reach out to HR if I had questions regarding my attire. I don't, but I will if I do.
> **ME:** I know you don't have questions. I do. Like why you think pink calms people.
> **VICTORY:** Look it up!
> **ME:** That dress is inappropriate.

VICTORY: How?

ME: Well, you can see every curve of your ass in it for one. Stevie's looked at it about 5 times today.

VICTORY: These are our company messages, Jett!

ME: I own the company, Pix.

VICTORY: Goodbye.

ME: See you at one.

Thankfully, she'd stopped smiling at Stevie. I'd burst her bubble in the next few hours, which shouldn't have been a goal of mine. Victory Blakely was interesting, but she was downright mesmerizing without her facade of happiness.

Bob stopped mid-sentence. "Are you okay, Jett?"

"Yes, why?"

Bob's bushy eyebrows formed a frown as he considered his next words. "You're smiling, son."

Bob had been with me for years and his balding head probably reflected the amount of stress I'd put him through. No one called me son except my father, mother, and him. "So what if I'm smiling?"

"You never appear happy when we discuss the Armanellis. Not like that, anyway."

I cleared my throat. "I don't know what you mean."

Bob glanced behind him to where I'd been looking. His bright-blue eyes that always seemed so damn friendly sparkled with recognition. "Ah. I see."

"You don't see anything, old man."

He looked down at his laptop with one side of his mouth quirked up. "She's whip smart and a beacon of light. I'm enjoying working with her."

"She's naive, Bob. We both know it. Not everything is sugar plums and lollipops like she thinks."

"Sure, but isn't it nice to have someone around every now and then who thinks it is?"

I looked out at the open office. Vick was flouncing around now. Like always, she shook off her anger faster than I could blink. Josie eyes sparkled at something she said, and Brey laughed when Vick gestured wildly in the air. The long petal-pink sleeves of her dress flared at the edges and Brey picked at one of them as if admiring the fabric. Vick nodded quickly, eyes wide.

No doubt those two were discussing clothing and not business. "It'd be nice, Bob, if everyone worked so we're prepared for the Armanelli meeting."

Bob closed his laptop as slow as a sloth would. "We'll be fine, Jett."

I sighed and ran my hand through my hair. "Get back to work, old man."

"Like you say, I'm old. I've got to take my time." He rustled around in his seat for a minute longer.

"You just ran a damn marathon, Bob. Get the hell out of my office."

He sprang up from his chair, laughing. He might have been pushing seventy but no one would guess it by his upright stance, athletic build, and spry gait. "Get some sleep, son. You're cranky."

I straightened a few papers on my desk as he left, not wanting to reply. I wasn't sleeping well. The only nights I'd gotten sleep had been the ones after a certain woman blew my mind and those were few and far between. I needed to get back to random women and regimented routines. It was the only way I was going to survive taking over this company.

Thirty minutes before the meeting, I made my way to our conference room with the team I'd assigned. Brey followed closely behind me, making an effort to stay professional and not look at her husband. Vick, on the other hand, bounced around near Bob and took a seat near him. Eyeing the projector and technology in the room, I mumbled, "They'll just want to talk."

Brey nodded. "I agree. I made the PowerPoints in case, but I don't believe you'll need them."

"Not sure it was worth the time. Your PowerPoints are burned into our brains. We'll know the stats if needed."

Brey pursed her lips to hold in a grin. She knew that was as good a compliment as she was going to get from me.

"Brey, your PowerPoints were on point," Vick chimed in.

Bob nodded, eyes damn near twinkling. "I agree. They really helped me understand the data."

"Good job, Peaches," Jax said as he sat down next to me and leaned around me to look into his wife's eyes. Hers widened and she shook her head once. The woman seemed to think she could control a Stonewood.

"Babe, everyone knows we're married. I can call you Peaches here."

Bob and Vick snickered while two other people on my legal team ruffled through their notes, trying to make like they hadn't heard.

"Let's focus on preparing for the meeting, Jax," Brey clipped out.

"Sure." He nodded. Then looked at everyone else in the room. "Anyone have any questions for Mrs. Stonewood? She made the PowerPoints earlier this week at home. In my bed."

Brey's cheeks turned red with anger and embarrassment. Across the room, Vick practically sighed with giddiness before she raised her hand. "I have a question."

Bob mumbled, "This ought to be good."

"I'm just wondering if Mrs. Stonewood created the PowerPoints before or after—"

"Victory," I blurted her name loud and my whole team turned to look at me. I took a breath. No one knew how important this contract was except me. They sat here joking while I reworked the damn numbers in my head and noted the different outcomes. This partnership solidified who was a king or queen in Chicago and who was a pawn. I glared at the woman who thought work was a game. "I don't think we need to finish that sentence."

Caden and Sebastian Armanelli strode in with Gloria. "Oh, I would love for Victory to finish her sentence," Sebastian said, scanning the room, sizing us up, calculating the dynamics. "Victory, seems you've made Jett Stonewood a little perturbed. I heard your name through the door. Tell me, was the sentence that bad?"

He looked her up and down, his eyes scanning that bubblegum-pink dress like a damn kid on Christmas morning. He wanted to unwrap the present.

She smiled at his perusal and glanced at me. "I'm never bad."

I mouthed, I fucking told you.

CHAPTER
SEVENTEEN

VICK

JETT TRIED EVERYTHING he could to rattle me, but I wouldn't scare that easily. He'd invited me to this meeting just to show me I couldn't handle it, that my positivity would die here because I was incapable of actual work. Jett didn't know me though.

I had more drive in my pinkie finger than most people had in their entire body. Doctors had told me to take a year off from high school, that I could sit back a grade. Those days, I remember clinging to my mother's words like a lifeline. "My daughter is seventeen and at the top of her class. Where she will stay. Because she's a Blakely. I didn't raise a daughter who couldn't handle it."

Handle it, we did. Even through late nights of throwing up from the chemo and emergency hospital visits and losing my hair along with my friends and my whole damn life, I'd stayed at the top of my class. I'd outdone everyone and gotten into every college I'd applied to.

Then my mother's words got the best of me the day I'd told her I could go to school in California and conquer the world on my own. "You almost died, Victory. You can't risk catching something and not being close to home. You have a compromised immune system. Your father and I can't lose you. Not after we almost lost you before. Stay close, honey. You can live a great life here."

The words propelled me now in the conference room. I was a Blakely, and I was living my life. Not stuck at home anymore. I finally took the step to leave and I would take another. I could handle this meeting and show I had a right to one of these seats as much as anyone else on the legal team.

I cleared my throat and stood to greet the two beautiful men along with their own legal team. Bastian and Cade had gone swimming in their Italian gene pool and come out soaked in the best of it. Their curled brown hair and dark eyes caught most women's attention. Bastian wore those curls a bit longer, a tad unruly. Like he wouldn't conform to the usual standards or rules. Cade followed behind his brother and held himself more rigidly. Rules must have applied to him.

"Just a joke between colleagues, Mr. Armanelli." I nodded at him and went to shake his hand as Jett strode over to welcome them also.

Bastian looked at my hand like it was offensive. "Vick, you partied with me and that little dancer over there," he gestured toward Brey who smiled wide. "One of the best nights I had in a long time. Don't revert to professionalism now."

Truth be told, a long time ago, before I knew they were mobsters, I partied with them because I thought they were celebrities hanging out with Jaydon. We drank way too much and danced way too hard. The memory of the night calmed some of my nerves. He wasn't *The Godfather*.

Him referring to our night out could have been awkward. I could have stumbled over my words and looked at my boss in trepidation.

But I didn't do awkwardness well. I stepped into his open arms. I was scared by the idea of Katie dating him, but I had forgotten how unintimidating Bastian was. The news stories painted darker and darker pictures of these men, and their sweet demeanors got stained with the images depicted.

When I pulled back, Cade stood behind his brother, his eyes bouncing from Jett, to me, to Bastian. He shot his hand out for me to shake like he wanted no part in the prior hug exchange. I nodded at him as I slid my hand in his.

He mumbled something about it being a pleasure to see me again, but his gaze stayed on Jett.

Jett. The formidable man who sucked the life out of the room. The boss of it all.

The man I'd screwed the night before.

The man I could find in a room with my eyes closed because the scent of him lingered with me through the night, mixed with my dreams, and stole away my thoughts.

"So, it seems you've all met." He finally spoke, staring at Bastian like the cards had been laid on the table and they both had an equal winning hand.

Bastian nodded. "Seems the Stonewood men keep marvelous company."

Jett grunted, and instead of shaking their hands, he spun to go back to his seat. As he made his way there, everyone else followed suit.

Jett maneuvered a few pieces of paper around the table before leaning back in his chair. "Your father isn't here."

Cade jumped in no doubt ready to right the ship. "He wanted to be here but thought since your father stepped down, it was best for us to handle it. Sons to sons."

"This isn't a family reunion, Cade. I don't sit at the kid table while the adults talk business. It isn't son to son. It's owner to owner. You own the business now?"

Cade's eyes narrowed just like his brother's did next to him. Bastian sucked on one of his teeth, making a squeaking noise. It was the only noise in the room as the tension shifted. Both Armanellis scanned their surroundings, and my stomach dropped. Suddenly, these men weren't as approachable. Suddenly, I wondered if the news story about bodies being hidden was true.

Jax sighed. I glanced at Brey with my eyes wide.

She quickly shook her head, signaling not to look her way. But I needed her reassurance. We were dealing with the mob. Someone needed to let me know I wasn't dying today.

"I took over the city if that's what you're asking." Bastian folded his hands on the table and pointedly moved a ring around one of his fingers. It matched the one on Cade's ring finger.

Jett's eyebrows raised in surprise. "When?"

Bastian laughed, but it felt hollow. "Dear old dad handed it over right before this meeting."

Reading between the lines of two men who ruled the business and mafia worlds wasn't my strong suit. I knew there was more to the story as Jett nodded solemnly. "Well, then. Let's me and you talk business, Sebastian."

"Our contract stays the same. We don't have time to negotiate a change in terms."

"That contract was outdated the day our fathers shook hands."

"There's no record of that handshake," Bastian quipped.

"I don't have time for this," Jett sighed, shoulders slumping as if the world's weight had become too heavy. "You know I'm trying to develop a way of maintaining a clean water supply in third world countries. It's time sensitive for people who live there. This isn't as important."

He pinched the bridge of his nose, and everyone fell silent. His words echoed through the room, shifting the focus from the power struggle between men to the struggle of humanity. A man's pride should have been measured by what he did for the world, not by who might have been a bigger man in the conference room.

Maybe both Bastian and Jett knew that. Maybe the two saw and fought battles so much larger than the rest of us could fathom that they could put aside whatever differences they had to make their partnership work.

"I'm here to keep working with you, Jett," Bastian said, his words precise, clear, and starkly honest.

Jett's blue eyes scanned the room. "We're all here for that. Let's make it work. What do you need?"

"I need backing on the pharmaceutical company, Levvetor."

Sheets of paper ruffled throughout the conference room as our team scrambled to find the relevant information.

"Not even on the table, Bastian," Jett grated out. "You didn't send any information on that. It's a curveball I'm not willing to entertain."

The air shifted, I saw it before anyone else or they didn't care to see it. Bastian rolled his shoulders once and flicked his gaze to his brother.

"We should do it," I blurted.

Every single blue eye, green eye, Italian eye, and brown eye swung my way. The attention of the whole room was on me.

And not in a good way.

Maybe a concerning one from Brey and a curious one from Bastian and Cade's side of the table. Everyone else wanted to kill me, burn me at the stake, shove me out of the conference room and apologize for the idiot. I understood it. I wanted to take back my words as soon as I'd unleashed them.

"She's new," Jett explained and waved away my comment.

"She's also intelligent. Hear her out." Brey sat up tall, head turned to face Bastian. And to avoid Jett, no doubt.

"Anything for you, little dancer," Bastian smiled as he murmured it. Partying with Bastian and Cade one night had ended mostly in Bastian wanting more from Brey than she could give him because her heart already belonged to Jax. Bastian flaunted his soft spot for Brey every time he encountered the couple now.

"Drop the name, Bastian," Jax warned.

Jett cleared his throat. "Let's keep this about business."

I stopped him. "Investing in Levvetor would not only benefit the company from a publicity standpoint, it's also a good company. And if that solidifies the contract we want with you ... " I glanced at the Armanelli team and then looked at Jett. His shoulders sat stiff and straight under his suit jacket. He glared at me while he clicked his pen in and out. The sound matched my heart's beat. Fast. Rapid. Alive. "I think it's a deal we shouldn't pass up."

Beep. Beep. Beep.

Stepping in to take the decision out of a powerful man's hands so I could give my opinion washed away any feeling of weakness, fragility, or deficiency. Normally, I worried over whether my cells would divide abnormally one day. It took one simple imperfect DNA mutation and I would go back to wondering if I would get to see another day.

I hated that anxiety.

I wanted to keep waking up to the sun, go to work and fight the city sidewalks to get there, sit across from the most beautiful man I'd ever slept with and go head to head with him.

I wanted to feel alive.

I let it creep across my face, the smile that I felt through my whole body.

Jett leaned back in his chair, raised a dark eyebrow and clicked the pen one last time. He searched the room. "Anyone else think it's a good idea?"

"We need to do some research but it could work," Jax nodded at me and winked. Brey beamed at him like he had redeemed himself for the conversation minutes ago.

I almost jumped out of my seat when I heard a soft clipped voice from the corner speak up, "Levvetor Pharmaceuticals has outsold competitors for two quarters now. They're gaining attention and relevance as they are pricing their drugs higher than competitors and still selling. It's a solid investment."

Jett watched Gloria as she rattled off more statistics about the company. The company I knew all about. I could have rattled off those statistics along with ten others and given a firsthand story of my experience with them. A Levvetor drug saved my life.

Jett interrupted Gloria. "I'm not interested, Gloria," he ground out loudly. His perfectly sculpted jaw flexed as he stared at her, daring her to continue. When she closed her laptop and snapped her mouth shut, he eyed the rest of his team. Every single person's head went down, submitting to their king, not willing to argue, share thoughts, build ideas. This wasn't Stonewood Enterprises, it was Stonewood Autocracy.

"Jett, we must already be watching them with those numbers and—"

"Whether we are or aren't watching them, Ms. Blakely, has nothing to do with this meeting. We aren't backing a company that wasn't even on the table to pacify you, Sebastian."

"Then the contract stands as is." He shrugged and closed his folder, ready to leave.

Jett moved to stand as well. The hardened line of his jaw and cold blue eyes glaring out at no one in particular showed me he was just as ready for them to leave.

Blurting out my feelings hadn't helped. Pushing Jett's boundaries definitely hadn't helped. I knew after this meeting the deal would be dead in the water. I'd overstepped my place.

Yet, I was a Blakely. My mother taught me not to fold even when I encountered the impossible.

I stood and smoothed the soft fabric of my dress. "What exactly do you want invested in Levvetor, Bastian?"

He stopped moving and looked at me with curiosity. "Without Stonewood Enterprises, I can only invest sixty percent of what I'd like. It would give me a share but not the voting share needed."

I took a deep breath and tried to figure out if we could swing it. "If I had another investor … "

"They want Stonewood."

"I'll call Harvey. He'll consider it."

"You'll call Harvey? You have a direct line to the CEO of Levvetor?" Jett sneered from behind me. His breath was hot on my neck. Everyone in the room was watching us as I looked over my shoulder at him. He was closer than he should have been. Too close for a business relationship.

I noted that. Noted that everyone in the room would be speculating on whether we'd had relations after this meeting.

I sidestepped Jett dramatically, hoping our team noticed that too. "Yes, as I said, I'll call him."

Bastian outright laughed at our exchange. Then he clapped his hands together. "Well then. You and I have business to discuss. Everyone else can go back to work."

Jett's lip curled, his muscles bunching like he wanted to lunge for me. I'd seen them poised that way before, but this stance was filled with rage instead of desire.

"We don't make deals without my business involved, Victory. There's a reason we're in Stonewood Tower right now." His words dropped rock after rock into the pit of my stomach. The blood rushed through my veins with my heart jackhammering under his stare.

"You don't want your business involved." My voice sounded meek and timid. I lifted my chin and flipped my hair once to reinforce my confidence. "I think helping a company even if we can't invest in them would be the best thing for everyone."

"So, now the Armanellis are a company to you?" He lifted an arm and extended it to look at his watch. "I don't have time for you or this. The meeting is over."

Bastian cleared his throat and the bubble around Jett and me popped. "I'd like a word with Ms. Blakely alone."

Everyone filed out quickly, nodding or mumbling a thank you to their bosses and colleagues, excited to get out of the room before they got in as much trouble as I had.

Brey walked by and grabbed my hand briefly while she leaned in to whisper, "Good luck."

Jett didn't walk out with his team. He crossed his arms over his expansive chest and stood there with his feet shoulder width apart. He looked unmovable and protective. Hot.

"Victory works for me."

"She does, but the business we have together isn't a part of Stonewood Enterprises."

"Then you can have dinner with her outside of her working hours."

"Don't be a prick, Jett. I just need a minute with her." When Jett still didn't move, Bastian sighed and ran a hand through his dark curly hair. "Oh, for fuck's sake, I'm not trying to date her or get her into business with me. She's safe, she's yours, she's untouchable. I get it."

"I'm what?" I stammered out. "I'm not ... We're not ... "

"Don't fucking forget it, Bastian." Without looking at me, he stormed out and slammed the door.

Bastian groaned and mumbled, "Jesus."

He sat back down in his chair and waved at the one next to him.

I glanced around, searching for cameras or something in case he really did try something mobster-ish. Nothing looked remotely like security, and I found myself tensing back up.

"I don't want to hurt or scare you, Vick. It's just me."

I nodded and pulled the chair out but moved it a little further away before sitting.

He grumbled something low and then his hand shot out to the leg of my chair so fast I nearly jumped. He dragged the chair close enough that we were inches apart and said softly, "You danced with me a whole damn night, woman. And now I'm dating your friend. Katie isn't scared of me. You shouldn't be either."

"Katie isn't scared of anybody."

A laugh burst out of him as he sat back. "Got that right. I'm fucking scared of her sometimes."

I slumped at his assessment of my friends. I remembered that laugh he had—so intoxicating, I told Brey to have fun with him in the club, not knowing a thing about him. Now that I knew so much more, I wondered how I could accept Katie dating him.

News outlets consistently followed the Armanelli men, and while they never did the dirty work themselves, there was so much done in the streets of the city they controlled. Taking over for his father meant he could make a call and literally have someone killed. That power and feeling of godlike control could only lead to abuse.

"Everyone should fear you. Power breeds fear."

"I don't have power like you think."

"Don't you though?"

He stared out the windows. "It's a beautiful city. I'm not here to paint it red. My dad gave me power because he wants me to clean up the red that's already been spilled."

Was he saying what I thought he was saying? This was for movies or books. Not my life. Not my carefully protected life.

"Look, I don't want to be involved in this thing between you and the Stonewoods." I sighed. "Levvetor is a good company. Does that mean you should back it? I'm not sure. I don't know if you are looking to corrupt it or help it."

"Help. Promise."

"I don't know how much weight that holds. A promise between us is—"

"Cross my heart, I'll bleed out on the streets of Chicago for you if you find me lying."

I looked him up and down, took in his expensive suit, the way his body leaned toward me in a way that didn't feel creepy but earnest. He wanted me to believe him, maybe even wanted me to be friends with him. Some yearning was there, but it was definitely platonic. "Why Levvetor?"

"I could ask you the same question. Going up against Jett isn't for the faint of heart."

"Meh…" I shrugged a shoulder.

He smiled. "More to that story, I see."

"You don't see because there isn't anything to see," I scoffed.

"If you were just working under him, you wouldn't have gone up against him."

"Yes, I would have," I countered, and I meant it. "I believe in Levvetor."

He measured me up this time, and I didn't shrink under the assessment. "Why?"

"You first," I blurted. I didn't want to share my story, didn't want to see the pity or the sympathy in his eyes. I didn't share my story with anyone anymore. I'd learned quickly in high school that no one really wanted to hear it. No one wants to know how you're actually doing when they ask the question. They want comfort, and it is completely uncomfortable to talk about cancer.

He sighed. "Aside from the fact that it will make us all a lot of money, my father knows the founder. They are good friends of the family." Before I could ask, he added, "And yes, I mean that in every sense of the word. We don't want competitors shutting them down, and that means we need to pour more money into it when the government starts to back the bigger companies."

"Their drugs are working. The government can't…"

"Big companies can make smaller ones go away even if they are finding cures, Vick. You know that."

"Okay. So, if Stonewood Enterprises won't back you, then I'll lean hard on my mother's company."

"Blakely Fashion? Interesting. You'll be tanking your career at Stonewood Enterprises and doing something completely illegal. And …" He dragged the word out as his eyes tracked over my face. "You don't care one bit."

"Nope." I stood up, ready for the conversation to be over.

"I need an explanation."

"Can't me wanting to save lives be enough?" I turned toward the door.

"Nope." He stepped in front of me, his height and presence worked to his advantage, overwhelming my space and my confidence. "Tell me why."

"I've used a drug they make," I whispered the admission.

His eyes jumped back and forth between mine. Then he scanned my body, surely looking for the evidence of my cancer.

He wouldn't find any. My cancer hadn't left scars on the outside. It festered in my bones, flowed through my blood, and weighed down my soul instead. Cancer wasn't always apparent but it was always lurking. If not in you, then it lurked in someone you loved, morphing the way they looked at you, treated you, saw you. It morphed and marred every aspect of your life.

"You don't…" He stopped. "You aren't sick. You don't look…"

"I'm in remission. Have been for years."

His brow furrowed. And his gaze turned harder, more solid. "You're a fighter then."

His words, they weren't a question but a statement, and I stood taller with it. The belief in his voice or possibly the cemented conviction made me want to hug a mafia boss. "I'm a fighter then."

We let the time pass. Minutes went by. I crossed and uncrossed my legs, fidgeted with my pen. I didn't feel the need to make him feel comfortable or fold under the awkwardness of it all.

"You don't tell people."

"It doesn't go over well," I admitted.

"That's a lot of baggage for one person."

"I'm sure you have a lot of baggage for one person too."

Bastian's shoulders tensed. Then he cracked his neck, as if trying to release the secrets he had no doubt stashed away.

"We follow your lead when it comes to Levvetor." He licked his lips and buttoned his suit jacket.

"I'm sorry?"

He looked up at the digital clock on the wall. "We need your expertise."

My thoughts acted like hair full of static and shot in twenty million different directions. I could do this. It was the opportunity of a lifetime and a way for a pharmaceutical drug I believed in to move forward.

Also.

I would be working for the mob.

I would be going against on Stonewood Enterprises. Jett would flip out. He would literally lose his shit.

"I'll do whatever I can."

"Get Jett to back it. I don't want your mother's company involved. Government can get dicey." He licked his full lips. "Mean. Stonewood Enterprises has the manpower to handle mean."

"My mother's company ... "

"Doesn't know what mean really is, Vick." He grinned, showing his teeth like a wolf all of a sudden, they held a sort of snarl so vicious I wanted to take a step back.

"And you think I do? That I can handle this?"

He walked to the door, opened it, and motioned me through. His smile was slow as I made my way through it. "You're a fighter."

I met his gaze. "Damn right I am."

CHAPTER
EIGHTEEN

JETT

VICK AND BASTIAN.

Vick. And. Bastian.

I opened my laptop but couldn't focus. I rearranged the paperweights on my desk. My father had given me three of them, all perfectly round. All blown glass. All from a little shop in Italy. The colors rippled, flowed together, and then pooled in just the right spots.

I liked the detail in them, the smoothness, the feel of the substantial weight in my hand. I grabbed one and fisted it.

One of a kind. They were all unique, and they all had their purpose. I kept them on my desk, set up for every person to see when they came and sat there. Some would focus on the red one, some on the blue, but most were drawn to the colorful one fisted in my hand, the captivating one swirling its damn color everywhere.

153

I needed to name that paperweight Victory Blakely. She *was* color, entertaining the whole world and not stopping for a second to think about all the attention she attracted.

And the woman was one of a kind, that's for sure. No one else on my team had the audacity to push a partnership forward with the Armanellis knowing I didn't want to. Leave it to her. And leave it to her to grab the attention of one of the most dangerous men in the city.

Sebastian Armanelli definitely appeared harmless. His charm was instrumental in sweeping his family's business under the rug. And the man worked like a panther in antelope's clothing. He was new mob, new money, new power. He didn't technically do any dirty work. Most of the business he and his family did was clean, legal, maybe a little risky and hovering near criminal, but most often fighting for good.

Even if that meant going up against the government.

I had no doubt this backing would put me in a shitstorm with the FDA and other pharmaceutical companies. I didn't have the bandwidth, my team didn't have the bandwidth. Not with my father stepping down.

I squeezed the paperweight, contemplating the place I worked at day in and day out. We moved companies forward, we pushed healthcare, we pushed tech. Hell, I'd found a company to navigate bottling water without plastic and instead using biodegradable material. Now, some of the largest brands were following suit.

I had to work harder than ever to pave the way for good in my city, and I hoped it would spread to other cities across the world. I believed in my team. I believed we had the ability to change the world.

Vick breezed in, bouncing about like a ball that was as pink as cotton candy. Everyone's eyes tracked her around the office like she was some sweet as hell candy too. She stopped by Josie's desk and they both laughed at something she said. Then she hovered by Bob as though she didn't have a pile of work waiting for her.

I waited for her to look up, I willed her ass to look my way.

She didn't.

Fine.

I called my dad. "What the fuck do I need to know about Levvetor and the Armanellis?"

"Jett Stonewood," my mother bellowed. "You're on speaker and if you think I raised you to speak that way—"

"Dad, why do you have me on speaker?"

He chuckled. "We're in the car, and she's your mother."

"She's an enforcer is what she is."

"Watch your mouth, young man," she said but the tone was lighthearted.

"Love you, Mom. Dad, I really need to know what I'm dealing with here."

He sighed. "I'm trying to enjoy my time with your mother."

"And I'm trying to not go into the lion's den completely blind."

The silence on the other end told me all I needed to know. "Avoid it if you can."

Vick was back at her desk, typing away, and I could have been imagining it but I saw a new posture, a new purpose. "And if I can't?"

"Don't go in blind."

I hung up when I heard him end the call.

I stared out at the cityscape for a minute, glanced at the cotton candy below, then shoved away from my desk. "Screw it," I grumbled as I walked out of my office and to her desk.

"You want to discuss the meeting here or in my office?"

She jumped like she'd anticipated my coming but still couldn't prepare herself. Good. She needed to learn who was boss. The damn company had my name behind it, not hers.

"Bob and I are working on another contract that—"

"That can wait."

"I don't think it can," she shot back and eyed me with those whiskey-colored eyes that delivered the same bite as a shot of the liquid.

"Vicky," Stevie hissed, his eyes wide as they ping-ponged between the two of us.

She glared at him for a second, and then she folded back into her old posture like Mr. Stevie wanted. She cleared her throat and clicked a window closed on her screen. "I'm sorry. Yes, we should discuss it in your office."

Stevie's smile was instant, like a proud boyfriend. I filed away his look and my feelings toward it for another day.

I turned on my heel and heard her shoes clicking after me.

I opened the glass door and waved her in. She avoided looking at me and walked right to one of my chairs. I closed the door and sat behind my desk.

The silence stretched between us. I made her wait while I pressed the privacy button. My windows tinted, and she rolled her eyes at the effect.

"Why are you rolling your eyes, Vick?"

"I'm not."

"Cut the shit. Time is money around here, you know that."

"Okay. Then we probably shouldn't focus on my eye rolling."

I rearranged the paperweights, trying to curb my temper.

She eyeballed me while I did it, not looking at any of them for even a second. "Levvetor needs you to back them."

"Oh, really?" I sat back and folded my arms over my chest. "What about you finding Bastian a different company? I'm pretty sure an employee offering to hook a client up with a competitor isn't in our handbook."

"You have every right to fire me, and I'm happy to resign if you feel I need to after my display in there."

I started to tell her I wouldn't be firing her, but she stopped me.

"I don't care about my job." She hesitated when I lifted an eyebrow. "Of course, I want to keep working for your company. It's Stonewood Enterprises where la-di-da the sky's not the limit. Although I must say, today, in that room, it seemed like your standpoint was the limit and no one wanted to overstep it or share a damn idea."

I tried to say why that was. People needed to know who the boss was, when to be innovative, and when to shut up, but she barreled on. "Either way, yes, I want to keep my job, but I'm happy to step down and move on if you want. I just want you to reconsider Levvetor."

"I won't ask why. You know you need to explain yourself."

She nodded, wringing her manicured nails in her lap. "A couple of years ago, the government tried to shut them down. Now, of course, no one ever came out and actually said that, but the FDA released a statement after a meeting they had with one of Levvetor's biggest competitors. Levvetor appealed, lost millions, and just barely scraped by. I followed the news of it all very closely. Coincidently, I was doing a thesis on the company at the time. Their drugs work, Jett. They are saving lives at an extraordinary rate."

"So do other pharmaceutical companies," I said. It was the truth. But it was also the devil's advocate in me. I had to come at it from all angles.

"Yes. At extremely expensive rates and by monopolizing the market half the time and sometimes to the detriment of their customers' health. That competitor has a higher death rate with more side effects than Levvetor ever had and they know it. That's why they tried everything in their power to shut them down."

"And they will again."

"Yes, they will again. And without you backing them, they'll win. You and I both know it."

"This happens all the time, Vick."

"But maybe this time we can stop it."

"I need you to be realistic at some point, Victory."

"And I need you to disappear into my damn dream world for a second, Jett, and take a chance. Shoot for past the sky. Get into the damn stratosphere with me and save some lives here."

"You were warning me about that mobster last night and now you want to get in bed with him."

"It'll be strictly business with them."

"You sure about that?" The question shot out of my mouth loaded with a ton of different meanings, and I wanted her to answer every one.

She cleared her throat and broke eye contact with me. "Of course. Steven asked me to dinner tonight, and I'm ... well, you know I'm committed to that. I'm not getting into bed with the mob."

"Committed to what exactly?" I didn't know why I was asking the question.

"I want a relationship, Jett."

"Oh, and Stevie will give you one." My tone was condescending. "He'll also keep you nicely packed in a Stepford wife box."

"What's that supposed to mean?"

I mimicked Stevie's gormless face and whined, "Vicky."

She stood up and paced back and forth in front of my desk. "This is irrelevant. Back to the meeting, please? Levvetor needs us, and Bastian doesn't think it is a good idea to have any company other than Stonewood Enterprises invested in them."

"Then, he should have put it on the table for me to take into account before the meeting."

"So, you're saying no based on principle?"

"It's a matter of respect, Vick."

"Levvetor is saving lives. Has it occurred to you that maybe lives are a little more important than you getting respect? Can we focus on that?"

"I focus on that every single day."

She halted as my voice boomed out louder than I intended. I rose from my desk and faced the city I fought for every day, instead of that infuriating woman. "Have you noticed the work we do, what we stand for?"

"Jett." Her voice was a whisper. "I know you do a lot ... "

"I don't need reassurance, Victory. Or praise, for that matter. I need you to see the bigger picture. If I fold to a man like that without him giving me respect, my company will fold a lot faster for a lot less. We can't afford that. The city I work for can't afford that."

"The world can't afford that," she continued for me. She'd made her way over to the window and stood beside me. "I see you scooping up wounded passengers and putting them on your overloaded boat to carry them to shore. You're their captain, Jett. And you spend every hour of your day making sure everyone has a life vest."

I glanced over at her, and her honey-colored eyes shone with sincerity.

She continued, "I'm ecstatic to be a part of that. And I know Bastian is asking for one more passenger on a boat that could sink at any moment because it's beyond capacity. Everyone here works extremely hard. I know everyone enjoys it, but you have to trust them to be able to handle more. The boat can take on more than you think. They are the best of the best, after all. And then reward them for it."

"I do reward them," I retorted.

She exhaled loudly. "Really? With what?"

"Money. A good salary. A very good salary."

She nodded and nudged my shoulder with hers. "True. But sometimes people like to have a little fun. They want to feel a part of the family. The Stonewood name shines bright, Jett, and I bet if you give your people a little release, they will come back rejuvenated and ready to kick even more ass."

"They're rejuvenated now."

"We've all been working extra-long hours since your father stepped down, and not one person is going to complain, partially because they're scared to but also because no one has the energy."

My jaw worked and I pulled on the cuffs of my shirt, considering what she'd said. At the bottom of my tower, figures rushed back and forth, and I was reminded of how this city drained people, how you could get swallowed up by its pace. My company operated the same way. "Fine."

"Fine, what?" Her eyes widened.

I smiled at her surprise. "You think my team needs something. Halloween is in a few days. Throw a party. The Monday after, I'm holding a meeting to discuss Levvetor. If the team agrees it's something we want to take on, I'll do it. If they're hungover and nonresponsive, I win. You drop it."

"Deal." Her smile beamed radiantly.

"And."

She groaned when she realized I wasn't done.

"You wear black every day for the rest of the year."

"Seriously?"

"Dead serious, Vick. Your colors are too damn bright."

"Oh my God," she mumbled, starting to walk out. "I have to plan an epic party. Please, for the love of all that is holy, loosen up before then."

The rest of the afternoon, I gazed at the damn paperweights, except for the moments I glanced up to see pink fluttering around down below.

By the end of the day, I wondered if the smell of strawberries would ever leave my office. Josie, Bob, and others turned off their computers as the sun set. I wondered if Vick would stay late, if she'd wait to see if I wanted a repeat of our other night.

A rude reminder came when she closed down her computer and walked out with Stevie. A feeling pooled in my belly and burned its way through the rest of my body, a feeling I wasn't much accustomed to.

I got back to work. And after a couple more hours of work and research on Levvetor, I texted Bastian and Vick together.

> **ME:** I'm considering Levvetor for the next week. I'm not committed, and I sure as hell want warning next time.
>
> **BASTIAN:** You think my pops gave me a warning before the meeting? I meant no disrespect.
>
> **ME:** Lie to someone who will believe it, Bastian.
>
> **VICK:** Is there a reason I'm included here?
>
> **ME:** Bastian seems to think you're a part of this.
>
> **BASTIAN:** She is and will be throughout.
>
> **VICK:** Happy to do what needs to be done.
>
> **ME:** We need more research on the company to start.
>
> **VICK:** I'll pull everything I have and begin in the morning.

> **BASTIAN:** We can meet next Wednesday. Sounds like there's a Halloween party, so guess I get to see you both this weekend.
> **ME:** Guess so.
> **VICK:** YAS!

I walked out of my office and shut off the lights as I made my way to the elevators. A large sign hung right above the elevator buttons and it read:

Halloween Frights and Costume Party
THIS SATURDAY
Meet at Farmland Haunted House
Costume Party 10 p.m. at Stonewood Tower
Dress to IMPRESS
Jett Stonewood is giving away $1000 for best costume

"Are you fucking kidding me?" I grumbled as I stabbed the elevator door and then dialed Vick's number.

She ignored my call.

I called again, and she sounded out of breath when she answered. "I'm a little busy."

"You were just texting. A little busy doing what?" My mind went right back to the pool in my gut, and I wondered if she was out of breath from doing shit with Stevie she should only be doing with me.

"I told you I was on a date!" she whisper-yelled.

"Oh, like Stevie gives a shit. He'd probably come if he knew you were on the phone with me."

"What do you want?"

"Where are you?"

"Seriously?"

"Yeah, you at dinner or at his place already?"

"I'm not a cheap date."

"Could have fooled me."

"We've never been, nor will we ever go, on a date."

"Fine," I sighed and walked out of the elevators as they opened up. "I didn't say you could book a haunted house for the party and offer a thousand-dollar prize."

"I know. Your brothers said I could."

"Those assholes—"

"Know how to have fun. Now, is there something you actually need?"

"Use common sense when you make your way home," I grumbled and then winced at my words.

"Steven"—she emphasized his name—"is a gentleman, Jett. He'll make sure I get home safe if and when I want to go home."

"Let me know if the night's as enjoyable as it is with me."

"Already is."

"Don't lie, Pixie."

There was silence for a beat, and I knew I'd struck a chord. I heard a breath of defeat leave her. "I'm trying to enjoy this, Jett. Is that so bad?"

"If you really need him to be happy, then no. It isn't bad. I don't know that you need him though."

"I need someone," she whispered.

I pinched the bridge of my nose. Something about Victory Blakely was broken. I heard it in the brief whispers and glimpses of her reality she let me see. She hid it so well that she was the chameleon blending into everyone's entertainment. I found myself drawn to those broken parts, the beautiful jagged edges she didn't want the world to acknowledge. "All right, Pix. Make sure that someone deserves you."

I hung up. I let the idea of her go.

Because I knew I didn't deserve her.

CHAPTER NINETEEN

VICK

"**B**REY, YOU HAVE to have some costume that will work better than that."

Full disclosure: I've dressed up year after year for Halloween. If I didn't have a friend throwing a party, we found someone who did. If somebody didn't have a costume, I conjured one up. If someone wasn't excited, I hyped up the party.

Halloween let you be someone else for the night. You could hide behind a mask or expose yourself with the mask. The possibilities were endless.

"I'm a black cat." Brey looked at me and shrugged.

"You are wearing a black dress and ears! And I know for a fact that dress wasn't purchased as a costume."

Brey smoothed back some of her long dark hair. She did that every time she was uncomfortable. "I just don't want to wear anything weird when it's a work party."

I slumped a little as I looked at all the costumes laid out on my bed. "I hate that everyone will toe the line because Jett is a tight ass and this is a work party."

She nodded and eyed my outfits like they were bombs. In her defense, most were extremely revealing or outrageous.

"I'm being Tinker Bell," I stated, and her eyes bulged. "Oh, come on, Brey. It's not that bad."

"It's a work party, Vick."

"You're wearing my Catwoman leotard."

"Absolutely not." She shook her head. "I'm way shorter and wider than you."

"You'll look hot. Just try it on."

She sighed because she knew I wouldn't let her out of at least trying it on. She snatched it and went to change as I slid out of my tank and jeans to shove on the green leafy bra that connected to a sequined corset and skirt. I had been smaller when I'd bought it two years ago. Now, I filled out the costume and was fully aware I was stepping over a work line.

I wanted to.

"Are Jax and Jaydon coming to pick us up?" I yelled to Brey in the bathroom.

"Yep. They should be here in an hour."

"Katie?"

Brey poked her head out and made a face. "Bastian is escorting her."

"'Escorting'?" I repeated and scrunched my nose.

"Her words, I swear."

"Weird," I mumbled. Katie and Brey had been high school best friends. I stumbled into their friendship in college, but they knew each other much better than I did. They'd all grown up together with Brey living right next door to the Stonewood boys. Jaydon still donned the title of her best friend, and I liked to think I came in at a close-ish third after Katie.

I loved them both but Katie had so many secrets, so many personalities, and a dark side that made her a moving target. I couldn't always read her, and didn't know if I wanted to. Some dark places were better left hidden, away from view.

"So, does she know that Bastian is heading up Chicago's *Cosa Nostra*?" I asked Brey because I knew if anyone could talk sense into Katie, it was her.

"I should ask you the same thing," Brey grumbled on the other side of the door.

"Oh, care to elaborate on that comment?" I did my hair in front of the mirror, trying to act as nonchalant as possible. She probably knew I told Bastian I would help. The Stonewoods rarely kept things from one another, and she was a Stonewood now.

Our conversation was cut off by the ringtone I loathed. Miranda sang about Mama's broken heart, and I about threw my phone across the room.

"Don't you think you should answer?" Brey mumbled. It was the third time my mother had called while Brey was over.

"You forget that my mother takes giving in as a weakness. If I answer, she'll assume her strategy was effective and ring me twelve times in a row the next time she wants to get a hold of me."

"Your mom is not that bad," Brey emphasized.

That was true, and I saw the way Brey fidgeted while my phone kept ringing. So, I grabbed and silenced it. "She's absolutely not that bad. We just don't see eye to eye on some things. You know she's extremely overprotective of me. She's obsessed with telling me I shouldn't be living in the city. Don't you know how dangerous it is, Brey?"

She laughed at my widened eyes. "I honestly wish I had parents who doted on me like yours do."

I cleared my throat, not knowing what to say but picking my words carefully. Aubrey had lost her mother in a house fire her father had started. She didn't go visit him in prison, and they didn't get along.

My relationship with my parents was nowhere near that complicated. I grabbed her hand and squeezed. "I'm sorry, best friend. You can call my parents any time."

She laughed and shrugged, "I have Jax's parents. The Stonewood family is priceless."

"I bet." After assessing myself in the mirror, I asked, "Do I look the part?"

"The part of what? Tinker Bell in *Peter Pan*?"

I scoffed. "No, do I look slutty enough to make all the boys look my way but professional enough to be at a work party?"

She sighed. "Yes to the first, not so much to the second."

"Great! Exactly what I'm going for. Steven will die when he sees me," I proclaimed.

"He won't be the only one," she said. Then she asked, "Do you really care what Steven thinks?"

"Of course," I replied a little too quickly. "Why do you ask?"

"I just…" she cleared her throat and smoothed a flyaway hair. "He's a bit boring, Vick."

"Brey!"

"I know. I'm not enjoying telling you, but it's the truth."

I giggled at her discomfort. "That's so rude. He's not boring, he's just not complicated. You, of all people. I wouldn't have expected that coming from you."

"I know. I'm a bit bitchy today."

"Care to share?"

"Not yet," she sighed. "Soon. Just not yet."

I nodded and let it go. "So, it's just him being boring you don't like?"

She winced. "You had to ask, didn't you? Honestly, I think I'm starting to hate hearing him call you Vicky about as much as Katie does."

"It isn't that bad," I countered as I put on a little more eye makeup to match the green on my costume.

"Not now. But imagine in a year or two, it might drive you nuts."

I shrugged and smoothed some of the leaves into place on my skirt. "He's nice, and he wants to be married in a year or so. He told me on our date."

Brey wrinkled her nose at herself in the mirror next to me. "He told you that on your first date?"

"To be fair, we've known each other for years, Brey."

"True." She waved at her face. "Paint me, please."

I smiled because Brey never did her makeup when she was going somewhere with me. I took it as a compliment to my past life as a hair stylist and makeup artist during college.

As she closed her eyes, she pointed to my leotard. "I don't think I can wear this."

"Oh, you are wearing it. You will be jaw-dropping after I finish your makeup. We are going to win this costume contest."

"You are." She cracked open one of her big green eyes. "Or Jett is going to drag you out of the party because of your inappropriate costume."

"Drag me?"

"Yup." She laughed a little.

"Hold still. What's funny?"

"He's going to drag you out and have his way with you."

"Oh, God. Please. That was a mistake that won't be happening again. Nor do I want it to." Even as the words left my lips, I knew they were a lie.

"You don't have to hide it from me. I'm married to one. I get it."

"Stonewood men, right? Except Jaydon." I finished her eye shadow.

"Ew. Definitely not Jaydon." Brey almost gagged, and I knew it was genuine. He was as close to a brother as she could get.

"Steven's been perfect though. Seriously." I sighed and sat down on the bed atop the glitter of my Victoria's Secret flight attendant costume. That one was much too revealing even if it was one of my favorites. "He and I go way back. We were able to just comfortably talk and enjoy each other at dinner. He loves working with me, and oh my God, he loves the Stonewoods. Double dates would be amazing."

"Or kind of weird. He kind of sucks up to them."

I rolled my eyes. "They're the Stonewoods. You don't get it, but I was a little starstruck at one point too."

She sighed and sat down next to me. "That might be true. It doesn't really matter if you like him and are comfortable with him though."

I nodded and assessed both of us in the mirror. "I'm definitely more comfortable with him than Jett Stonewood."

That was the biggest problem. I liked Steven. But when I'd gotten home after our date, I'd poured myself a glass of wine, laid out my pills, and pondered why I didn't like him more. Maybe we were uncomfortably comfortable. I didn't want to be so comfortable with someone that I didn't feel a damn spark when I looked at them. With Steven, it felt like a soft, cozy fabric brushing up against me. Nice, but not a spark of fire that excited the hell out of me.

My apartment buzzer sounded. "Speak of the devil men…"

I buzzed them up and when I opened the door, Jax gave me a brief hug before looking for his wife like an animal starved.

When he saw her, his eyebrows slammed down, and he stalked over to her. "Oh, no," he growled as he waved at her outfit.

"Oh, yes!" I exclaimed, clapping as I saw his dangerous look. It meant we did her up perfectly. "I love that you're Batman. This is so perfect, you two."

"She's not wearing that, Vick." He glared at me and then at his wife. "You're not wearing that, Whitfield."

"You mean Stonewood?" Brey smirked and crossed her arms over her chest. "We think my outfit's cute."

"Your outfit is a second skin, and that fine ass is mine. Not for anyone else's eyes."

"It is a fine ass, Brey," Jaydon added.

I laughed. Jax looked like steam was about to come out of his ears.

"Avert your eyes, you asshole," Jax grumbled at his brother.

"Oh, come on, man. You know I'm joking with you." He winked at Brey and smirked at me, "Not really though."

I grabbed my coat. "You boys clean up nice. Jaydon, the Joker costume." I nodded my head. "You even have the makeup on point."

"I got a friend to do it." He waggled his eyebrows.

"Gross." I rolled my eyes and waved them toward the door. "We better get going. I don't want to miss the haunted house. It's supposed to be three floors of hell and then they bury you alive for ten minutes. People are going to freak the hell out."

"We're going to stay here for a minute while Brey changes." Jax stood cemented in place like an immovable wall.

"You stay," Brey replied, completely unfazed as she walked out the door and yelled over her shoulder. "I'm going to see who does like my costume."

He growled, but made his way after her with a grin on his face. That man loved her even when she was testing him, maybe more so.

Brey and I chatted with the driver while he navigated the streets to pick up Steven and then take us to the Farmland Haunted House. The road darkened, twisting and turning like a snake until we pulled up to the old barn.

Ghouls and monsters hovered around our group as we waited outside the haunted house. They were letting our team in only ten at a time. Turned out, a lot of people from Stonewood Enterprises wanted to attend the impromptu Halloween party.

Brey nudged me. "Probably should have worn something a bit warmer." She laughed, but Jax had already wrapped his Batman cape around her. He looked happy as hell to have an excuse to.

Steven hadn't been so thoughtful, or rather, he was in the same position as me with his green attire and no coat. He shivered near us. Jaydon unbuttoned his purple jacket. "You'll freeze, Vick."

I held up my hand. "No can do. Purple clashes with my green."

Jaydon snorted. "So, take it off when we get inside."

I couldn't admit the real reason I wouldn't put on his coat. Waiting for a man I wasn't with to see my outfit before I covered it up would be silly. Still, I shook my head.

"Vick," he grunted as he held out the purple blazer. "Put the damn thing on."

"She enjoys living on the edge," the voice I'd been dying to hear responded to his brother.

I turned to take in the vision that Jett Stonewood had warped into on Halloween. The black silk suit reflected a slight shimmer under the moonlight. The clean lines and tailoring showed off his athletic build. He lurked in the shadows but the bold-white mask covering half his face drew everyone's attention. His collared shirt was the same onyx as his belt and shoes. And even in the darkness, his eyes sparkled and commanded me to look straight at him.

"A modern Phantom of the Opera?"

"A risqué, over-the-top Tinker Bell?"

The light green corset cut into my breasts as I took a deep breath.

Jett's eyes laser-focused on my quivering cleavage. "Take Jaydon's coat."

Steven took that second to finally act concerned. "Vick, when we planned this, I didn't think to wear extra layers. Wish I would have brought a coat to match for you."

Jett's eyes didn't wander over to Steven or anyone else. He unbuttoned his black jacket and slid it off. Without saying a word, he stepped behind me, grabbed my wrist, and stuffed my arms into his jacket.

I protested, but it wasn't in earnest. "Hey! I'm really not that cold."

"No one gives a shit. You're making us all uncomfortable," Jett hissed, and that shut me up.

Tonight wasn't about making anyone uncomfortable. It was about proving that everyone could be more comfortable and would work better when they were.

I had to remember that even as our line moved, and I smiled to myself at having Jett's smell all around me. The jacket was warm and felt like melted butter over my skin. I glanced at the tag. Yup, this cost him a fortune.

Steven stayed glued to my side as he talked with the Stonewoods, and I tried my best not to salivate over Jett. He'd pocketed his hands, but that was the only sign the cold affected him. He nodded at all the right things, talked at all the right times, and genuinely looked like he was trying to have a pleasurable time for once.

The night had kicked off perfectly. A few employees came out of the haunted house laughing and screaming. Ghouls and monsters leapt at them one last time as they made their way over to the concession stand.

We moved forward in the line, just one group away from going in. Right then, Gloria walked up, her white dress flapping in the wind behind her. Her dark hair fell loosely around her face, framing her rosy cheeks and red lips. As she leaned in toward Jett, my stomach twisted.

The Phantom of the Opera and Christine.

They'd come as a couple.

My boss and his assistant.

My boss who I'd slept with and secretly had a stupid crush on even though I knew we could never be anything.

He'd come with her just as I'd come with Steven.

Jett looked at me as Gloria whispered something in his ear. He put his hand on the small of her back to steady her while she leaned into him. His eyes held no remorse, no guilt.

Nothing.

We'd fucked. That was it.

What a perfect reminder.

I spun toward my friends to hear Brey saying, "I'm not doing the burying-you-alive part. I just can't. Small spaces. Just no."

Jax pulled her close. "We'll do hot cider, Peaches. No worries."

Jaydon nodded. "I'm doing it all. Vick you're doing it all right? YOLO?"

I winked at him. "Only live once."

The line shifted as a masked man ushered us in. Chains clattered and the door shut us in. Pure darkness descended. My heart rate instantly rose. I liked scary movies, and I'd been to haunted houses but I always, always went with someone I could hold on to.

Tonight, I wasn't sure if Steven wanted me to hold him and Brey was holding onto Jax. I folded my hands together and walked forward. A light, dim and flickering, switched on. I glanced around to find all of us were in a small metal cage, the door to the next room closed. I looked up and my stomach dropped as I stepped back, stumbling into Jett. It looked like snakes slithering above us. "Oh, God."

Jett grabbed one arm to steady me. "They're fake," he said dryly.

I glanced back, and he was smiling a little at my horror.

I mumbled a sorry for falling on him and righted myself. It occurred to me that Gloria hadn't come into the haunted house, but even so, I moved over toward Steven.

In that cage, more creepy-crawly reptiles sprang out at us. The sound effects had me flinching at every single one. Steven jumped along with me, and at one point shoved me forward to save himself.

He whispered, "Sorry. That one got to me too."

"It's fine. All in good fun." And it was. Some people handled these sorts of things better than others. I wasn't one of them but this was for the company, and this haunted house boasted some of the best reviews.

When the door opened for the next room, I let everyone else walk in. I figured that way I'd know what was coming, seeing as I had to fend for myself. Brey would have been more understanding of my fear and hung back with me, I was sure, had she thought Steven wouldn't be a great partner. As it turned out, he crossed his arms to shield himself from the rest of the frights and hurried through, leaving me behind.

I waved Jett forward. "I'll go last."

"Pix, the last one always gets scared from behind."

My eyes widened.

"Go on. I'll protect you." He waggled his eyebrows and puffed up his chest, teasing me as if the haunted house was absurd.

In the next room, a man with a melted face handed us 3D glasses. The room's graffiti suddenly popped out menacingly. The monsters lurking behind dark objects jumped out, snarling and grabbing at us. The 3D paint enhanced their disfigured faces and made them appear much closer than they were.

Our group dispersed, each man for himself. It felt like life and death. Run or be killed. Some of us rushed forward but I stumbled back and screamed as a green goblin whose head hung from his body lunged at me.

Jett steadied me again and whispered in my ear, "He matches your costume. You come with him or Stevie?"

I glared up at him. "You're joking right now?"

"It's just staging, Pix."

A chainsaw revved in the distance. I cursed the stilettos I wore as I tried to back up further.

"No. Go forward. We have to get through the haunted house. Not go backward."

"I probably shouldn't keep going," I mumbled as I looked for an exit. "Do you think they'll let me out if I say I have a heart condition? My heart's beating really, really fast."

Jett laughed. It rolled out of him like he couldn't contain it, and his smile stretched so wide that I wondered if the real Phantom of the Opera would have ever appeared as beautiful as he did. "Your heart is fine, Victory. Move your ass. I got you."

He didn't know if my heart was fine. I counted the days back to when I'd last taken my heart medicine. I tended to avoid it. The meds made me feel like I had a weakness, and I wanted to forget about it. Cancer lingered, and ignoring it felt better than dwelling on it.

Still, I moved forward, feeling a little more confident with Jett's arm to hold on to. "We should probably try to catch up to our group."

"The group that ran as fast as they could and left us for dead?"

"They didn't leave us."

"Stevie ran so fast, baby. And his face was whiter than my mask."

I tried not to laugh. I really did. "In his defense, I'm just as scared."

The next hallway pulled more screams from me as lights flashed and shined on a morbid-looking skeleton covered in cockroaches.

Jett retracted his arm from my death grip.

"Jett, fine. I'm scared! Please don't…"

He wrapped his arm around me, tucking me in close to his chest like he was ready to fight off all the damn haunted house demons for me.

I squinted at him to see if I could read the expression he had under the mask. "Should I be reading into you staying behind to walk me through this?"

"No. It's the best use of time for me to usher you through so we can get tonight over with as fast as possible."

"Efficient."

A man with a mask jumped out and revved a chainsaw right in my face. I yelped into Jett's chest and he pulled me close before glaring at the man in front of us. "That was too close. Back the fuck away from her."

The man must have witnessed a Stonewood stare because the chainsaw died and he moved out of our way.

"I'm officially keeping my eyes closed the rest of the way," I mumbled into his shirt.

"I don't know why you booked this when you hate it."

"Because other people love it. But I don't usually do things like this."

"Seems like some stupid shit you would want to do all the time."

"I didn't indulge in stuff like this for a long time," I admitted.

"Interesting," he murmured but didn't ask me to elaborate.

Something loud clanged near us. I squeezed my eyes shut tighter and gripped Jett's arm like it was my only lifeline. He announced, "That was an angry clown. Scars all over his face."

"Um, thank you?"

"Well, if you're not going to look, I guess I'm obliged to help you experience it somehow."

A scream sounded on our left. "A child being held hostage by an angry witch."

We stepped up onto what felt like wood boards that creaked under our feet.

"In a room full of decapitated dolls. The angry little girl with long black hair is coming at us with one of the heads."

"Oh my God." I shoved him forward to get out of the room as fast as possible.

He laughed at my antics. "You can't even see them, Victory. She's probably ten years old."

"And could be completely deranged."

"You still want to be buried alive at the end of this?" he asked. That tone, snide as hell, made me want to let go of him and walk the rest of the haunted house on my own.

Almost.

I was too chickenshit.

"Maybe I shouldn't." I meant it too. My heart rate wasn't slowing down. I made a mental note to take those pills tonight.

"Yes. Maybe you shouldn't."

"But they say it's a once in a lifetime feeling."

"Oh, for fuck's sake," he sighed as we walked through another creepy sounding room. "We don't have to do everything that's once in a lifetime."

"You don't," I replied. But I did.

I had to live.

We reached what seemed like the end. A man asked if we wanted to be buried alive, and I opened my eyes to see he was dressed in jeans and a sweater, completely normal.

"We need full consent to do this. You can go in with four other people, but it looks like it is only you two right now."

"Did my friends go in already?" I asked about Brey and the others.

"They opted out after their walk through, which is very common."

I cleared my throat. "I think I'd like to do it."

"Before you go into the room, I have to let you know we do require you to lie down flat like you're in a coffin. Then, we drop hollow plastic balls on you for a couple minutes. They are the same type of balls that can be found at Chuck E. Cheese's and Discovery Zone. After the allotted amount of time, the walls are shifted so the pressure will give your body the illusion of being buried alive. The experience is about ten minutes."

I cleared my throat, trying to shake my anxiety. I glanced at Jett to see if he was contemplating going in with me. "You don't have to come with. I'm going to do it."

I couldn't tell what he thought with the mask covering half his expression. He shrugged his shoulder and then wrapped his arm around my neck to pull me close to him. He whispered into my ear, "I'm not happy about you laying down on the ground in my jacket." Then he said to the man, "We're ready when you are."

Beep. Beep. Beep.

The beeping this time was fast as hell to match my heart. I walked into that dark room with a man I wasn't sure I would ever fully not want but definitely sure I trusted more than most. He watched me lie down on the ground and grumbled something about how filthy it must be.

Then he squatted down beside me and lifted up his mask. "You really okay doing this, Pix?"

My hand, completely disregarding my mind's command, searched out his and held it. "I think I just need to do it and not focus on it."

He slid the mask back onto his face and laid down right next to me. Then he pulled my body up against his. Turning on his side, he faced me and wrapped one arm around my waist.

"You're supposed to lie on your back, Jett."

"I'm supposed to be doing a lot of things I'm not doing tonight, Victory."

"Like what?"

"I'm supposed to leave you and your damn fantasies alone."

I sighed, waiting for something to happen. And avoiding looking over at the man I wanted way too much. "Then why don't you?"

His hand slid from my waist up to my cheek and turned me to face him. "Because you make it your mission to glitter and shine brighter than every single object around you."

"I don't."

He shook his head slowly, and then his lips were on mine and an eerie version of an Evanescence song began to play as balls fell on us. His hands held my face, and I lost myself in the way his tongue slid over mine, the way his body fit up against me, the way he didn't let me up for air through the whole song. He wrapped his arm around my waist and pulled me closer, like our bodies needed to be right up against the other, like we were two molds that slipped into each other perfectly.

It seemed like just a small moment in time. Maybe a second or a minute that his lips brushed over me. Yet, the balls rolled off of us and he pulled away to stand. "Good enough distraction from being buried alive?"

The Phantom of the Opera glowered down at me from above, one of his large hands outstretched. He didn't look at all tousled or shaken from what we had just done.

I, on the other hand, felt my heart stuttering as my mind disassembled all my hopes and dreams of a future with someone I could count on to be with me, stay with me.

"Pix?" he questioned when I didn't immediately move from the ground.

I grabbed his hand and pulled myself up. Hurrying forward, not wanting to look at him anymore, I shoved through the exit doors, so ready to find Steven.

A werewolf—a real one, I swear—snarled at me as soon as I turned the corner. I screamed and toppled right back into the Phantom's arms as the werewolf ran back into the forest on four legs, no joke.

Jett laughed so hard, his eyes scrunched closed behind his mask. I wiggled out of his grip and straightened his jacket as I huffed at him. "It's not funny. That thing was real."

"That thing was a fifteen-year-old kid. You're scared of a fifteen-year-old." Then he laughed hard as hell again.

I wanted to scream at him, but this was one of the few times I'd seen him relaxed and jovial.

Jett worked. He didn't play.

Then and there, looking at him, I found something I was more afraid of than haunted houses, werewolves, or even getting sick again.

I was losing my heart to the Phantom of the Opera.

CHAPTER
TWENTY

JETT

HAUNTED HOUSES HAD never appealed to me. I'd never gone to one before. I didn't have time to waste on people trying to scare me when there were actual real and scary problems in the world.

Yet, tonight, I could appreciate the appeal. I saw my team completely engrossed in their terror, thus discovering about a million weaknesses of my employees.

One in particular interested me.

Victory Blakely was a timid little thing.

She didn't enjoy ghouls or monsters or frights. Again, she surprised me with that revelation. Had I known she was going to be as scared as she was for this event, I probably would have told her to wait it out. Yet, she'd planned it and gone in full throttle.

I watched her, hanging on Steven as she sipped some hot cider that Brey had ready for her when we walked over.

Everyone apologized for ditching us in the haunted house, and I let Vick reply with her canned response of it not bothering her. Nothing anyone did ever bothered her, except when it came to me.

She shook off every damn ounce of discomfort, let it shatter on the floor, and picked it up to restructure it into a fun disco ball. "Don't worry about it! Jett and I got buried alive. We conquered the fear and are still alive to tell you about it."

Stevie laughed. "Was it intense?"

That asshole should have been the one to stay with her and wrap his arm around her. He'd beelined his pansy ass out of there as fast as he could.

Vick shrugged her shoulders. "Could have been worse." She eyed me. "Could have been better."

"I highly doubt it," I replied, suddenly wondering if she was kissing other men and if they were better than me. I shouldn't have considered it; I knew she was dating Stevie. I knew, and yet I wanted to pry.

I spun around to look for Gloria. I was developing a problem and a surefire way to circumvent it was to focus on something else. "We'll see you at the office," I mumbled and left them.

Gloria appeared in her white get up. She'd planned our outfits and made sure we had transportation for the night.

"You enjoy the haunted house?" she asked when I ambled up and told her I was ready to leave.

"I'm not enjoying any of this."

"You are and you should," she corrected. "Victory Blakely isn't all she seems, you know."

"I don't know what you mean by that."

Gloria always cut to the chase and cut people off at the knees while she did it. The woman didn't dance around facts or observations. It was the reason she was my assistant. We understood each other.

So, as she wiggled a bit after we'd slid into the SUV before answering me, I questioned her. "What aren't you telling me?"

"Something I will continue to not tell you. I'm just saying the woman is more than a pop of color in your office."

"I'm not discrediting her intelligence and value, Gloria. Do I think she necessarily belongs on my team? I'm not sure yet. I know she has the credentials."

"I vet every person on your team. Thoroughly. I'm telling you, she's more than just credentials. She belongs here. The party is an unfortunate but perfect example. The team will do well next week after this burst of goodwill from you."

I narrowed my gaze at her. "You think the party is working?"

"It's genius. They'll have ideas for Levvetor after this. And quite honestly, we should have thought of the party in the first place."

I didn't hide my growl as I looked out the window.

Gloria didn't even flinch at my blatant dismissal. "I'm fighting for that deal. It's the right thing for our company to do. I'm telling you now so you're fully prepared for it next week. I don't intend to hold myself or Ms. Blakely back."

I let one side of my mouth lift at the tenacity this woman could bring to the game. She didn't mess around, and I respected her for it. "You're one in a billion, Gloria. Remind me why we aren't together."

"Because we fuck well but aren't compatible. You and Ms. Blakely most likely are. Keep that in mind before you go pushing her away. You'll regret it in the end, and Steve will be more than willing to let her run into his arms as he begs for your approval over her shoulder."

"So, I'm not imagining that man's desire to be with her is only to get closer to us Stonewoods?"

"I think Vick's the only one not able to see it."

I sucked on my teeth. "She sees it. She just has her daydream glasses on to filter out the glare of his every annoying move."

Gloria nodded as we pulled up to Stonewood Tower. "I suggest you dispose of those glasses of hers before she ends up in the wrong man's bed for good."

The woman slid out of the SUV to leave me with one thought.

Victory Blakely had turned into a reality I wanted.
And what I wanted, I got.

CHAPTER
TWENTY-ONE

VICK

JETT: You set up a bar and music in the office? Wasn't the haunted house enough?

SMILED. THE MAN was fuming but an epic party meant drinks, music, dancing. We'd piled back into our SUV to make our way to Stonewood Tower. After Jett had disappeared so quickly, I slid out of his jacket, uncomfortable that I wanted to be in it even when he didn't want to be anywhere near me.

Yet, I sat there smiling at his text and smoothed my hand over the jacket on my lap before I responded.

ME: Don't sabotage it by standing there looking unapproachable. You gave me one night to motivate this team. It has to be fair.

JETT: This is getting ridiculous.

ME: Oh, just you wait. ;-)

I tried to curb my excitement. I imagined tons of people would show up at the Tower even if they didn't opt in for the haunted house.

Steven pulled me close in the SUV. I waited for an explosion of feeling or even a small spark. But my stomach didn't flutter, my palms didn't sweat, my heart didn't beat any faster.

Steven wasn't Jett.

That was a good thing, I told myself. But my body didn't agree, it recoiled from him much like he'd deserted me in the haunted house.

I tried to romanticize the moment. I smoothed my hand on his chest. "I love you as Peter Pan."

We were the cute couple finally. After our date, we'd decided to go as a pair to the party. Tinker Bell and Peter Pan had been my idea.

Steven smiled at me so wide, I could practically see his molars. Was his smile always this cheesy, this docile, this boring?

I glared at Brey, her words echoing in my ear. She'd planted the idea in my head, planted my mediocre reaction. I snuggled closer to him and pushed my long ponytail to the side.

"You look fantastic, Vicky." His chuckle burst out of him. "Jax, I have to wonder if Jett's fine with the ladies dressing like this for a work event?"

Jax eyed him for more than a second. Jaydon chuckled to himself while typing on his phone, no doubt very aware of his brother's overprotective nature with Aubrey. "My brother shouldn't be looking at my girl's outfit and neither should you."

Steven's smile died while Brey face-palmed in embarrassment. "No, I just meant…"

"Stop while you're ahead, bro," Jaydon chimed in, still texting.

I grabbed his phone and turned it off. "Don't be a dick." He sighed and slumped back into his seat. "We're dressed to make jaws drop, Steven. You saw people at the haunted house. We're all fine."

He looked my outfit up and down again. For the first time, his incessant need to please the Stonewoods and be part of the pack irked me. I wiggled in place, suddenly uncomfortable.

Jaydon leaned into my ear and whispered, "Don't, Tinker. You look hot as hell, woman. Perk up."

I gawked at him, concerned Steven had heard, but Jaydon rolled his eyes like he didn't care at all.

Steven rambled on to Jax, trying to make up ground, but the frown that crossed his face every time he looked at my outfit reinforced something in my mind. The man I was dating was more concerned that my boss would frown upon my outfit rather than enjoy taking in the view.

We pulled up to Stonewood Tower, and I vaulted out of the SUV. The environment was toxic, and I wanted out. Brey dashed after me. "That was awkward, right?"

"So awkward," I agreed.

Jax appeared behind her. "Fuck me. This is still not a good idea."

We turned to see Jax staring directly at her ass.

"Jax, we're in public. Try to have a filter," Brey suggested.

"Try to wear some clothes," he shot back.

I snickered at their bickering. Jax attempted to control Brey, but she had him by the balls. The man followed her into a fire to fetch her for God's sake.

As we approached the elevator, Brey looked concerned and asked him, "Do you want to go home?"

He beelined for the door. "Yup. Good idea."

"Great. Vick will make sure I get home safe when the party's over."

Jax froze, and his muscles bunched. "Are you kidding me?"

"No. I'm going to enjoy myself. If you can't,"—she shrugged—"I suggest you go home."

"God damn it," he grumbled but then slid his hands around her waist and leaned onto her shoulder to kiss her neck. "Love you, Peaches."

I looked over at Steven but he was nervously adjusting his green T-shirt and watching the elevator numbers. When the doors opened, he stepped in and smiled. "I'm excited to see what you all planned."

Brey shrugged. "This is all Vick's doing."

"I can't believe Jett agreed to this last minute." He looked baffled. "We're all so busy."

"Yep. That's why we need a break," I explained. "We work hard and so we should play hard when possible."

My heart rate climbed with the floor numbers though. This wasn't playing for me. It had been constant planning and organizing for the past couple of days. A business was on the line. A business that saved my life.

The elevator doors opened to strobing lights and fog. The buzz of the employees was damn infectious. Excitement hummed in the air and I turned to Steven and smiled. He looked shocked at what we'd done. I took it as a good sign that I'd pulled off the office party of the century.

Josie shot straight over. "Brey!" She grabbed Brey's hands. "This is fantastic."

Brey smiled. "I honestly didn't do much. Mostly this was the beautiful Tinker Bell, here."

I bowed a little and Josie's eyes went wide. "Vick, you look hot as hell. And everyone's already having a great time." She leaned in to whisper to both of us, "Also, I'm not supplying drinks. So, that's always a plus."

A laugh bubbled out of me, and I relaxed a little. Josie never made it past small talk with me, but her short spunky haircut and positive attitude—even when she was just getting coffees for everyone—made me think we could get along. "How are the drinks?"

"So spooky!" Josie squealed, waving us in.

We left the guys behind so we could admire our hard work. Luckily, Stonewood Enterprises had the space and resources to whip this together in a flash, something Samson and Sons could never have done. Brey and I had worked with Stonewood's on-site catering and bar, along with a bunch of other vendors, to enhance the party experience. Ghouls served drinks with faux spider webs in them. Vampires proffered trays of eyeballs. Our team's laughter roared over the "Monster Mash"—the only compliment we needed. Brey beamed along with me as our fellow employees continually thanked us. Most of the company Jett had absorbed was here too. I'd made sure everyone saw the invites and knew this was a big deal.

Gloria stopped us after we each grabbed a Witchy Whiskey Sour, served in a cup that looked like a cauldron. "You ladies pulled this off."

Brey nodded and peered cautiously between Gloria and me. If I hadn't been positive about Jett and Gloria's intimate relationship before, I was now. I shrugged, and my leafy bodice bobbed up and down. "We had a lot of help. When Stonewood Enterprises has mostly everything—"

"Don't downplay planning it on such short notice. You've earned many people's respect here."

I glanced at Brey, trying to gauge the sincerity of Gloria's compliment. The woman didn't give commendation or talk to me at all, really. She ran the office like clockwork and, as I now knew, had a relationship with Jett. My ankles wobbled in my stilettos as we faced off.

Then she smiled at me. Every severe line in her face disappeared, the tight fist she always held at her side loosened. She rubbed that hand over her other forearm, up and down. "I'm really looking forward to helping you close the deal with Levvetor."

"I'm sorry. You knew?" I questioned, not sure if she knew this party was a test or if she just wanted me to know that she was on board.

As if she could read my thoughts, she said, "I'm aware of pretty much everything Jett does. His life is work and I am his right-hand man, the hand of the king."

I furrowed my brow. "Okay." I dragged out the word, waiting for her to continue.

"The party is a test. He'll say you failed, but he knows you passed. Also, I told him I'm pushing that deal as hard as I can come next week. I'm loaded and ready to go. We'll get Levvetor on our books. I promise you."

The last thing I pictured myself doing that night, I did right then. I closed the distance between Gloria and hugged her. She stood completely still, frozen in shock or discomfort but, for once, I didn't care. "You won't regret it. I promise you the company is saving lives."

"I did my research." Gloria nodded and took a large step back. "I'll see you Monday."

With that, she smiled at us again and walked away.

"I might cry," I confessed to Brey.

"Me too," Brey blurted out. "She's amazing to work with. She's so reliable, you know? But also sort of different. I just ... didn't picture that happening."

Jax appeared near Brey. "Whiskey sour, huh?"

She smiled like the two of them had a secret. I scanned the crowd for Steven, ready to give those two the alone time they wanted.

Steven was glued to Jaydon's side, talking his ear off, and I winced knowing that I would be the one feeling like a third wheel if I joined them. I moved from table to table and took in the costumes and fun everyone was having instead. Coincidentally, Bob had dressed as Captain Hook, so we posed for a picture together.

"You pulled off the costume perfectly," I told him.

He held his oversized belly and laughed. "I barely made it out the door looking like this, but all in good fun. My wife told me she's always had a thing for pirates."

He winked at me, and I felt it. The happiness. The unwinding.

Beep. Beep. Beep.

Music pulsed around me, and cobwebs swayed above us. The drinks were over-the-top, as was the costumed waitstaff and the decorations. But one thing wasn't exaggerated: the spontaneous smiles, the hum of amusement, the unrestrained laughter. I inched myself up against the back wall and people watched for far too long.

"You're smiling like you think you've won," the Phantom whispered into my ear.

Goose bumps skittered over my skin, and I closed my eyes to quell the attraction his voice sparked. "Haven't I, dear Phantom of the Opera?"

He crossed his arms, flashing the Oystersteel of the Rolex he normally wore. Even his thicker-than-average wrist, peppered with dark hair and veins in all the right places made my mouth water.

I sighed. "I set your jacket down on the table back there. I didn't have a chance to give it to you before you disappeared."

He raised an eyebrow at my accusing tone. "Surprised you noticed my departure. Stevie seemed to have all your attention."

"And Gloria had all of yours," I snapped and then winced. "Not that I care. I don't. I can't and I won't. Tonight isn't about that."

"You're right. It's about you proving a point." Jett turned toward the crowd. "You think you're doing a good enough job? You think they'll come ready to work on Monday? Rejuvenated?"

"I have no doubt. Especially after you crown the costume queen or king with a thousand dollars."

"I'm guessing you don't want to announce my vote yourself?"

"Absolutely not." I clapped my hands together and vibrated with joy. "I want to have everyone line up and show off their outfits to you one by one."

He winced.

"To music, of course," I added.

"No one wants to do that."

"We have fifty-plus employees who signed up beforehand."

"Jesus," he grumbled and slid his hand over his face. "You went overboard, woman."

"Not possible."

"Completely possible. Look at your outfit, Pix. It's a damn plant corset wrapped up in sparkle and glitter. Did you dye your hair?"

I threaded my fingers through the tips of blonde that I'd paintbrush-dyed pink and shrugged. "I figured if I lost and had to wear black, at least my hair would pop."

"Jesus. No one went to the lengths you did for a damn costume. Can't we just say you won?"

That was all the compliment I needed from him. I pushed off the wall and spun slowly. I knew my corset shimmered and the leaves over my ass and boobs swayed as I rocked my hips to the music. "I'm freaking happy and proud of my Tinker Bell, Jett."

"And half the room is damn happy you wore it too."

I winked at him. "Which half?"

He pinched the bridge of his nose. "You know it's the male half. It's completely inappropriate for work."

"Exactly!" I exclaimed and clapped my hands. "This isn't work! That's the point."

"You should have kept my jacket on."

"You're kidding, right? Do you honestly care that much who's looking?"

"More than I want to, Pix. A lot more than I want to."

I licked my lips and quivered with his admission. "I'm not too happy about the way your date looks at you either."

"Ah, at least I get one honest response from you tonight."

"I'm always honest."

"You're always *happy*, Victory. Even when you're not. You never let the raw side of you breathe and it's suffocating in there." He sighed and pulled at one of my pink strands. "Let's get this voting going, shall we?"

His words twisted my insides. My throat constricted, my chest tightened, my mind short circuited. Feelings, ominous and wretched, curdled in me. Fears I worked so hard to suppress clawed at the walls I'd built around them.

Would all this be good enough? Would I be happy with my life if I took a turn for the worse the very next day?

I swallowed the questions down and buried them deep where they belonged. If I was suffocating the raw part of me, I hoped I would snuff it out completely.

I went through the motions of emceeing the costume contest, and Jett sat there smiling as person after person showed off their attire.

My mind was on his words though. Had I adopted a positive attitude to the point of my own detriment? Was I losing my grip on reality by denying what I truly felt?

I yelled into the microphone, "I think that's everyone. Let me go talk to the Phantom."

Brey in her Catwoman suit sidled up to take the microphone. "Oh, no. Ms. Blakely, you will do your walk in your outfit. You do not get to opt out just because you emceed."

"Girl,"—I whispered—"this isn't for me."

She covered the mic. "I know. It's for Stonewood Enterprises. Look at them. They want to see you, Vick."

My fellow employees erupted as I walked over to the runway they'd outlined with their bodies in front of Jett. He sat there, subdued and smiling.

Brey cut to a favorite song of mine. I twirled and swayed to the deep beat of the bass. I rolled my hips a little and got a few hoots and hollers from the crowd. Jett's eyes burned into me, goading me to end my walk as quickly as possible. Instead, I backed up and dropped low to the floor, running my hands down my body and back up to my glittering wings. I waved a pretend wand, and just as the tempo picked up, random employees threw green glitter into the air above me. Brey held out a bag of it, letting people grab more.

Everyone was laughing, the lights were shining, my heart was beating.

The Phantom was watching.

I made my way to him, leaned over, and gripped the arms of his chair. Glitter fell over both of us as I whispered, "I just think of a happy little thing."

"Pix," he grumbled, jaw clenched.

"It's the same as having wings."

"Clip your wings, woman. Fall back to the ground where the rest of us are."

"I don't need them, Jett. I can already fly."

His blue eyes held mine as he barked at the crowd, "Tinker Bell wins." Then he whispered, "Monday, we come back from Neverland, Pix."

I grinned at him and shook my head of pink locks. "Not a chance, Phantom. We belong here."

CHAPTER
TWENTY-TWO

VICK

MY HEAD POUNDED as Miranda Lambert belted out her song from my phone.

It was a distinct reminder that I hadn't followed any part of my health regimen the night before. I'd drunk alcohol, consumed sugary hot apple cider, and ignored all my vitamins and pills.

Again.

The nutritionist my mother hired years ago would have said I was feeding the cancer that lived deep in my bones still. His warning used to haunt me.

Now, I shoved the thought aside along with my sheets to stretch on my bed. I rolled over to grab my phone and silence it, but hit a wall of man.

I recoiled fast.

Oh, no. Jett had looked so good last night. How would I explain myself to everyone? I went home with the boss, I slept with him again, and Steven would … Oh, Jesus. Steven. We were going to be over. He would never talk to me again.

For some reason, the idea came as a sort of relief.

I lifted the sheets to wake up my Phantom and saw green tights. My stomach dropped.

Green tights traveled up to a green shirt and a symmetrical face with blond hair.

Steven had come home with me.

I glanced down and took inventory. I was still in my costume. I'd blacked out.

Our first time together wasn't forgotten because it never happened.

We were still definitely together, and I needed a freaking mind reset.

Jett probably went home with Gloria. I rewound the night. I'd danced for the crowd, won the contest, had more drinks. Brey and Jax left shortly after. Bastian arrived.

Bastian Armanelli—he'd come with Cade and Katie. They'd dressed as grim reapers. If they'd come earlier, I would have crowned them winners; their costumes killed it.

We drank so much. I remember climbing onto a banquet table at one point to bottle feed shots down people's throats.

I winced at that. Steven got me down from the table and must have stuck by my side the rest of the night.

I nudged him. "Steven?"

He groaned and cracked an eye open. "Morning."

I cleared my throat. "Yeah. Good morning. How are you feeling?"

"Probably about as good as you're feeling."

"Right." I stood up from the bed and wiggled my corset around so I could breathe. "I'd love for us to get breakfast or something but you're still in costume, and I have a killer headache."

"Agreed." He got up and grabbed his things off my nightstand. "Rain check?"

The man was cutting and running out of my house faster than I could kick him out. "Sure." I shrugged because I didn't know if either of us wanted one. "Uh, tell your family I say hi. I'll see you at work."

"Right. Right. See you there." Just when I thought he was about to leave, he French kissed the hell out of my face, morning breath and all. "I think the party went well. The Stonewoods seem to love you." He paused. "And me too."

He turned on his heel and strutted out my front door.

I wiped the back of my hand across my mouth, grabbed my vitamins and pills from the kitchen, and went to brush my teeth. I peeled off my costume and studied what was left of me in the mirror. Glitter stuck in my matted pink hair, and my milky skin sagged. Dehydrated. I leaned on the counter where the vitamins and pills for Saturday and Sunday sat.

"I hate you," I whispered. Then I popped the cases and downed everything except the medication. My heart medication. A little red pill that was supposed to be mandatory and for that very reason it was the hardest to swallow.

Literally and metaphorically.

I was better. I was living. I was enjoying life. And the life I'd mapped out was coming together. I had an impressive job, exceptional friends, a banging body (if I said so myself), and not one damn scar from the cancer.

The pain and turmoil were where they should be—packed away and hidden.

And I planned to be in a committed relationship, marry, and have kids. Steven was a step in the right direction. He'd commit, he'd try, and maybe he'd tackle the hurdles with me.

I gripped the counter, glowering at the pill. I'd paved my way through the chemo, through traveling to Chicago, to this job, to freaking Hawaii.

I swiped the pill over the edge of the counter, into the toilet bowl, and flushed it away.

I didn't need that reminder. I was sure there would be millions of other little reminders in my life.

I took the rest of the day to prepare for Monday, the day of our meeting. I wanted everyone primed with Levvetor information and happy to serve it up to Jett.

Video chatting with Gloria and Brey regarding tactics and PowerPoints helped ease my worries.

On Monday morning, I slid on my Louboutin black stilettos. The red soles matched the fierce red dress I zipped up. Commuting on the L, I rehearsed my points again. Everyone had received an updated version of the PowerPoint and files to review before the meeting at 1 p.m.

I scoped out the workplace when I arrived. Nothing seemed much different. Josie handed me a coffee and smiled at me as I sat down. "Everyone is still talking about the weekend."

"Oh, great," I replied and lifted my cup. "Thanks for the coffee."

"Sure. Also, I pulled a few notes on our marketing efforts for the meeting later. I think if we discussed merging one of our other pharmaceutical company's branding with Levvetor's and consulted the finance team regarding what we could afford, the Levvetor acquisition would be beneficial."

"Great idea." I pulled up a file on my computer to make note of her suggestions. "Thanks so much for looking into it. I wasn't sure anyone would have the time to review any of this before the meeting."

Josie patted my shoulder. "We're all part of Stonewood Enterprises, Vick. If we don't have time, we make it. I think it will be a great work session. See you later."

Gloria popped up out of nowhere to repeat Josie's description. "'Work session'? I saw that in the meeting reminder you sent this morning. Nice touch."

I groaned and tapped a red manicured nail on the desk. I'd painted my acrylic nails the night before to match my look. "I thought it might help but now it seems silly."

"It'll help. Everyone here is competitive. They'll all try to one up each other."

"Let's hope so," Brey whispered as she stopped at my desk. Steven glared over his computer at us like we might get him in trouble.

"We're talking about the meeting later, Steven."

"Oh. That's great. It's just, we're right in front of Jett's office. I don't want him to think we're just..." He shrugged like his thought was obvious.

I dropped my eyes to make sure I didn't roll them dramatically. Gloria pivoted to face his desk. "You think my boss would ever believe I'm..." She shrugged as if to shake off Steven's ridiculous comment and turned her red lips down. "Please. Go back to work."

Both Brey and I stared at each other with eyes wide as an owl's in complete shock. Steven opened and closed his mouth like a guppy before turning back to his computer.

Gloria continued as if we were discussing the weather. "I'll go set up the conference area for later. Do not be afraid. Jett smells fear. Brey, you know exactly what I'm talking about."

She walked off before I could respond. "I'm more than a little frightened now."

"At least she's on our side," Brey reassured me.

"The deal is ours to lose."

"And you've never lost a thing, Vick," Brey said, each word pronounced like she had everlasting belief in me.

If only she knew.

My friends would never know though. I wasn't there to present my sob story to them, and I'd never willingly share that I had beat my first round of cancer.

Because that's all it was. The first round.

I didn't need them looking at me differently, like I was a poor little thing who'd barely survived. I didn't need them worrying that

I'd somehow get cancer again either. I didn't want to be stuck in the padded room my friends would definitely build for me if they knew.

Living with the secret of having had cancer was lonely. It was lonely when you had it, and it was lonely if you survived it. I worried about it coming back more than enough for everyone; I didn't want them worrying too. Sure, it would be lonely if I had to go through it again, maybe not surviving this time. Dying slowly.

Yes, I hadn't lost a thing by keeping it to myself. Not yet.

But I worried every single day that I would.

CHAPTER
TWENTY-THREE

JETT

SHE WORE RED. Not a dark red either. It was a blood-smeared-on-the-walls red, a fighting red, a bold, bright mockery of my recommendation to tone down the color.

Fine.

She wanted war. This was a battle to her. It was just business to me. I straightened my tie and tugged down my shirt cuffs.

Our conference room overlooked the lake, providing a calming atmosphere before the storm of each meeting. A large crystal chandelier hung above, and the brown wood mixed with glass and touches of gold on the seating gave the room a lavish look.

I witnessed Gloria align with Brey and Vick as they each presented points on Levvetor to the top people on my team. Every single person listened like lives depended on it.

And they absolutely did depend on it, but we couldn't save everyone.

After they wrapped up the presentation, Vick stepped forward with some colorful Post-it notes because she couldn't possibly have used plain old white ones.

"I'm hoping you can each write down a question or concern you may have in regard to backing Levvetor on the pink Post-it. On the blue, let us know a reason you think it may be a good idea. Then, let's go through them."

Brey passed around the pads along with pens. Gloria told the team they could work together if they wanted to. That opened up conversation.

I didn't normally take this approach in meetings. We discussed it as adults; we didn't write it down. Yet, here I was following their orders because Brey pointedly put the pads in front of me before she sat down at my side.

On the pink Post-it, I wrote:

SAVE LIVES

On the blue, I wrote:

BURN OUT

Gloria collected everyone's ideas and stuck them up on the whiteboard. And one by painstakingly one, we went through them. I put my chin in my hand and let the team duke it out. Quite frankly, I was surprised by their enthusiastic responses.

I raised my eyebrows when Jon, someone who prided himself on being monochromatic, jumped up to exclaim that he knew how to solve one of the problems.

Vick glanced at me when Bob high fived him and said he knew Jon was the man to do it after his dance-off on Saturday.

"Great." I clapped my hands when Vick took the last Post-it and stuck it over to the resolved side of her whiteboard. She folded her crimson nails over her hands and waited for me to continue. "It seems we have a lot of great ideas on how to make the Levvetor acquisition work. So, are we all in agreement that we should invest a significant amount of our quarterly budget in this company, even knowing that the FDA may rule against it?" I pushed a finger into my temple, trying to hold in the frustration. "The CEO of their biggest competitor is on that board of advisors."

The balloon of enthusiasm that was surely the same red as Vick's outfit deflated.

Gloria stepped forward to take me on. She would too. She'd told me she would come in guns blazing, but Vick held up a hand.

"Do you think we can't handle it?" Vick asked.

"I've never taken on a venture we were incapable of handling, Ms. Blakely."

"And yet you're hesitating on this one. I realize that the FDA is a very large government entity. But Stonewood Enterprises doesn't have a limit, right?"

"While limits are made to be broken, they also serve as a reminder to evaluate the options. I'm not questioning my team's capabilities because I want to. I'm questioning them because I have to."

"If you're risk averse on this, then tell the Armanellis we can't handle it. Someone else will, and they'll do it carelessly. Our team is methodical, dependable, and innovative enough to manage it. Without us, lives will be lost and this company will most likely not stay afloat. That'll be on you."

And wasn't it always on me?

My team would go to the very brink to save a company. Our mission was to turn them into profitable enterprises. I had the greatest minds on my team, working in tandem to make the machine more than well-oiled.

Yet, at the end of each meeting, each phone conference, each day, *I* made the call. When to say yes and when to say no. My father had handed over the gavel because he'd had enough of the stress of playing God, of choosing whether to back massive industries or let their flame die out. That choice sometimes meant thousands of workers would lose their jobs, meant they might not be able to feed their families.

The ripple effect was astronomical every single time.

The weight, the guilt, the pressure often proved to be too much. Most people weren't cutthroat enough to handle it.

I was. I had to be.

My team had to be also.

It didn't mean they should shoulder the burden every time though.

"Victory, you proved a very good point this weekend when we all let off a little steam. We do better with a workload we don't have to push ourselves to handle." I held up my blue Post-it. "If we're overworked, we burn out. We need time to unwind so we can come back refreshed like we did after the party. Right, everyone?"

Most of the team nodded and quietly agreed.

"My father built this tower and company only by putting together the hardest working teams he could find. We all know that my father lost his wife for a very long time because he sacrificed putting her first. The company was his love, and he mulled over every single decision he made like it was his child. Every time you go in hard, you risk everything else coming second. But"—I held up the pink Post-it and looked at Vick—"we'll save lives."

I moved the backing of Levvetor to a vote, and Victory Blakely beamed like she'd won an Oscar.

I lost the competition. She'd be able to dress like a damn rainbow for as long as she wanted. And Bastian got to come to our meeting right after this one and smile smugly at me when I told him we would do it.

None of it mattered though.

I was a Stonewood. The city needed me just like it had needed my father. I'd seen others put things first before their career and the career suffered. Stonewood Enterprises wouldn't suffer. We wouldn't falter. I knew because I'd found my weakness in plain sight.

She wore red and her smile shined brighter than the damn sun.

The few weeks after our meeting with the Armanellis passed by in a blur as I flew in and out of town. I managed some large mergers and handled other business matters. I lasered in on my company and handling my father's loose ends. Every call turned into one more and every conference time extended. Business boomed, and we'd passed our stretch goals halfway through the month.

Gloria waltzed into my office to celebrate the excellent news with a bottle of champagne. A rare smile formed across her face, and I took in how symmetrical the woman was. She perfectly filled out her dress and had her hair pulled back in a tight pony. It emphasized the angles of her face, the slant of her eyes. "You're staring, Jett."

"You look good today." I shrugged.

She eyed my privacy button, and I hit it without her having to ask. She slumped a little and swayed her hips as she walked over to my desk. "I'm tired today."

"I see that." I nodded at her now relaxed posture.

She scooted her ass up onto my desk, something she would never do if the windows weren't tinted. Without eyes on us, though, Gloria relaxed much more. "Armanellis can be bitches to handle, and Levvetor is proving to be a big ass beast."

"You knew that going in."

"I knew that going in." She tapped one finger on the bottle. "You're working harder than usual. The goals being met attest to that."

I straightened a paper she'd knocked askew when she sat down. "If I'm running the place, I'd better provide an impeccable example, right?"

Her hands slid to her thighs. "Agreed. I've been working harder under the knowledge that I'm now the assistant to the sole owner of Stonewood Enterprises. Your father resigning motivated me."

I laughed. Her blatant honesty about slacking before could have rubbed someone else the wrong way, but Gloria's silver was most anyone else's gold. "You ready to quit yet?"

"No. I'm tired and wound up for sure." When her eyes grew languid, I knew the question she would ask. "Care to unwind me now?"

My dick jumped a little at the prospect of fucking her on my desk. We were familiar, I'd had her in my office before and there had never been any mention of me not having her there again. Today, I would probably make that clear.

I glanced behind her to where I knew Victory Blakely sat even though she couldn't see us through the darkened glass. I'd avoided her for weeks now, knowing my business would always come first and she needed someone to put her first instead.

My world didn't match hers.

I saw the light and dark of the world and focused on where the light came from, how it energized itself, and how I could produce light in the dark. I thrived on making my city whole.

She focused on the color of it all. She burst into the office day after day in greens and blues and pinks and reds and one day orange. Bright-as-a-sunset orange. She announced it was the color of the ribbon for a specific leukemia, one that Levvetor produced a treatment for. That day she handed out orange wristbands and orange frosted cupcakes too. For no specific reason.

Just to make everyone happy, she'd said.

Her outright confidence in staying positive morphed our office into a workplace of energy. Enjoyment. Enthusiasm.

She claimed it was fun. And fun, according to her, was one of the best ways to motivate people.

I, no lie, looked it up. She was right.

"I've lost you." Gloria slid off my desk and straightened her dress. "I'm glad."

"Sorry, I'm distracted." I rolled into my canned apology only to halt at her words. "What? You're glad?" I stood from my chair and walked around the desk. I stopped just a few feet from her and glanced at my paperweights. Her eyes followed mine.

"Blue is still my favorite," she offered.

"It's a mesmerizing color."

"And yet your gaze always wanders back to the explosion of color."

I didn't deny it. "They're all beautiful."

"Yes. You're absolutely right. But … " She sighed and shrugged. "I've lost you to the explosion of color. I told you once before, we work well physically, but she can offer you so much more."

"I'm not pursuing her." I ran my hands through my hair, denying attraction to another woman as I let this one down easy.

She gave me a sideway glance. "I'm not too mad about it, actually. Just needed an outlet right now." She tapped the blue paperweight and then smoothed her hand over the colorful one. "Ms. Blakely, huh?"

"No one right now, Gloria. Stonewood Enterprises needs me."

She waved away my concern and then pointed at the champagne on my desk. "Drink this and invite her to drink it with you."

"I'm here to work, not play."

"Glower at someone else, Jett. I'm too tired to act like I care." She turned to walk out of my office. "Enjoy the drink. Take a load off. The team's working like they're on ecstasy or something. Vick's fun vibe is working, which means you get to work less. Enjoy it."

"Yeah, yeah," I grumbled.

She wasn't done. "Enjoy her. Before some mediocre idiot does it instead."

CHAPTER
TWENTY-FOUR

VICK

MY DAY WASN'T going how I wanted it to. I woke up late. Miranda kept screaming out of my phone. Decline. Decline. Decline.

Steven wouldn't shut up about us all having Thanksgiving together. Brey took a day off, which meant I couldn't complain to her.

Josie had set coffee on my desk and, it being the day that it was, I spilled it.

I tried to maintain my composure as Steven jumped up to grab some napkins. I sighed and closed my eyes for a second.

I hadn't spilled on my clothes or my computer. I at least had coffee to spill. I had a job to drink my coffee at.

Not that I was even supposed to drink coffee according to the nutritionist. Not that I should be putting myself under this kind of stress. Not that I even belonged here.

I shoved back from my chair, ready to take a minute in the bathroom. Or an hour.

A message popped up on my computer.

> **JETT:** Calm the fuck down. It's coffee.

My eyes shot up to the man's office. He hadn't talked to me since we'd told the Armanellis we had a deal. He'd nodded at me, walked out, and gone back to being the ever elusive, completely driven and dedicated businessman everyone knew.

A Phantom to us all. He hovered above us with the power, a stark reminder that we all had realities to face. I couldn't figure out if his presence was actually a healthy dose of realism everyone needed or if it was a complete downer.

I sat back down somewhat violently. And my fingers flew over the keys before I could stop them.

> **ME:** Please don't interrupt your oh so busy schedule to worry about me and my little problem over here.
> **JETT:** Is that hurt I'm reading under your snarky ass reply?
> **ME:** It's not. I just know you have work to do.
> **JETT:** What's wrong with you today? Where's the radiant delight our team normally gets?
> **ME:** I need some coffee.
> **JETT:** And I'm sure Stevie will find you some along with some napkins to clean up the mess. Chill. Out.
> **ME:** Go back to work and leave me alone.
> **JETT:** I'm unusually interested in why you're not smiling.
> **ME:** You're a dick.
> **JETT:** You know this is the company message system.
> **ME:** Well, hopefully, the owner doesn't fire me.
> **JETT:** The owner's asking you what's wrong.
> **ME:** I just spilled my coffee and I'm tired.
> **JETT:** Take the morning off then.

ME: No. Like you said, Steven will be back with more coffee.

JETT: Forget I said that. I'll go with you. See if we can destress together or if you're tired and need to sleep, I'm happy to sleep with you.

ME: Get fucked, Jett.

JETT: You said that to me your very first day on the job. And I told you that day, Pix, that's exactly what I'm trying to do with you.

ME: I'm in a relationship with Steven. Find somebody else to harass.

I slammed my laptop shut, and it effectively shut down my monitor as well. Then my phone went off and Steven arrived.

With napkins.

And no coffee.

I exhaled a lengthy breath as I silenced my phone. I grumbled a thank you when he handed me the napkins and sat back down at his desk.

"Need help?" Looking up would have served as a reminder that I could barely resist the broad shouldered, beautiful specimen of a man that was Jett Stonewood.

I let my blonde-pink hair act as a curtain while I soaked up the dark liquid. "I have it under control."

He hummed. I heard him shift and stole a quick peek at him leaning his hip on Steven's desk. "So, Stevie, how are the numbers this week?"

The question was unnecessary; everyone knew the numbers. Still, Steven perked right up. "Oh. Great. No worries about meeting our goals."

"Well, we want to surpass those, right?"

"Right, right. We will. We will." He didn't sound as confident. "With Levvetor being in the forefront now though ... "

My gaze trailed to him. I could barely believe my ears as my so-called boyfriend rattled off an excuse about everyone focusing more on that company than his. He'd thrown us under the bus to save himself and the sorry ass job he was doing.

"Levvetor is not stealing away any employee's time," I blurted, rage fuming from every part of my body.

Jett laughed, but it rattled out like a canned reaction. He leaned a little toward Steven and murmured, "Women, right?"

Steven puffed up like he'd won a damn award and laughed. "Right."

I should have shut down the conversation then and there. I saw the setup from a mile away. Yet, I stopped myself.

Blame curiosity. Maybe even self-destruction. I guess a subconscious need to veer from my original dream. I couldn't quite put my finger on the reason.

But I let Jett ruin it all. Let him dismantle what Steven and I had. He did it quickly, effortlessly. Casually.

"I'm going to hit the bars after work. Gotta let off some steam. You in?" Jett asked him.

"Yeah. Sure. Sure. Ready when you are," my supposed boyfriend replied much too eagerly.

"You two aren't exclusive, right? I need a wingman tonight, not a kept man." Jett put the question out there, offering Steven a brick he could use to either reinforce our foundation or throw at a window, shattering what little we'd built.

"Oh, no. We're not exclusive." He chucked the brick and our relationship along with it. So fast. So easily.

My stomach plummeted along with the brick. I'm sure my face fell too, but Jett didn't give me any time to dwell. He nodded at the dumbass who was my nonexistent boyfriend. "Great. I'll let you know a time later today."

Then his eyes cut to mine. A vivid blue ocean burst from them, inviting me to come swim. "Victory, as discussed over messaging, we have things we need to do today. Let's go."

With those words, he spun on his oxfords and headed toward the elevator.

Maybe I should have tried to discuss my feelings with Steven, but then his whiny voice sighed my name with the damn Y that I should have shut down the first time he used it and said, "We can talk about it later. You know I enjoy being with you, I just really want this in with Jett."

I held up a hand as I walked toward the elevators. "I don't do nonexclusive. So, we're exclusively done."

The words ruffled his feathers to a level of discomfort he'd never experienced from me before. He squirmed and scrunched his face in a way that would normally have me consoling him. "Now, Vicky, just wait."

My body almost surged in his direction to do just that. Instead, I curtailed my damn instinct. The one that made me smooth out the kinks, stop the rattling of nerves, settle the unsettled. I stopped doing everything for everybody else and stepped back, away from the person who only made the slightest effort and toward the person who took what he wanted.

"I'm not in the mood today, Steven. Just so not in the mood." I rubbed a hand over my forehead and then ran fingers through my hair. "We're over. And it's Vick. No Y."

I met my Phantom at the elevators where the smile he wore was as big as it was victorious. He appeared younger, approachable, less ruthless. He'd lost the tie he'd been wearing and the top two buttons of his white collared shirt were undone. My mouth watered at a glimpse of that chest.

"I hope you're happy with yourself," I muttered, trying my best to stay mad at him.

"Quite pleased with how easy he made it. I've always told you he bends with the damn wind."

I punched the elevator button even though Jett already had. "Don't gloat. It doesn't suit you."

He leaned in to me. "Relax, Pix. I'm taking the morning off to help you let go of whatever the hell is bothering you. Your tension is making everyone else tense."

We walked into the elevator as the doors opened. When they closed behind us, he studied me. "My team has somehow stopped being mine and started being yours."

"Huh?" I asked.

"You buzz in and they buzz up. You barrel forward and they do too. Bob called me the other day to explain a new take on a contract. He nailed it, and then proceeded to tell me about the cookie he was eating that you'd brought in. They move with you whether you're happy or in a funk like you are now."

I slumped onto the elevator railing. "If that's true, I feel shitty about how I'm acting today."

He eyed me leaning against his elevator and dragged his gaze up and down my black skirt and blouse. "I was surprised to see you in black today."

"Well, I felt witchy this morning," I snarled.

He hummed and then said, "What do you want to do?"

"You had us take the morning off. You pick what you want to do."

The elevator doors opened, and he set his hand on my lower back to guide me out of the lobby to a black SUV. "Great. I wasn't going to do what you wanted anyway."

He opened the car door and I slid into the back seat, greeting the driver. He was an older man I hadn't met before who'd begun driving for Stonewood Enterprises a few weeks ago.

"Well, don't let Jett here fool you. He doesn't work that hard, and he's always up for a good conversation if you're driving him." I winked at Jett who rolled his eyes.

"Jerome isn't an idiot, woman. He knows better than that."

"He's right, miss. I do, but I'm happy to try and annoy that man out of working any day I get him in my car."

"That's what I like to hear!" I rubbed my hands together and leaned back in my seat. Jett's arm rested across the top of it and he curled his hand around my shoulder to pull me closer. "So, part of your problem today was being in the office. You're out and smiling already."

"It's just the sun. Fall's been cold so far, and I'm a sucker for sun and a warm day," I admitted as I looked out the window. "Where are we going?"

"To Garrett's Popcorn Shop," Jerome announced. "That's where you wanted to go, right, boss?"

"You're correct."

I scrunched my nose. "What if I hate popcorn?"

"You love anything sweet. Also, no one hates popcorn. Not this popcorn anyway. You been there?"

"Nope. I've only been here for a few months. Can't do it all when I'm working for a boss who never sleeps."

"Your ass stays later than me half the time. You love working just as much as I do."

I smirked as I watched the park pass us by. The trees were changing colors; the reds bled into the yellows and oranges, painting the type of autumn scene everyone imagines when October or November is mentioned. "I appreciate doing something I believe in."

"Jerome, pull up to the park," Jett commanded softly.

I raised my eyebrows in question, but he winked at me like he wanted to make me happy. I shook the idea away. Jett Stonewood wanted some ass, he didn't want anything more from me. Without a boyfriend, I was in the same boat. I didn't mind us sleeping together, but I needed to draw a line for my heart's sake.

"Walk in the park, Jett Stonewood?" I teased him.

"We only get to enjoy the autumn colors for a few damn days. Entertain my little whims, woman. You got big ones I have to deal with daily."

My laugh skittered out as I jumped from the SUV and waved to Jerome.

The breeze blew around us, ruffling feathers of the ducks on the lake. The smell of the lake and maple trees invaded my nose. The sun warmed my skin just enough that my long sleeved blouse kept me comfortable rather than chilled. Jett unbuttoned his suit jacket and slid it from his shoulders to offer it to me. I shook my head. "I enjoy feeling the wind on my skin."

"You would, Pix." He draped the jacket over his arm and offered his elbow to me. I took it and fell into step with him. We walked along the park sidewalk, listening to the lake lapping against the rocks. In the middle of the work day, the park was empty, secluded.

Ours.

"This is one of my favorite places," Jett murmured as he gazed off into the distance.

"It's a beautiful one." The statues, the green grass, the fountain, and the view of the city—I'm sure it was many people's favorite place.

"I used to come here when my dad pissed me the hell off at the office. It's always desolate during work hours. Chicago absorbs its humans into the buildings from eight to five."

"Hard workers that we are."

"Yep. Sometimes I forget everyone needs a break, needs motivation."

"You do exemplary work. Your personnel needs to see that in their boss."

"I'm happy I kept you in my damn office space."

"I'm happy too."

"Now, Stevie, on the other hand…"

"Oh my God. Can we not talk about him right now? And can you stop calling him that?"

"Vicky—" he began.

"You're such an asshole."

He chuckled and pulled me close. Before I could stop him, before I could remember that this was just foreplay for a good lay later, he kissed me like he meant it, like we were meant to be.

And I lost myself in that park. Lost my heart and my dreams to him. I tumbled into a new reality, his reality. A place I was scared of because I didn't know if I could withstand the hurt, the pain, the heartbreak that most definitely would come with it.

I told myself I could avoid it, or at least get over it. Maybe I could even morph it into something I really wanted.

I opted to look on the bright side, and we made our way to the popcorn shop he swore was the best.

"The popcorn ... No, it's the smell. Oh, God. The taste of it," I mumbled as we finally got through the line and took our first bites while leaning against the exterior brick wall. I shoveled more into my mouth. "No, it's seriously the best thing I've ever experienced in my life."

"I know that's not true." He stood there, arms crossed, with a challenging grin on his face.

"It is true." I wasn't paying attention. The caramel from the corn was melting in my mouth like it wanted me to know what heaven truly was.

All of a sudden, Jett loomed over me, pressing his body against mine so I was sandwiched between him and the brick wall. "Victory Blakely, *I'm* the best thing you've ever experienced."

The sun lit him up from behind like a damn god. His hair curled on the top where it was longer, and his five-o'clock shadow accentuated that strong jawline. When a man like him towered over a person, they normally shrank back, but I leaned into him. He smelled like fall and caramel popcorn and a hint of expensive cologne. "Sure you're the best?"

"Positive." His voice vibrated through me, low and dark. He transformed from the working man who'd bought me popcorn after a walk in the park to the Phantom. Lurking, wanting, taking. His look shook up my insides, and I almost orgasmed just from gazing at him.

I hummed. "Show me what you're made of then, Phantom."

He descended on me, ready to haunt me, ravage me, terrify me.

I let him. I didn't even put up a fight.

CHAPTER
TWENTY-FIVE

JETT

BACK AT THE office, I checked with Gloria on the calls she'd held for me while we were out. Vick waved me off and made a beeline for her desk, shining even brighter than she did on her best day.

"She seems happy," Gloria blurted. "You seem happy too."

I tore my gaze from the little pixie. "She needed a pick-me-up. I delivered one."

"Make sure you're delivering more than just one."

"Are you her best friend all of a sudden? Remember we've known each other for years, woman."

"She's climbed the ladder and passed you on the totem pole pretty fast in my book."

"Great. I'm going back to work."

As I walked back to my office, I saw Vick sliding the decline button on her phone again. This time I didn't wonder if it was Mr. Stevie. The man wasn't even looking her way.

The hum of the office had reached the normal level now that Vick bustled about reinvigorated. I dove into my work with new energy, too, knowing full well that Ms. Blakely had infected me.

I just wasn't sure it was something I wanted to be infected with. Work came first, yet my mind wandered to her more than it should have.

By the time peoples' desks started to clear and the sun began its descent in the sky, I'd spun every possible scenario for our relationship in my mind. We were complete opposites. She was the damn kid on the other side of Neverland where time didn't exist and fun overpowered everything. Yet, somehow, her fun was getting better results than my serious approach.

> **ME:** Come to my office when you get a minute.
> **VICTORY:** Why don't you come to my office?
> **ME:** I was attempting to give you the option. Now, that seems ridiculous. Get your ass in here. Now.

She fluttered over to Bob's desk as he was packing up and talked with him for a good five minutes. Then she meandered in. "Yes, Phantom?"

"Drop the name. It's not Halloween."

"Not happening. It suits you when you get all perturbed like this."

"You realize the Phantom of the Opera was a recluse consumed with self-loathing, right?"

"So, what? You a generic phantom haunting all of us with the facts of the day? We don't care about the details of the actual musical." She crossed her legs and folded her hands as if her word was final.

"This is a ridiculous conversation." I straightened my tie to get back to what needed to be said. "I think we need to have dinner together."

Her mahogany eyes opened to the size of saucers. Then she back-pedaled toward the door and shook her head. "Nope. No. No. No."

She'd made it to the door, about to pull the handle open and walk out when I pressed the privacy button. "Why?"

She yanked the door, and it didn't budge. She jiggled the handle. "Seriously?"

"Answer me."

"No. Let me out."

"Not happening, Pix."

"After all this time? What happened to reality? Me in the clouds and you on the ground?"

"Figured we'll meet in the middle."

She huffed. "I had a plan, you know? I was going to date a nice, competent guy with a suitable job and get married. He would love me, and we would fit perfectly in a sweet little saltbox house." She paced and rubbed her forehead. "It was a good plan. Solid. And Steven checked all the boxes. He's sweet enough and nice enough and he obviously has a good job."

"He's an annoying shell of a man. You and I both know it. He bent over backwards and was willing to sleep around on you just to have a bro night with me."

She rubbed her forehead and avoided meeting my gaze as she said, "Whatever. He was perfect for me."

I leaned back on my desk. "What's it you said to me earlier in our messages? Oh, right. 'Get fucked' because that's a lie."

"I was trying to get fucked by Steven," she sputtered and threw up her hands.

Her words—or maybe the day, or maybe my whole thought process—finally caused my temper to erupt. "In that case, lift your skirt, woman," I bellowed back. "I'm happy to show you that he will never be able to fuck you like I do."

I saw the shiver run through her, and her nipples tightened under the thin material she claimed was a blouse. "We need this conversation to be over, and we probably need to stop what we're doing."

"You're that scared?"

"I'm not exactly excited about falling for you and having my heart broken. I'll fall too. Like an idiot seeing all the stop signs and still going full speed ahead."

"You do have a tendency to do the opposite of what the signs say. Hawaii, for example…"

"This isn't a joke, Jett."

"For once, you don't want to lighten up. Fine. Entertain my idea for a second. You can live on the edge a little, we can see where it goes. Don't you want to see where this goes?"

"Can you honestly say you think it'll go somewhere?"

"I don't know."

"And that's the problem. I want someone to know. I could know with you. If you wanted it, I could know."

"You're trying to check off boxes, Vick. And that's not the fairy tale you want. You could know with anyone because you just want the life you planned. That's you shooting for the sky but you work for me. We go above and beyond the sky. Me and you, if we end up working, we'll be beyond, Pix."

Her eyes glistened at my words. She eyed the paperweights that had mocked me all day with their colors. "Who gave you those?"

"My dad."

"You stare at them a lot."

"They open my eyes to what people want and need."

"What do I want and need? Can you tell just by me looking at them?"

"You want the world, Victory Blakely, and I'm going to try and give it to you."

She stopped pacing and set one shaky hand on her hip. The orange band on her wrist looked completely out of place next to her expensive outfit but also perfectly placed because she was Victory Blakely. Without color, she wasn't her.

"You're mixing up my thoughts, Jett. I sat in that chair"—she thrust a finger toward her desk—"all day telling myself we don't fit. I chose the right words with the right reality this time. I didn't fabricate it or fluff it up. I flew down from the clouds you think I'm on to get to your level. I told myself we will never ever work."

"Let's go past the sign that says Imminent Shitstorm Ahead, Pix. Let's see if we can."

She stalked up to me and grabbed the back of my neck to take my mouth in hers. The woman kissed like she approached life. The color blasted through me, making me wonder if I'd only been living in gray scale all of my adulthood. She pulled back. "Don't disappoint me, Phantom."

I smiled. "I wasn't joking when I told you to lift your skirt."

She stepped back and slid it slowly up her hips. My dick stood to attention immediately. Her long legs looked smooth as silk, and when I grabbed her by the waist, she wrapped them around me and tightened her hold. "Is this room somewhat soundproof?"

"Doesn't matter if it isn't. I expect you to scream my name, Pix. And I don't care if everyone hears it."

She moaned and yanked what little hair of mine she could grasp, then dove in for another kiss. This was long overdue. I swiped my tongue across her plump bottom lip. "Still taste like strawberries."

She bit my lip and ground out, "And you still taste like the Phantom in my dreams, the one I couldn't shake even though I wanted to."

I'd pictured her on my desk for days now, pictured taking her everywhere in Stonewood Tower. When she murmured those words, I almost dropped her, almost ran the other way. Something deep in me stirred, and I wasn't sure if I could handle it. I was used to managing everything, and not being able to control this feeling, this relationship with her, put a frigid fear in me.

Her nails dragged across my back, and she looked up at me. Her brow furrowed like she was just as nervous, just as scared, like she knew the chemistry between us would erupt and destroy us or be a phenomenon we could never come back from.

I swooped one arm across my desk and files flew to the floor along with all but one paperweight. I dropped her ass on the edge of the oversize desk and placed that brilliant rainbow of glass next to her. She and I looked at it for a second.

"Do I want to know?" she whispered.

"If we don't work out, I'll name this piece after you." I unbuckled my belt and slid it slow and deliberate from my waist. She watched my every movement and then leaned forward to unbutton my pants and lower my zipper. I took my dick from my briefs and said, "You're swirling around in my damn head, and I swear it looks just like this. Color everywhere, warring and fighting and fucking with me."

"Jett, I can't … you can't say things like that to me and expect…"

I stopped her by sliding my fingers up her thighs and moving the lace thong she wore to the side. "I say what I mean, and I mean every word."

She hissed when one finger slid in. "God, I'm so wet already."

"Because I'm here to fuck you, Victory Blakely. I own this part of you."

Her eyes flew open as she ground her pussy into my hand. "No one owns any part of me, Phantom. I belong to me." She grabbed my wrist and worked herself faster as I slid another finger in. She rode my hand like she was chasing her dreams, her head falling back. With her eyes closed and her pinkish hair cascading down around her, swaying to her rhythm, she captivated me. "You're mine, woman."

"I'm mine. I own me." Her damn drive and determination to be herself, to push herself, to stand up and shine bright as the sun hooked its claws into me. My armor melted, bled down onto the floor and dissipated.

"If you say so, Pix. If you say so," I murmured as she hit her high and I watched, riveted by the way she writhed against me.

She came back to me quick, eyes wide and alert. A sheen of sweat glistened on her skin, and she yanked my hand from her sex to bring it to her lips. She tasted herself on my fingers and I almost came right there as she sucked them clean. "I do say so, Phantom. And don't you ever forget it."

I plunged into her like I could overpower her or manage her rapture over me by working her into a frenzy again. I delivered the high she craved and swam in the dream she'd invented for me. I didn't know how she'd gradually hypnotized me, but she had. I wondered if I could do the same to her, if I could charm her into indulging me for a bit longer.

When she screamed my name, I gripped the paperweight next to her and used the edge of my desk as leverage to bury myself deep into her as I came.

We both forced in deep breaths, relishing the post-orgasm sensation. I pushed up on my forearms and peered down at her.

"You good?" I asked, voice softer than it had probably ever been after sex.

She glanced down at our bodies, still wrapped up in each other. She cleared her throat. "Yeah, fine."

I looked down, too, with a sinking thought. "Shit." I pulled out of her and off her in the same motion. "I didn't protect you."

"Or yourself," she declared and waved at my junk.

"Shit." I had messed up. "I'm clean, Pix."

"Me too." She waited a beat. "I also have birth control. Not trying to trap you or anything. No worries."

She hopped off the desk and righted her clothes.

"I'm not worried about that. I never said you would," I blurted, somewhat angry she had the audacity to come to that conclusion.

"Your mind works that way. Darkest reality ready to present itself at any moment. So, I'm reassuring you."

"That's bullshit." I grabbed my belt off the floor and pushed my dick back into my briefs. "Don't pin that accusation on me."

She shrugged and finger-brushed her colorful hair. "Okay, Jett." She smoothed her hands down her outfit and sighed. "Thank you for the good day. I was convinced it would be terrible."

My gut and heart clenched at her soft omission. "Looking forward to making a few more of your days the best you've ever had."

"I wouldn't go that far," she swiftly threw back, but she was smiling.

"I would. I intend to. Get ready for me, Victory Blakely. I'm about to own you like I own my company."

"Now that would be an experience, but I highly doubt it, Jett. You can only have one real lover, and that's the company for you."

I picked up the paperweight and tossed it up. We watched it spin in the air before I caught it. "I intend to prove your statement wrong."

"I intend to enjoy watching you try." With that, the woman, confident as hell in her exits, left me without a backward glance.

CHAPTER
TWENTY-SIX

VICK

MY WORLD WAS shifting, morphing, and ramping up. I found myself enjoying the hell out of it too. I wanted to tempt fate and push destiny to the point where I could say I had lived even if death was closer for me than for others. I hoped every day it wouldn't be, but I chose not to remind myself that it might.

I stashed the vitamins and pills far, far away in the back of a cupboard and opted to forget it all.

My mother's number still popped up on my phone. She called more and more in the next few days, but I was dancing with the devil.

Jett Stonewood.

The day after our desk liaison, I dressed in a risqué, cobalt dress with a plunging neckline. The color reminded me of Jett's eyes right before he took me. He took me that day too. Over and over again.

He came home with me that night and we escaped into our own reality together, far away from the world.

The next night, he tried to drag me to his place, but I wasn't ready to invade his personal space. My eyes were already filled with stars, my mind with irrational hopes, and my core chanted his praises. I had him over and over again, and he worked me just like he said he would. I was overwhelmed with what I felt was love, and he took care of me as assiduously as he did his company. Quite possibly the most ruthless businessman in the world, he didn't disappoint me.

Our Friday at the office proved to be less than productive work wise. I revised a response to the FDA that Bob had written up for Levvetor. One ingredient wasn't meeting the FDA's standards, and Levvetor's competitors were roaring from behind the FDA's title. We needed to focus.

"Thanksgiving is only a week away. I mentioned to my family that you might join us for dinner. And what about your family, Vicky? We should give things another try," Steven whined from his side of our corner. The man had tried to make up for his stupid actions.

I didn't look up from my computer. "Vick, Steven. Vick."

He nodded. "Fine. What do you say?"

"Honestly, I'm not worried about the holiday right now, Steven. The CEO of Levvetor will be meeting with us in a couple days and we haven't resolved things with the FDA."

"Leave that to the chemists. They can figure out an alternative."

My teeth ground together, holding in my response. Maybe I couldn't work this closely with him. I thought we were friends, that we could move on from the train wreck that was the beginning of our relationship, but I found him more and more aggravating.

"If the chemists could find an alternative, they would have."

He sighed. "So, I really screwed up my chances with you."

I glanced over to see a stricken man, and he looked too damn miserable to deny him a minute of attention. "We wouldn't have worked either way."

"Really? I thought we were looking pretty good."

"I was pretending to be happy when I wasn't."

"Huh," He replied, his face turning pensive.

"You're a great guy. And, honestly, Josie always brings you your coffee first." His eyes shot up. "Just saying."

"I've been wondering," he murmured, a small smile on his face.

I laughed at how happy he looked. "She's so pretty too."

The man preened at being given a go-ahead. I almost rolled my eyes at how easy it was to change his mind.

"Ms. Blakely." The darkness in his voice had me jumping. My Phantom stood behind me with a scowl on his face. "Can I see you in my office?"

I peered up at him, trying to decipher his expression, but he shuttered the emotions I'd been able to read so well the past few days. "Uh, sure. Let me just finish up this memo."

"I'd appreciate you coming now," he ground out and then stalked off.

"*Pfft.* Boss is being a little bit of an ass today, huh?" I said to Steven, trying to lighten the situation, but he'd ducked behind his computer as if he wanted nothing to do with my getting in trouble.

Of course he didn't. The man still kissed up to the Stonewoods every chance he got.

The frills of my red skirt swayed as I made my way to Jett's office. The black polka dots matched my black silk blouse as I waltzed in there. "Can I help you, Oh, Mighty One?"

"Really?" he quipped, one dark eyebrow raised. "You referring to me as your God now, Pix? Because I can be that for you. I'll rain heaven and hell down on you every day if you want."

I tried my best to roll my eyes, but he'd twisted up my stomach and caused the ache between my legs to start. His drive to all of a sudden be the man in my life excited me.

My nipples tightened and my muscles automatically strained toward him. He looked like a god, standing there with the sun cascading in through the windows to illuminate him from behind. His dark hair had grown out a bit, and I knew his five-o'clock shadow would leave beard burns on my skin when he kissed me. I resisted shivering in front of him. "What do you want, Jett?"

"We need to discuss the fifth section of the HR handbook."

I racked my brain for what section that was. Normally, I would have known off the top of my head; I prided myself on recalling legal regulations. But I was too busy salivating and panting over him in those damn blue slacks to remember a thing. He had draped his suit jacket over his desk chair. His sleeves had been rolled up to show his muscular forearms and the Rolex he always wore.

"I'm sorry. What section is that?"

"The code of conduct section as it seems you're flirting with Stevie out there and fucking me in here."

"Excuse me?" I blinked once, twice. My drool at his appearance dried up while I recovered from the blatant insult. "Are you kidding me?"

"No." He used his hip to shove off the desk and walked behind it so it stood between us. Then he sat down in his big leather chair and languidly curled his large hands around the armrests. "Although our handbook doesn't condemn fraternization within the company, we frown upon it."

"Well, you … I … good to know, Jett," I sputtered.

"Do you want the handbook to review?" He opened a drawer and slapped a file onto his dark, enormous desk.

"I don't need to review anything," I hissed.

"Are you sure? There are concerns."

"Oh, well, if the concern is about me fucking my boss on his desk, you can rest assured, I'm fully capable of not fucking him again."

He narrowed his eyes. "You know that's a lie."

The menace behind his blue eyes I knew well. I'd shot the same sentiment his way the past few days each time Gloria had stood next to him, even though she'd been nothing but nice to me.

That actually made it worse. She was beautiful, kind, and operated like a perfect assistant under Jett.

I ground my teeth just thinking about it. "I'm not lying. I don't need you between my legs. Especially if your handbook frowns upon it."

He ran his tongue over his teeth and sucked on them as if sharpening the retort that he was about to make. His hand moved to the privacy button and instantly, I was wet. He stalked toward me and grabbed my neck with one large hand, getting a good hold on me. "If my handbook flat-out denied you of it, I'd still be there because it's where I belong. And you damn well know it."

"Then stop talking about it and prove it."

He shoved me up against the doorway. "You and having me prove shit. You know I don't have to prove a damn thing."

"If you say so."

He grunted and then dropped to his knees, sliding his hands under my skirt. "You drive me insane every time you look at him, Pix."

"Who? Steven?"

"Stop calling him that. No one on God's green earth calls him that. *Stevie*"—he emphasized the name he knew was patronizing—"doesn't deserve your attention."

His hand skimmed up to my panties. He growled when he realized how wet I was.

"You know you were the one who arranged for us to sit across from each other."

"Colossal mistake," he murmured. Then he breathed me in and I shuddered at the brush of his exhalation. He looked up at me and those azure eyes held me captive. He looked like he belonged to me, kneeling before me, hands up my skirt, and an expression of need across his face. "We aren't fucking around anymore, Victory Blakely."

I searched his gaze, trying to understand his words, but he raised my skirt higher and moved my panties to the side. Then, his mouth was on me and I forgot everything else. Jett Stonewood was truly a god, and heaven and hell were his lips and tongue working me to orgasm.

I gripped his brown hair, trying desperately not to yell his name. I let him consume me and swirled into an oblivion of ecstasy. He pushed me over the edge when his fingers glided fluidly into me.

"Damn. You taste sweet everywhere," he murmured more to himself than me as I tried to steady myself and open my eyes.

He picked me up, not at all ready to be done with me. My legs wrapped around him like they belonged there. After the week we'd had, they practically did. He kissed me and I tasted myself on him, mixed with his own flavor. That was better than anything I'd tasted in a long time.

"This is definitely condemned in the workplace," I said as I unbuttoned his pants and grabbed him. I steered him into me and moaned.

"Good thing I'm the boss, Pix."

I rode him hard, back against the door.

Our muscles tightened together, our eyes glazed over together, and we fell over the edge together. It was the edge of the unknown, and I didn't know if we'd ever reach the ground. If we did, would the ground be jagged rocks or a pillow of clouds?

A woman's voice sounded overhead. "Gloria has set up a meeting for you in fifteen minutes. Make sure you arrive with your clothes on."

Jett winced as my eyes bulged. "What the hell was that?" I blurted out as I shoved my blouse back into my skirt.

"Jax's stupid new app, Alice. She's some sort of artificial intelligence and we're beta-ing her right now."

"Well, she's a little bitchy, no?"

"She's intuitive," he chuckled. "I don't need to show up to the meeting with my dick hanging out."

"Hopefully our CEO can figure that out without a snippy app telling him," I retorted.

He laughed harder, and I giggled.

"At this rate, woman, I'm not sure I can figure out shit with you working so close to me. I'm walking around with a semi hard-on all damn day. Help a guy out, and wear something a little less appealing."

The picture he painted had me in hysterics, and I waved at him to stop.

"I'm serious, Pix. I can't go to another meeting arranging myself."

"Oh my God." I wiped tears from my eyes. "How are you funny all of a sudden?"

"I'm always funny. I just don't share it out loud," he admitted, somewhat sadly.

I sobered a little and asked, "Why? Funny Jett is likeable."

He stared at me staring at him. "People need a boss."

"An approachable one. I told Steven today—"

"That reminds me." He rubbed one hand over my cheek before he sauntered toward a hidden speaker. "Alice, tell Gloria to move Stevie's desk."

"What?" I exclaimed and then yelled up to the woman in the ceiling. "No, Alice. Do not."

Alice replied, "Done."

"Alice!" I yelled. "What happened to sisters over misters!"

"She only listens to the person she's programmed for," Jett chuckled.

"Why did you do that?" My hands went to my hips.

"I'm not interested in watching you stare at your ex and flirt with him all day."

"You were willing to stare at us after you fucked me in Hawaii."

"I wasn't under the impression we would be continuing our relationship at that time."

"So, what was your impression at that time? You just really wanted us on your team, right in front of your face?"

"Honestly?" he asked as if I wouldn't want to hear his answer.

I nodded, waiting for the blow I knew he was about to deliver.

"I liked making you squirm and dismantling your little vision of a perfect life."

"That's really messed up, Jett."

"Admittedly, I still enjoy it. You're cute always, but when you're pissed, you're a brilliant flame of red and black or whatever the hell color you're wearing that day." He paused. "Or when you feel like that world is crumbling."

I crossed my arms over my chest, trying to block out the flutter in my stomach. Jett didn't know that most of the time my world was crumbling or that I was chasing time, fighting the clock, living around the possibility that I might not get a clean bill of health the next time I went to the doctor.

"What are you thinking?" he whispered.

"Nothing," I replied way too fast and then changed the subject back to what was important. "Moving Steven is ridiculous."

"Probably. But I need to maintain my productivity level, and I can't do that if I'm glaring at you laughing at his shitty jokes."

"Are you jealous?"

"I'm territorial." He shrugged and sat down behind the desk I was starting to realize he used as a barrier between us.

"Do I get to be territorial?" I asked. "Because I know for a fact you and Gloria have a relationship."

He harrumphed and avoided eye contact by having his blue eyes on those paperweights. "Had. Past tense. And she's the best assistant I've ever had."

"That's fine. I'm not asking you to do anything about it. I just don't think you need to do anything about Steven either."

"Stop calling him that."

"Okay. Don't move him and I will."

I saw him physically mashing his teeth together. "He doesn't contribute anything to the team."

"He's sort of the guy that everyone likes to think they are doing better than though, right?"

He squinted at me and then chuckled. "I mean, I guess."

"Let him stay, Jett."

He sighed. "Don't laugh at his jokes."

"Done." I smiled at his petty jealousy. Truth was I felt the same. "Can I ask you not to ever look at Gloria again too?"

"I barely look at anyone and you know it."

That was probably true. Jett had a tendency to be doing something on his laptop or his phone while he worked with you. He just worked constantly, and we accepted that as his employees.

"I still imagine that you might be."

"You imagine fantastical shit all day but you decide to worry about the negatives with me?"

"You bring that out in people." I shrugged.

He smiled and then licked his lips. "I'm becoming possessive of you, Pix. I'm not admitting that lightly. It isn't a joke anymore. Like I said before, not fucking around. Don't sleep with other men. I mean that."

"Same goes for you then. I'm my own person, and if I find you doing something you shouldn't, I will buzz through the men in this city just to prove to you I'm the most desired woman out there that you can't have."

"That's mature," he growled.

"I'm not claiming to be mature at all."

He dragged his eyes up and down my body. "I don't want to do anything with anyone else right now, anyway. All I want is you screaming my name and laughing only at *my* jokes."

I smiled. "I wasn't laughing at Steve's joke, by the way." I emphasized the name. It was my compromise to his demands.

"What was funny then?"

"We were agreeing that Josie seemed like a good match for him."

"Josie?" he questioned.

"Yup." I started backing out of his office. "He's totally into her. Not me."

"Everyone's into you, woman. Tone down your likeability."

"Never going to happen, boss. Never ever."

I spun around fast to hide my giant smile. Jett and I were getting somewhere, and I couldn't help but wonder if somewhere could be the ending I wanted it to be.

CHAPTER
TWENTY-SEVEN

JETT

"I WANT MY BOYS home for Thanksgiving. And you never come home. Your father will talk business with you if you want. But you will be here, Jett."

My head fell back to rest on the leather of the SUV's seat. Jerome hummed up front and ignored my growl of frustration. "Dad wants to talk business after he left me to run this one? No thanks."

"I have better things to do than argue with my son, Jett." My mom's voice was laced with warning. "And I don't have to. Because my sons listen to me. Get your ass home by Thursday."

True to being a Stonewood, she didn't wait for a reply before she hung up.

"What's traffic like if I make a stop at Vick's, Jerome?"

His shoulders lifted slightly. "Won't be much different. I'll reroute."

I nodded and went back to staring out the window. Thanksgiving with the family meant Jaydon acting like a child, Brey and Jax pawing at each other, and for the first time in years, my parents probably doing the same.

I wasn't enduring the night without backup.

I waited for Vick to buzz me into her apartment lobby and took the stairs two at a time. Better than waiting for the elevator that seemed slower than a sloth on one of its lazy days.

When she didn't open the door immediately, I pounded on it.

"Give me a minute," I heard.

A minute for what? I pounded again. "A minute for what? You just buzzed. Let me in."

She opened the door and poked her head out to look down the hall. Then glared at me, her face scrubbed free of makeup. "Rude."

"Think I care about winning over your neighbors? I don't like waiting."

She sighed.

I blurted. "I need you with me on Thanksgiving."

She frowned. "I don't ... I'm sorry. What?"

"I'm going home. My mother's request. I want you with me." I walked in as she opened the door fully.

"That's probably not a superb idea."

I turned to assess her again. She looked young, cute. No makeup allowed a few light freckles to show on the bridge of her nose. "Did you just shower?"

"Yes." She bowed her head and then looked toward her living room. "Like I said, I need a minute."

"For what?"

She waved at her face. "To get ready."

"We aren't going anywhere. Stay how you are."

She cleared her throat and then her hand moved to her neck. "I just ... I'd rather put some makeup on."

"No." I blocked her path as she moved towards her hall. I tipped her chin up. "You remember the light in Hawaii? How you thought the sunset changed things?"

"Yes," she answered quietly.

"It doesn't. Just like some makeup on your face doesn't change anything for me either."

"I don't know if I should take that as a compliment."

"Take it how you want. You're beautiful upside down and fucked or right side up and put together. It's a waste of time for you to put makeup on now. Especially since I plan to take you in your shower later tonight."

Her body shuddered. Then she pushed back the wavy blonde hair that fell to the base of her shoulder blades, completely undone. "I didn't expect you, so my place is a little out of sorts."

She headed to the living room, and I followed. "I'm not worried about it, Pix. You told me you were staying here for Thanksgiving. I thought I was too. So, come home with me."

"I have work to do."

"So do I. Work with me there."

"Why?" She stopped what she was doing and straightened. In her white tank and black shorts, she looked so damn fuckable I barely contained the need to rush her.

"I don't want to be alone dealing with the damn happy life everyone is living."

Her head tilted just enough that the pink ends of her hair swayed over her tits. "Aren't you living a fortunate life? The life you want?"

"Sure but it isn't the one they want me to live."

"So, are you ashamed?"

I raked my hands through my hair. "No, woman. Just come with me."

"Why would I go sit with your family on a holiday, Jett? I'm not your girlfriend. It's weird."

"You aren't?"

"No!" she practically spit back at me, busying herself with straightening her already tidy living room.

"So what the hell are you then?"

"I just figured ... I don't know. I was the person you were sleeping with."

"We established we weren't just messing around. You're the only person I'm sleeping with, and I better be the only one you're sleeping with too."

"I have family to see on Thanksgiving."

"You specifically told me this week you weren't going to see them."

"Well, maybe I changed my mind."

"Pack a bag for Wednesday. We're staying over two nights."

"I don't want to go."

"Tough shit. I want you there and you don't need to be eating Thanksgiving dinner here all by yourself. You're coming."

"Can you be any more demanding?"

"Absolutely. Take off your top, hop up on that counter of yours, and spread those legs." I pointed over to her kitchen. "I need to fuck some sense into you for thinking you could ever tell me no."

Always up for a good time, my little pixie did exactly as she was told.

CHAPTER
TWENTY-EIGHT

JETT

WE SPENT THE next few days at Vick's place working like dogs on a deadline. Bastian called her Monday night, and I heard her continually agreeing with him.

Then, she said something like, "Yeah, I'm still healthy. What do you mean?"

The turn of conversation made me drop what I was doing and listen harder. She glanced over at me and got up from where she was parked on the couch to walk down the hall.

"No, Bastian. I'm not concerned because the product was and has always been good."

I wanted to follow her, but I waited for her to come back into the room and jumped right in. "Why is he asking you how you are? That a personal call?"

"Jealousy doesn't suit you, Phantom."

"I beg to differ. If I put my hands down your pants right now, I'd find you wet."

She glared at me. "Overconfidence doesn't suit you either."

I chuckled. "Answer the question. He call you for more than business?"

She sighed. "It's all business. He's just—"

She got cut off by her phone ringing. She silenced the unique ringtone. It was the ringtone she always silenced.

I eyed her with a question on my face.

"I haven't told my mother that I'm not coming to Thanksgiving yet."

"That's not going to be a fun conversation, I'm guessing."

"No. It won't be. We don't really see eye to eye on a lot, so…"

Her phone rang again. This time, I snatched it from her and pressed the green button. She lunged for me, but I swung out of her way and walked to her bedroom. "Hi, Ms. Blakely. How can I help you today?"

Her mother sniffed. "Well, I called to talk with my daughter who owns this phone. Who is this?"

I smiled. She sounded older but just like Vick. "Jett Stonewood. Her boss."

Her voice was high when she replied. "It's past seven. She's still at work? You keep her that late?"

Interesting. The woman didn't even pause for a second to consider that she was talking with a Stonewood. She rolled on like the name meant nothing to her at all.

"We're not working." I got straight to the point. "Also, I invited her to my family's Thanksgiving."

Silence stretched over the line. I waited her out as I'm sure she was waiting me out. Finally, she replied, "I'd like to speak with Victory now." Her tone was clipped.

"Mrs. Blakely…"

"Give my daughter her phone." The woman's voice had taken on the same tone as my mother's when she'd reached the end of her rope.

"If it's any consolation, I hope to meet you at some point. You've raised a hell of a woman and you managed a great company."

The woman didn't have the same need to ease someone's discomfort as Vick did. She harrumphed, and I handed the phone over to Vick who had been hiding her face in her hands for the past minute.

"Hi, Mom," she said, shooting daggers at me. "No, Mom. I'm not ...Yes. No, Steve and I weren't ... right. I understand he's part of the family ... I agree that dating my boss isn't the smartest."

She sighed and went to sit on the couch where she rubbed her head, and with every passing minute, I realized the mistake I had made.

Victory Blakely was being managed by a brilliant and ruthless businesswoman. Her mother obviously tried to run her daughter's life the way she had run her company.

"Mom, I just can't talk about that right now ... Because ... no, it isn't anyone's business but mine. And I can take care of myself. I've been doing just fine here."

She paused and then shot up from the couch. "No. I don't want you to come visit. I'll come home in a few weeks. I promise ... Of course Dad needs to see me."

Her body relaxed and her eyes started to glisten a bit. "Mom, he has to deal with you daily, I know he needs me there now more than ever. You'll run him into the ground otherwise. I won't make plans for Christmas."

She glanced at me. "I don't know Mom. We aren't ... it isn't really like that. He just wants me there for Thanksgiving."

I walked up close to her and the phone. "I'll come for Christmas. Happy to."

Vick shoved me away and put her finger up to shush me. "Yeah, okay. Well, we can talk about it later, Mom. I'm not committing to bringing him. I love you," she singsonged. "Goodbye."

She hung up so fast I was sure her mother was trying to say more.

"What in the actual fuck, Jett?"

"You silence that phone every single time she calls."

"And for good reason."

"She micromanages your life?"

"Among other things." She curled in on herself, her eyes shuttered closed.

"Care to elaborate?"

"Not really."

"You know, if you were a business deal, I'd say the whole thing was off. You can't hide your hand like that."

"I'm not a business deal, Jett. And I'm sure you're hiding things too."

"Ask me anything you want to know."

She stared at me like I'd just suggested wearing our clothes inside out. "Really?"

"Ask."

She picked at an imaginary fuzz on her shirt and combed the strands of her hair with her fingers in her mirror. "Why are you so against relationships or marriage or happiness in general?"

"Why wouldn't I be?"

"Because normal people want a happy ending."

"I get that all the time when I sleep with a woman."

She rolled her brown eyes. "You know what I mean."

"Why do I need a reason to believe in reality? It's a fact that all relationships end at some time or other. You break up or you die."

"That's morbid."

"I had a great childhood, if that's what you're asking. Everyone knows that. They've printed it in magazine after magazine."

"You could have told them to print that. Is it the truth?"

I didn't even have to think about it. "My parents fought when they separated, sure, but there was always love there. I wasn't deprived as a child. I didn't have a traumatic relationship, maybe one or two women scorned but nothing life altering. I don't have a reason for the way I am. I don't need one, Vick. I honestly believe it makes the most sense."

"I just think it's a sad way to live. With no hope for something better."

"I hope to make other lives better. I try to run a successful business. I try to push this city forward."

"Ah. You don't want the complication. You do realize being happy doesn't mean you have to quit putting one hundred and ten percent into your company, right?"

"We'll agree to disagree." I shrugged. "My turn. You want to answer the question about your mother or your whimsical lifestyle?"

"Can't a girl dream?"

"You take it to an extreme and you know it."

"At one point in my life, I was wrapped in a lot of darkness, so much so it felt like tar clinging to every piece of my mind and dragging me into the pits of hell. I don't want to be there again. I won't be there again."

"If you don't confront the dark, you can't ever get to the light."

"Now that, Phantom, is the most profound thing you've ever said to me."

"Yeah, well, I have to come at you from different angles."

"Come at me straight on and you'll probably get me naked in that bed over there."

She was avoiding the tough questions. She was still hiding her hand. But I'd worked a one-in-a-million deal before. I knew how to play the long game, and as I looked at her, I knew I wanted to play.

I wanted to win.

And I would.

CHAPTER
TWENTY-NINE

VICK

"I NEED A DRINK," I admitted to Brey as we had lunch together before Jett and I would head off to the Stonewood home.

"I can't believe you are telling me this now, hours before you leave. On a work lunch." Her green eyes practically bugged out of her head.

"Well, when did you want me to tell you?"

"Probably right when it happened." She shifted in the cafe's white chair. "Or the next day. Or even a call this morning would have been nice. A text with a brief summary that you would see me at my husband's family's Thanksgiving dinner because you are dating his brother." She paused to glare. "I'm honestly too shocked to go back to work I think."

I ignored most of what she'd said. "You could probably tell your brother-in-law you're feeling sick."

"Jett doesn't care if anyone is sick because he would work through it and expects us to do so as well," she seethed.

"Truth," I agreed and took a bite of my salad. "In his defense, we all love the work almost as much as he does."

Brey nodded. "We're killing it at the Tower lately."

"I completely agree. I feel everyone's energy, and it just rubs off on me. I so enjoy our team."

She smiled. "I'm not dropping this topic, Vick. You might be enjoying the team but you're definitely enjoying the boss."

"Really?" Brey surprised me with how much she'd grown over the past year. She never would have blurted that out before. Now she did it with a smile on her face. "You know I don't kiss and tell."

"You always kiss and tell," she retorted.

"So! I'm not doing it this time."

"No need." She pursed her lips and looked away. "I'm very aware you two are kissing. I feel it every time he glances your way. And he does, Vick. A lot." She waggled her eyebrows at me and sipped some of her water.

"Fine." I sighed and then admitted, "I want to believe he could be this committed guy who can put me before work. I want to be married and have what you have."

Her smile immediately died. She knew just as well as I did it wasn't plausible.

"I know it sounds stupid. But I want it so bad. I always have."

She took my hand. "I know you want those things and you deserve them, Vick. I just don't know if…"

"If Jett's the one for that? If he's just having fun?" I finished her thought, and she frowned and squeezed my hand like she didn't want to agree but knew she couldn't disagree. "Lately, there are so many moments where he says just the right thing and acts just the right way that I think he might want it too. And I believe him."

"He probably does want those things. It's just…"

"You aren't sure he's capable of getting them with how invested he is in the company?"

She shrugged. "I don't know."

I sighed. "I have to remind myself that I'm probably imagining all of it because I want it so bad."

"You aren't. And even if you are, it's okay to want things. It's okay to hope. I hope for both of your sakes that it works. The two of you seem so much happier."

"But we're happy until we're not. What if I'm still doing the same thing with him in ten years? What if he can't commit to anything more?"

"Have you asked him?"

"After just a few weeks of dating? I mean he did just claim I was his girlfriend, but that was in the heat of the moment. Honestly, I don't even know if we are actually dating." I groaned and looked up at the ceiling of the restaurant.

"Oh, you're dating. Jett's made it clear to Bastian. Very, very, very clear."

"What do you mean by that?"

"Bastian told Jax and Katie, I guess."

"Katie's still seeing Bastian?" I asked way louder than I intended to. "That must be why she hasn't returned my calls."

"She's in a weird place. I think something is going on with her and Rome, honestly. Don't say anything but I think they slept together."

I physically winced at her confession because, truth be told, I knew they had. I walked in on them fighting about it and they couldn't deny it.

Brey studied me and then nodded. "So, you knew? You didn't tell me because I've slept with him too?"

I didn't know how to answer that. "Honestly, Brey, you went through so much last year, you didn't need to know that the guy you'd slept with also slept with one of your best friends."

"We sound so messed up," she sighed.

"Aren't the best of friends always messed up?" I smiled at her.

"I like to think we'll figure it out one day. Until then, I guess we get to see how awkward Thanksgiving dinner is going to be."

"It'll be fine. I'm just a friend. Nancy loves me." Nancy—Mrs. Stonewood—loved everyone and everyone loved her. She could have run the world with her charm had she wanted to. Instead, she let her overly driven husband go live in the city so she could raise her kids in a small town, away from the chaos that was Stonewood Enterprises. The media followed them—after all, they were the American equivalent of the British Royal Family. Yet in Chicago, and their small hometown, people normally left them alone. They were the town's royalty and their natives. They were respected, revered, and probably feared too.

Brey nodded. "Nancy will be so happy you came. She'll wonder though."

"I'm going to need to drink a lot to get through this holiday, aren't I?"

Brey shrugged. "Depends on if you act like you're actually seeing the man. You could just be tagging along."

"Yes!" I jumped on the idea. "That is perfect. I drove home with him because we got off work at the same time, and we thought it would be fun to have me tag along because I wasn't going home."

"As long as Jett—"

"He doesn't care." I waved her off. "It will just make everyone more comfortable. No awkward vibes."

"It probably—"

"Thank you. I was worried. I didn't know what to think. When he asked... I just thought... Does he normally bring women back for Thanksgiving?" The words flew out of me before I could stop them. It'd been the question on my mind for the last few days. I recoiled at my own outburst. "Oh, God. Don't answer that."

"It's probably something you should just ask him, Vick. He's never been too closed off."

"Just blatantly open and honest and straightforward even when it's painful. The answer could be really, really excruciating at this point." I waved the waitress over, knowing we needed to get back to work and also not wanting to discuss how easily I could get my heart broken.

"If that's how you feel, then you need to tell him. You need to be just as candid with him."

"I'm not sure I can be."

"You better try. Or you will end up losing more than you think you have."

I bit my lip and handed our waitress some cash as she walked up. When Brey tried to add more money, I stopped her. "You got last lunch." Then I turned to the waitress. "Keep the change."

We headed back to Stonewood Tower, and I slid into my chair, prepared to make a few calls for the next hour.

My desktop pinged just as I scooted my chair forward.

> **JETT:** Ready to head out?
>
> **ME:** It's pretty early. I was going to make a few more calls to prepare for the holiday weekend.
>
> **JETT:** They can wait. Everyone's checked out anyway.
>
> **ME:** That go for the whole office?
>
> **JETT:** Leave it to you to try get everyone an extra half day off.
>
> **ME:** People want to give thanks for their families and enjoy their company now. Like you said, everyone's already checked out.

I waited for a response but didn't get one. I looked up to the man's office but like the Phantom he was, the windows were dimmed.

I opened an e-mail and pulled my colorful ponytail over my shoulder. I worked the strands into a braid as I thought over a response to the e-mail Bob had sent me. We needed to smooth the waters with the FDA if we wanted Levvetor to gain any traction but I didn't know how to do that when they were blatantly choosing to back a different company.

Gloria's voice sounded over the office's built-in speakers. "On behalf of Stonewood Enterprises, I'd like to thank you all for your hard work this month. We've done some outstanding work. To avoid holiday traffic and spend as much time with our families as possible, please take the rest of the day off and enjoy the long weekend. Again, thank you."

"Are you ready?" His deep voice rumbled low from behind me.

I jumped. "Jesus, Jett." I glanced across my desk to see Steve scrutinizing me. "I'm sorry. Mr. Stonewood. You scared me."

"Mr. Stone—" His eyes flicked to Steve's desk, then his smile curved across his face, slow and calculating. "You're referring to me as Mr. Stonewood now, Victory?"

I shot up from my chair, alarm bells silently ringing from his look. We needed to exit the building now before people found out I was sleeping with the boss. People, yes, but more specifically, Steve.

"Of course." I grabbed my bag and motioned toward the elevator. "You were going to give me a ride to see Brey and Jax over the holiday, right?"

"Was I?" Jett asked, walking much slower than I wanted him to. "I was under the impression I was giving you a ride to my family's house so you could meet them."

I laughed, but it came out high and strained. I turned to Steve. "Tell your family I said hi and happy Thanksgiving."

"Uh, yeah. Sure," he replied, studying me as if I'd grown horns. Then, a smile so slimy slid across his face as I saw the pieces of the puzzle fall into place for him. "Vick, did I mention I might have left my watch at your place on Halloween night?"

I saw his comment for what it was, a blatant pissing contest, one where he got to insinuate that he'd placed a flag down on me before a Stonewood.

Both Jett and I tensed, my muscles coiled to attack him for such an asinine move. "No, you didn't mention it because that was about a month ago and I can assure you that you didn't leave it there. Goodbye, Stevie."

Thankfully, Jett followed me as I stomped to the elevator and didn't say a word as we stepped in. I pressed the lobby button repeatedly until the doors closed. As soon as they did, I turned on him. "Are you trying to make it everyone's business that I'm sleeping with you?"

"I don't really care one way or the other," he answered, completely unfazed by the annoyance in my voice.

"Well, I do." I poked at his large shoulder. "You can't just start acting like we're intimate. People are already suspicious."

"Suspicious? Or territorial? Seems Stevie wants to make it known that he slept with you."

"Oh, please. Who cares if he's doing that? It's not like he actually wants to be with me. It's only about impressing you or being the bigger man. If people think we're dating, *that's* a larger issue. The team is starting to trust me, and I want their trust. I like the career I've started here. I have more respect than I've ever had anywhere else."

Jett moved forward and swiped his FOB before pressing a red button. The elevator slowed to a stop.

"What are you doing?" I pushed the lobby floor button again but the elevator didn't move.

"Making something clear to you. I want your full attention for it."

I waved at the doors. "That's a little dramatic."

"You told me before you don't belong to anyone, right?" He raised an eyebrow.

I crossed my arms over my chest. "Right."

"Then I never want to hear another man try to metaphorically piss all over you in front of me again."

"You're being ridiculous. You want me to call him out?" I widened my eyes when he didn't immediately shoot down the idea. "You know how painful that would be for everyone?"

"You and making everyone feel at ease," he mumbled under his breath before crowding me up against the wall and breathing into my ear. "I don't care whether it makes my whole office uncomfortable, Victory. I don't enjoy hearing a man imply that about you. I'm not proud to say it just about nearly killed me to not fire him on the spot. If you're worried about making someone feel uncomfortable, know that I'm twisted up inside listening to him being an asshole."

"Phantom," I smoothed his chest, trying to calm him. I saw his anger for what it was. He didn't like the disrespect Steve put out there. I didn't either. "I made it pretty clear that no watch was left at my place. I'm done with him and he knows it. And for the record, I never slept with him. There's nothing left for him to say. So, he won't do it again."

"No. He won't. Because I'm coming to realize if you belong to anyone other than yourself, it's me. You better realize it fast too. I will remove anyone from our lives who claims otherwise."

I brushed my fingers over his jawline, soothing away the tension and anger. "Okay, Phantom."

He leaned toward the buttons and swiped his FOB. Then, instead of pressing the lobby, he pressed the underground parking button. He stepped away from me and cleared his throat. "I'm driving. My vehicle's in the garage."

I folded my hands together, not sure where we stood but sure it wasn't on the same ground we'd stood before. "Don't you have work to attend to?"

He pointedly slid his phone from his pant pocket and turned it off. "You've got my full attention."

"Oh." I leaned against the elevator railing, and my hands gripped it like it would help stabilize my spiraling feelings. "I don't need it. I could work too."

"You also mentioned you're concerned people won't respect you in the office if we're in a relationship."

Even with the admission he'd just made, I still felt that way. "I just think that we aren't sure this relationship will work out. We aren't even sure if this is a relationship. So, I don't think everyone needs to know about it. And by everyone, I sort of mean no one. No one needs to know."

He rubbed the shadow of stubble on his chin. "Interesting approach, Pix. What do you expect me to tell my family then?"

"Will they ask?"

He chuckled. "Someone will ask, woman. You think I bring all the women I sleep with home for Thanksgiving?"

I cleared my throat and the frustration at hearing about the other women he slept with away. Watching the doors, I said, "I'm Brey's friend. We'll just go with that." The elevator doors opened, and he lifted his chin as he held the doors open for me. The blue in his eyes was deep, dark, and masked any emotion he felt toward my words.

My heart galloped faster than a horse chasing a damn dream. And maybe I was chasing one too. But Jett didn't dismiss my idea. He didn't want to claim me as his.

The moment in my apartment a few days ago had been a fluke and his anger in this elevator was just jealousy. Even so, there was a whisper of hope in the back of my mind that wished it could be real.

"I'm this way." He turned left, and we walked down the row of luxury cars on sleek cement.

"I've never been down here."

"It's pretty absurd in Chicago. Having a car is inefficient."

"And yet you do," I teased, trying to lighten the mood.

He pressed a button on his keychain and a black F-150 truck chirped in front of us. The ground clearance was ridiculous and the wheels were so big, it took up more than one parking slot.

My mouth dropped. "You're kidding me, right?"

"About what?" He rounded to the passenger side and opened my door.

"This is grotesquely extravagant." I scrunched my nose and walked over, ready to get in. "Why would you have this big ass truck in the middle of Chicago where you can't even fit into a damn parking spot?"

One side of his mouth kicked up as he grabbed my hips to lift me into the seat. A spark of heat shot straight through me, and I gasped.

He wedged himself between my legs before I could turn in my seat to face forward, his eyes on my open mouth. "I enjoy getting my hands on you any way I can. If I get that reaction every time I lift you into this dumbass truck, I'm driving it to work from now on."

"Get real, Phantom."

He rubbed his hard length against me, and my nipples tightened. "I'm the most real thing you're ever going to have between your legs again, woman."

He grabbed my jaw and devoured me. I clawed at his shirt and pulled him closer, needing the taste of him more than I'd needed anything in days. My body hummed for him, was becoming attuned to him and starting to thirst for him like it did for water. I drank in as much as I could as fast as I could before I pulled back to catch my breath. "We're in the workplace."

He murmured, "My workplace," before diving in again and pulling at the bottom of my dark green top. Then his hands were on my skin and my pussy clenched, so wet and ready to have him in me again. "I swear you're trying to drive me insane with these outfits," he mumbled as he worked at a tie that cinched my waist in to form an hourglass figure.

"It's conservative and very work appropriate."

"It's a fucking maze to get off you and looks like porn for the guys at work. Stevie stared at you all damn day," he growled into my neck as he focused on undoing the knot at the side of my top.

"Steve can stare all he likes, Jett, as can most men, if it helps get them through the day." I shrugged.

Jett's head whipped up from my neck. "Victory,"—his jaw popped and the stare he gave me held warning—"those men don't get to eye fuck you on company time. Especially not when it's my company."

I didn't know if he was madder about them doing it to me or doing it on his company time.

Another car beeped, signaling someone else was in the garage with us. Jett's hands went to my thighs and his head dropped like he was trying to pull it together.

"Guess party time is up," I said, teasing him because he started the party thinking he'd be able to finish it.

"Give me a minute," he grumbled under his breath.

I leaned forward and rubbed my legs against his as I breathed into his neck, "That all it takes, big man?"

"You're a devil wrapped in intoxicating clothing, woman." He stepped back and pushed my legs over to face the front. Then the passenger door was slammed a little harder than I'm sure it would have been on any other day.

We drove to my apartment where I teased him about the fuel economy of the massive truck he claimed was logical.

He teased me about it being very logical with all the shit I had to bring. Which was only three suitcases. Two of which were tiny ones. In my defense, I didn't know what to expect of the holiday so different clothes for different possibilities was warranted.

The drive to the Stonewoods' home only took two hours as Jett navigated around the city traffic and had a toll pass.

"This is Greenville," he announced as we passed a large carved wood sign that read Welcome to Greenville, Population 5,439.

"Small town," I said while taking in the widened and curved roads where the speed limit had dropped to twenty five. Admiring the backdrop of red-leaved maple trees and rolling hills of green grass, I wondered if he missed this lifestyle.

He pushed the button that controlled the windows, lowering them to let the autumn wind whip in. His elbow popped out right as the top of the window reached the door. A smile stretched across his face, the most genuine one I'd ever seen on him. "Yup, so small that every damn person is up your ass all day every day."

"Seems frustrating."

"It's home."

My elbow went to the middle console, and I set my chin in my hand to study him. "You kind of look like you fit here with this big pickup and your hair getting all blown around in the wind."

He glanced at me and chuckled. "My mom raised small-town boys. We couldn't shake it if we tried."

"You don't look it in your suit and tie."

"I'm still in part of my suit now," he said, eyebrow raised as he turned down another street.

He was. He'd lost the jacket and tie, but he still wore slacks and his white collared shirt didn't hold a damn wrinkle. The sleeves were rolled up and his big hands gripped the steering wheel of a F-150 now. The Rolex glinted in the sun, but it was on the wrist of a man who looked perfectly able to chop wood out here in this small town. My mouth watered at the vision of him in this truck, on this country lane where kids played outside and the sun shone on every golden leaf.

He chuckled, and the sound shook my whole stupid, fantastical soul. "What are you thinking, Pix?"

I snapped up straight in my leather seat. "Nothing worth mentioning."

"I like your not-worth-mentioning thoughts. Hit me."

"Small towns make me think of big dreams of my picture-perfect future, Jett."

"Hmm." He nodded but didn't ask me to elaborate. I didn't want to either. We both knew that road ended in a fork where our paths and ideas split off in opposite directions.

We pulled up to an expansive home with white-stained cedar siding and a wraparound porch. Round, ribbed pillars stood tall, holding up a balcony above them. The lush, manicured front yard boasted enough green acreage for two more houses of the same size. "Ready?" he asked as he hit the gravel drive and inched forward until we were parked behind another pickup.

My eyebrows shot up at the other vehicle.

"My dad's. And yes, probably every man in town has one."

"Ah. It makes more sense now."

"What makes more sense?" He opened his door.

"Every man needs a bigger truck than the man down the road."

"I got the biggest, babe. Don't worry." His door shut, and I found myself laughing at the rare snapshot of humor he graced me with.

He took his time lowering me to the ground, and I immediately felt relief that I'd changed when we stopped at my apartment. I wore cream flats to match my blouse and dark jeans. The flats made navigating the gravel drive easy, and my long sleeves combated the chill of the wind.

Jett rounded the truck's bed to grab our bags. As he did, both his parents waltzed out from their heavy, oak double doors to meet us.

"Vick!" Nancy shouted and waved at me as she hurried forward. The black maxi dress flowing around her legs matched her long ebony hair.

I tried to grab one of my suitcases, but Nancy waved me away. "Let the men handle it."

I glanced at Senior Stonewood, who was an older but just as good-looking version of his son. He could be classified as the silent type. He took one look at me, making his assessment, and I tried not to shake under it. This man had single-handedly restored a large city's economy. He masterminded every pitfall and escaped every recession. My mother, an extremely intelligent businesswoman herself, considered his accolades some of the best in the history of entrepreneurship.

Every time I'd encountered him, I'd hid behind Brey or Jaydon. Today, I had no one to hide behind. "I'm Vick." I stuck my hand out for him to shake.

He didn't move, and the wind died, the sun dimmed, my heart raced. He was a stone wall standing taller than anyone I'd ever encountered, more forbidding than I'd ever imagined. Then he chuckled, and the wall crumbled with the rumble of it. His hand clapped me on the shoulder as he pulled me in for a hug.

"I know who you are. You're Brey's best friend. I know my daughter's best friends."

His words warmed my heart to him immediately. They had taken Brey into their family after her father went to prison for burning down their home with Brey's mother in it. Some wouldn't have accepted her as a daughter so quickly. After Brey married into the family though, there wasn't a doubt. She was a Stonewood, and Senior Stonewood obviously took notice of his daughter's life.

"Right," I nodded. "Thanks for having me."

"Thank you for coming." He motioned to his son and they moved in sync to get the bags. I heard them grumble to one another about women and their belongings as Nancy pulled me in for a hug. "I'm so happy you could make it."

"Yes. I was happy Brey invited me," I mentioned loudly for everyone to hear.

Nancy pulled back. "Oh, honey. Don't do that. Jett told us he was bringing you. I'm happy he's dating someone," she singsonged as she hooked her arm in mine and guided me toward her home. "Otherwise he'll end up just like his father."

"You're still with me, aren't you?" Senior Stonewood grumbled.

"Legally, we're still separated," she quipped back without turning around. Smirking at me, she whispered, "Make them work for it. It's what they deserve when they put in five hundred hours a week as if life outside of Stonewood Enterprises doesn't matter."

We stepped up onto her porch and I barely had time to take in the expansive foyer as we walked in. The smell of tea drifted through the house as she steered me toward the kitchen.

"I'll show you to your room later. You're staying with Jett, right? Now that we've addressed the elephant that shouldn't have been in the room in the first place?"

"I ... um ... " I stuttered, glancing back to see if Jett could answer for me.

He winked at me from the foyer where he and his father were setting down bags. "She's staying with me, Mom. Give her a little breathing room."

I rushed to amend his statement. "I can stay wherever. If it's Jett's room, he'll obviously sleep on the floor."

"Of course he will." Nancy winked at her son. Then she let go of my arm to pour some tea. She proceeded to add a splash of liquor into the hot tea before handing it over. "Take the edge off if you want. Just remember, you've been known to drink with me and Brey before dating my son. I'm still the same person, Vick. I just have more ammo to equip you with in the dating field."

Truthfully, I'd always enjoyed a night out with Jaydon and Brey in college. Sometimes, Nancy would roll into town to see her son and join us. She was that woman who could fall in step wherever, completely comfortable and accepted anywhere.

"I'm trying to process everything," I admitted. "I had a whole story prepared for today."

Her smile warmed the room, and as I sipped the spiked tea, I relaxed a bit. "Isn't it so much better to stick with the truth?"

The temptation to give an answer that would appease her was strong, but I gave the honest one instead. "Maybe. I'm not sure what to expect."

"No one in love does." She contemplated her estranged husband and my Phantom walking toward us. I would have corrected her—Jett and I weren't in love—but I had a feeling she wasn't talking about us anymore.

"A lot of traffic on your drive in?" Senior Stonewood asked.

Jett shook his head no. "Want to get settled in?" he whispered near my ear.

"Don't steal her from me already. I barely get any woman talk around here," Nancy pouted.

"You wanted this old man here with you all the time, Mom. Now you got him." His dad scoffed at him as he steered me toward the stairs. "We'll come have a drink once we get unpacked."

At the top of the massive staircase, portraits of the Stonewood boys lined the walls. Their dark hair and blue eyes made them heart-stoppingly gorgeous children.

I halted to point at a picture of them dressed up in baby suits with their hair combed to the side. It captured my eye because they were all covered in mud—Jett, with his arms crossed, glared at Jax and Jaydon who were smiling ear to ear while smearing more dirt on each other. "This is the cutest thing ever."

"Easter Sunday. My little brothers thought playing in the mud was a wonderful idea."

A laugh escaped me, and Jett rolled his eyes as he held up my bags. "Bedroom's this way, Pix."

I scanned the wall. "Give me a minute. I have to absorb your childhood."

He disappeared and then was back without our bags. His arms slid around me, and his scruff tickled my ear as he said, "See. No glaring issues in my childhood."

I rubbed his forearms as I examined another picture with Jett on the side, glaring at his family again. This time, his mother and brothers were covered in paint while he sat casually on the side, completely untouched, in jeans and a white T-shirt. I pointed to it. "When was this taken?"

"I don't know. Probably when I was fifteen. My mom hired a photographer to capture the family dynamics."

"They captured them all right."

"Getting paint everywhere for a picture serves no purpose."

"What about enjoying yourself?"

"Washing all that shit off was not enjoyable. I guarantee it."

I sighed and squeezed his arms before I turned to have him lead us to his room. "We're so different."

"Water and oil."

"It must be something much more destructive."

"No. Yin and yang. We're working well together."

"We'll see."

Our dinner that night was light. Nancy claimed to be preparing for the feast the next day. Brey and Jax showed up late that night after we'd retired to our bedroom.

As we got ready for bed, Jett slipped into dark shorts right in the middle of the room.

"Seriously?" I lifted an eyebrow at him and glanced at the window. Then the open door. "Go to the bathroom to change."

"What for?"

"What if someone sees us in here with you naked?" I hissed.

"We're staying in the same bed. What do you think they expect, Pix?"

"Oh, no. You're sleeping on the floor. I told your mother." I grabbed a white fluffy pillow and threw it down. "You can have the comforter though."

He grabbed the pillow off the floor and the comforter from my hand to shove them back on the bed. "Not happening, Pix."

"We're not sleeping in the same bed, Jett. It's disrespectful to come into your parents' home and do that when we're barely together." I tried to snatch the pillow again, but he shoved it further onto the queen-size mattress.

"If you're in the same house, building, or even on the same fucking block as me, we're sleeping in the same bed."

"I don't want to disrespect your parents."

"Technically, they aren't even married. They can't be mad at us. And I don't care about disrespecting them. I have been for years," he retorted and grabbed his bag to unpack.

My chest flared at his confession. If he was saying he'd been bringing women here for years, it meant I wasn't anywhere near as important to him as he was to me.

I told myself to accept that. I grabbed one of my suitcases and moved toward the bathroom. "I'm just going to freshen up."

He let me go. In the bathroom, I remembered I was here to enjoy myself, enjoy him, enjoy what I had for the time I had it. I grabbed some of my makeup remover and took a cotton wipe to rub it over my face. I wiped away the layers that held my happiness in place. I peeled away my clothes and slipped into soft cotton pajamas with long sleeves.

After tying my hair back and packing away my belongings, I sighed at the reflection in the mirror. After long work days and long hours searching for the joy in everything, there were these moments where I felt exhausted and all I wanted was to just be.

I didn't want to be happy or sad. I wanted nothing but to relax and let time pass instead of worrying that I wasn't reveling in the gratification of being alive.

I fisted my hands and then grabbed my suitcase.

When I reemerged into the bedroom, Jett was under the comforter and sheets, laptop open, typing away. He looked up and smiled. His broad chest was free of clothing, his abs defined even though he slouched, and his biceps looking bigger without a suit jacket hiding them.

"Ready for bed?" his voice rumbled softly. He licked his lips as he looked me up and down and I watched the motion, knowing how much pleasure they alone delivered.

"Sure." I ground out because I knew I wouldn't be getting any of that pleasure while we were here. I wouldn't try anything with his family under the same roof. I set my suitcase down harder than I intended and got to my side of the bed. I slid in and stayed on the very edge.

He clicked off the light. "Vick," he whispered.

"Jett?" I whispered back.

I heard a soft laugh from him before one of his powerful hands grabbed me around the waist and pulled me close to him. "You belong here. Next to me."

My heart thumped.

It didn't sound like a *beep*. It was raw and low and powerful, like the muscle somehow knew it had a fresh purpose: to beat and live on for something that felt a lot like love.

CHAPTER THIRTY

JETT

SHE CAME OUT of that bathroom like a spirit stripped bare. When I pulled her close, she didn't fight me. Asking her if something had changed or was wrong wouldn't have worked.

Her happy wall would fly back up, and I didn't want it between us in the dark of the night. I'd opened the window so the cool breeze rustled in. The air in this town smelled greener, like fresh-cut grass and forest. If I could smell that mixed with strawberries, I'd contemplate giving up just about anything to keep it forever. I buried my nose in her hair and sighed.

She turned to me, her whiskey-colored eyes as dark as chocolate in the night and murmured, "I think I might be falling in love with you."

Those words should have scared me. They would have coming from any other woman. I had become more attached to this woman than I'd ever planned and knew that meant one thing. Something else would suffer. Relationships were give-and-take.

Her hands curled up over her chest, and she shrank back from me, shrank back from the words. None of it was supposed to be romantic. She lay there, a vision with pink-blonde hair encircling her, eyes glistening in the moonlight, and confessed to me like a sinner in a confessional. A tear streamed down her face.

"Victory, don't cry."

"It's just … I can't stop it. I've told my heart not to. I have thought of every logical reason we won't work. Still, my mind keeps restructuring the narrative." She took in a shaky breath. "Now we're here at your parents' like we're serious, and I'm in your childhood room and this house and this town and everything is so damn perfect."

"You're painting a pretty picture, Pix," I reminded her, reminded myself. Still, the picture was starting to feel very real.

"That's the thing. I'm not. For once, what I'm saying, I'm not even exaggerating." She sighed. "I just need you to know. I'm falling but I'm trying not—"

I took her pouted lips in mine and didn't let her finish her sentence. Victory Blakely was quickly becoming the thing I wanted most. More than Bastian not bothering me about Levvetor, more than my job, and more than Stonewood Enterprises thriving.

I threaded my fingers through her hair and memorized the silken texture. Her hands gripped my shoulders as I took the kiss deeper and moved closer to her, rubbing my length against her. Her leg slid up my thigh like she couldn't stop herself.

My hand pushed her shirt up, and I dipped it into her bottoms, groaning when I realized she didn't have panties on. "Are you trying to kill me?"

"I wanted you to sleep on the floor."

"Damn," I grunted and rolled my thumb over her clit.

She hissed.

"Quiet, Pix. Or you won't get to come in my bed."

"This shouldn't be happening."

I ran a finger over her pussy and she was so wet, I knew she didn't mean it. "Want me to stop?"

"We should," she whispered as she arched her tits against my chest.

"Right." I moved to her neck to suck at her collarbone and she gripped my hair as I worked her clit just the way she liked. "Remember to stay quiet."

She moaned into the pillow.

Her hands flew over me and then she was down by my shorts, but I leaned away. Her eyes fluttered open, "Jett?"

"This is for you. I get you in my old room where I used to not worry about a damn thing in the world. I want the same from you right now."

"I'm not worrying. I just want to make you feel good like you—"

"That's the thing, Pix." I slid my hands to her waist and she protested. I hushed her and turned her around so that her ass was right up against my dick. I rubbed the peaks and valleys of her curves and whispered into her neck, "I'm making *you* feel good now. Forget everything else."

Her ass pushed into me, and I nipped at her neck as I slid my hand back in her shorts. When she started to pant and moan louder, I sucked the sensitive skin right below her ear.

"Oh, God," she breathed out.

"Your god, woman. I'm here to deliver you to heaven, and you'd better go willingly."

Her hand crept back toward my shorts. I bit her ear. "Remember I can fuck you to hell too, Victory. Do what you're told. Tonight, take the pleasure."

She chanted, "Yes, yes, yes."

I covered her mouth. "I'm starting to think you want them to hear."

Her thighs squeezed tight around my wrist as my fingers slid in and out of her. I picked up the rhythm.

"From now on, you take what you want from me. You don't worry about what I want or need. Understand?"

She didn't respond at first so I slowed my pace.

"Jett!" she ground out and rolled her ass back into me.

"Say it, Pix. Tell me you understand."

"Fine. I understand, you prick."

She didn't. Not really. But I was going to make sure to teach her.

CHAPTER
THIRTY-ONE

JETT

THE SUN SHINED in on my woman, and my mind played tricks on me because she looked better under it. She looked better every time I looked at her. Long blonde hair and smooth sun-kissed skin. Her bruised lips were evidence that I'd kissed her enough last night. Still, I wanted another taste.

I shifted up on to an elbow to stare at this perfect specimen of womanhood. She'd fallen asleep not long after I'd brought her to a final high of many. Then she woke me up by straddling me and admitting that my dick was the only thing she wanted. She told me she wasn't taking no for an answer. Suffice it to say, I let it happen.

My dick didn't give me much of a choice.

The white sheets were tangled around her now and I had every intention of taking her again before we joined the family downstairs for breakfast.

"Man, my flight got delayed and you should have seen this guy—" Jaydon swung open my bedroom door.

"Jesus." I pulled the comforter over Vick whose eyes popped open at Jaydon's voice. Then she smiled like it was no big deal.

"Jaydon!" She grabbed the sheet and leapt up to hug him.

Naked.

"Are you fucking kidding me?" I grumbled and wiped a hand down my face.

"Vick, you can't be serious. You're sleeping with Jett?" He pulled back from his hug but kept his arms around her waist to puppy eye her like he could win her over. "I lost Brey to Jax. Jett's worse, babe."

She gazed up at him and laughed. "Maybe if you hadn't left us for LA and the big screen."

"I'll fly you out any time you want."

"Prove it," she replied coyly, like proving it wasn't *our* private joke.

"Vick, go put some clothes on," I grunted.

"Or leave your clothes off." Jaydon waggled his eyebrows.

"Jaydon, get the hell out of my room." I leaned over the bed to find my shorts.

He kissed Vick's cheek. "I'll see your fine ass and his grumpy one downstairs for breakfast soon."

"Sounds good." She beamed and once the door was closed, she turned to glare at me. "Don't tell me what to do like that in front of someone ever again. It's disrespectful and rude."

"Don't hug men in front of me while you're naked then."

"First, I'm not naked. I have a sheet wrapped around me. Second, even if I was, it isn't something your brother hasn't seen before. Three,"—she dropped the sheet—"you want to keep seeing it, don't be an ass."

She turned and slipped into the bathroom before I could compile my thoughts.

I heard the shower turning on and barged in. I whipped open the shower door. "What do you mean my brother has seen you naked?"

"Exactly that."

"If you screwed him, Vick…" Warning heated my voice. I didn't have a threat to follow through with though. Water cascaded off her hair, tits, waist, and ass. I drank in the picture, the glistening pebbles and tracks decorating her skin. I wanted to lick them off and fuck her against the shower wall.

"Then what, Jett?" she asked pointedly as she rubbed shampoo into her hair. "I'm not asking you who you've slept with before me."

"Because there's no way in hell I'd sleep with a sister of yours."

"Well, to be fair, I'm an only child, so I guess we will never know the truth of that claim." She laughed at her own joke, trying to lighten the mood. When she saw I wasn't laughing, she sighed, "I haven't slept with Jaydon. Jeez."

"Thank God." I shucked off my shorts and stepped into the shower with her. "Now bend over so I can fuck some sense into you."

Her hands were already on the shower tiles. "I've been friends with him for years. It makes complete sense that he's seen me naked once or twice. You know I don't care if guys look."

My hand grabbed an ass cheek to pull her hips out toward me. "Start caring, woman. Your body isn't up for display unless you're displaying it to me. Privately."

"You're so damn territorial," she mumbled, but she was losing herself to my hands rubbing her everywhere.

I slammed into her. "Damn right I am. Territory marked and owned."

I screwed her hard. She needed to remember who she was dealing with.

When Vick finished getting ready, she disappeared to find my mother for tea.

I took a few work calls because Thanksgiving didn't mean I was completely free. Then I meandered down the hallway, hoping to catch Vick alone so I could drag her down to the lake behind our home.

Instead, Brey popped up out of nowhere, her dark hair down and her green eyes glowing with determination. She stood in my path, and I tilted my head in question.

"Brey?"

"Hi." She cleared her throat and placed her hands on her hips. "So, we aren't at work."

"So it seems," I replied, somewhat amused. Brey and I had always gotten along just fine. I didn't love her like either of my brothers, but I'd learned to appreciate her presence within the family and her intelligence within my company. She had a knack for spotting risky investments and an eye for problematic business ventures. "I'm happy we both get the weekend off."

She nodded once. Then she nodded again and cleared her throat. "I'm not bothering you to discuss work. I hope you can set aside the fact that you're my boss for a second and just be my brother-in-law."

I examined her squirming under my gaze. Brey always appeared slightly uncomfortable, but now she fisted her hands tightly on her hips and her breath was somewhat erratic.

"You know I'm always your brother-in-law?"

"Well, yes." She waved away my question. "We just … we work together. That's our relationship."

I shook my head slowly. "No. We're family."

Apparently, I hadn't made that clear to her. I was hard on her at work and didn't say much to her outside of it, but she'd married Jax and I respected that. I commended her for all she'd been through as a kid and as a woman too.

"Okay, well, then. As a part of your family, I'll let you know a little bit about mine."

I waited and widened my eyes to encourage her to continue.

"Vick's not a toy. Don't play with her like one. If you do, I'll never forgive you, and that might not mean much to you, and you might not care, but I'm in this Stonewood family for life. So, for the rest of your life, I will make every single family event you attend a train wreck. It isn't polite or nice, but I'll do it."

"Brey, I'm not—"

She held up a hand. "Just don't play with her. That's all I'm asking." Her eyes pleaded with me, her dark eyebrows bunching a little.

I nodded once, and that was all she needed. She pushed past me to head to her own room. My phone rang on my way down the stairs, Bastian's number popping up on the screen.

"It's Thanksgiving," I answered, my voice low with frustration.

"FDA wants to push one of Levvetor's ingredients in one drug to the forefront. Seems they are willing to drag the brand name through the mud, even with Stonewood Enterprises attached to it."

I stopped midway down the steps. "You're sure?"

"I wouldn't call you on Thanksgiving for shits and giggles."

"Vick and Bob scrutinized the letter to them for hours before sending. They received it?"

"You saw the copied e-mail with the attached letter as well as I did, Jett."

I hummed and looked down at myself in the hall mirror. The lines on my face had deepened over the years and the muscles through my body were this tense most of the time. The business took its toll and then it kept taking.

"I can take care of it my way or we can do it your way."

"My way's cleaner," I answered, but I hated to do it.

Vick rounded the corner at the base of the stairs and looked up with a smile on her face. It died when she saw my expression. She moved to my side and rubbed a hand over my chest. "You okay?" she whispered.

Bastian blurted, "That Vick with you?"

"Doesn't matter."

"It does. Let me talk to her."

"No. We do this my way. I'll pull investments and revoke the partnership on the dairy company the FDA is backing." My stomach should have bottomed out. I'd essentially rolled down my window and started throwing stacks of hundred-dollar bills out of it.

"It'll be a tremendous loss," Bastian warned.

"I'm aware, and I'm the only one capable of handling that loss without it bankrupting me."

"It takes me a lot less to—"

"Bastian," I stopped him. "My company. My rules. You pulled me in. Now fuck off. It's Thanksgiving."

I hung up, and Vick squinted at me. "Levvetor's deal is going to shit."

"It's handled."

"Handled with how many millions?" she pried.

"Lots." I put my arm around her shoulders and turned her back toward the bottom of the stairs. "Now, let's go get interrogated by my family."

She didn't move. She grabbed my bicep to stop me. "You're sure about this?"

"You said we were saving lives with this company, right? You wanted this, right?"

She recoiled at my words. I knew she would. "I did but…"

"Don't ever second-guess yourself if you wanted it badly enough to fight for it in the beginning. If it was worth it then, it's worth it now."

Her eyes searched mine. Then she straightened up and squeezed my bicep. "I think it's worth it."

"And you're worth it." I winked at her and she looked at me completely confused. I pulled her down the stairs. "Let's go. I'm hungry."

CHAPTER
THIRTY-TWO

VICK

THANKSGIVING DINNER COULD be tacos, a salad, or even McDonald's. So long as you were with a family that loved one another, it was special. Holidays brought waves of frustration and happiness for me.

My mother called just before we sat down to dinner.

"Happy Thanksgiving, Mom."

"Happy Thanksgiving, Victory," she replied softly, her heartfelt tone completely genuine. My mother loved me. She just loved me so much she smothered me and tried to protect me from the one thing she couldn't. "How's your day?"

"Great." I glanced up at Jett who nodded at me and left me in the foyer to give me privacy. "I'm having a great time with my friends. I needed it this year."

"I get that." The softness in her voice carried over as if trying to appease me. "I understand we don't see eye to eye on your care, honey."

"It's okay, Mom. It's the holiday. We don't have to discuss it now."

"I don't know when to discuss it though," she confessed, her voice breaking a little.

The guilt trapped me, weighted me down in a way I couldn't escape. I closed my eyes and leaned into the wall, hoping it would provide even the least bit of support. "Maybe you can come visit me this weekend."

"Okay!" She spat out so fast, I instantly regretted it. "I'll bring your father. We'll make a day of it. The nutritionist said he's had a hard time getting ahold of you."

I opened my mouth to give an excuse.

She rushed on though. "No worries. I told him you got a new job, sweetie. It's hard to keep up with everything. I made a list of the changes he felt might help. And your doctor's appointment is tomorrow, right?"

I winced because I'd lied about setting up that appointment. I needed to find a new doctor in the area and make one. The idea of revisiting my whole medical history made me nauseous. "Yeah. Um, it was a day I had off. So, I figured I would get it out of the way."

"That's so wonderful. Have you called the doctor's office to send over your medical history or is that something I can help you with?"

My mother was a businesswoman on a mission. She knew just the right question to ask. "I have it handled, Mom."

"Just making sure." She laughed lightly. "I'm so excited to see you on Saturday. Text me your address, and we'll be there by lunch, okay?"

"Sure, Mom."

"I love you so much, Victory. Have a wonderful Thanksgiving. Make sure you follow your dietary guidelines tonight. I know it's hard on the holidays but—"

"I'm fine, Mom." I kept a firm hold on my voice to stop the aggravation from bleeding through.

"Oh, your dad wants to talk with you, of course."

I peered around the corner, and all the Stonewoods seemed to be carrying on just fine.

"How you doing, Ms. MIA?"

"Oh, you know, still here."

"Damn right you are. Thanksgiving isn't the same without you here," he grumbled, and I knew he was walking away from my mother.

"I know, Dad."

"I miss you. She misses you. She might not say it outright, but she's just coping in her own way." He always felt the need to explain her to me, as if I didn't understand.

"There's no need to cope with anything. I'm fine here. I'm really, really enjoying the city and my job."

"I know, Vick. I know. She doesn't have her job or you to manage anymore though. She's an empty nester on steroids," he chuckled.

My gut clenched a little at hearing the deep rumble that was so friendly, so soothing, so much a reminder of what home and the holidays were with him. "I'll be home for Christmas. We'll decorate the tree together. I'll come home for it, okay?"

"Yeah, yeah. Don't come for my benefit. I can handle her. I just think you need to face each other soon. Something's gotta give."

"Okay," I whispered.

"She's getting antsy. So, if you mean for her to visit this weekend, mean it. But just know, she's antsy."

'Antsy' was code for my mother losing her sanity.

I hummed into the phone and told him I loved him. I didn't want to think about the weekend now or how to deal with my mother. I needed to enjoy the today. Every holiday deserved enjoyment, deserved loved ones laughing together if they had the good fortune to be in one another's company.

My mouth watered at the rich aroma of roasted turkey as I entered the dining room. The warmth from the gathered bodies intensified the scent of the sweet apple candles, dissolving every concern weighting down my shoulders. I smiled at Brey and Jaydon laughing over their drinks.

"You guys," I waltzed over to them and eyed the liquid steaming from their mugs. "I'm behind already, aren't I?"

"Nancy spiked the tea hard this time," Brey admitted with a giggle. "Jaydon, go get her one."

He winked and clapped me on the shoulder, "I got you."

As he disappeared into the kitchen, Brey whispered to me, "Nancy wants us girls to take a walk. Jax and Jett are off somewhere talking about his app."

"Oh." I ran my hand over the mahogany dining room table. The grain pooled beautifully in places, and yet the gloss smoothed the surface to glass. "Are we eating in here?"

Brey straightened her black jumpsuit. "No. Nancy thinks the table is too big. I think Jax's dad had this room decorated for business dinners back in the day."

The rich tones and dark woods definitely screamed luxury and wealth. "Where are we going to eat then?"

Brey pointed toward the kitchen. "There's another dining area on the other side of the kitchen."

Nancy breezed in with Jaydon, who held a drink for me.

"Should we go for a walk?"

Jaydon handed over a white mug with dark steaming liquid inside it. "I'm coming for the walk," he announced.

"It's just us girls," Nancy softly corrected him.

"Girls are my best friends, Mom. I'm coming." Jaydon held his ground and when his mom didn't say anything, he started toward the door. "You're all going to need coats. It's getting chilly."

We bundled up and stepped into the cool outdoors. Brey and Nancy discussed a few of the neighbors as we strolled the small town's streets. I listened quietly while I absorbed the suburban atmosphere.

Brey had grown up next door, but the house was long gone. It had been torn down a few years after the fire and someone had built a brand new place on the lot. She glanced at it as we passed, and I wondered if she felt erased or forgotten.

Maybe she wanted that, to feel that part of her life was gone, but grappling with the invisibility of something so traumatic rattled a person.

I wanted to forget my cancer. Every hospital I passed, every clinic I avoided going to, every nutritionist phone call I declined popped holes in my confidence of being able to move on from my past.

The wind picked up, and we burrowed further into our sweaters and scarves. Leaves flew circles around us and the crisp autumn air reminded us that winter could, and most likely would, be bitingly cold.

We rounded their block, and a lake rippled with ducks and geese up ahead.

"This is my favorite place," Brey said, then sighed at the view. The sun reflected millions of diamonds off the surface of the water. She continued on, "I found myself and my family here."

"We found you too." Nancy put her arm around Brey and squeezed. "Your mom would have been so proud of you. She'd think I need grandchildren soon, but ... "

We all laughed at Nancy's blatant entreaty. The woman was desperate for grandbabies and Brey had been like a daughter to her for so long that her marriage being only months old made no difference.

"Jax and I need time to work on ourselves before we bring a little human into this world."

"That never stops, Brey," Nancy sighed. "You'll be working on yourselves forever. Look at me and Joe."

I couldn't control my eyes widening a bit. No one called that man by his first name. To hear her do it felt wrong, and yet she did it with no hesitation, like she wasn't at all intimidated by him.

"Dad needs to work on himself, Mom," Jaydon blurted out. "Not you."

"You were a mama's boy from the second I birthed you, Jaydon," Nancy teased.

"And I'll be one till the day I die," he chuckled.

"You might take my side, but I need to work on myself too. I need to work at a lot of things if we are going to really give this relationship a go. Everyone compromises in relationships."

Nancy said the words while looking at me, like I needed to read between the lines.

"Your dad quit the company, but he'll never quit working. He loves it too much." She sighed. "I love that about him too. We needed balance when you were children though."

"You Stonewoods don't balance anything very well," Brey murmured.

Jaydon bumped his shoulder into hers. "You're a Stonewood, too, Sass Pot. You don't balance well either."

"I do too," she contested.

"You work long hours and you're barely considering making me an uncle and my mom a grandma."

Her green eyes flared, and she shoved her shoulder harder into his. "I'm supposed to give you a niece or nephew when you're barely in town? No thanks."

"That's what uncles do! They fly into town, spoil the kids, and fly out. I have to make movies. I'm over there trying to make this world feel something."

"Your rom-coms are really making people feel things, all right," she mumbled and looked at me. "Did you see his last rom-com? He barely said two words."

"Well, in Jaydon's defense, no one really wanted him or his costar to talk anyway. Them walking around in their swimsuits the whole movie was enough for everyone." I smiled sweetly at Jaydon and he glared at me with betrayal in his eyes.

"You love my abs just like every other woman in the world."

I shrugged and sipped on the remains of my hot spiked tea. "I'm not denying that. It's why the movie did so well."

"Agreed," Nancy chimed in. "You got paid solely for your work-out schedule and not your acting skills with that one. Hopefully, you'll pick a better story line for the next movie."

"Mom!" Jaydon whined but the smile creeping across his face said he could take the heat and knew we were right. "You're supposed to be on my side always."

"I'm a mother of truth. Not lies. That movie was awful, honey."

He guffawed at that, and the sounds of the holiday—of us laughing and sharing jokes—rolled through the wind and over the lake.

"LA is expensive and that movie paid the bills," he admitted.

Brey shrugged. "You have more talent than that, Jaydon. The world is waiting to see it."

He sobered and stared out at the lake. He didn't comment, but I saw the look in his eyes. I saw the doubt we all carry in ourselves. "If you say so, Sass Pot."

I waited for Nancy to jump in and push him. My mother would have. She would have driven home my talent, explained what it was to be a Blakely, and ground my doubt into dust.

Nancy didn't say a thing. She rubbed her son's back and then she turned toward her beautiful home to announce, "Let's get back, huh? Dinner should be ready soon."

We walked back through some woods and up a hill. Nancy fell into step beside me as Brey and Jaydon chatted behind us.

"I meant what I said before," she murmured, not facing me.

I tilted my head, trying to remember her words. "I'm sorry?"

"Everyone compromises in relationships."

"Oh. Right," I agreed, not knowing where the conversation was going but sure this woman was going to try to mold me into the person she wanted for her son. I didn't blame her for it. Every mother wanted the best for their child. I just didn't know if I would agree with her, if I could compromise any more of my life for Jett. I had compromised so much just to be here.

"He works too much. He doesn't bend. He's insanely controlling. He used to make his two brothers sit down for class in the middle of summer, I kid you not. He would instruct them. He was born to be the businessman he is. I know that. I just honestly don't know if he has it in him to be anything else."

I wanted to say something to make her feel better, but her words dried up the water that had fed the hope flower blooming in my soul.

"I love him. It's why I'm warning you. He never brings women home for the holidays. He wants something with you. I can't quite figure out if he has it in him to give a woman what she needs though." Her laugh skittered into the wind, filled with sadness. "I'm not sure because he's like his father, and I still struggle every single day to figure out if that man can give me what I need. I see that look in your eyes. It's the same look I've had for years. You love him."

I stopped her. "I don't." I was falling but I wasn't there yet. Or so I kept telling myself.

"You may think that now. But you'll see. You will if you don't already. You're worried that you'll never get the love you put in returned, and I'm here telling you I honestly don't know that you will. I wish I could say differently because I really, really want grandkids."

A sad laugh burst out of me. I let it overtake me so it could suppress the sudden need to cry.

Nancy grabbed and held my hand the rest of the way home.

Dinner with the Stonewoods didn't make me feel any better. We sat at a small table in a brightly lit room, everyone shoved together so close our legs touched the person next to us. Jett took advantage and held my thigh through most of the dinner. The crackling fire added to the cozy ambience. I drank extra liquor and tried to immerse myself in the comfort of a close family that loved one another.

Jett left the window open that night and we snuggled close, keeping warm with just our body heat.

I stayed up much later than anyone else in that house. I'd smiled through dinner and enjoyed everyone's company, but Nancy's words echoed through me; they played on repeat over and over again.

As Jett held me close, I wondered if it was better to risk the time I wasn't sure I had on a man who made me feel like life could be firework after firework, each time with him a flash of sparkling color. Or was that time a waste? Would it be better spent on a man sure to deliver my dream of marriage and what I thought was ultimate happiness?

My mind spun a web of possibilities.

Jett and I drove home late Friday. I sent him off with the excuse that my parents were coming to town the next morning.

Yet, that weekend I cocooned myself away from the world. I didn't answer Jett's call, and I didn't invite him over. I ignored every one of my mother's calls and didn't text her my address. I retreated into myself, swallowed up by the what ifs and the angry voice inside that said maybe I had no time to waste, maybe that terrible enemy that was cancer would take me quicker than I had anticipated.

The fear overcame me and I let it.

I let the dread and the anxiety and the depression creep back in. I dug through my closet, pulled out the old photos and hospital papers and proof of the wreckage that had been my life. I shed ugly tears, drowning myself in the tragedy. I wanted to be happy. I should have been happy. Yet, I let the cancer I was supposed to have beaten consume me and dictate my life.

I was to blame for the days that came after, no matter what anyone says. I was responsible for the devastation that found me.

CHAPTER
THIRTY-THREE

JETT

SOMETHING HAD SHAKEN Victory Blakely.

I didn't navigate shaken women well. I didn't navigate them at all.

Work always came first. But somehow, over the course of the past few months, Victory had become more important than work. Thanksgiving with her solidified it.

Yet, over the weekend, my doubts crept back in. She was avoiding me, and I couldn't figure out why. I didn't know if I wanted to, if this was the shit I was going to have to go through. Women were difficult. Business, I'd learned. I'd wrestled with it and won, I knew how to handle it.

Victory wasn't business.

And even in my business, she'd taken what I thought I'd known, put it in a jar, added her freaking pixie dust, and shaken it all up. My team ran better with her. They practically ran for her.

I got to work early Monday.

Bastian called to let me know the head of Levvetor wanted a meeting with us that morning, and of course a board member of the FDA wanted in on it since I'd threatened their dairy trade. Cards fell fast when the strings you pulled had money attached to them.

When I walked through the lobby doors, I was surprised to see Vick. She normally arrived early, but today, she'd shown up at the same time I did—hours before anyone else got there.

"You're early," I said to her back when I reached the elevator.

She didn't turn around. Her long blonde hair fell from a high ponytail, straight down her back to a pink point. I knew better than most that hair felt like silk, moved like liquid, and was easy to wrap around my knuckles before I fisted it.

Today she dressed in a muted gray, but her shoes popped bright orange and matched the band she always wore on her wrist.

"Victory," I growled out her name, wanting her attention as the elevator made its way down toward us.

Her back slumped like she knew she had to turn.

When she did, I almost took a step back. Her eyes searched mine and ripped through my soul, stealing all the happiness from it. "Are you … " I trailed off, not knowing how to ask the question, not knowing this side of her.

"I'm aware I ignored you this weekend. I'm struggling with some personal things. I—" The ping of the opening elevator doors cut her off. We walked in, and the doors closed on us. She faced the wall and grabbed one of the rails. "I'm good at bliss, Jett. You know this about me."

"Mm-hmm," I agreed, waiting for her to continue. When she didn't, when I realized Vick may not be able to get through the workday, I stepped forward and swiped my FOB. It shut down the lit floor buttons, and the elevator shot up to my penthouse instead. Each of us had a floor to ourselves, one that was our own private haven if we needed it.

"I want so much to be just fun."

She shoved off the railing and turned toward me. She stalked over and slammed her hand onto the wall close to me. "I earned the fun. I bled for it, agonized over it, worked my ass off to build a place I could have it. All for what? For this?" She motioned at me. "To feel this for you? The one guy who can only give me a 'maybe' when I deserve a 'hell yes'?"

I took her by the elbow and walked her into my living space. She didn't even look around. Her glare stayed on me, waiting for me to respond. "Nothing is that concrete, Pix."

"Some relationships are."

"If you think that—"

"I do."

"Where's all this coming from? We had a good time over the holiday," I countered, trying to bring her down off the ledge of disdain she was on.

"That's just it. I want holidays like that every single holiday. I want a big family around, people laughing, telling stories, bickering over nothing. I want it all for as long as I can have it."

"Then come to the holidays at my house," I said, confused. "You don't get those at yours? I'm happy to have you come."

She shook her head slowly. "You don't get it."

"Don't get what?"

"You couldn't possibly get it, and I'm not sure you ever will."

"Explain it then."

"No!" she screamed. Her eyes widened, and she took a step back. "No, Jett. This isn't something I can explain to you." All the emotion, all the pain disappeared from her face as she slowly blinked and took a deep breath.

"Where do we go from here then?"

"Back to what you're good at, Jett."

"What's that?"

"Work." She turned back toward the elevator and her display of yo-yoing emotion pushed me to just concede and follow her. We had a damn long day ahead of us. I'd figure it out with her later. I'd make sure she understood that we had something.

Today, we just had to get through the meeting.

We rode the elevator in silence, and when we got to our floor, Gloria greeted us. "You're early today too."

I nodded to her, but she buzzed about her desk, not paying me much attention.

When she saw Victory, she shot forward though.

"Harvey from Levvetor will be at the meeting today. He requested that both of you be there," she announced.

Her eyes were on Vick like she desperately needed the woman to know something. And Vick responded by freezing. Her whole body turned rigid. "Why me? How does he know I work here?"

Gloria softly responded, "Bastian told him."

"Great," Vick grumbled.

"The FDA rep will be there too. Gloria, please make sure we have the room set up. I don't intend for the meeting to go on long."

Vick's phone went off, the ringtone signaled her mother was calling. I wasn't surprised when she silenced it and pushed past me to get to her desk.

"I'll have the room ready," Gloria murmured. "And Jett?"

"Yes?"

"Your day is about to become very difficult. Remember, it's worth it."

Gloria sometimes got that way with me, giving foreboding advice. At first, I ignored it, but when it became a reality every single time, I started paying close attention. Now, I took her words like the gospel they were.

"What aren't you telling me?"

"Exactly what I can't tell you."

At 1:15 p.m. on the dot, Bastian and Cade Armanelli waltzed in wearing all black suits with two large guys trailing them. Their presence today was purely to intimidate, not negotiate. I saw it in their eyes, in the fact that they didn't bring a corporate team but a mob team.

I shook my head at Bastian. "Your muscle isn't necessary here."

"And yet, I feel better having it just in case."

"Suit yourself," I shrugged and waved them into the conference room. I'd asked Bob, Gloria, and Jax to be at the meeting. No one else needed to be present, but Harvey had requested Vick. She waited at the table, stock-still. Her thick gray-speckled dress looked as stiff as she did. The last thing I needed on my mind was an angry woman—especially the one I was sleeping with—during one of the most important meetings of the year.

Mr. Young, the rep from the FDA, was ushered in by Gloria. She let him know he could take a seat wherever he liked.

"Jett Stonewood." I offered my hand and he took it in his meaty one. His firm handshake didn't linger or squeeze me too hard. After our research, I knew he was only about ten years older than me. For the type of position he held in the FDA, I was surprised by how young he was.

"Weston Young. Nice to finally meet you. Little unfortunate that it's under these circumstances."

"Agreed." I turned toward the conference table. "Have a seat and as soon as Harvey gets here, we'll talk."

"Sure." As he introduced himself to people around the table, Vick stood up and gave that terrible fake smile that I knew was bull-shit. My team followed suit, and then Weston got to the Armanellis. I saw the way his hand trembled as he took Bastian's.

He knew exactly who was at the table and exactly the risk he took by being here.

After a few moments, laughter could be heard in the hall; voices of both a man and a woman. Levvetor's main man, Harvey, strutted in, a sparkle in his eye as he announced himself and the woman next to him.

"Everyone,"—his voice boomed, boisterous as ever—"I can't thank you enough for coming out today. We need this. Levvetor needs this. Right?"

He turned to the tall blonde woman who stood in front of us as if on a stage, hands folded perfectly in front of her, nails painted the same color as her dress, and her amber eyes scanning the room just the way Vick's did. When they landed on Victory, they hardened.

Like mother, like daughter. Vick's body jolted with an emotion I'd never seen on her. She glanced at me in dread and then back at her mother. She mouthed, "No," trying to silently communicate something before the meeting started.

Harvey rambled on though. He saw nothing transpiring. He'd come to put on a show, and he would do it, come hell or high water.

"Mrs. Blakely was wonderful enough to accompany me to the meeting. The FDA has concerns about our product. Isn't that right?"

Mr. Young stood and introduced himself. Then he went on to say, "We thoroughly test every product that we make available to cancer patients. I'm a part of that team. I'm happy to meet you today and discuss it."

"It'll come to a vote within your administration, but I want you to know the side you should be voting for. I think we can do that without Jett discussing dairy and without Bastian here, huh?" He tried to nudge Weston gently into his court.

"I hope so. Right now, I need to see more evidence. We're working on testing, and I hope your teams are working on alternative ingredients too."

Harvey nodded vigorously and then turned to Mrs. Blakely again. "I wanted to introduce you to Mrs. Blakely. She and Vick here, who is an employee of Stonewood Enterprises, can provide you with a perfect example of why this drug needs to be an option for patients with leukemia."

Since the age of eighteen, I'd been privy to major negotiations. I'd been in conference rooms where people screamed at one another, threatened each other's lives, negotiated billions of dollars, voted down saving thousands of lives. I watched my father never, ever show his true feelings in those meetings. He was the boss. The unwavering, rock-solid foundation of Stonewood Enterprises.

Harvey's words tested my composure as the new boss. No part of me should have portrayed surprise at his words. Quite frankly, I should have already had the information. But my mind scrambled to catch up, snapping up bits of memory to come to a quick conclusion: Victory's mom must have had leukemia. It all made sense—her desperation to save the company that saved her mother, her knowledge of Levvetor when Bastian brought it up, avoiding her mother's calls, unable to cope with their new relationship.

I studied her picking at the corner of one of her nails, head down. Going over to shake her and ask why she never confided in me wasn't a possibility now. Wasn't a damn option.

Mrs. Blakely took a breath and her voice cut through the air with precision and purpose. "My family doesn't go to great lengths to share our story because it doesn't define us. We're Blakelys. We define ourselves. When we battle something as terrifying as cancer, we're humbled. Vick, Harvey wants our family to do a commercial," she whispered the last statement.

My pixie shot up from her chair, no longer a little bundle of fun. Her eyes bounced around the room, finally resting on her mother. One word bled from her, a world of emotion packed into it. "No."

Her mother stepped forward, ready to argue. "This is for the company, Vick. It's for others who've gone through the same thing."

"It's not fair to ask me to do that."

Harvey jumped in. "If you can't…" He hung his head like he understood. The man came in loud and proud but it seemed the Blakelys held a special place in his heart, one he didn't want to tarnish by capitalizing on their experience.

"She can," Bastian said from the end of the table. His eyes were dark, his words final. "She will. If the commercial puts this drug in a place where people trust it. We do it."

Vick turned on him, a wounded animal, fighting for her life. "You know what I went through, and you want to put me through more?"

"I want you to fight for this even if it means bleeding for it," he countered.

She searched the room, and her eyes fell on me. Unshed tears pooled in them like she knew something was about to change, like we were approaching something she couldn't turn away from. She blinked once and one tear spilled over as she said, "Okay."

I understood not wanting her family in the spotlight but people would appreciate that her mother had survived this. They would respect the woman more. There was no downside.

None that I could see.

Harvey pulled out a laptop and explained they'd already actualized a commercial they felt was a great start. Weston asked if this had anything to do with the ingredients, and Harvey put him off by saying this was a better testament to the drug's effectiveness.

The commercial started.

The first five seconds of the video showed Victory, probably high school aged, with family and friends on her birthday, laughing and enjoying the celebration. The music changed as it faded to black. A long, low note from the piano signified we were about to see Mrs. Blakely stricken with cancer.

When the screen revealed Victory in the hospital, my body convulsed with shock. My blood ran cold, the tips of my fingers tingled. I lost the air in my lungs along with the ability to think. I lost the ability to comprehend.

I was supposed to sit, apathetic, like a damn rock, but a tsunami of confusion, frustration, and some emotion I couldn't put my finger on barreled through me.

"Get out," I whispered.

Victory was probably the only one who heard because she stared at me with those same desolate eyes.

My body felt like a damn grenade had gone off inside it. I was supposed to sit there and not react, not feel the shards of emotion puncturing the insides of my soul. She'd never told me. She'd never thought to confide in me, to help me understand her. She'd never wanted me to really know her. She'd worn a mask better than I ever could. She'd painted a picture like Picasso. She'd had me living in a reverie I never, ever wanted.

"Get the fuck out!" The words thundered out of me like a cannon releasing its fury.

Everyone but Vick exchanged confused stares, except for Bastian, who nodded and ushered his crew out. "Let's give them a minute."

They filed out just as the commercial ended, leaving us in silence.

I waited. And waited, recognizing the calm before the storm. I knew the eerie silence before a battle must have felt just like this.

Still, I waited.

Her hair cascaded down over her face as she hid from me, looking down at the table.

Her small frame curled in like she finally, finally was afraid of something.

A fear gripped me too. Because I'd been hit with the realization that I loved her and didn't know a thing about what she'd been through. The fear that I could lose her wasn't just a trick of jealousy anymore. Cancer. Ugly. Deathly. Too fucking real to ignore. Cancer gobbled up jealousy and presented a truly terrifying opponent, one I wasn't sure I could control.

"So, Victory Blakely, turns out you're the Phantom behind the mask and I've been the one living in Neverland."

CHAPTER
THIRTY-FOUR

VICK

LIFE FLASHES BEFORE you sometimes. In snippets, on a film reel, in a damn commercial if your mother decides to put it out there for the world to see. And, God, did they ever see it.

I remember each of the moments before the coma and, savvy marketer that she was, she made sure there was a clip of me in that coma too. The summer before I found out I had cancer, we celebrated my sixteenth birthday. I was getting my driver's license. I was going to go to homecoming. I was potentially going to be voted onto the homecoming court. I played tennis, I cheered, I had so many damn friends. I looked like the cute, happy, all-American teenager. With two loving parents who made good money and no siblings, I was spoiled rotten.

When the doctor called with irregular blood results, we didn't think anything of it.

At sixteen, hormones are all over the place. I was tired for no other reason than my busy sports schedule and maybe some fluctuations due to the birth control I was on.

The doctor ordered more tests. The worst one was the bone marrow biopsy. My mother held my hand. I didn't scream because I was a Blakely, but I saw the way my mother's face tightened, how her jaw flexed and felt how her hand squeezed mine. Blakelys felt pain just like everyone else, and we both endured it at that moment.

Every single pain I went through, my mother did as well. I learned very quickly how much she loved me. How much she cringed and broke with each of my treatments.

I tucked that pain away from my parents because I loved them too. I held on to my family when my friends turned away, when they realized they didn't know how to act around the girl who couldn't play volleyball anymore, who was in a coma during prom, who was in the hospital for weeks.

I cleared my throat. "It isn't something I talk about to most people, Jett. Obviously, a Levvetor drug saved my life."

"Am I 'most people'?" The question wrenched out of him.

I finally lifted my head and pushed my hair behind my ear to look at him. I had avoided this exact encounter with so many, knowing I'd see the pity or the change in their eyes. I didn't want any of it. I wanted to be treated exactly the same as I had been before they knew I had cancer. But no one could do that. And Jett wasn't any different. His azure gaze drowned in pity and sympathy, but there was another emotion there.

Anger.

"Jett, people don't want to hear about a disease that tormented me. Cancer makes people squirm."

"I'll ask the question again. Am I 'most people' to you?"

I sighed and bent the paper in front of me. I focused on lining up the edges and creasing it neatly in two as I said, "I don't know what you are to me."

"Well, I'll inform you then. I'm the guy who screws you into oblivion and then stays to see the sun rise on your skin. I'm the guy who wakes up thinking of you and goes to sleep only to dream about you. I'm your boss, but I'm also your lover. I'm definitely your only boyfriend, and I'm the one who you've been contemplating spending your life with even if you don't want to admit it."

I crumpled up the folded piece of paper. It had Levvetor facts on it which I didn't need to know. I already knew that three out of every five of their terminal leukemia patients recovered in some way. Did they go into remission like me? Not always. And mostly, the companies didn't track patients past the five-year survival point.

I was a statistic, and I was a damn good one in their eyes. None of it mattered if I couldn't find a way to live with it though.

"Most days, I wake up wondering if it will be the day I start to feel a little more tired, if I'll maybe get a pain in my bones that will signal the cancer is back. Most days, I'm determined to wake up and avoid every reminder of that looming statistic, the one that Levvetor and all those pharmaceutical companies promote. I'm a damn good stat in their eyes. I've survived past their five-year studies, and they don't even follow up any more. To them, I survived and their job is done. Yet, every single day, I feel like I'm dying. Like I'm not living big enough, well enough, not experiencing enough. So, yeah, I don't want the reminder from you, or anyone else, that I'm a survivor or that I had leukemia. I want to forget it."

"Who's to say I'm going to remind you?" he whispered.

"You'll remind me every time you look at me with pity in your eyes. And even if you aren't thinking about my past, I'll wonder if you are whenever you ask me how I'm doing or how I've been feeling. My paranoia will creep in, and I'll never feel like the invincible girl you saw before they played that godforsaken commercial."

"I never thought you were invincible. I thought you were naïve," he stated matter-of-factly.

"Well, I don't know if that's better or worse than what you think now." I shoved away from the table and stood. "Does it matter? We should never have come this far. I should have walked away before I started falling in love with you."

His nostrils flared, but I didn't care anymore. None of this mattered. He wasn't going to be my perfect ending because I wasn't going to get a perfect ending. No one did. We came into the world alone and we would leave it alone. In between, I'd continue to find ways to stave off the anxieties.

"Yes. You should have walked away. I'm not going to baby you and tell you that you shouldn't have. I'm not a damn prince or a knight in shining armor. I have a business to run, Victory."

"Then run it! I'm not asking you to do anything else."

"Yet, here we are: me screaming at everyone to get out of a very important meeting because my girlfriend didn't care to enlighten me about the video of her deepest secret being shown to the whole office."

"I had no idea my mother was coming today. You have to believe that. That footage was all her doing."

"I do believe that, unfortunately." He rubbed his fingers over his eyes. "You don't have to sign off on that commercial."

"I do," I countered and turned away as I said the words. "Bastian's right. He knows I can handle this. I should handle it."

"Bastian had no idea what they were going to show. He wouldn't expect—" He stopped mid-sentence. His jaw worked, and I saw how his muscles tightened as the truth plowed into him. "You told Bastian."

I didn't have to agree or disagree. My silence amplified his rage. It rolled through the room, building like a snowball, like an avalanche, ready to suffocate and swallow us whole.

"You told Bastian! Fuck, woman!" he yelled and his fist flew down onto the table. The crack of bone hitting solid wood didn't deter him from pounding it again.

"You're going to break your hand," I murmured.

"Will that wake you up?"

"Wake me up to what?"

"To the fact that you jeopardized our relationship before it even started. You didn't come to me about this. You went around me and under me and over me but never *to* me. You never gave me the option to have an opinion, and you never showed me the respect of telling me what was really going on with this deal."

"So, it's about the business now?"

"It's about everything." The pain of his stare ripped through me. "You had cancer, Pix."

He emphasized the word, and I knew it was gutting him. My mother and father got that same look when they couldn't help me but wanted to, when they wanted to mask their pain and fear but couldn't.

"I'm still here, Jett," I whispered. I wasn't dying any faster than before, I wasn't any different. I was just me with a past he hadn't been expecting. He scanned me up and down like he would be able to see the disease, like the scars were visible, like the cancer that had lived deep down in my bones might crawl out and attack. "It's just me."

He walked up so close, his chest was a hair's breadth away. I smelled his cologne, and his exhalation was a whisper on my lips. He lifted one hand as if he was going to hold my face.

Yet, he didn't touch me, my skin was different to him now. Maybe it was tainted; maybe I was too ruined, too damaged. He curled his hand up and fisted it as he drew it back to his side and squeezed his eyes shut.

"I was trying to get to know you, I was falling for this vibrant being who lived on the edge, not knowing why. And then"—his eyes shot open—"I find you didn't trust me with some of the most important pieces of your life. You trusted a stranger though. You trusted someone I don't even trust with my business. You gave him sensitive information about yourself—my girlfriend—and the deal."

"You make it sound so bad." I shook my head and tried to process how to meet his argument head-on. "The information was on a need to know—"

"Don't come at me with some bullshit. I don't care what it was." He collapsed into his chair like I'd defeated him, like he wasn't the most ruthless businessman in all the world. His face had fallen. His downturned mouth and his closed-off eyes made me wonder if we could come back from this. "You were supposed to be the light with no dark. You weren't supposed to have all the complicated bullshit of reality, Pix."

"And you were supposed to be able to handle all the complicated bullshit, Phantom."

He grunted but didn't look my way. He stood from the table and started toward the door. "Do what you want with the commercial. It's your life."

My heart splintered. His words felt final. The darkness that had crept in over the weekend seeped further into my soul. The depths of despair clawed at the surface. Shadows stole in, doubts and fears and things that shook me awake in the night.

He asked everyone to reenter the room and apologized for his outburst as they filtered back in.

I nodded as the meeting continued. I said all the right things. I smiled. I put on the show I needed to put on as the grief swallowed me whole.

My mother stopped me after the meeting. "I'm sorry, Vick. I had to come. Harvey called. I tried to contact you. I tried to see you this weekend. But you didn't answer or text me back."

"It's fine." My tone was clipped, but I knew I'd pushed her away. I had ignored her so much that this was my fault. My heart wasn't in it to be mad at her. My heart wasn't in anything anymore. It was broken, shattered on the ground, smashed to little fragments I was sure I wouldn't be able to piece back together.

"Honey,"—she cupped my jaw the way I had wanted Jett to—"I love you. You're hurting, and it isn't that commercial that hurt you. Maybe you should come home for a few days."

I sighed and tried my best not to let the tears fall. I looked toward the ceiling. "I should get back to work."

I didn't talk to Jett the rest of the day. He disappeared into his office, and I couldn't find the strength to face him, to know he was done with me, to know we were over.

I went home early that night. I didn't stick around to talk with anyone. My phone rang once or twice, but I didn't answer.

I took a long shower. I drank a few glasses of wine. I cried quietly. I didn't break though.

I told myself the next day I would get up and go to work with a damn smile on my face even if the boss was my ex. I'd had him and not even really known.

Sleep never came. I tried counting sheep but the only things hopping over a fence were my regrets.

The next morning, I got ready like it was any other day. I put on bright yellow to channel the sun, to illuminate my smile, to appear lighter than my soul would ever feel again. I repeated to myself how I'd known Jett and I wouldn't last. I told myself I would handle it. But it was like barbed wire had coiled itself around my heart, constricting everything. The blood wasn't pumping right, the oxygen wasn't circulating.

As I got onto the train, I felt it. The jump in my heart. The little skitter, not even really a skip. The light flutter that should have signaled to me that something was off. I didn't pay it any attention. Health anxiety consumed me when I was first told I didn't have cancer anymore. I conditioned myself to ignore the signs, to curve my mind's attention away from my body's symptoms. I took a deep breath and reminded myself that my heart was breaking, the crushing weight was normal.

I remember stepping off the train. I remember how the clouds looked so, so gray. Like the rain was coming. Like the bleakness and the turmoil swirling in them wanted out, wanted to dampen the world and bring us all down.

The first drop was the one that did me in. It hit my cheek harder than a bullet, and I couldn't take any more pressure.

Witnesses say I looked confused, disoriented as I made my way across the street, that I stopped to look up at the first drops of rain. When the car hit me, I went down without a fight. My eyes rolled to the back of my head before I even hit the ground.

CHAPTER
THIRTY-FIVE

JETT

I **HADN'T LOOKED UP** from my computer since I'd arrived that morning, long before anyone else. I'd blacked out the windows and put my focus where it needed to be.

Victory Blakely had stolen too much of my attention already. She'd muscled her way into my thoughts, my dreams, and my damn hopes for the future.

And I wasn't a man who planned happily ever afters.

In the conference room, we'd gone back and forth about her keeping the one secret she should have told me. But I understood why she hadn't. I saw the fear in her eyes, the way she'd seized up during that commercial.

Like a puzzle piece clicking into place, it all made sense. She rushed into life head-on, afraid she'd run out of time to live. She focused on the good, the positive, the brightness of life because she didn't want to waste time with the crushing darkness of the reality she'd already endured.

I couldn't sleep thinking about how she drew people in with her magnetic optimism, the force actually helped her maintain a buoyant momentum despite her depressing past. My heart ached.

My pride held on to being right with a death grip. She should have told me. I should have been the first person to know. Not Bastian. Not a damn stranger.

I sighed and took two of the paperweights in my hand to roll round and round.

Brey shoved the door to my office open so violently it would have smacked the wall had we not installed a door stopper. "What did you say to her?"

I raised my eyebrows at the dark-haired woman my brother married. Her face was tight with emotion, and her green eyes blazed bright against her olive skin. She shook with anger. I knew she wanted to lash out—her claws were sharpened, her fangs bared.

I didn't reply. I waited. Just as in business, waiting pushed people to open up, even when it was personal.

"She didn't come to work, and she didn't answer my calls last night. Jax told me about the…" Her eyes closed momentarily in pain. "I should have known. She never told me. But you did something. She wouldn't have skipped work because of this."

I looked back at my keyboard, pride rearing its ugly head because she hadn't called me either, and I wanted her to apologize. I knew I should be apologizing too. I wanted her to do it first though. "Maybe she's sick."

"Get real!" Brey bellowed.

I jumped at the volume of her voice. "Woman, we are at work."

She folded her arms across her chest. "You think I care about that more than I care about the well-being of my friend?" She waited a beat and when I met her with silence, she stalked toward my desk and slammed my laptop closed. "Call her right now!"

"I'm not calling her, Brey."

She narrowed those blazing emeralds at me. I set down my paperweights and lined them up. "You should get back to work."

Maybe she contemplated it as she chewed the inside of her cheek, but I doubt it. Because the next thing I knew, she swiped the paperweights off my desk so forcefully, the burst of color shattered everywhere.

Then she slammed her hand down on the desk. "Call her and find out where she is. Now."

Getting emotional over a phone call wasn't worth all this. I picked up my phone and dialed her number.

No answer.

Of course.

I hung up. "She's ignoring me." When Brey glared at me, I figured I would do a check. "Alice, ask Gloria why Vick's not here."

Alice responded a moment later. "Gloria is coming to your office now."

"Why…" I started to grumble but then Gloria strode in. "Gloria, I didn't ask—"

"Victory's in the hospital." She cut me off with four words that shot fear as cold as absolute zero dry ice into my veins.

I shot up from my desk. "What?" My feet wouldn't move; my body wouldn't cooperate. Brey was already heading out the office with her phone to her ear.

Gloria marched up to me and forcefully grabbed my elbow. "Move," she commanded. "Your driver's out front."

"I'm supposed to fly out to…" I blanked, not knowing for once in my life where I was supposed to be going for work.

"None of it matters." She dragged me to the elevators and jackhammered the down button. "She'll need you there when she wakes up."

"Wakes up?" The words jarred me, my autopilot screeched to a halt. "What the hell happened? Is she okay?"

"Her mother didn't give many details. She's passed out. They're monitoring vitals and running tests."

I left Gloria with instructions to cancel appointments indefinitely and manage the team. Jerome went double the speed limit when I told him. She'd impacted his life just like she had my office, my family, my business, everything.

She touched it and it glittered—that was the brilliance of Victory Blakely. An enigma of a woman so in love with the world, I thought her sheltered to believe in all that goodness. But her approach to life had grown on me. I began to find her naivete refreshing.

Now, her outlook on life was striking, blinding, and shockingly beautiful. Like the amount of pressure that creates a diamond, she'd been put in extreme circumstances. She came out shining so damn vividly, the world took notice.

The world wanted every ounce of the light she gave, but I'd seen that light drained. I saw the way she persistently gave it out, even when she was sapped of energy, emptied of all power.

I wondered when she'd get a break, if she'd ever get one.

I wondered if the fact that she might not was my fault.

I jumped from the vehicle before Jerome could bring it to a full stop and ran into the hospital. After finding her room, I shoved open the door.

Her parents sat on one side of the bed. Harvey perched on the couch in the corner. Brey and Jax arrived a few minutes later, holding hands. We watched my Pix sleep, a bruise and a couple stitches on her forehead. An IV was in her left arm and a heart monitor beeped on her right.

The room was quiet except for the sound of the machines operating. Her hair was matted around her face and dark shadows encircled her eyes. In the white hospital gown, she looked small.

Helpless.

Void of life.

I cleared my throat, trying to clear away the fear too. "What happened?"

Her mother's eyes didn't leave her daughter's face. She whispered, "Something to do with her heart. They think it caused her to falter on the sidewalk and a vehicle hit her. I … " She choked on her words. "We weren't safe enough."

Her husband hushed her and told her nobody was at fault.

She whispered something about medication and diet.

Brey whispered softly to Jax and then went to stand by Vick's mother. She said a few things and listened. Brey relayed the information, "The car grazed her." Then she shook her head a bit as her eyes started to glisten. "Well, she looked dazed according to the person who called 911. The driver must have not been paying attention. The doctors are running tests."

"She woke up for a few minutes. She remembers a little," Vick's mother whispered. "They sedated her though. Her heartbeat is irregular."

The woman broke down again.

Jax's phone rang and he took the call, face grim. When he handed it to me, I shook my head. "I'm not taking work calls."

"This one you have to," he sighed and shoved the phone into my chest.

I glanced at the caller ID. "Bastian, I don't care about the deal."

"That hit was the FDA."

The words registered slowly, nailed themselves into me like a torture device. The pain was real, the recognition of it excruciating, and the desire for revenge stronger than everything else.

"Be clear," I commanded. As I stared at my brother, seeing his tight jaw, his tense neck, his eyes burning with the same rage that was in me, I knew. I knew what Bastian's next words would be.

"The FDA's guy, Young, put a hit on her so the commercial wouldn't work. My guys are doing some digging. I'm not sure if they pulled this because of a grudge against my family or solely because of greed. We're lucky she hesitated on that sidewalk."

His words rocked me as I stood in that hospital room with the woman I loved, her family and friends buzzing about. I loved her and I had almost lost her to the stupidity of the business. Like a steel anchor hitting the bottom of the jet-black sea, the importance of my place within my city and business dropped to exactly where it needed to be. "Do what you have to do. I want Mr. Young to know who owns this city."

"Is that you or me?" Bastian asked snidely.

"Partners, Sebastian. I'll offer you that. That's all." I stared at Vick and knew I needed a partner if I was going to give her everything anyway. And I would give her everything.

"Done." With that, he hung up.

After the call, doctors and nurses filed in and out.

Brey and Jax went to look for a few more chairs. Harvey tried to make small talk. My woman was a statistic to him. He couldn't run a commercial if she wasn't in good health. I wanted him gone but didn't want to aggravate Vick's already drained mother.

I kept my mouth shut.

I pulled a chair up to Vick and took her small hand in mine. I didn't say a thing. I didn't have to. With my hand in hers and my other rubbing up and down her arm, she had to know I was there. I was never one to make idle talk with her. I wouldn't now.

I'd be her rock when she needed me most.

CHAPTER
THIRTY-SIX

VICK

B*EEP.*
Beep.
Beep.

This time the sound wasn't a memory. And it wasn't just the thumping I'd started to hear, not the real, raw sound of my blood pumping through my heart on its own.

Mechanical.

High.

Beep.

Beep.

Beep.

I was back. Somehow, I was back in the hospital. The place I absolutely hated.

The pace of it quickened, and I tried my best to breathe in and breathe out, to slow my racing heart. I heard my mother talking. I heard Harvey.

I needed to be okay.

Okay with whatever the doctors were going to say was wrong with me. Okay that I wasn't as healthy as I wanted to be. Okay that I was a girl in her twenties contemplating the fact that death might be closer for her than for an eighty-year-old.

I was sick, unhealthy, broken, damaged.

My happily ever after was just an end without flowers and fairy tales and kids laughing and life bursting through.

A strong hand, one I'd memorized and obsessed over, squeezed mine. I felt the callouses, the strength of it. How it swallowed my hand and how it held on as if it wasn't letting go.

I turned toward that hand and cracked my eyes open just a bit.

"Hi," I mouthed to him.

Jett Stonewood sat there with a white hospital room as his backdrop. It faded away when I focused on him though.

The thumping of my heart came back loud, louder than the beeping in my mind.

He was here.

Maybe as just my boss, maybe as a concerned citizen. Maybe more, maybe less. It didn't matter.

I needed his unshakeable matter-of-fact attitude in that moment.

His other hand smoothed the skin of my forearm and he mouthed back, "Hi." His blue, blue eyes gazed at me with something new in them.

"Oh my God," my mother gasped from the other side of the bed. She turned to my father as she laid a hand on my arm. "Get a doctor! She's awake! Oh, honey, we're here. We're going to figure this out."

She leaned over, and her head fell on my shoulder. She squeezed my arm, and I hit her with the same comment I made to her all the time. "I'm fine, Mom. It's all going to be fine."

The canned response barely registered. She nodded her head vigorously and waved Harvey over. "Harvey, she's okay. God, she's going to be okay. You look like your color's returning, honey. The doctors said your blood levels are all great. You're just fine. This car accident was a blessing in disguise … We'll just change up your heart meds, okay?"

Her voice shook, and tears shimmered in her eyes. She looked like a mother about to lose her child. Desperate, fearful, clinging to a thread of hope and staking everything on it.

I'd caused that pain. My sickness took the badass business-woman and diluted her down to this. She used to walk into a room and heads would turn, people would whisper in awe, and I would smile with pride. She'd been stripped of all that to take care of me.

The promises I made weren't good enough, but I tried my best. "We'll do what we need to, Mom. It'll all be okay."

She clung to my every word, like a starved being snatching up any scrap she could. "Harvey has ideas too. He thinks there might be other medications that could—"

"Stop." Jett's voice shot through the room like an arrow released from a powerful crossbow. Fast, succinct, almost deadly.

My mother and Harvey jumped.

Jax and Brey had waited at the foot of my bed but Jax strode to his brother's side. "Bro, it's her family."

"I don't give a fuck." Jett cut him off. He glared at my mother and Harvey. Then he glowered at Jax. "I'm her family now. I'm the one. Her man. Her everything. What I say goes. Everyone stops. Now."

My mother's eyes widened along with Harvey's.

Jett stood and my hand slipped from his as he leaned over me and put his hands on the opposite side of the bed. He caged me in and looked like an animal protecting his territory. "Get out." The sound was low and vicious.

My mother straightened, and I saw the woman in her who I'd admired before all my ailments took their toll. She wore a black Armani blazer with satin peak lapels that were held together with one button. The white blouse beneath matched her fitted pants. I got my style from her and splashed color in. She didn't need the color. Her presence was enough. "I'm not going anywhere. You pushed us out of the room yesterday, and I shouldn't have gone then. I'm definitely not going now. She needs me. She practically had a heart attack. We need to figure out why and how to avoid that in the future."

"Great. Have a field day with the doctors outside her room. She needs a minute."

"A minute? From what?" My mom looked affronted.

"From you. From all of you." He motioned at the whole room. "She's trying to make everyone in this goddamn room feel better. You're not giving her a second to even digest what's happened. So. Get. Out."

My mom stared at him. Drilled holes in his eyes, dug away at the man he was. I saw the fight in both of them and was surprised to find I wasn't sure who would come out on top.

I said the words I knew she needed to hear. "Mom," I sighed. "I'm a Blakely. I got this."

One movement from my mother, a small step back, showed me the truth in her soul: she wanted what was best for me. She touched a hand to my shoulder and whispered, "I'll be outside."

Then she motioned for everyone to follow her. And Harvey, Brey, and Jax didn't argue.

Jett sighed and hung his head, still encircling me with his body. Then he sat back down and took my hand in his.

"Jett, I—"

"No, Pix." He squeezed his eyes shut like my voice physically caused him pain. "Don't say a damn word. Just be, woman. Just be."

I shut my mouth. An ocean of fear rolled in and swept me into the anguish and helplessness of lying there listening. The waves washed up memories of other hospitals, of waking up to loved ones beside me and not knowing how to soothe them when all I wanted was to be alone and soothe myself.

Beep. Beep. Beep.

The sound I never wanted to hear again but the sound I couldn't escape. It was the sound I covered up with awe-inspiring experiences so as not to remember the miserable ones.

My first tear dropped. And the ocean, dark and deep with all my anxieties and pain, dragged out every tear out thereafter. I gasped for air, trying to center myself, trying to stop the tears.

I glanced at Jett who still held my hand. His face hadn't changed; he looked unmoved, unshaken. Like a lighthouse. Strong enough to withstand the most violent storm and still guide me, be there for me, stand tall for me.

"Let it all out, Victory. They're going to come back in here and you're going to want to make them all happy again. I'll probably have to leave. I'm not sure I have the patience for any more of it today."

I laughed and it turned into a hiccup and then a cry again. He squeezed my hand and nodded as more sobs racked my body. I was down in the depths of a sea so cold and black with the misery I'd pushed down there for years that I don't know how long I cried.

He sat there with me the whole time, his hair mussed, his blue eyes steady, and his broad chest hunched over my bedside. The sleeves of his shirt were rolled up and I saw that watch ticking away in sync with the beeping in the room. The sound faded as I stared at my Phantom, the man who'd finally set my voice free. His thumb tapped the back of my hand in time to the beep and his stare switched between me and the door, as if to watch for any unauthorized entry.

I squeezed his hand as my crying subsided. "Thank you for letting me fall apart."

"Hm. Still fucking beautiful in the hospital light, even after crying for what must have been at least an hour," he stated, like he was reading the news.

I smiled because I loved his compliments even if they were shrouded in insults. "Thank you, Phantom."

He smiled back. "Thank you for letting me see you fall apart for once. Your enthusiasm for life is draining."

I rolled my eyes. "It's either love life or fear it."

Those words sunk in, penetrating my soul, taking root and growing quickly into the mantra I knew I would live by. I'd just seen my parents, the man I loved, and my best friend here to stand with me. I could fight whatever the doctors said, I could move another mountain of sickness if I needed to, because I had people that cared about me, that would fight with me.

Life was worth the struggle, worth the pain, worth the anguish when you shared it with others, when you saw fear and stared it down before barreling forward. Fear was a ferocious monster, meant to tower over you, drain you of your courage, and rob you of your life. You had to meet fear with your own ruthless vigor to live, stand taller, and beat it into submission.

I was a Blakely, and as I laid there listening to the beeping, encountering the fear again, I knew I was stronger.

I squeezed Jett's hand. "I'm choosing to love life."

"You don't just love life, you tempt death and stare it in the face, woman." He grunted. "I still think you have a death wish, and I'm not looking forward to protecting you from it."

His words alluded to a future for us, one I wasn't sure he wanted even if he was here. My heartbeat picked up, my palms started to sweat. I pulled my hand from him and folded it into my other hand to hide my worry.

"Look," I began. "All cards on the table?"

The smirk that flickered across his face didn't help my anxiety. "Sure, Pix. Hit me."

I let out a shaky breath. "We're probably over." I glanced at him, and he didn't deny it. My heart plummeted but I kept on. "I can't give anyone an amazing relationship or a great love story with my health issues."

"Are you going to apologize for telling Bastian about your cancer before you told me?"

"What?" I stuttered.

"It's really all I want." He glanced at the clock. "I missed my flight to New York for you today."

"Oh, I'm sorry. I didn't expect—"

"I'll probably be missing a million more flights for you over the years."

I looked at him, confused. He wasn't making sense at all. He was jumping around, and I couldn't keep up.

"I once almost fired a guy for putting his wife before my business."

"Okay?" I dragged out the question.

"I'm happy I didn't. I now see why people put the ones they love before work. I'm going to miss a lot of flights for you, and I'm going to expect a damn apology for you confiding in a stranger before you confided in me. I'm going to expect a lot from you."

He stood up and started pacing at the foot of my bed.

"Jett, I don't expect anything from you. You don't even have to be here."

"Oh, I will always be by your side from now on. Make no mistake."

"What are you talking about?" I narrowed my eyes at him, wanting to believe but not sure I could. "I might be sick, Jett. I had cancer. I just got sideswiped in traffic probably because, in all honesty, I haven't been taking my vitamins or my heart meds. I'm a mess!"

He chuckled and shook his head as he continued to pace. "Yeah, you really are. Well, we will see what the doctors have to say."

I glared at his assessment of me. Sure, I could say it, but I didn't need him to confirm I was a mess. "Well, thank you but you can go. I'll see what the doctors have to say and I'll take care of myself. I've done it this long. I don't need my boss helping me out. Thank you very much. I get that we had a thing, and that we screwed it all up. I don't need you swooping in. I have it under control."

He stopped and pinned me with his intense gaze. He scanned me from the tips of my toes all the way up to the crown of my head. When our gazes met, his was filled with anguish. "I actually believe that you do have it under control. For some reason, you could tempt the grim reaper and he'd probably walk away from you smiling. You're a walking beacon of life. Still, you need me to be there when that beacon needs a recharge, Vick, and I'm going to be. For me, it's you before everything else from now on. When I thought for a second your flame might have been extinguished, mine was too. The business, the life I lived, nothing mattered. You've been the damn sun I've been orbiting for a while now, and I just didn't see it."

The words I tried to form wouldn't come. His confession rendered me speechless.

"I just agreed to a partnership with Bastian."

"You what?" I gasped.

"You need more from me. I'm putting my girlfriend first. He'll help."

"He's the freaking mob!" I yelled.

"Jesus. Do you have to be so damn loud?"

"Okay, this was a verbal agreement, right? He can't hold you to—"

"Don't rack your brain, woman. I don't want you to lawyer me out of my decision. Plus, like you said once before, the mob doesn't care about legalities."

"So, you're in the mob now?" The question sounded ridiculous, and yet, I was absolutely serious.

"I'm thinking if you're dating me, you probably are too."

The thumping of my heart drowned out the beeping.

He leaned on the foot of my bed. "I'm serious when I say I need to trust that you're going to put me before everyone and everything like I'm going to do for you. My business will come after you. I will be there for you. I'll shield you from brightening everyone's day when you're having a shitty one. You get to cry with me and sometimes I hope you laugh with me too. We're going to be a family, Victory Blakely, and my family doesn't have the sky as the limit."

"You know I want to be married with 2.5 kids and a white picket fence in a few years, right?" I threw back at him, testing how serious he really wanted this to be. "Even if I'm in the mob…"

"You want a proposal now?"

A laugh bubbled out of me. "You better not, Phantom. I hate hospitals."

He smiled and rounded the bed to sit beside me. "If you want all that, we'll get all that."

"I can't have kids." The confession flew out of me before I could stop it. The one secret I'd hidden from everyone, the bone-crushing burden, the empty void that seemed to stop my fairy tale before it had even begun. I shrugged when he raised his eyebrows. "All cards on the table, right? The cancer took that from me."

"If you want them, then we adopt them. Sky's the limit for some, Pix. Not us. You get me?"

"I get you."

EPILOGUE

VICK

"**W**E'RE NOT HAVING a barbecue without meat, Jett." I stormed in from the Stonewoods' kitchen after rifling through the grocery bags.

Nancy eyed her husband and Jett. "I told you both to get hot dogs, burger meat, and steaks."

I crossed my arms. "There's none of that in there."

Senior Stonewood rolled the whiskey in his tumbler around and pointed at his son. "I had it in the cart. He put it back."

"Are you the father, or is he?" Nancy quipped.

"Dad came to his senses. A vegetarian lifestyle is better for the environment and our health," my boyfriend announced as he sipped tequila.

"It's the Fourth of July!" The words burst out of me. I held onto my anger even though I felt it slipping. "We're having everyone here this afternoon and you decided to make a play on health? Are you insane?"

Jett's eyes sparkled with mirth as he lounged next to his father in a red T-shirt and blue jeans. Completely casual and completely sexy. "Pixie, no need to raise your voice."

"I swear to God, you're going to kill me."

"No," he deadpanned. "The meat would kill you. I'm saving your life so I can keep annoying you for the rest of it."

I motioned to Nancy. "We have to go get something to cook."

She grabbed her phone. "I'll text Brey."

Senior Stonewood got to his feet and said he needed to cut the grass. Jett ambled over to me as his mother left the room, still typing on her phone. He wrapped an arm around my waist where my white-and-blue striped maxi dress cinched. I shoved it off. "You're on my shit list."

"I'm always on your shit list." He nuzzled into my neck. "Come upstairs with me. You need to unwind."

I narrowed my eyes and said what I always did when he pushed me too far. "Get fucked, Phantom."

He laughed as his hands slid to my jaw to cup my face. "You know that's exactly what I'm trying to do."

I sighed. "I don't like having parties where people aren't happy."

"They'll be happy," he said with so much conviction I almost believed him.

"People like steaks at a barbecue."

"They'll be healthy too."

I growled but he kissed me, took what was officially his, and reminded me of what I got to have with him every day.

We fought like banshees half the time, and Stonewood Enterprise's team knew how to pinpoint our weaknesses when they wanted something. Bob pleaded his case for everyone to have a week off after the Fourth of July weekend to me, not Jett.

After a fight within the tinted windows of Jett's office and some great make up sex, Gloria announced that everyone was getting a week off.

We balanced one another.

I was the light to his dark, and he was the steady rock to my unstable ground.

After my stay in the hospital, Jett didn't really leave my side. We argued over everything I did that was, in his eyes, dangerous. The overprotective side of him that he never wanted to turn off got a constant workout with me.

We needed to live and enjoy every experience. Jett wasn't used to doing that. He wanted to work to make experiences better for everyone else.

And he did work. A lot. I was aware that he and Bastian had a partnership that allowed him a little more time, but it wasn't much. The partnership remained unpredictable, risky. Dangerous. But we didn't shrink from danger. As I constantly reminded him, we barreled full speed ahead even when the signs told us to stop.

I pulled back from him. "I love you, but we're having burgers today."

"I'm not." His mouth turned down. "And I thought you wanted to try being a vegetarian."

"I tried it for a day and decided it was terrible."

"Jesus," he grumbled as he slid his hand in mine and pulled me toward the front doors. "Let's go get the damn cardiac arrest food then."

I skipped along with him and beamed when we made it to his massive pickup. He swung open the door and lifted me in. Yup, still got hot all over when he did.

He rounded the hood of the truck and got in on his side. He turned the key in the ignition and then side-eyed me. "Victory."

"Yes," I answered with too much humor in my voice.

He growled and leaned past me to grab my seat belt and buckle it. "You're irritating me on purpose."

"Probably the same way you irritated me on purpose by not getting the meat in the first place."

He chuckled and backed out of the driveway. "I intend to get some on the side of the road before we get back home."

"Ah. Now, there's my fun-loving man. I see why you purposely left the meat now."

His smile was wolfish as we drove back to the store.

Unfortunately for both of us, my phone sounded on the way back. A new song. One for my mother. Aretha belted out that there wasn't a mountain high enough or a river wide enough to keep her from getting to us. And as if my mother knew that was her song, she rang Jett's phone when I ignored her call.

"Vick's answering service," Jett answered as I smacked his arm and glared at him. He was supposed to make me scream in ecstasy on the side of a small-town road. These were goals we needed to accomplish.

Instead, he chatted with my mother, window rolled down, breeze flowing through his dark hair, while he smiled wide with one tanned forearm on the door.

"She's here. You know she never answers that phone though. She thinks it'll ruin her fun." He winked at me. "I know you're fun, Annabelle. Something's wrong with your daughter. The sooner you get to this barbecue to straighten her out, the better."

I rolled my eyes at their ridiculous conversation. The man joked more with my mother than I had ever known he could joke in his whole life. Since my hospital stay and a family Christmas together, we'd all gotten along better.

We had a long way to go still because we were Blakelys. We pushed until we got what we wanted. My mother still wanted a cautious daughter. I still wanted a zero-to-sixty lifestyle. I wanted to live because I still didn't know how long my clean bill of health would last.

And it was clean. I made sure to do doctor check-ins now. I made sure to follow up with my nutritionist. I wanted to live long and be crazy healthy and crazy happy.

Loving someone did that to you, made you want to be better, live better, and live longer. It made you realize all you had to lose. I'd already been embracing the world and acknowledging its beauty, but with love, the world dazzled even brighter. I didn't want to miss a single sparkle of it.

Every piece of life was meant to be shared with someone you loved, and I shared it all with Jett. The highs and the extreme lows. He let me wallow on my bad days and protected me fiercely in those moments.

As we pulled into the Stonewoods' driveway, he hung up and reprimanded me for not answering. I rolled my eyes the whole time. We made quick work of getting ready for the barbecue, and then family started to show up.

As the sun descended over the lake, Jett announced we weren't going anywhere for fireworks. "I bought some for our lake this year."

"Shut up," I squealed. "You did?"

His mouth kicked up. "Told you everyone at the barbecue was going to have fun."

I barreled into him and gave him a huge hug as everyone laughed at my happiness.

We laid out blankets, and I sighed when we finally sat down on our own. Jett picked me up and set me in his lap. He wrapped his arms around my shoulders and I leaned my back into his chest. "I love you for doing this," I said as I looked up at him.

He nodded once and l scanned our family and friends. "Everyone seems happy."

"They are." I patted his arm and gave him a peck on the neck. "You did that. You always do that."

He hummed and pointed out the man in the distance on the lake. After a moment, a beautiful spark as bright as a hive of fireflies in the dead of night whizzed into the darkened sky. It left a trail of glitter and then burst into golden arcs raining down like a shimmering weeping willow.

Our family and friends *oohed* and *aahed*. My mother glanced over from her blanket with my father and mouthed a wow to me. I yelled out to everyone, "My boyfriend is the best!"

Brey and Katie laughed along with Jax and Jaydon.

Firework after firework lit up Greenville over the lake. I could have sworn my happily ever after couldn't get any better. Jett read my mind, and he wanted to prove one thing. The sky wasn't the limit for him. He would always, always get into the damn stratosphere with me.

Another firework sailed into the sky, I heard the hiss as the rocket shot up and when it burst, the color lit up the sky with words I had been waiting for.

In red: **Will**

In bright white: **You**

In blue: **Marry me?**

In green, a pixie fairy.

Thump. Thump. Thump.

Haven't read Aubrey and Jax's story yet?
Keep reading for a sneak peak of Inevitable.

SIX YEARS AGO

CHAPTER
ONE

AUBREY

THE FORCE OF his tackle knocked the wind out of me. Jax Stonewood wanted a reaction from me. I was brought up to never give one though. At fifteen, in a household where restraint was a key to survival, I had a pretty good handle on how to control myself when someone surprised me.

I controlled my desire to look at the boy who sat on top of me, ready to smash a snowball into my face.

I took my time looking up at the clouds and the snowflakes dancing around instead. They glittered and sparkled, mingling wildly. With liberty. And a freedom that I envied.

"Aubrey, I thought I told you the last time it snowed that face washes are a tradition if you get caught on Stonewood land," Jax said.

Finally, I turned my gaze toward him. "Don't you dare."

He smirked, one of his dimples revealing itself. Even catching my breath while lying in the snow, my heart still somehow melted.

Jax freaking Stonewood. My walking, talking sex-on-a-stick neighbor *always* warmed my blood even though I'd never admit it. Jay, his younger brother by two years and my senior by one, did little to nothing for me, but he was my best friend.

"Jax, come on, man. Mom said if you facewash anyone else, she'll lock your ass in your room for the rest of winter." Jay sounded out of breath, like he'd run up right beside us.

I wanted to thank Jay for coming to my rescue but couldn't take my eyes off of Jax.

I never could.

The three Stonewood boys moved in next door four years ago, and our quiet, undisturbed block morphed into a revolving hang-out for kids our age. The Stonewoods drew attention, and I didn't have much choice joining in when Jax and Jay tackled me one day to steal my candy. Their older brother, Jett, couldn't be bothered with their antics.

I admit, I cried to my mother, and they ended up having to apologize.

Jax and Jett tolerated me tagging along when they were in the neighborhood. After all, I was the homeschooled girl that their little brother had formed a bond with. Maybe the bond formed because we were close in age or because Jett and Jax left out their little brother a lot. Either way, it just happened.

Over the years, my crush for Jax just happened too.

Even right then, knowing he was going to smash snow in my face, I thought winter couldn't have agreed with him more. His normally broody, calculating eyes glittered like the snow with mischief and fun. The cold reddened his cheeks just right, and the wind tousled his dark hair to look unruly. The wind, the cold, the snow loved him like everything else in the world.

The only people immune to his charm were his family, and I appreciated that Jay tried to shield me from it. "You know Mom's not kidding either. She's going to be pissed if she finds out you facewashed Brey."

Instead of Jax acknowledging his little brother, his eyes stayed on mine. Then, they moved to my hat. With the hand that wasn't holding snow, he ripped it off. "What's with you and this bun all the time?"

I started to wiggle under him. "Let me up. My clothes are getting soaked from the snow."

"Right." His eyebrow quirked. "I guess I can't mess with your pretty little face."

My stomach dropped.

He was teasing me. I knew that. None of the Stonewood boys saw me as pretty. I'd seen the girls that paraded around them and in comparison … Well, there was no comparison.

They were tall. I was short.

They wore shirts that showed off their cleavage. I didn't have any cleavage to show off.

They were women. I still felt like a girl.

I wanted to believe him if just for a second though. I wanted him to want me even though I knew he was older, hotter, and had much better-looking options to choose from.

That thought ignited my temper.

I bucked under him, trying to get him off. His smirk thinned, his blue eyes darkened. His head tipped closer, and I felt his breath on my lips. I could smell the mint of the gum he always chewed. He stared at my lips and then glanced back at me, like he was assessing everything in me, figuring out what made me whole. For a second, I thought he might even lean the extra whisper closer to touch my lips with his.

Instead, he squeezed his eyes shut and crushed the giant snowball I forgot he was holding into my hair, grinding it just hard enough that my bun fell apart.

I screamed. Jay groaned.

Jax rolled off me, laughing hysterically.

My cheeks heated with embarrassment, and then it got even hotter as my embarrassment turned to rage.

Instead of dusting myself off and trying to save my bun, I scurried to scoop up as much snow as possible and slammed it into his face, smearing it all around.

"You're such a jerk!" I yelled.

Jay hauled me back quickly as Jax made a grab for me. He whispered in my ear, "Don't make it worse, Brey. Just go inside and get cleaned up. My mom just made lunch for us."

Jax was standing with another snowball ready to launch and glaring at both of us. "Would you stop babying her, Jay? After winter break, us upperclassmen get to teach the underclassmen a lesson. You know Sophomore Kill Day includes her too."

My eyes widened.

I'd heard about the water balloons launched at underclassmen on their way to school in the fall.

I'd heard about lockers being filled with pudding and about the lockers being stuffed with underclassmen as well. The high school administrators turned a blind eye to the bullying that happened. They called it just a little bit of good old fun.

I called it torture and wanted no part of it.

I whipped my head to Jay. "Please walk with me to school next week?"

Jay smirked at me like I was silly. "I got you. Don't worry about it." Jax grunted. "You can't walk her to school. It's tradition," Jax said, abandoning his snowball to glare at us like my idea was outrageous. "He can do whatever he wants," I screeched.

"People are going to start to think you two are dating with how protective Jay is of you."

Jay and I shrugged our shoulders in unison. Jay never really cared much about anything. He just wanted to have fun and wanted everyone to have fun around him.

For the first two years their family lived next door, he was the one who never asked why he couldn't ring my doorbell or why he couldn't come over. He mentioned once that he wanted me to hang out later than normal. When I said I couldn't, that my dad would be home, he didn't ask why that mattered.

After being homeschooled for so many years, he was the first friend I could trust and the breath of fresh air that I'd needed for a long time.

I begged and begged my parents to go to a public school after getting a taste of friendship. When they finally agreed, the darkness lightened up a bit, the clouds cleared.

The first day of sophomore year opened my eyes though.

I hadn't realized how mean people in school could be and how territorial girls were of the Stonewood brothers.

Jax distanced himself immediately. He didn't have time for Jay or me when he was captain of everything and enjoying every girl who looked his way in school.

Jay didn't miss a beat though. Our friendship was an immovable force even when every one of the girls he hooked up with hated me. His friendship made me unpopular. Girls didn't want to be my friend even when they realized my father mingled in all the same circles as their parents. I was the girl whose dad owned a big local business and who got to live next to the Stonewoods. That made me enemy number one.

I was a threat and a target.

And Sophomore Kill Day was going to be difficult to suffer through.

I felt the panic seeping in. It wasn't being stuffed into a locker or getting hit with paint-filled balloons that scared me. I could handle all that. I didn't even care if I got made fun of or picked on. If I came home from school looking a wreck or a phone call from the office was made, my father would resort back to claiming homeschool was the best option to raise a proper lady.

I knew better. He'd find something wrong with the studies my mother put together or he'd find fault in my work ethic.

He already found fault with so much.

Jay put his arm around my shoulders and told me he would walk me to school, that I shouldn't worry.

Jax grumbled behind us, "What the hell's she so quiet for? It's just one day out of the year."

I inhaled deeply, remembering that self-control was my friend. I grasped at that control so I wouldn't snap at Jax—until I saw my hair in the foyer mirror of the Stonewoods' house.

I froze and Jax ran right into me.

"What's wrong with you?" His voice rose, but I didn't glance at him.

My eyes were on my hair. My long, wavy brown hair had escaped the tightly tied bun that took a concentrated amount of time to do.

Both Jax and Jay stood on either side of me exchanging worried looks. My green eyes widened, glassing over as they stared back at me in the mirror. My face paled so much that it contrasted sharply with the dark brown nest that sat on my head.

I frantically started combing my fingers through it. "Oh my God. Do you have a brush? I need a brush."

They both stared at me like I was crazy.

"Okay, if you don't have a brush, I'll take a comb. I need to fix this right now."

Jay shook his head, and Jax stepped back.

"You guys, I need something! Anything!" Anything to make this look better. I felt control slipping through my fingertips. "Oh God. My father is going to kill my m—"

Both the boys kept staring, first questioningly, then with what appeared to be pity.

"Please!" I practically screamed.

I felt the air escaping my lungs. I squeezed my eyes shut and tried to focus on twisting up my hair to wrap it close to my head.

"Brey." Mrs. Stonewood appeared in the mirror. She stood behind me on the large staircase. "I have a brush right upstairs. Why don't you follow me?"

I tripped and almost fell at the bottom of the stairs. Jax's hand caught my elbow, and I turned to say thank you, to grab at any dignity I may have had left. When I saw his confusion at my panic, I couldn't bring myself to say a word.

He started to walk up the stairs with me, his hand still on my elbow.

I didn't care. I just needed to get my hair back in order.

"Jax, this is just us girls," his mother said, her voice stern.

Jax's hand left my elbow and for some stupid reason, I missed it. Probably because I knew after this, he wouldn't touch me with a ten-foot pole.

I followed her up the rest of the white marble stairs and down the hallway to a gigantic bathroom that I probably should have just run to the moment I saw the mess on my head.

She went to one of the drawers and pulled out a brush. Turning me toward the mirror, she calmly started brushing my hair without offering me the brush to do it myself.

I stiffened, staring at her head over mine in the mirror. Her eyes were the same blue as Jax's and they glistened with sympathy.

I didn't want it. I didn't need it. I had done just fine with my mother and my father so far. I stepped closer to the speckled granite countertop. "Thank you for finding me a brush."

Her brow furrowed. "I can help you with your hair."

She'd read my silent plea right. I wanted her to leave, but she wasn't budging.

"Is there a reason you can't wear it down?"

She knew the reason. Adults like Mrs. Stonewood were easy to read. They all held the same expression. The first time I encountered that look had been a day my mother picked me up from grade school. My teacher had seen a bruise on her arm when my mother reached for me.

She had gasped and we both stiffened. My mother pulled down her sleeve quickly but my teacher's eyes had already changed. They flicked to our car nervously, and she asked if everything was all right.

On the way home, my mother said she wasn't going to be dropping me off anymore, that I would have to walk. I read her thoughts. That day, I nodded my head in total agreement. Soon after, I was being homeschooled.

Now, Mrs. Stonewood begged me with her eyes to tell her something as she stroked my hair and brushed away the curls.

I didn't answer her.

She'd always been a sort of friend to me, the type of mother I never had. She yelled at the boys for me, let me eat cookies, she even told me to call her Nancy instead of Mrs. Stonewood. At this moment though, knowing that she wanted the truth, I figured not answering was my best answer. I just couldn't bring myself to lie to her.

She began to fold my dark curls over one another and said, "Whenever you're ready, we can talk. Just us girls." She always said 'just us girls' when she wanted me to understand it would be our little secret. My throat constricted and when I looked away from her, I felt wetness slide down my cheeks. I wiped the tears away quickly, hoping she didn't see.

If she did, she didn't say a thing. "All better."

I looked in the mirror and saw that my hair was French-braided, and it looked classy. Father wouldn't mind this. No curls. No frizz. No hair out of place.

"Thank you," I mumbled.

"Don't thank me when two out of my three boys did this to you." Her third and oldest son, Jett, was in college, living near his father. Thank God because I didn't think all three Stonewoods here would be good for the female population.

I let out a sigh and smiled a little. "Only Jax, really." We started our way back down the hallway.

"I'm going to have to ground him for eternity at this rate. To think, he's seventeen and facewashing girls. I doubt there's hope for him."

I laughed a little, feeling the weight of my braid swinging and realizing I felt a little freer with this hair style. "Not this time, Nancy. I got him good after he did this to my hair."

"Snow to his face?" Her eyes met mine again and they no longer appeared sympathetic, she was trying to make me smile.

I laughed a little and nodded.

"All right. He's off the hook this time. Go beat them in some of those video games." With that, she turned a corner and disappeared.

I made my way down the hallway and found both Jax and Jay sitting in the middle of their rec room, two empty plates beside them as they played a video game.

I moved to grab the plates to take them to the kitchen. Littered with crumbs, those plates would have been grounds for a fight in my home.

Jay grabbed my arm and yanked me down. "We'll clean up later."

I stared at the plates for a second longer, willing away the itch to clean it up. When Jax pushed another controller in my hand, I welcomed the distraction. "If you pick the character Peach again, I swear I'm going to make it my mission to throw every question mark I get at you," he mumbled.

I smiled, realizing that neither of them were going to comment about the hair incident.

I didn't care that both he and Jax got annoyed with me picking to be Peach every time. I didn't care that they would tease me the whole time. I only cared that they would be my friends knowing my faults. It mattered that they acted as if my panic attack hadn't happened at all. Real friends accepted you for who you were, not who you pretended to be. "You're just mad because I beat you every time I play her."

Jax groaned when I picked her as my character, like I always did. "Do you want to be her or something? We at least switch our characters. You are obsessed with her!"

Truth was, I wouldn't mind being her. She was a princess. "Whatever."

After a round I lost, Jax leaned toward me. "How's it feel to be losing, Peaches?"

I scrunched up my face. "Her name is Peach, and I'm not her."

"No. You're not. You're Peaches." He laughed to himself as he focused back on the screen. Jay started to laugh along with him.

"Peaches kinda fits you," Jay said.

Jax groaned. "Find your own nickname for her, man. Quit copying me."

"It's not a nickname!" My voice came out high and irritated.

"You kinda screech like her too."

"You want me to call you Bowser?" I said trying to get the upper hand, but as he crossed the finish line in first place, I slumped.

"No, Peaches. You can just call me winner."

I glared but kept my eyes on the screen. "You'll always be last place in my book. L.P. L.P. rolls off the tongue quite nicely too."

He grumbled something about showing me what could roll off my tongue nicely but I ignored him, so happy with my quick work on a degrading nickname for him.

We bickered and played again and again. Before I knew it, the sun was setting. I finished in first place only to throw my controller down, "I gotta go!"

Jax rolled his eyes. "You can't leave just because you finally won."

"Get over yourself, *L.P.* I won like ten times in the last hour."

He stood to his full height and crossed his arms, trying intimidation. "Peaches, let's be realistic."

Maybe it was the way everyone backed down from him or the way he commanded everything around him but I never wanted to give in to him, to let him have anything without a fight. I put my hands on my hips and stood a little straighter. "L.P.,"—I mimicked his tone—"realistically, Jay beat you last time, and he's the worst."

"Hey!" Jay jumped up. "I'm way better at Jax in most things. He plays this way too much."

I patted Jay's arm and glared at Jax for making me indirectly insult Jay who always stood up for me. He was the sweet one, the one I would call my friend. I held Jax's eyes. "Of course, Jay. We both know you're better than Jax at most *everything.*"

Jax's eyes widened as he took a menacing step forward. He searched my face again, analyzing me. "What the hell does that mean?" he ground out, a gravelly tone in his voice sending shivers up my body.

I stepped back quickly and turned as if unaffected. I didn't answer him because I didn't really know what it meant. Jay and I were friends, nothing more. I didn't know if he was better at anything than Jax, other than being my friend.

He was the absolute best at that.

"See you guys later!" I yelled over my shoulder as I bounded down the stairs.

Halfway out the door, Jax yelled from the stairs, "See you on Sophomore Kill Day."

I winced at the reminder.

Jay would protect me. I hoped.

What Jay wouldn't be able to protect me from was walking into my kitchen and seeing my father sitting at the table, glaring at the door.

"Where's Mom?"

"You mean Mother?" he asked, his voice louder than even his normal yelling voice. "I'm asking the questions, Aubrey."

I nodded, frozen in the doorway.

"Close and lock that door. You are letting in the cold."

I turned and did as I was told. I had no choice. Not when I didn't know where my mom was.

As the lock clicked into place, I felt my body start to shake. I couldn't turn back around. I willed myself to pivot, to face my father.

I pled with my self-control, begging it to help me stop shaking, to give me the courage to ask him again where he'd locked Mom up this time.

Control, that little friend of mine, wasn't needed though. Instead, my father yanked me back by my French braid and spit out, "What the fuck is this? She let your hair grow this long?"

Tears stung my eyes from the hair pulling.

The tears spilled over when he reached for the knife block and slid a large butcher knife from it. The metal glinted in the light. It shined as if it had been sharpened and primed for just this specific moment. When the metal sparkled as it swung toward me, I wondered if blood made it shine more brightly.

I wouldn't find out that day because my father only sliced it fluidly across my braid.

My hair unraveled and hung shoulder-length. He threw my twelve inches of braid into the trash and the knife into the sink.

The sounds of the metal hitting ceramic and the knife ricocheting forcefully around the sink drew my focus to the sharpness of the blade. How quickly it sliced through every strand of the hair. Gone, it was all gone.

"Don't blubber in my house," my father yelled and slammed his open hand upside the back of my head. I flew forward, seeing black. Just barely, I caught myself on the countertop.

The blade was closer now, my teeth just inches from the side of the sink.

My father, such a smart, successful man. People said we were lucky to have him. He'd saved my mother, Tala, from that home she'd lived in on the reservation.

That home though was my mother's sanctuary. Father didn't let her talk much about it but she shared with me how it saved her when her own mother vanished. One night, her mother went to work and the next she was gone like a beautiful star burning out in the galaxy.

"Go clean up your mother. She's in the office," he grumbled as he pulled the keys from his slacks and threw them at me.

I stood there wondering what he would do if I said no. If I didn't back down and pushed him just a little further.

My father, such a smart man. He never hit us where it would leave a mark for anyone to see.

His eyebrows raised. My shoulders sank.

Control was my friend and my enemy. I hated it for making me a coward and loved it for saving my mother and me from more pain.

My mother laid like a wounded animal on the floor when I opened the door. I hurried to her and smoothed her hair back. I slid my hands over her face as she cried and ran her fingers through my hair. "Oh, my little dreamer. All your dreams have been cut away."

Yes, every strand of my hair held another dream, another identity, another hope. My mother taught me those sorts of things about our heritage behind closed doors when my father wasn't around to listen. How the wind whispered to me to make me strong, how the water could wash away most anything, how my hair held a piece of me that connected me to every part of those before me, to her. A part of me I would never ever get back.

She cried for my loss.

I cried when I saw what he'd done to her ribs.

She cleaned up my hair that night as best she could. I cleaned up her back and ribs.

Nights like those, we were the closest and furthest from each other. No other person in the world could know exactly what we were going through in those moments. We were also so lost in our own nightmares, we were too scared to speak them out loud to one another.

I always thought our bond was indestructible, a desolate pair who would always make it through the worst trauma together.

CHAPTER
TWO

AUBREY

JAY CALLED SEVERAL times over the next week during our winter break from school, but I avoided him. I took care of my mother and kept an immaculate home instead. I didn't give my father a thing to complain about over the rest of my vacation.

Sophomore Kill Day descended on me more quickly than I would have liked, especially when I had no interaction with Jay. I couldn't be sure if he would walk me to school or if I would be on my own.

I put on makeup like it would help camouflage me. I wore the cutest skinny jeans I had and a dark flowy top to look nice, but not so showy as to call unwanted attention to myself. I pulled on some boots that would weather the snow and my puffy winter jacket. I'd mastered tying my hair in a bun that mirrored the same one I'd had before it was cut. I thought I looked good.

I could make it through the day as long as Jay helped me. When I left my house that morning, he stood at the end of my sidewalk, beaming.

He walked up like we'd been talking about this every day and swung an arm around my shoulder. Then he grabbed my backpack.

"I can carry my backpack, Jay."

"Not if the water balloons start flying once we reach school grounds," he said.

My eyes must have widened because I felt his chest shaking while he chuckled at me. I smacked his chest. "You're a jerk."

He squeezed my shoulder and reassured me. "No one's going to bother you, Brey."

I breathed a sigh of relief. "Thanks for walking with me."

"Wouldn't have walked with anyone else."

"You sure?" I teased, skipping ahead to face him and catch him in his lie. "Melanie or Sophie didn't want to walk with you? They weren't mad?"

He looked just past my shoulder toward our school coming into view. "They'll get over it."

"Probably, but I'm guessing your walk to school could have been much more fun this morning." I wiggled my eyebrows.

His eyes, such a lighter blue than Jax's, danced with humor. Then, he dropped my bag and lunged for me. He grabbed me around the waist and knees, carrying me like a baby where he hovered right over a snow pile. I screeched, "Jay, you better not."

"Say you enjoy walking to school with me just as much as I like walking to school with you. Or else."

I batted at his arm and tried to hold back my laugh. "Are you kidding right now?"

His smile widened. "Say it, Sass Pot, or I'm dropping you."

I laughed a little harder as he fake swung me toward the snow pile and screamed, "Fine. Fine! I love walking with you."

"Say you know I like walking with you too."

I chuckled as he set me down when I confirmed what he wanted.

Then we were walking again and I mumbled, "Guess I have to protect myself from you on Sophomore Kill Day too."

Another laugh exploded from him. "Yeah, what a monster I am."

I just smiled up at him. "You need to stop growing. You're already a whole head taller than me."

"Yeah, or keep growing so I can fight off the asshats that are lining up to bother you."

I rolled my eyes. "Yeah, just hundreds of them."

No guy had approached me all year. I wanted someone to make me forget about Jax next door. I wanted a Prince Charming, one who would overshadow Jax's effect on me. I'd dreamed he would bump into me on my first day of school, we would both have stars in our eyes and we would fall madly in love.

Instead, every guy pretty much ran away from me or ignored me. Jay mumbled more to himself than me, "You have no idea."

I blew a raspberry. "I do. The notches on your bedpost are at about a bajillion and mine … well, are none." I shrugged.

He held my backpack to his stomach as he bent over to laugh.

The genuine happiness that belted from him was infectious and made me forget how nervous I'd felt getting ready for school that day and how anxious I'd been to see him after a week, how terrible I felt the whole week without him.

He sighed and patted me on the back as we walked on, approaching the front doors of the school. "There's my girl."

I looked at him quizzically.

"Don't act like you haven't been jittery and nervous this whole morning."

I sighed, more relaxed when I admitted, "Well, it's supposed to be a rotten day for us sophomores."

He nodded and when we reached the school entrance, he stepped in front of me, ready to open the door. He hesitated, then turned to me as he cleared his throat. "When you're ready to talk about why I didn't see or hear from you all last week, I'm ready to listen."

I saw the hurt in his eyes. I could see him warring with himself over bringing it up and guilt washed over me. It was the first time he brought up that I hadn't returned his calls for a week or that I ignored him when he came to my house and threw stones at my window. He deserved for me to be as good of a friend to him as he was to me. "I'm so sorry, Jay."

He looked at my hands which were wringing themselves out. This was unspoken territory for us. I'd ignored him in the past when my father had lost his temper but never for this long.

He'd never called me out on it. We would simply pick up where we'd left off.

He pulled me to his chest for a hug and mumbled, "Missed you, Sass Pot."

When he pulled back, his megawatt smile was back in place, and the concern behind his eyes had disappeared. One day, I owed him an explanation, but relief washed over me knowing that he wouldn't push me anymore.

The first bell rang as I made it to my locker and Jay set my bag down. "You gonna make it the rest of the way?"

I rolled my eyes. "Thank you for walking me, Jay."

"A thank you from Brey." He held a hand to his heart. "Day's officially made now."

"Go to class, you idiot."

"See you at lunch." He spun to walk down the hall and within two steps, five people surrounded him. Shaking my head at how popular one person could be, I didn't think much about opening my locker.

When I swung it open and heard the hiss though, I jumped and looked toward the sound. Coiled in the corner sat a green snake. I stared at it as it stared at me, neither of us ready to make the first move. Its tongue darted out, and I jerked back. The snake probably took my movement as a threat and launched itself at me.

I screamed, flying back and trying to catch myself as I stumbled over my backpack. I wasn't sure if the snake was poisonous, but I acted fast as I fell to the ground and scrambled across the floor, trying to put distance between us.

When I glanced back at my locker, the thing was slithering toward a corner of the hall.

Away from me.

Thankfully.

I sucked in a relieved breath and closed my eyes as my panic subsided.

That's when my embarrassment set in as I heard the first laugh bubble up around me. I knew when I opened my eyes, they would all be staring. A hallway full of my classmates would be ready to get the best of their Sophomore Kill Day prank.

One chuckle I heard distinctly though. It was low, melodic like a siren's song, beautiful enough to lure someone in, but dangerous enough to ruin them as well.

When I searched out that laugh, I found him. Jax stood in the middle of his friends and slapped one of them on the back. "How'd you get Ms. Gering's snake in there? You went above and beyond, man. Above and beyond."

They high fived, and I saw red.

I shot up, snake and embarrassment completely forgotten, and stomped toward them.

They both stopped laughing as I shoved in between them and looked up at Jax.

His friend said from behind me, "Welcome back. Don't take offense, Sophomore Kill Day applies to everyone."

I wasn't paying him any attention. My tunnel vision was aimed directly at the boy in front of me whom I wanted to hate so badly but had a crush on instead. We were a breath apart, and I could smell his spearmint mixed with some sort of sandalwood aftershave.

I hated how he treated me, and I hated how I didn't hate that smell. "Do you have no shame?" I seethed, looking up at him.

His hand shot out, too quickly for me to dodge, and ran through my hair.

The angry red that I saw melted to black and white as I realized my bun must have come loose when I'd fallen. The rage pumping through my veins turned ice cold as Jax's gaze—always so calculated—flashed so many emotions in a second, I couldn't read even one.

Jax whispered so softly that I barely heard it, "Your hair, Peaches, what happened to your beautiful hair?"

The tears that hadn't come in days, that hadn't fallen when I combed my newly short hair or when I looked in the mirror or even from the embarrassment of falling in front of everyone at school, began to fall then.

I started to curl in on myself.

I felt my heart seizing from the cold in my veins, everything was black and white but him and me, and I wanted so badly to just tell someone.

To tell him.

I was ready to give in.

An unlikely ally showed up to save me from spilling my secrets. She had bright yellow and black hair, chopped lethally right at her chin. She looked like a bumblebee ready to sting when she stepped in front of Jax and shoved his hand away from me. "You are a piece of shit, Jax Stonewood," she seethed.

People were looking on, and I realized I'd lost a few tears in front of them. I turned away from them and toward her. This girl stood tall, ready to go to war for me even though we'd never talked before. Her anger radiated through the hall, blinding us with its brilliance.

"Next time you want to take Ms. Gering's snake, I'll make sure there's a poisonous one to inflict some serious pain on you. Get off your high fucking horse for once and act your age."

Everyone stood by silently, probably in a little shock that this girl was attempting to tell off the most popular people in our school.

Then, the guy who'd slapped Jax's hand before stepped forward. "Katie, it was just a joke. It's Sophomore Kill Day."

Katie just scoffed at him. "What are you? Ten? Don't come near me after school today, Nate. We are done."

Then, to my surprise, Nate looked crushed and stepped toward her. "Please, Katie…"

She just held up her hand and turned to look around on the floor. She saw the snake had slithered to a corner and badass that this Katie was, she hunched over and held out her hand. The snake slid up onto it and wrapped itself around her wrist.

The snake whisperer walked toward me, and I started backing up. I mean, she was holding a snake, but she was quicker than me. She hooked her free arm in mine and whispered, "Don't let them see your fear."

I stood a little taller and started to walk with her. "Thank you."

I looked back one last time to see Jax still there as everyone else disbursed. He looked a little shaken and a lot more interested than he ever had before. When he mouthed, "I'm sorry," I knew I was in trouble because I'd already forgiven him.

Katie and I walked to our first class together, because it turned out we had nearly the same schedule.

After thanking her one too many times, she looked over from her desk with her lightning yellow and black bob swinging my way. "You apologize too much, Aubrey."

"Oh, you can just call me Brey."

"Well, Brey, you're kind of too nice."

I cleared my throat and sat a little straighter in my desk before our third period bell rang. "I'm just being polite and thankful."

"K." She shrugged her shoulders. "Stop now though. It's creeping me out."

"Why?"

"Because, no one is ever that nice unless they're hiding something. Clowns and shit are nice."

I smiled, thinking it over. "Kind of like the people who whistle down the street."

"Exactly."

"How about Mr. Larson?" I mentioned our teacher. "He's extremely nice."

"Yup. Creepy as fuck." She finally cracked a smile. With that smile against her caramel-colored skin and her petite frame, I figured out why Katie had Nate pleading to forgive him. We were sophomores and usually guys like Nate and Jax didn't dabble in underclassmen.

"So." I glanced toward the door to see if anyone else was listening to our conversation. "You and Nate?"

"Ugh." She groaned. "Don't remind me. It was a fling, something to pass the time and kind of a place to sleep for a while."

I must have looked confused.

"Guessing you don't gossip much?" she asked somewhat surprised. "You seriously are the real Goody Two-shoes deal, aren't you?"

"Wha…what are you talking about?"

"You know? You're the homeschooled Whitfield everyone keeps talking about. I'm the foster kid who jumps from home to home. It's a small school, Brey. You haven't heard the shit these idiots think up?"

The teacher started setting up the materials in the front of the room and I watched him, realizing how stupid I must look. "I guess you could say I avoid gossiping to people and people avoid gossiping to me."

She shrugged. "Whatever. I'm done with that asshole."

"He seemed sorry."

"He's immature. I mean, for fuck's sake, I'm a sophomore and I had to tell him to grow up." She shook her head and her hair swung with her. "So, what happened to your hair?"

Man, she talked so fast and jumped topics so quickly, I had to hope I didn't get whiplash. "I'm sorry, what?"

"Jax was mumbling about your hair. What happened?" She didn't beat around the bush.

I smoothed my hand over my newly formed bun and shifted in my seat.

"Got it. It's private, I understand." She turned to face the front, and then her grayish eyes glanced at me sideways. "You can wait till lunch to tell me."

My lips thinned. "I just got a haircut."

She stared at me for a second. Then, burst out laughing. "Okay, you're officially one of the worst liars I've ever seen."

I just shrugged and wiped my now sweaty palms on my jeans.

She leaned in a little over her desk and whispered, "I think I like you. I think we're going to be really good fucking friends. So, I'll tell you a secret. I've been in foster care for a long time, seen a lot of shitty things, and I can tell when something is wrong with someone the moment I meet them."

My eyes must have been wide as I sat there, frozen, listening to her and not knowing what to say.

Her look altered from one of the fierce stinging bee she portrayed to a more wounded, understanding animal. "Your secrets will always be safe with me."

We stared at each other for a beat. For the first time ever, I sat next to another girl that shared the same look I did. I wanted to tell her everything right then and there. Maybe it was her brashness, the way she held herself tall as if neither of us had to be ashamed and we could be something more than the abuse that went on in our homes. I smiled at her and nodded in understanding.

For the first time ever, I wanted to tell Jay. I didn't even listen in my next two classes because I was planning a way to tell them both.

When the lunch bell rang, Katie and I weaved our way through the halls to the cafeteria.

Taking a table with our lunches proved to be easy as we were early. Katie's mile-a-minute mouth was going over our last class when I looked up and saw Jax approaching. A couple girls called out to him but he'd set his eyes on me. I could feel their determination across the room, raking over my face and trying to read me the way he always did.

As he neared, Katie glanced up and then grumbled. "Oh, for fuck's sake, doesn't he have a girlfriend? He's practically obsessed with you."

"Katie!" I whisper-yelled.

Before she could answer, Jax leaned against our table and set a peach in front of me. "Peace offering, Peaches."

I would have said thank you. I would have accepted it and we would have parted ways amicably. No lines would have been drawn. No people would have had to witness the war beginning.

Jay had other plans, as he barreled up to us and shoved Jax so hard, he stumbled into the other table.

"What the fuck, man?" Jax roared, stabilizing himself and coming back at him.

No one stepped in between them like I assumed some of their friends would. Everyone around us was fine with these beautiful guys destroying each other's faces.

"I told you not to fuck with her." Jay pointed to me, and it seemed everyone's heads in the lunchroom turned my way. "You gave me your word."

Jax glanced at me and back at Jay. His gaze hardened as he eyed his brother again. "Well, I'm sorry, Jay. Didn't know the little pixie was so important to you. If you'd have told me you two had a thing—"

Jay shoved him hard again, but this time Jax was ready and shoved him back harder. They were both strong, too strong and too charged to be in each other's faces.

Katie must have seen my panic as I slipped out from my seat and jumped between them because as I faced Jax to push him back, she faced Jay and pushed him back.

My hands were on his chest and I felt his heart beating so hard, I rubbed him there like I had the right to. "It's all right. Please stop, okay?"

His hands flexed into fists and his eyes remained trained on his brother, but Katie had reined him in. She spun around to me and spoke loudly, "Brey, were going. Leave these fuckers to their own shit."

I glanced at Jax again. His eyes were still on his brother. They held something other than anger though. His brows pulled down like he was acknowledging something, like he was worried.

The color drained from Jay's face as he glanced from Jax and then to me with wide eyes. I lifted a hand to smooth back my hair and realized it had slid from my bun again. My short hair was loose and Jay finally noticed.

Without another word to Jax, I rushed toward Jay.

He'd always known something was amiss in my household. Everyone did. I'm sure he'd assumed but the look on his face right then said his speculations were confirmed. It was recognition, and I knew that if I didn't tell him today and talk him down, he'd share his suspicions with someone he thought would help.

As I grabbed his arm and stormed out of the back doors of the lunchroom, Katie followed and brushed off anyone who tried to talk to us. When we sat at a secluded picnic table, I started at the beginning.

I confessed that the first time I remember my dad hitting my mom, I did nothing. Every time after, nothing. I ended my excruciatingly long confession with the shame of still not doing anything every time he hit her.

Jay asked about my hair, and I told him I deserved it and that I should have hidden it better because my mom paid a price for my negligence later on. He looked mortified, but Katie nodded her head solemnly, like she completely understood.

That day, none of my stones were left unturned and none of my secrets were left unsaid. Those stones built a wall between us and everyone else in that high school. My secrets fortified our friendship and lifted so much weight off my shoulders that I honestly believed I had enough strength to fly away from the problems I had at home.

Some problems though weighed enough to keep me firmly grounded.

CHAPTER
THREE

JAX

SUMMER FINALLY CAME after what had been a damn long year. That Sophomore Kill Day prank caused something to happen to my relationship with Aubrey. I saw her for more than just the little girl my brother hung out with and as part of my life.

Or part of me. I couldn't figure out which. Without her around, and with Jay protecting the hell out of her, I freaking missed the little spitfire.

So, week after week, I'd played nice. I said hi to her in the halls, I walked with her and Jay to school, I tried to eat lunch with them when Katie wasn't around.

I'd made a fucking effort the rest of the school year, even got her to go to a few parties with Jay and me.

Not that I needed her or him to talk to me or anything. Life was just better when she did. Plus she was my friend too.

Kind of.

I'd found during the rest of the school year, I sort of saw red every time she was with my brother alone.

So, about a month into summer, I took another step in making peace. I called her to invite her to a bonfire party.

Aubrey's dad was the one who answered the phone. He never answered.

He must have come home early, and I was shit out of luck because he said she couldn't do anything. Frustrated and confused, I hit end on my cell phone harder than I wanted.

Jay came up behind me. "Who'd you just call?"

"I called Aubrey's house. Thought maybe she'd want to go to the party. Why doesn't she have a goddamn cell phone?" I mumbled, still staring at my phone.

"She coming?" Jay said, climbing up on one of the kitchen barstools.

"No, her dad answered."

"Frank answered?" he almost yelled. "Yeah, man. Weird, right?"

Jay looked a little panicked. Then his mouth snapped shut like a locked box. He shrugged his shoulders and looked away.

"What's wrong?"

"Nothing." He scooted off the barstool and headed toward the foyer. "Let's go upstairs and get ready for this party."

I grabbed his arm. "What aren't you telling me?"

He tried to yank his arm free, but we both knew I was stronger. Jay wasn't weak, but I was still older and meaner. Jay had always been the baby, the one everyone loved, the perfect child who never got into fights. Fights had their benefits though. I could beat Jay in a fist fight any day.

He glared at me when my grip tightened. "Jax, you're eighteen. Act like an adult. Let go of me, and let me get ready. I'm not telling you shit."

My baby brother's eyes iced over like mine did when I was set on something.

"Fuck," I mumbled and let him go. I knew I wasn't getting anything out of him.

We both got ready and went to the party in silence.

We pulled up to a huge bonfire in the woods and saw two kegs set up, our friends all drinking. Bottles of liquor had been scattered around the fire, and everyone looked like they'd been partying most of the night. The moon was bright, the bugs were staying away, and beautiful cheerleaders had put on their shortest dresses to dance around the flames. The scene should have made me happy. I should have been throwing back a drink and smiling when one came up to slide her arms around my waist. I should have been happy as hell that Jay had found one of the other cheerleaders and was cozying up next to her by the fire.

Instead, I couldn't shake the feeling of dread. Something wasn't right.

Aubrey's dad never answered the damn phone.

After an hour, I knew my mood wasn't going to change. I found Jay and nudged his shoulder to stop his make out session. "I'm going home, bro."

Jay looked confused. "We just got here."

"I'm not feeling it."

Jay ran his hands through his dark hair, most likely torn between wanting to fuck his cheerleader and making sure I got home. Times like this reminded me of how great a brother he was. He never fucked anyone over. He cared. I knew ultimately if I didn't give him a way out, he'd drive home with me to make sure everything was all right.

"Jay, I didn't drink. You can stay and hitch a ride later or call me." He squinted at me trying to gauge the situation.

"Seriously, man. I'm fine." I laughed to diffuse his concern. "You wanna smell my breath?"

He relaxed then. "No, dude. Don't be a dick. I was just making sure." He pulled his cheerleader for the night closer to him. "Text me when you get home."

I nodded and left the party.

The drive back was quick and quiet. My Ford F150 drove like a dream. I hadn't been surprised when my father gave me the gift once I turned eighteen. I'd been begging for a truck since I started driving, and after pulling good grades for a year and doing some research on investments, my dad claimed I'd earned it.

Technically, I hadn't because my dad's associates, who included my older brother Jett, didn't actually invest the money where I'd recommended them to do so. Instead, they'd patted my back and told me I'd done good work and research. Come to find out, had they invested where I'd said to, they'd have been all the richer. Investment, risk, and math came easily to me. My dad finally witnessed it, and the man probably would have bought my ass anything at that point.

I rubbed my hands over the steering wheel and smiled to myself. The long nights of research had been worth it. I planned to take care of this truck for years. It was special to me, the first real thing I'd earned.

So, when I turned the corner to our block and hit the gas full speed—not thinking about whether or not I'd crash or worrying about rocks flying up and denting the metal—it was for a damn good reason.

I saw fire. Fire dancing like a tyrant taking over Aubrey's house. Red.

Scorching.

Burning.

Fire.

I should have called 9-1-1. I should have stood back and waited for the fire department. Instead, I floored the gas, drove right up her driveway and jumped from the truck.

It wasn't heroism that fueled me, but fear. It damn near swallowed me up, flooded my lungs and drowned me. My fight to get to Aubrey was a fight against that fear. It choked me and had me struggling to break free. She could be in there. She could be hurt. She could be…

I didn't think about anything but her.

I ran towards the door. I heard someone in the distance yelling my name, but I didn't turn, I didn't hesitate. I tried to open the door but it was locked. I roared and kicked it in near the handle.

Smoked billowed out of the house and I plowed in. I paused in the living room, realizing I had no idea of the layout of her house. I had never been in it. The fire swayed, furious with the wind that had entered the room with me. The smoke invaded my lungs and eyes immediately. I scanned the room, trying to make out hallways, searching for Aubrey. The flames and smoke created a maze, one I wasn't sure I could navigate. As I stood in the middle of the room, overwhelmed with my dilemma, the flames seemed to crackle in laughter at me.

Through a cough, I yelled, "Peaches, where are you?"

I heard coughing coming from a room to my left and darted for it down a short hallway.

"Aubrey?"

I heard a whimper on the other side and tried to open the door.

It was locked. Triple locked. I stepped back to kick it in, but it didn't budge. The door echoed a metal sound back at me. It was as if the door was sarcastically saying to me, "I'm made of steel, dumbass," while the fire continued to roar in the background.

Smoke joined in, taking over the hallway. I coughed harder and harder. I tried to take in a breath but choked on it.

I sunk to the ground and whispered, "Aubrey, the door. It's locked. I can't get it open."

Another whimper.

"Peaches," I coughed. "Where are the keys?"

All I heard was, "Dad."

Everything clicked then. The weird phone call. The anger on the other line. How weird Jay had been acting.

Her father was a fucking psychopath.

We all knew it. We just didn't know it to this extent. I crawled farther down the hallway to another door. This one was unlocked and as I opened the door and crawled in, I realized the air wasn't saturated with smoke but with the smell of alcohol. I welcomed it as I gasped and gasped until I could stand.

That's when I saw Frank—passed out facedown on his bed—completely oblivious to the chaos engulfing his home. A bottle of Macallan was tipped over next to him, and it looked like only a few drops had made it onto the floor rather than down his throat.

Finding those keys had to be my top priority, even as I considered pummeling him over the head with that empty bottle. I snatched them from his pocket and turned to make my way back to Aubrey.

Some might hope I thought over my choices, weighed leaving a man to die, or that I considered my decision.

I didn't.

The only hope I had for him was that he burned to death.

I took my shirt off, put it over my nose and ran back to the locked door. I unlocked it and shoved it open. She was curled up by the door, her face too swollen to even see her eyes. Her mother's face was worse, if possible. I picked Peaches up and whispered, "I got you." Then to her mother, I yelled, "Let's go!"

The woman just paced back and forth in front of the window that was barred on the inside. "He will come. He will come," she mumbled.

The smoke invaded the room like a snake of fury. It slithered in, ready to attack any space it could. I kept beckoning to Aubrey's mother, but she wasn't snapping out of whatever the fuck was wrong with her.

With Aubrey still in my arms, I lunged in front of her mother's pacing. Her dark eyes clashed with mine and I saw recognition ignite in them.

"My husband didn't come?" She all but accused me.

I just shook my head and coughed out, "We have to get out of here." She glanced at her daughter in my arms and a silent plea passed between them. It was the first time I saw Aubrey really communicate with her mother. I noticed the fake conversations she had with her in front of us all the time, the poised looks, and the hollow smiles.

This time, I felt her body curl in on itself and saw her clenching her fists. Then, she spread her fingers like they might give her the courage she needed. Aubrey's green eyes widened, even with the swelling around them. They held determination and strength through pain. And I'd be damned if they didn't beg her mother to feel the strength too. The look warped to bleeding desperation though, as we both saw the resignation in her mother's eyes.

Aubrey reached her arm out and started to lean toward the fire and her mother, who was backing away from both of us into it. "No, Mom. Don't."

Her mother's eyes snapped to mine. "Take care of her."

With that, she darted out of the room and down the hallway.

Then, Aubrey started screaming. She was a daughter losing her mother and she fought me like it.

I ran for the front door, opposite the direction her mother went. I didn't waste energy comforting her. I saved it to keep her safe, all while she wailed on me and squirmed to go after her parents. The maze of flames had grown, and I decided to make a run right through it.

We burst through the front door, Aubrey crying in my arms, fire trucks pulling up, and my mother crying on the front lawn. I dropped to my knees on the grass beside her, and we exchanged knowing glances. She must have seen something in my expression because instead of crying tears of joy that we'd made it out alive, she laid her hand on Aubrey's cheek and shushed the screams coming from her.

That night, those screams ricocheted through my very being and they became the ones that haunted my sanity, making me question everything. I kept hold of her until she calmed down.

Paramedics continued to check our vitals and ask questions. I would never remember what they asked me, but I remember staring at that house. I remember the crackle and popping of wood that descended once Aubrey stopped screaming.

She didn't look at me, and I didn't look at her.

We stared at the house, and I felt my mom wipe tears from my eyes when firefighters appeared with two bodies, neither of which looked like they had life in them.

"She left us, just for him," Aubrey said. Her voice cracked and sounded numb, void of emotion. It didn't sound like her at all. Her mother's decision had changed her.

My decision changed me too. I left both of Aubrey's parents to die to save her. I left them to burn to death, and I felt void of guilt.

That was the day I realized I'd do anything for that girl.

It was the day I realized I loved her.

BUY INEVITABLE NOW OR
GET IT FREE ON KINDLE UNLIMITED HERE:
https://amzn.to/2MOsJa0

ABOUT SHAIN ROSE

FACEBOOK PAGE:
facebook.com/author.shainrose/

INSTAGRAM:
instagram.com/author.shainrose/

SHAIN ROSE IS an author of Contemporary Romance and New Adult novels. She fights for love one word a time. Those happily ever afters can sometimes be a bitch to get to.

When she isn't writing, she's spending the days with her husband, daughter, son, and terrible cat. She and her husband drink way too much coffee, eat way too much candy, and laugh way too much. Life is good when the kids are behaving.

On the off chance she's not writing or spending time with family and friends, she's calling them to talk. And if no one answers, then she's reading and watching trashy TV.

LET'S STAY IN TOUCH

RECEIVE UPDATES ON all things Shain Rose and get an email once the pre-order is live! Subscribe to Shain Rose's newsletter here so you can be the first hear about all the news:
shainrose.com/newsletter

JOIN SHAIN ROSE'S Lovers of Love Facebook Group to keep in touch and get sneak peeks into the Stonewood Brothers' lives:
facebook.com/groups/shainroseslovers

AMAZON AUTHOR PAGE:
amzn.to/37Nfejt

BOOKBUB PAGE
bookbub.com/authors/shain-rose

GOODREADS PAGE:
goodreads.com/shainrose

WEBSITE:
shainrose.com

ACKNOWLEDGMENTS

Bloggers, readers, every single person taking a chance on me: thank you for reading my words. Thank you for helping me do what I love and believing in me. Sharing my dream with you is one of the most amazing things I've ever had the privilege to do.

I have family and friends that consistently show up and show out. Ride or die.

Always have to give it up for my hubs. I don't put him out there on blast as the best husband ever because he's private as hell. Still, I have to say I love him for being the best at everything. He's my number one fan, my ride or die, my best friend, and my absolute favorite.

Everyone knows how difficult these last few months have been with the pandemic and so many changes to our world. I seriously couldn't have finished this book without my family. Shamiah, Mom, Karah, I love you.

My children were literally no help. The only thing I can thank them for is proving to me that I could write a book on no sleep. #stilllovethemtimesamillion

Ladies, you know who you are. I might not be answering your phone calls (I'm a terrible friend) but you'll always be my besties.

Author ladies! Andrea, Dannie, Heather and Harloe (H-squared), Kate, the whole sprint chat (.........here are more than four periods for you) I'm in: THANK YOU for listening to me, for pushing me, for letting me freak out with questions, for looking at a million covers with me, for going on this journey with me. I seriously couldn't do this without you!

Printed in Great Britain
by Amazon

45734054R00205